CONSTANCE F. WOOLSON

Rodman the Keeper: Southern Sketches

The American Short Story Series

VOLUME 87

GARRETT PRESS

Library of Congress Catalog Card No. 69-11928

*This volume was reprinted from the 1880 edition
published by D. Appleton & Co.
First Garrett Press Edition published 1969*

The American Short Story Series
Volume 87
©1969

Manufactured in the United States of America

ISBN: 978-1-4344-1978-1

GARRETT PRESS, INC.
Publishers
250 West 54th Street, New York, N.Y. 10019

PREFACE.

THE sketches included in this volume were written during a residence in the South, which has embraced the greater part of the past six years. As far as they go they record real impressions; but they can never give the inward charm of that beautiful land which the writer has learned to love, and from which she now severs herself with true regret. Two of these sketches have appeared in the "Atlantic Monthly," four in "Appletons' Journal," and one each in "Scribner's Monthly," "The Galaxy," "Lippincott's Monthly," and "Harper's Magazine."

C. F. W.

CONTENTS.

RODMAN THE KEEPER.

The long years come and go,
    And the Past,
The sorrowful, splendid Past,
With its glory and its woe,
    Seems never to have been.
——Seems never to have been ?
    O somber days and grand,
    How ye crowd back once more,
Seeing our heroes' graves are green
By the Potomac and the Cumberland,
And in the valley of the Shenandoah !

When we remember how they died,—
In dark ravine and on the mountain-side,
In leaguered fort and fire-encircled town,
And where the iron ships went down,—
How their dear lives were spent
In the weary hospital-tent,
In the cockpit's crowded hive,
          ——it seems
Ignoble to be alive !

            THOMAS BAILEY ALDRICH.

" KEEPER of what ? Keeper of the dead. Well, it is
easier to keep the dead than the living; and as for the gloom
of the thing, the living among whom I have been lately were
not a hilarious set."

John Rodman sat in the doorway and looked out over his
domain. The little cottage behind him was empty of life save
himself alone. In one room the slender appointments provided by Government for the keeper, who being still alive
must sleep and eat, made the bareness doubly bare; in the
other the desk and the great ledgers, the ink and pens, the

register, the loud-ticking clock on the wall, and the flag folded
on a shelf, were all for the kept, whose names, in hastily written, blotted rolls of manuscript, were waiting to be transcribed
in the new red-bound ledgers in the keeper's best handwriting
day by day, while the clock was to tell him the hour when the
flag must rise over the mounds where reposed the bodies of
fourteen thousand United States soldiers—who had languished
where once stood the prison-pens, on the opposite slopes, now
fair and peaceful in the sunset; who had fallen by the way in
long marches to and fro under the burning sun; who had
fought and died on the many battle-fields that reddened the
beautiful State, stretching from the peaks of the marble mountains in the smoky west down to the sea-islands of the ocean
border. The last rim of the sun's red ball had sunk below
the horizon line, and the western sky glowed with deep rose-
color, which faded away above into pink, into the salmon-tint,
into shades of that far-away heavenly emerald which the brush
of the earthly artist can never reproduce, but which is found
sometimes in the iridescent heart of the opal. The small
town, a mile distant, stood turning its back on the cemetery;
but the keeper could see the pleasant, rambling old mansions,
each with its rose-garden and neglected outlying fields, the
empty negro quarters falling into ruin, and everything just as
it stood when on that April morning the first gun was fired
on Sumter; apparently not a nail added, not a brushful of
paint applied, not a fallen brick replaced, or latch or lock repaired. The keeper had noted these things as he strolled
through the town, but not with surprise; for he had seen the
South in its first estate, when, fresh, strong, and fired with
enthusiasm, he, too, had marched away from his village home
with the colors flying above and the girls waving their handkerchiefs behind, as the regiment, a thousand strong, filed
down the dusty road. That regiment, a weak, scarred two
hundred, came back a year later with lagging step and colors
tattered and scorched, and the girls could not wave their
handkerchiefs, wet and sodden with tears. But the keeper,

his wound healed, had gone again; and he had seen with his New England eyes the magnificence and the carelessness of the South, her splendor and negligence, her wealth and thriftlessness, as through Virginia and the fair Carolinas, across Georgia and into sunny Florida, he had marched month by month, first a lieutenant, then captain, and finally major and colonel, as death mowed down those above him, and he and his good conduct were left. Everywhere magnificence went hand in hand with neglect, and he had said so as chance now and then threw a conversation in his path.

"We have no such shiftless ways," he would remark, after he had furtively supplied a prisoner with hard-tack and coffee.

"And no such grand ones either," Johnny Reb would reply, if he was a man of spirit; and generally he was.

The Yankee, forced to acknowledge the truth of this statement, qualified it by observing that he would rather have more thrift with a little less grandeur; whereupon the other answered that *he* would not; and there the conversation rested. So now ex-Colonel Rodman, keeper of the national cemetery, viewed the little town in its second estate with philosophic eyes. "It is part of a great problem now working itself out; I am not here to tend the living, but the dead," he said.

Whereupon, as he walked among the long mounds, a voice seemed to rise from the still ranks below: "While ye have time, do good to men," it said. "Behold, we are beyond your care." But the keeper did not heed.

This still evening in early February he looked out over the level waste. The little town stood in the lowlands; there were no hills from whence cometh help—calm heights that lift the soul above earth and its cares; no river to lead the aspirations of the children outward toward the great sea. Everything was monotonous, and the only spirit that rose above the waste was a bitterness for the gained and sorrow for the lost cause. The keeper was the only man whose presence personated the former in their sight, and upon him therefore, as representative, the bitterness fell, not in words, but in averted looks, in sudden silences when he approached, in withdrawals and avoidance, until he lived and moved in a vacuum; wherever he went there was presently no one save himself; the very shop-keeper who sold him sugar seemed turned into a man of wood, and took his money reluctantly, although the shilling gained stood perhaps for that day's dinner. So Rodman withdrew himself, and came and went among them no more; the broad acres of his domain gave him as much exercise as his shattered ankle could bear; he ordered his few supplies by the quantity, and began the life of a solitary, his island marked out by the massive granite wall with which the United States Government has carefully surrounded those sad Southern cemeteries of hers; sad, not so much from the number of the mounds representing youth and strength cut off in their bloom, for that is but the fortune of war, as for the complete isolation which marks them. "Strangers in a strange land" is the thought of all who, coming and going to and from Florida, turn aside here and there to stand for a moment among the closely ranged graves which seem already a part of the past, that near past which in our hurrying American life is even now so far away. The Government work was completed before the keeper came; the lines of the trenches were defined by low granite copings, and the comparatively few single mounds were headed by trim little white boards bearing generally the word "Unknown," but here and there a name and an age, in most cases a boy from some far-away Northern State; "twenty-one," "twenty-two," said the inscriptions; the dates were those dark years among the sixties, measured now more than by anything else in the number of maidens widowed in heart, and women widowed indeed, who sit still and remember, while the world rushes by. At sunrise the keeper ran up the stars and stripes; and so precise were his ideas of the accessories belonging to the place, that from his own small store of money he had taken enough, by stinting himself, to buy a second flag for stormy weather, so that, rain or not, the colors should float over the dead. This was not patriotism so called, or rather miscalled, it was not sentimental fancy, it was not zeal or triumph; it was simply a sense of the fitness of things, a conscientiousness which had in it nothing of religion, unless indeed a man's endeavor to live up to his own ideal of his duty be a religion. The same feeling led the keeper to spend hours in copying the rolls. "John Andrew Warren, Company G, Eighth New Hampshire Infantry," he repeated, as he slowly wrote the name, giving "John Andrew" clear, bold capitals and a lettering impossible to mistake; "died August 15, 1863, aged twenty-two years. He came from the prison-pen yonder, and lies somewhere in those trenches, I suppose. Now then, John Andrew, don't fancy I am sorrowing for you; no doubt you are better off than I am at this very moment. But none the less, John Andrew, shall pen, ink, and hand do their duty to you. For that I am here."

Infinite pains and labor went into these records of the dead; one hair's-breadth error, and the whole page was replaced by a new one. The same spirit kept the grass carefully away from the low coping of the trenches, kept the graveled paths smooth and the mounds green, and the bare little cottage neat as a man-of-war. When the keeper cooked his dinner, the door toward the east, where the dead lay, was scrupulously closed, nor was it opened until everything was in perfect order again. At sunset the flag was lowered, and then it was the keeper's habit to walk slowly up and down the path until the shadows veiled the mounds on each side, and there was nothing save the peaceful green of earth. "So time will efface our little lives and sorrows," he mused, "and we shall be as nothing in the indistinguishable past." Yet none the less did he fulfill the duties of every day and hour with exactness. "At least they shall not say that I was lacking," he murmured to himself as he thought vaguely of the future beyond these graves. Who "they" were, it would have troubled him to formulate, since he was one of the many sons whom New England in this generation sends forth with

a belief composed entirely of negatives. As the season advanced, he worked all day in the sunshine. "My garden
looks well," he said. "I like this cemetery because it is the
original resting-place of the dead who lie beneath. They
were not brought here from distant places, gathered up by
contract, numbered, and described like so much merchandise ;
their first repose has not been broken, their peace has been
undisturbed. Hasty burials the prison authorities gave them ;
the thin bodies were tumbled into the trenches by men almost
as thin, for the whole State went hungry in those dark days.
There were not many prayers, no tears, as the dead-carts
went the rounds. But the prayers had been said, and the
tears had fallen, while the poor fellows were still alive in the
pens yonder ; and when at last death came, it was like a release. They suffered long ; and I for one believe that therefore shall their rest be long—long and sweet."

After a time began the rain, the soft, persistent, gray rain
of the Southern lowlands, and he staid within and copied another thousand names into the ledger. He would not allow
himself the companionship of a dog lest the creature should
bark at night and disturb the quiet. There was no one to
hear save himself, and it would have been a friendly sound as
he lay awake on his narrow iron bed, but it seemed to him
against the spirit of the place. He would not smoke, although
he had the soldier's fondness for a pipe. Many a dreary evening, beneath a hastily built shelter of boughs, when the rain
poured down and everything was comfortless, he had found
solace in the curling smoke ; but now it seemed to him that
it would be incongruous, and at times he almost felt as if it
would be selfish too. "*They* can not smoke, you know, down
there under the wet grass," he thought, as standing at the
window he looked toward the ranks of the mounds stretching
across the eastern end from side to side—"my parade-ground,"
he called it. And then he would smile at his own fancies,
draw the curtain, shut out the rain and the night, light his
lamp, and go to work on the ledgers again. Some of the

names lingered in his memory; he felt as if he had known the men who bore them, as if they had been boys together, and were friends even now although separated for a time. "James Marvin, Company B, Fifth Maine. The Fifth Maine was in the seven days' battle. I say, do you remember that retreat down the Quaker church road, and the way Phil Kearney held the rear-guard firm?" And over the whole seven days he wandered with his mute friend, who remembered everything and everybody in the most satisfactory way. One of the little head-boards in the parade-ground attracted him peculiarly because the name inscribed was his own: "—— Rodman, Company A, One Hundred and Sixth New York."

"I remember that regiment; it came from the extreme northern part of the State. Blank Rodman must have melted down here, coming as he did from the half-arctic region along the St. Lawrence. I wonder what he thought of the first hot day, say in South Carolina, along those simmering rice-fields?" He grew into the habit of pausing for a moment by the side of this grave every morning and evening. "Blank Rodman. It might easily have been John. And then, where should *I* be?"

But Blank Rodman remained silent, and the keeper, after pulling up a weed or two and trimming the grass over his relative, went off to his duties again. "I am convinced that Blank is a relative," he said to himself; "distant, perhaps, but still a kinsman."

One April day the heat was almost insupportable; but the sun's rays were not those brazen beams that sometimes in Northern cities burn the air and scorch the pavements to a white heat; rather were they soft and still; the moist earth exhaled her richness, not a leaf stirred, and the whole level country seemed sitting in a hot vapor-bath. In the early dawn the keeper had performed his outdoor tasks, but all day he remained almost without stirring in his chair between two windows, striving to exist. At high noon out came a little black bringing his supplies from the town, whistling and shuffling along, gay as a lark. The keeper watched him coming slowly down the white road, loitering by the way in the hot blaze, stopping to turn a somersault or two, to dangle over a bridge rail, to execute various impromptu capers all by himself. He reached the gate at last, entered, and, having come all the way up the path in a hornpipe step, he set down his basket at the door to indulge in one long and final double-shuffle before knocking. "Stop that!" said the keeper through the closed blinds. The little darkey darted back; but as nothing further came out of the window—a boot, for instance, or some other stray missile—he took courage, showed his ivories, and drew near again. "Do you suppose I am going to have you stirring up the heat in that way?" demanded the keeper.

The little black grinned, but made no reply, unless smoothing the hot white sand with his black toes could be construed as such; he now removed his rimless hat and made a bow.

"Is it, or is it not warm?" asked the keeper, as a naturalist might inquire of a salamander, not referring to his own so much as to the salamander's ideas on the subject.

"Dunno, mars'," replied the little black.

"How do *you* feel?"

"'Spects I feel all right, mars'."

The keeper gave up the investigation, and presented to the salamander a nickel cent. "I suppose there is no such thing as a cool spring in all this melting country," he said.

But the salamander indicated with his thumb a clump of trees on the green plain north of the cemetery. "Ole Mars' Ward's place—cole spring dah." He then departed, breaking into a run after he had passed the gate, his ample mouth watering at the thought of a certain chunk of taffy at the mercantile establishment kept by Aunt Dinah in a corner of her one-roomed cabin. At sunset the keeper went thirstily out with a tin pail on his arm, in search of the cold spring. "If it could only be like the spring down under the rocks where I used to drink when I was a boy!" he thought. He had never walked in that direction before. Indeed, now that he had abandoned the town, he seldom went beyond the walls of the cemetery. An old road led across to the clump of trees, through fields run to waste, and following it he came to the place, a deserted house with tumble-down fences and overgrown garden, the out-buildings indicating that once upon a time there were many servants and a prosperous master. The house was of wood, large on the ground, with encircling piazzas; across the front door rough bars had been nailed, and the closed blinds were protected in the same manner; from long want of paint the clapboards were gray and mossy, and the floor of the piazza had fallen in here and there from decay. The keeper decided that his cemetery was a much more cheerful place than this, and then he looked around for the spring. Behind the house the ground sloped down; it must be there. He went around and came suddenly upon a man lying on an old rug outside of a back door. "Excuse me. I thought nobody lived here," he said.

"Nobody does," replied the man; "I am not much of a body, am I?"

His left arm was gone, and his face was thin and worn with long illness; he closed his eyes after speaking, as though the few words had exhausted him.

"I came for water from a cold spring you have here, some-where," pursued the keeper, contemplating the wreck before him with the interest of one who has himself been severely wounded and knows the long, weary pain. The man waved his hand toward the slope without unclosing his eyes, and Rodman went off with his pail and found a little shady hollow, once curbed and paved with white pebbles, but now neglected, like all the place. The water was cold, however, deliciously cold. He filled his pail and thought that perhaps after all he would exert himself to make coffee, now that the sun was down; it would taste better made of this cold water. When he came up the slope the man's eyes were open.

"Have some water?" asked Rodman.

"Yes; there's a gourd inside."

The keeper entered, and found himself in a large, bare
room ; in one corner was some straw covered with an old
counterpane, in another a table and chair ; a kettle hung in
the deep fireplace, and a few dishes stood on a shelf; by the
door on a nail hung a gourd ; he filled it and gave it to the
host of this desolate abode.   The man drank with eagerness.

"Pomp has gone to town," he said, "and I could not get
down to the spring to-day, I have had so much pain."

"And when will Pomp return ? "

"He should be here now ; he is very late to-night."

"Can I get you anything ? "

"No, thank you ; he will soon be here."

The keeper looked out over the waste ; there was no one
in sight.   He was not a man of any especial kindliness—he
had himself been too hardly treated in life for that—but he
could not find it in his heart to leave this helpless creature all
alone with night so near.   So he sat down on the door-step.
"I will rest awhile," he said, not asking but announcing it.
The man had turned away and closed his eyes again, and
they both remained silent, busy with their own thoughts ; for
each had recognized the ex-soldier, Northern and Southern, in
portions of the old uniforms, and in the accent.   The war
and its memories were still very near to the maimed, poverty-
stricken Confederate ; and the other knew that they were, and
did not obtrude himself.

Twilight fell, and no one came.

"Let me get you something," said Rodman ; for the face
looked ghastly as the fever abated.   The other refused.
Darkness came ; still, no one.

"Look here," said Rodman, rising, "I have been wounded
myself, was in hospital for months ; I know how you feel.
You must have food—a cup of tea, now, and a slice of toast,
brown and thin."

"I have not tasted tea or wheaten bread for weeks," answered the man ; his voice died off into a wail, as though
feebleness and pain had drawn the cry from him in spite of

himself. Rodman lighted a match; there was no candle, only a piece of pitch-pine stuck in an iron socket on the wall; he set fire to this primitive torch and looked around.

"There is nothing there," said the man outside, making an effort to speak carelessly; "my servant went to town for supplies. Do not trouble yourself to wait; he will come presently, and—and I want nothing."

But Rodman saw through proud poverty's lie; he knew that irregular quavering of the voice, and that trembling of the hand; the poor fellow had but one to tremble. He continued his search; but the bare room gave back nothing, not a crumb.

"Well, if you are not hungry," he said, briskly, "I am, hungry as a bear; and I'll tell you what I am going to do. I live not far from here, and I live all alone too; I haven't a servant as you have. Let me take supper here with you, just for a change; and, if your servant comes, so much the better, he can wait upon us. I'll run over and bring back the things."

He was gone without waiting for reply; the shattered ankle made good time over the waste, and soon returned, limping a little, but bravely hasting, while on a tray came the keeper's best supplies, Irish potatoes, corned beef, wheaten bread, butter, and coffee; for he would not eat the hot biscuits, the corn-cake, the bacon and hominy of the country, and constantly made little New England meals for himself in his prejudiced little kitchen. The pine-torch flared in the doorway; a breeze had come down from the far mountains and cooled the air. Rodman kindled a fire on the cavernous hearth, filled the kettle, found a saucepan, and commenced operations, while the other lay outside and watched every movement in the lighted room.

"All ready; let me help you in. Here we are now; fried potatoes, cold beef, mustard, toast, butter, and tea. Eat, man; and the next time I am laid up you shall come over and cook for me."

Hunger conquered, and the other ate, ate as he had not eaten for months. As he was finishing a second cup of tea, a slow step came around the house; it was the missing Pomp, an old negro, bent and shriveled, who carried a bag of meal and some bacon in his basket. "That is what they live on," thought the keeper.

He took leave without more words. "I suppose now I can be allowed to go home in peace," he grumbled to conscience. The negro followed him across what was once the lawn. "Fin' Mars' Ward mighty low," he said apologetically, as he swung open the gate which still hung between its posts, although the fence was down, "but I hurred and hurred as fas' as I could; it's mighty fur to de town. Proud to see you, sah; hope you'll come again. Fine fambly, de Wards, sah, befo' de war."

"How long has he been in this state?" asked the keeper.

"Ever sence one ob de las' battles, sah; but he's worse sence we come yer, 'bout a mont' back."

"Who owns the house? Is there no one to see to him? has he no friends?"

"House b'long to Mars' Ward's uncle; fine place once, befo' de war; he's dead now, and dah's nobuddy but Miss Bettina, an' she's gone off somewhuz. Propah place, sah, fur Mars' Ward—own uncle's house," said the old slave, loyally striving to maintain the family dignity even then.

"Are there no better rooms—no furniture?"

"Sartin; but—but Miss Bettina, she took de keys; she didn't know we was comin'—"

"You had better send for Miss Bettina, I think," said the keeper, starting homeward with his tray, washing his hands, as it were, of any future responsibility in the affair.

The next day he worked in his garden, for clouds veiled the sun and exercise was possible; but, nevertheless, he could not forget the white face on the old rug. "Pshaw!" he said to himself, "haven't I seen tumble-down old houses and battered human beings before this?"

At evening came a violent thunderstorm, and the splendor of the heavens was terrible. "We have chained you, mighty spirit," thought the keeper as he watched the lightning, "and some time we shall learn the laws of the winds and foretell the storms; then, prayers will no more be offered in churches to alter the weather than they would be offered now to alter an eclipse. Yet back of the lightning and the wind lies the power of the great Creator, just the same."

But still into his musings crept, with shadowy persistence, the white face on the rug.

"Nonsense!" he exclaimed; "if white faces are going around as ghosts, how about the fourteen thousand white faces that went under the sod down yonder? If they could arise and walk, the whole State would be filled and no more carpet-baggers needed." So, having balanced the one with the fourteen thousand, he went to bed.

Daylight brought rain — still, soft, gray rain; the next morning showed the same, and the third likewise, the nights keeping up their part with low-down clouds and steady pattering on the roof. "If there was a river here, we should have a flood," thought the keeper, drumming idly on his window-pane. Memory brought back the steep New England hillsides shedding their rain into the brooks, which grew in a night to torrents and filled the rivers so that they overflowed their banks; then, suddenly, an old house in a sunken corner of a waste rose before his eyes, and he seemed to see the rain dropping from a moldy ceiling on the straw where a white face lay.

"Really, I have nothing else to do to-day, you know," he remarked in an apologetic way to himself, as he and his umbrella went along the old road; and he repeated the remark as he entered the room where the man lay, just as he had fancied, on the damp straw.

"The weather *is* unpleasant," said the man. "Pomp, bring a chair."

Pomp brought one, the only one, and the visitor sat down.

A fire smoldered on the hearth and puffed out acrid smoke now and then, as if the rain had clogged the soot in the long-neglected chimney; from the streaked ceiling oozing drops fell with a dull splash into little pools on the decayed floor; the door would not close; the broken panes were stopped with rags, as if the old servant had tried to keep out the damp; in the ashes a corn-cake was baking.

"I am afraid you have not been so well during these long rainy days," said the keeper, scanning the face on the straw.

"My old enemy, rheumatism," answered the man; "the first sunshine will drive it away."

They talked awhile, or rather the keeper talked, for the other seemed hardly able to speak, as the waves of pain swept over him; then the visitor went outside and called Pomp out. "*Is* there any one to help him, or not?" he asked impatiently.

"Fine fambly, befo' de war," began Pomp.

"Never mind all that; is there any one to help him now —yes or no?"

"No," said the old black with a burst of despairing truthfulness. "Miss Bettina, she's as poor as Mars' Ward, an' dere's no one else. He's had noth'n but hard corn-cake for three days, an' he can't swaller it no more."

The next morning saw Ward De Rosset lying on the white pallet in the keeper's cottage, and old Pomp, marveling at the cleanliness all around him, installed as nurse. A strange asylum for a Confederate soldier, was it not? But he knew nothing of the change, which he would have fought with his last breath if consciousness had remained; returning fever, however, had absorbed his senses, and then it was that the keeper and the slave had borne him slowly across the waste, resting many times, but accomplishing the journey at last.

That evening John Rodman, strolling to and fro in the dusky twilight, paused alongside of the other Rodman. "I do not want him here, and that is the plain truth," he said, pursuing the current of his thoughts. "He fills the house;

he and Pomp together disturb all my ways. He'll be ready
to fling a brick at me too, when his senses come back; small
thanks shall I have for lying on the floor, giving up all my
comforts, and, what is more, riding over the spirit of the place
with a vengeance!" He threw himself down on the grass
beside the mound and lay looking up toward the stars, which
were coming out, one by one, in the deep blue of the Southern night. "With a vengeance, did I say? That is it exactly—the vengeance of kindness. The poor fellow has suffered horribly in body and in estate, and now ironical Fortune
throws him in my way, as if saying, ' Let us see how far your
selfishness will yield.' This is not a question of magnanimity; there is no magnanimity about it, for the war is over,
and you Northerners have gained every point for which you
fought. This is merely a question between man and man;
it would be the same if the sufferer was a poor Federal, one
of the carpet-baggers, whom you despise so, for instance, or
a pagan Chinaman. And Fortune is right; don't you think
so, Blank Rodman? I put it to you, now, to one who has
suffered the extreme rigor of the other side—those prison-
pens yonder."

Whereupon Blank Rodman answered that he had fought
for a great cause, and that he knew it, although a plain man
and not given to speech-making; he was not one of those who
had sat safely at home all through the war, and now belittled
it and made light of its issues. (Here a murmur came up
from the long line of the trenches, as though all the dead had
cried out.) But now the points for which he had fought
being gained, and strife ended, it was the plain duty of every
man to encourage peace. For his part he bore no malice; he
was glad the poor Confederate was up in the cottage, and he
did not think any the less of the keeper for bringing him
there. He would like to add that he thought more of him;
but he was sorry to say that he was well aware what an effort it was, and how almost grudgingly the charity began.

If Blank Rodman did not say this, at least the keeper im-

agined that he did. "That is what he would have said," he
thought. "I am glad you do not object," he added, pretending to himself that he had not noticed the rest of the remark.

"We do not object to the brave soldier who honestly
fought for his cause, even though he fought on the other
side," answered Blank Rodman for the whole fourteen thousand. "But never let a coward, a double-face, or a flippant-
tongued idler walk over our heads. It would make us rise in
our graves!"

And the keeper seemed to see a shadowy pageant sweep
by—gaunt soldiers with white faces, arming anew against
the subtle product of peace: men who said, "It was nothing! Behold, we saw it with our eyes!"—stay-at-home
eyes.

The third day the fever abated, and Ward De Rosset noticed his surroundings. Old Pomp acknowledged that he
had been moved, but veiled the locality: "To a frien's house,
Mars' Ward."

"But I have no friends now, Pomp," said the weak voice.
Pomp was very much amused at the absurdity of this.
"No frien's! Mars' Ward, no frien's!" He was obliged to
go out of the room to hide his laughter. The sick man lay
feebly thinking that the bed was cool and fresh, and the closed
green blinds pleasant; his thin fingers stroked the linen sheet,
and his eyes wandered from object to object. The only thing
that broke the rule of bare utility in the simple room was a
square of white drawing-paper on the wall, upon which was
inscribed in ornamental text the following verse:

> " Toujours femme varie,
>   Bien fou qui s'y fie ;
>   Une femme souvent
>   N'est qu'une plume au vent."

With the persistency of illness the eyes and mind of Ward De
Rosset went over and over this distich; he knew something
of French, but was unequal to the effort of translating ; the

rhymes alone caught his vagrant fancy. "Toujours femme varie," he said to himself over and over again; and when the keeper entered, he said it to him.

"Certainly," answered the keeper; "bien fou qui s'y fie. How do you find yourself this morning?"

"I have not found myself at all, so far. Is this your house?"

"Yes."

"Pomp told me I was in a friend's house," observed the sick man, vaguely.

"Well, it isn't an enemy's. Had any breakfast? No? Better not talk, then."

He went to the detached shed which served for a kitchen, upset all Pomp's clumsy arrangements, and ordered him outside; then he set to work and prepared a delicate breakfast with his best skill. The sick man eagerly eyed the tray as he entered. "Better have your hands and face sponged off, I think," said Rodman; and then he propped him up skillfully, and left him to his repast. The grass needed mowing on the parade-ground; he shouldered his scythe and started down the path, viciously kicking the gravel aside as he walked. "Wasn't solitude your principal idea, John Rodman, when you applied for this place?" he demanded of himself. "How much of it are you likely to have with sick men, and sick men's servants, and so forth?"

The "and so forth," thrown in as a rhetorical climax, turned into reality and arrived bodily upon the scene—a climax indeed. One afternoon, returning late to the cottage, he found a girl sitting by the pallet—a girl young and dimpled and dewy; one of the creamy roses of the South that, even in the bud, are richer in color and luxuriance than any Northern flower. He saw her through the door, and paused; distressed old Pomp met him and beckoned him cautiously outside. "Miss Bettina," he whispered gutturally; "she's come back from somewhuz, an' she's awful mad 'cause Mars' Ward's here. I tole her all 'bout 'em—de leaks an' de rheumatiz an'

2

de hard corn-cake, but she done gone scole me ; and Mars'
Ward, he know now whar he is, an' he mad too."

"Is the girl a fool?" said Rodman. He was just beginning to rally a little. He stalked into the room and confronted
her. " I have the honor of addressing—"

" Miss Ward."

"And I am John Rodman, keeper of the national cemetery."

This she ignored entirely ; it was as though he had said,
" I am John Jones, the coachman." Coachmen were useful
in their way ; but their names were unimportant.

The keeper sat down and looked at his new visitor. The
little creature fairly radiated scorn ; her pretty head was thrown
back, her eyes, dark brown fringed with long dark lashes,
hardly deigned a glance ; she spoke to him as though he was
something to be paid and dismissed like any other mechanic.

" We are indebted to you for some days' board, I believe,
keeper—medicines, I presume, and general attendance. My
cousin will be removed to-day to our own residence ; I wish
to pay now what he owes."

The keeper saw that her dress was old and faded ; the
small black shawl had evidently been washed and many times
mended ; the old-fashioned knitted purse she held in her hand
was lank with long famine.

" Very well," he said ; " if you choose to treat a kindness
in that way, I consider five dollars a day none too much for
the annoyance, expense, and trouble I have suffered. Let
me see: five days—or is it six ? Yes. Thirty dollars, Miss
Ward."

He looked at her steadily ; she flushed. " The money will
be sent to you," she began haughtily ; then, hesitatingly, " I
must ask a little time—"

" O Betty, Betty, you know you can not pay it. Why try
to disguise— But that does not excuse *you* for bringing me
here," said the sick man, turning toward his host with an attempt to speak fiercely, which ended in a faltering quaver.

All this time the old slave stood anxiously outside of the door; in the pauses they could hear his feet shuffling as he waited for the decision of his superiors. The keeper rose and threw open the blinds of the window that looked out on the distant parade-ground. " Bringing you here," he repeated— "*here;* that is my offense, is it? There they lie, fourteen thousand brave men and true. Could they come back to earth they would be the first to pity and aid you, now that you are down. So would it be with you if the case were reversed; for a soldier is generous to a soldier. It was not your own heart that spoke then; it was the small venom of a woman, that here, as everywhere through the South, is playing its rancorous part."

The sick man gazed out through the window, seeing for the first time the far-spreading ranks of the dead. He was very weak, and the keeper's words had touched him; his eyes were suffused with tears. But Miss Ward rose with a flashing glance. She turned her back full upon the keeper and ignored his very existence. " I will take you home immediately, Ward—this very evening," she said.

" A nice, comfortable place for a sick man," commented the keeper, scornfully. " I am going out now, De Rosset, to prepare your supper; you had better have one good meal before you go."

He disappeared, but as he went he heard the sick man say, deprecatingly: " It isn't very comfortable over at the old house now, indeed it isn't, Betty; I suffered "—and the girl's passionate outburst in reply. Then he closed his door and set to work.

When he returned, half an hour later, Ward was lying back exhausted on the pillows, and his cousin sat leaning her head upon her hand; she had been weeping, and she looked very desolate, he noticed, sitting there in what was to her an enemy's country. Hunger is a strong master, however, especially when allied to weakness; and the sick man ate with eagerness.

"I must go back," said the girl, rising. "A wagon will be sent out for you, Ward; Pomp will help you."

But Ward had gained a little strength as well as obstinacy with the nourishing food. "Not to-night," he said.

"Yes, to-night."

"But I can not go to-night; you are unreasonable, Bettina. To-morrow will do as well, if go I must."

"If go you must! You do not want to go, then—to go to our own home—and with me "— Her voice broke; she turned toward the door.

The keeper stepped forward. "This is all nonsense, Miss Ward," he said, "and you know it. Your cousin is in no state to be moved. Wait a week or two, and he can go in safety. But do not dare to offer me your money again; my kindness was to the soldier, not to the man, and as such he can accept it. Come out and see him as often as you please. I shall not intrude upon you. Pomp, take the lady home."

And the lady went.

Then began a remarkable existence for the four: a Confederate soldier lying ill in the keeper's cottage of a national cemetery; a rampant little rebel coming out daily to a place which was to her anathema-maranatha; a cynical, misanthropic keeper sleeping on the floor and enduring every variety of discomfort for a man he never saw before—a man belonging to an idle, arrogant class he detested; and an old black freedman allowing himself to be taught the alphabet in order to gain permission to wait on his master—master no longer in law—with all the devotion of his loving old heart. For the keeper had announced to Pomp that he must learn his alphabet or go; after all these years of theory, he, as a New-Englander, could not stand by and see precious knowledge shut from the black man. So he opened it, and mighty dull work he found it.

Ward De Rosset did not rally as rapidly as they expected. The white-haired doctor from the town rode out on horseback, pacing slowly up the graveled roadway with a scowl on his brow, casting, as he dismounted, a furtive glance down toward the parade-ground. His horse and his coat were alike old and worn, and his broad shoulders were bent with long service in the miserably provided Confederate hospitals, where he had striven to do his duty through every day and every night of those shadowed years. Cursing the incompetency in high places, cursing the mismanagement of the entire medical department of the Confederate army, cursing the recklessness and indifference which left the men suffering for want of proper hospitals and hospital stores, he yet went on resolutely doing his best with the poor means in his control until the last. Then he came home, he and his old horse, and went the rounds again, he prescribing for whooping-cough or measles, and Dobbin waiting outside ; the only difference was that fees were small and good meals scarce for both, not only for the man but for the beast. The doctor sat down and chatted awhile kindly with De Rosset, whose father and uncle had been dear friends of his in the bright, prosperous days ; then he left a few harmless medicines and rose to go, his gaze resting a moment on Miss Ward, then on Pomp, as if he were hesitating. But he said nothing until on the walk outside he met the keeper, and recognized a person to whom he could tell the truth. " There is nothing to be done ; he may recover, he may not ; it is a question of strength merely. He needs no medicines, only nourishing food, rest, and careful tendance."

" He shall have them," answered the keeper briefly. And then the old gentleman mounted his horse and rode away, his first and last visit to a national cemetery.

" National ! " he said to himself—" national ! "

All talk of moving De Rosset ceased, but Miss Ward moved into the old house. There was not much to move : herself, her one trunk, and Marí, a black attendant, whose name probably began life as Maria, since the accent still dwelt on the curtailed last syllable. The keeper went there once, and once only, and then it was an errand for the sick man, whose fancies came sometimes at inconvenient hours—when Pomp

had gone to town, for instance. On this occasion the keeper
entered the mockery of a gate and knocked at the front door,
from which the bars had been removed ; the piazza still showed
its decaying planks, but quick-growing summer vines had been
planted, and were now encircling the old pillars and veiling all
defects with their greenery. It was a woman's pathetic effort
to cover up what can not be covered—poverty. The blinds on
one side were open, and white curtains waved to and fro in the
breeze ; into this room he was ushered by Marí. Matting lay
on the floor, streaked here and there ominously by the dampness from the near ground. The furniture was of dark mahogany, handsome in its day : chairs, a heavy pier-table with
low-down glass, into which no one by any possibility could
look unless he had eyes in his ankles, a sofa with a stiff round
pillow of hair-cloth under each curved end, and a mirror with
a compartment framed off at the top, containing a picture of
shepherds and shepherdesses, and lambs with blue ribbons
around their necks, all enjoying themselves in the most natural and life-like manner. Flowers stood on the high mantel-
piece, but their fragrance could not overcome the faint odor
of the damp straw-matting. On a table were books—a life
of General Lee, and three or four shabby little volumes printed
at the South during the war, waifs of prose and poetry of that
highly wrought, richly colored style which seems indigenous
to Southern soil.

   " Some way, the whole thing reminds me of a funeral,"
thought the keeper.

   Miss Ward entered, and the room bloomed at once; at
least that is what a lover would have said. Rodman, however, merely noticed that she bloomed, and not the room, and
he said to himself that she would not bloom long if she continued to live in such a moldy place. Their conversation in these
days was excessively polite, shortened to the extreme mini-
mum possible, and conducted without the aid of the eyes, at
least on one side. Rodman had discovered that Miss Ward
never looked at him, and so he did not look at her—that is,

not often ; he was human, however, and she was delightfully pretty. On this occasion they exchanged exactly five sentences, and then he departed, but not before his quick eyes had discovered that the rest of the house was in even worse condition than this parlor, which, by the way, Miss Ward considered quite a grand apartment ; she had been down near the coast, trying to teach school, and there the desolation was far greater than here, both armies having passed back and forward over the ground, foragers out, and the torch at work more than once.

" Will there ever come a change for the better ? " thought the keeper, as he walked homeward. " What an enormous stone has got to be rolled up hill ! But at least, John Rodman, *you* need not go to work at it ; *you* are not called upon to lend your shoulder."

None the less, however, did he call out Pomp that very afternoon and sternly teach him " E " and " F," using the smooth white sand for a blackboard, and a stick for chalk. Pomp's primer was a Government placard hanging on the wall of the office. It read as follows :

IN THIS CEMETERY REPOSE THE REMAINS

OF

FOURTEEN THOUSAND THREE HUNDRED AND TWENTY-ONE
UNITED STATES SOLDIERS.

" Tell me not in mournful numbers
Life is but an empty dream ;
For the soul is dead that slumbers,
And things are not what they seem.

" Life is real ! Life is earnest !
And the grave is not its goal ;
Dust thou art, to dust returnest,
Was not written of the soul ! "

"The only known instance of the Government's condescending to poetry," the keeper had thought, when he first read this placard. It was placed there for the instruction and edification of visitors; but, no visitors coming, he took the liberty of using it as a primer for Pomp. The large letters served the purpose admirably, and Pomp learned the entire quotation; what he thought of it has not transpired. Miss Ward came over daily to see her cousin. At first she brought him soups and various concoctions from her own kitchen— the leaky cavern, once the dining-room, where the soldier had taken refuge after his last dismissal from hospital; but the keeper's soups were richer, and free from the taint of smoke; his martial laws of neatness even disorderly old Pomp dared not disobey, and the sick man soon learned the difference. He thanked the girl, who came bringing the dishes over carefully in her own dimpled hands, and then, when she was gone, he sent them untasted away. By chance Miss Ward learned this, and wept bitter tears over it; she continued to come, but her poor little soups and jellies she brought no more.

One morning in May the keeper was working near the flag-staff, when his eyes fell upon a procession coming down the road which led from the town and turning toward the cemetery. No one ever came that way: what could it mean? It drew near, entered the gate, and showed itself to be negroes walking two and two—old uncles and aunties, young men and girls, and even little children, all dressed in their best; a very poor best, sometimes gravely ludicrous imitations of "ole mars'" or "ole miss'," sometimes mere rags bravely patched together and adorned with a strip of black calico or rosette of black ribbon; not one was without a badge of mourning. All carried flowers, common blossoms from the little gardens behind the cabins that stretched around the town on the outskirts—the new forlorn cabins with their chimneys of piled stones and ragged patches of corn; each little darkey had his bouquet and marched solemnly along, rolling his eyes around, but without even the beginning of a smile, while the elders moved forward with gravity, the bubbling, irrepressible gayety of the negro subdued by the new-born dignity of the freedman.

" Memorial Day," thought the keeper; " I had forgotten it."

" Will you do us de hono', sah, to take de head ob de pro-
cessio', sah ? " said the leader, with a ceremonious bow. Now,
the keeper had not much sympathy with the strewing of flowers, North or South ; he had seen the beautiful ceremony more
than once turned into a political demonstration. Here, however, in this small, isolated, interior town, there was nothing
of that kind ; the whole population of white faces laid their
roses and wept true tears on the graves of their lost ones in
the village churchyard when the Southern Memorial Day came
round, and just as naturally the whole population of black
faces went out to the national cemetery with their flowers on
the day when, throughout the North, spring blossoms were
laid on the graves of the soldiers, from the little Maine village
to the stretching ranks of Arlington, from Greenwood to the
far Western burial-places of San Francisco. The keeper
joined the procession and led the way to the parade-ground.
As they approached the trenches, the leader began singing
and all joined. " Swing low, sweet chariot," sang the freedmen, and their hymn rose and fell with strange, sweet harmony
—one of those wild, unwritten melodies which the North heard
with surprise and marveling when, after the war, bands of
singers came to their cities and sang the songs of slavery, in
order to gain for their children the coveted education. " Swing
low, sweet chariot," sang the freedmen, and two by two they
passed along, strewing the graves with flowers till all the
green was dotted with color. It was a pathetic sight to see
some of the old men and women, ignorant field-hands, bent,
dull-eyed, and past the possibility of education even in its
simplest forms, carefully placing their poor flowers to the best
advantage. They knew dimly that the men who lay beneath
those mounds had done something wonderful for them and
for their children ; and so they came bringing their blossoms,
with little intelligence but with much love.

The ceremony over, they retired. As he turned, the keeper
caught a glimpse of Miss Ward's face at the window.

"Hope we 's not makin' too free, sah," said the leader, as the procession, with many a bow and scrape, took leave, " but we 's kep' de day now two years, sah, befo' you came, sah, an we 's teachin' de chil'en to keep it, sah."

The keeper returned to the cottage. " Not a white face," he said.

" Certainly not," replied Miss Ward, crisply.

" I know some graves at the North, Miss Ward, graves of Southern soldiers, and I know some Northern women who do not scorn to lay a few flowers on the lonely mounds as they pass by with their blossoms on our Memorial Day."

" You are fortunate. They must be angels. We have no angels here."

" I am inclined to believe you are right," said the keeper.

That night old Pomp, who had remained invisible in the kitchen during the ceremony, stole away in the twilight and came back with a few flowers. Rodman saw him going down toward the parade-ground, and watched. The old man had but a few blossoms; he arranged them hastily on the mounds with many a furtive glance toward the house, and then stole back, satisfied; he had performed his part.

Ward De Rosset lay on his pallet, apparently unchanged; he seemed neither stronger nor weaker. He had grown childishly dependent upon his host, and wearied for him, as the Scotch say; but Rodman withstood his fancies, and gave him only the evenings, when Miss Bettina was not there. One afternoon, however, it rained so violently that he was forced to seek shelter; he set himself to work on the ledgers; he was on the ninth thousand now. But the sick man heard his step in the outer room, and called in his weak voice, " Rodman, Rodman." After a time he went in, and it ended in his staying; for the patient was nervous and irritable, and he pitied the nurse, who seemed able to please him in nothing. De Rosset turned with a sigh of relief toward the strong hands that lifted him readily, toward the composed manner, toward the man's voice that seemed to bring a breeze from

outside into the close room; animated, cheered, he talked
volubly. The keeper listened, answered once in a while, and
quietly took the rest of the afternoon into his own hands.
Miss Ward yielded to the silent change, leaned back, and
closed her eyes. She looked exhausted and for the first time
pallid; the loosened dark hair curled in little rings about her
temples, and her lips were parted as though she was too tired
to close them; for hers were not the thin, straight lips that
shut tight naturally, like the straight line of a closed box.
The sick man talked on. " Come, Rodman," he said, after a
while, " I have read that lying verse of yours over at least ten
thousand and fifty-nine times; please tell me its history; I
want to have something definite to think of when I read it for
the ten thousand and sixtieth."

> " Toujours femme varie,
>   Bien fou qui s'y fie ;
>   Une femme souvent
>   N'est qu'une plume au vent,"

read the keeper slowly, with his execrable English accent.
" Well, I don't know that I have any objection to telling the
story. I am not sure but that it will do me good to hear it
all over myself in plain language again."

" Then it concerns yourself," said De Rosset ; " so much
the better. I hope it will be, as the children say, the truth,
and long."

" It will be the truth, but not long. When the war broke
out I was twenty-eight years old, living with my mother on
our farm in New England. My father and two brothers had
died and left me the homestead ; otherwise I should have
broken away and sought fortune farther westward, where the
lands are better and life is more free. But mother loved the
house, the fields, and every crooked tree. She was alone, and
so I staid with her. In the center of the village green stood
the square, white meeting-house, and near by the small cottage where the pastor lived ; the minister's daughter, Mary,

was my promised wife. Mary was a slender little creature
with a profusion of pale flaxen hair, large, serious blue eyes,
and small, delicate features; she was timid almost to a fault;
her voice was low and gentle. She was not eighteen, and we
were to wait a year. The war came, and I volunteered, of
course, and marched away; we wrote to each other often;
my letters were full of the camp and skirmishes; hers told of
the village, how the widow Brown had fallen ill, and how it
was feared that Squire Stafford's boys were lapsing into evil
ways. Then came the day when my regiment marched to
the field of its slaughter, and soon after our shattered remnant
went home. Mary cried over me, and came out every day to
the farmhouse with her bunches of violets; she read aloud
to me from her good little books, and I used to lie and watch
her profile bending over the page, with the light falling on her
flaxen hair low down against the small, white throat. Then
my wound healed, and I went again, this time for three years;
and Mary's father blessed me, and said that when peace came
he would call me son, but not before, for these were no times
for marrying or giving in marriage. He was a good man, a
red-hot abolitionist, and a roaring lion as regards temperance;
but nature had made him so small in body that no one was
much frightened when he roared. I said that I went for three
years; but eight years have passed and I have never been
back to the village. First, mother died. Then Mary turned
false. I sold the farm by letter and lost the money three
months afterward in an unfortunate investment; my health
failed. Like many another Northern soldier, I remembered
the healing climate of the South; its soft airs came back to
me when the snow lay deep on the fields and the sharp wind
whistled around the poor tavern where the moneyless, half-
crippled volunteer sat coughing by the fire. I applied for this
place and obtained it. That is all."

"But it is not all," said the sick man, raising himself on
his elbow; "you have not told half yet, nor anything at all
about the French verse."

" Oh—that ? There was a little Frenchman staying at the
hotel ; he had formerly been a dancing-master, and was full
of dry, withered conceits, although he looked like a thin and
bilious old ape dressed as a man. He taught me, or tried to
teach me, various wise sayings, among them this one, which
pleased my fancy so much that I gave him twenty-five cents
to write it out in large text for me."

" Toujours femme varie," repeated De Rosset ; " but you
don't really think so, do you, Rodman ? "

" I do. But they can not help it ; it is their nature.—I
beg your pardon, Miss Ward. I was speaking as though you
were not here."

Miss Ward's eyelids barely acknowledged his existence ;
that was all. But some time after she remarked to her cousin
that it was only in New England that one found that pale
flaxen hair.

June was waning, when suddenly the summons came.
Ward De Rosset died. He was unconscious toward the last,
and death, in the guise of sleep, bore away his soul. They
carried him home to the old house, and from there the funeral
started, a few family carriages, dingy and battered, following
the hearse, for death revived the old neighborhood feeling ;
that honor at least they could pay—the sonless mothers and
the widows who lived shut up in the old houses with everything falling into ruin around them, brooding over the past.
The keeper watched the small procession as it passed his gate
on its way to the churchyard in the village. " There he goes,
poor fellow, his sufferings over at last," he said ; and then he
set the cottage in order and began the old solitary life again.

He saw Miss Ward but once.

It was a breathless evening in August, when the moonlight flooded the level country. He had started out to stroll
across the waste ; but the mood changed, and climbing over
the eastern wall he had walked back to the flag-staff, and now
lay at its foot gazing up into the infinite sky. A step sounded
on the gravel-walk ; he turned his face that way, and recog-

nized Miss Ward. With confident step she passed the dark cottage, and brushed his arm with her robe as he lay unseen in the shadow. She went down toward the parade-ground, and his eyes followed her. Softly outlined in the moonlight, she moved to and fro among the mounds, pausing often, and once he thought she knelt. Then slowly she returned, and he raised himself and waited; she saw him, started, then paused.

" I thought you were away," she said; " Pomp told me so."

" You set him to watch me ? "

" Yes. I wished to come here once, and I did not wish to meet you."

" Why did you wish to come ? "

" Because Ward was here—and because—because—never mind. It is enough that I wished to walk once among those mounds."

" And pray there ? "

" Well—and if I did ! " said the girl defiantly.

Rodman stood facing her, with his arms folded; his eyes rested on her face; he said nothing.

" I am going away to-morrow," began Miss Ward again, assuming with an effort her old, pulseless manner. " I have sold the place, and I shall never return, I think; I am going far away."

" Where ? "

" To Tennessee."

" That is not so very far," said the keeper, smiling.

" There I shall begin a new existence," pursued the voice, ignoring the comment.

" You have scarcely begun the old; you are hardly more than a child, now. What are you going to do in Tennessee ? "

" Teach."

" Have you relatives there ? "

" No."

" A miserable life—a hard, lonely, loveless life," said Rodman. " God help the woman who must be that dreary thing,
a teacher from necessity ! "

Miss Ward turned swiftly, but the keeper kept by her side.
He saw the tears glittering on her eyelashes, and his voice
softened. " Do not leave me in anger," he said ; " I should
not have spoken so, although indeed it was the truth. Walk
back with me to the cottage, and take your last look at the
room where poor Ward died, and then I will go with you to
your home."

" No ; Pomp is waiting at the gate," said the girl, almost
inarticulately.

" Very well ; to the gate, then."

They went toward the cottage in silence ; the keeper
threw open the door. " Go in," he said. " I will wait outside."

The girl entered and went into the inner room, throwing
herself down upon her knees at the bedside. " O Ward,
Ward ! " she sobbed ; " I am all alone in the world now.
Ward—all alone ! " She buried her face in her hands and
gave way to a passion of tears ; and the keeper could not
help but hear as he waited outside. Then the desolate little
creature rose and came forth, putting on, as she did so, her
poor armor of pride. The keeper had not moved from the
door-step. Now he turned his face. " Before you go—go
away for ever from this place—will you write your name in
my register," he said—" the visitors' register ? The Government had it prepared for the throngs who would visit these
graves ; but with the exception of the blacks, who can not
write, no one has come, and the register is empty. Will you
write your name ? Yet do not write it unless you can think
gently of the men who lie there under the grass. I believe
you do think gently of them, else why have you come of your
own accord to stand by the side of their graves ? " As he
said this, he looked fixedly at her.

Miss Ward did not answer ; but neither did she write.

"Very well," said the keeper; "come away. You will not, I see."

"I can not! Shall I, Bettina Ward, set my name down in black and white as a visitor to this cemetery, where lie fourteen thousand of the soldiers who killed my father, my three brothers, my cousins; who brought desolation upon all our house, and ruin upon all our neighborhood, all our State, and all our country?—for the South *is* our country, and not your North. Shall I forget these things? Never! Sooner let my right hand wither by my side! I was but a child; yet I remember the tears of my mother, and the grief of all around us. There was not a house where there was not one dead."

"It is true," answered the keeper; "at the South, all went."

They walked down to the gate together in silence.

"Good-by," said John, holding out his hand; "you will give me yours or not as you choose, but I will not have it as a favor."

She gave it.

"I hope that life will grow brighter to you as the years pass. May God bless you!"

He dropped her hand; she turned, and passed through the gateway; then he sprang after her.

"Nothing can change you," he said; "I know it, I have known it all along; you are part of your country, part of the time, part of the bitter hour through which she is passing. Nothing can change you; if it could, you would not be what you are, and I should not— But you can not change. Good-by, Bettina, poor little child—good-by. Follow your path out into the world. Yet do not think, dear, that I have not seen —have not understood."

He bent and kissed her hand; then he was gone, and she went on alone.

A week later the keeper strolled over toward the old house. It was twilight, but the new owner was still at work.

He was one of those sandy-haired, energetic Maine men, who, probably on the principle of extremes, were often found through the South, making new homes for themselves in the pleasant land.

"Pulling down the old house, are you?" said the keeper, leaning idly on the gate, which was already flanked by a new fence.

"Yes," replied the Maine man, pausing; "it was only an old shell, just ready to tumble on our heads. You're the keeper over yonder, an't you?" (He already knew everybody within a circle of five miles.)

"Yes. I think I should like those vines if you have no use for them," said Rodman, pointing to the uprooted green-ery that once screened the old piazza.

"Wuth about twenty-five cents, I guess," said the Maine man, handing them over.

SISTER ST. LUKE.

She lived shut in by flowers and trees,
And shade of gentle bigotries ;
On this side lay the trackless sea,
On that the great world's mystery ;
But, all unseen and all unguessed,
They could not break upon her rest.
The world's far glories flamed and flashed,
Afar the wild seas roared and dashed ;
But in her small dull paradise,
Safe housed from rapture or surprise,
　　Nor day nor night had power to fright
The peace of God within her eyes.

JOHN HAY.

THEY found her there. "This is more than I expected,"
said Carrington as they landed—"seven pairs of Spanish eyes
at once."

"Three pairs," answered Keith, fastening the statement
to fact and the boat to a rock in his calm way; "and one if
not two of the pairs are Minorcan."

The two friends crossed the broad white beach toward
the little stone house of the light-keeper, who sat in the doorway, having spent the morning watching their sail cross over
from Pelican reef, tacking lazily east and west—an event of
more than enough importance in his isolated life to have kept
him there, gazing and contented, all day. Behind the broad
shoulders of swarthy Pedro stood a little figure clothed in
black; and as the man lifted himself at last and came down
to meet them, and his wife stepped briskly forward, they saw
that the third person was a nun—a large-eyed, fragile little
creature, promptly introduced by Melvyna, the keeper's wife,

as "Sister St. Luke." For the keeper's wife, in spite of her
black eyes, was not a Minorcan; not even a Southerner.
Melvyna Sawyer was born in Vermont, and, by one of the
strange chances of this vast, many-raced, motley country of
ours, she had traveled south as nurse—and a very good, energetic nurse too, albeit somewhat sharp-voiced—to a delicate
young wife, who had died in the sunny land, as so many of
them die; the sun, with all his good will and with all his
shining, not being able to undo in three months the work of
long years of the snows and bleak east winds of New England.

The lady dead, and her poor thin frame sent northward
again to lie in the hillside churchyard by the side of bleak
Puritan ancestors, Melvyna looked about her. She hated the
lazy tropical land, and had packed her calf-skin trunk to go,
when Pedro Gonsalvez surprised her by proposing matrimony.
At least that is what she wrote to her aunt Clemanthy, away
in Vermont; and, although Pedro may not have used the
words, he at least meant the fact, for they were married two
weeks later by a justice of the peace, whom Melvyna's sharp
eyes had unearthed, she of course deeming the padre of the
little parish and one or two attendant priests as so much dust
to be trampled energetically under her shoes, Protestant and
number six and a half double-soled mediums. The justice
of the peace, a good-natured old gentleman who had forgotten that he held the office at all, since there was no demand
for justice and the peace was never broken, married them as
well as he could in a surprised sort of way; and, instead of
receiving a fee, gave one, which Melvyna, however, promptly
rescued from the bridegroom's willing hand, and returned
with the remark that there was no "call for alms" (pronounced as if rhymed with hams), and that two shilling, or
mebbe three, she guessed, would be about right for the job.
This sum she deposited on the table, and then took leave,
walking off with a quick, enterprising step, followed by her
acquiescent and admiring bridegroom. He had remained ac-

quiescent and admiring ever since, and now, as lighthouse-
keeper on Pelican Island, he admired and acquiesced more
than ever; while Melvyna kept the house in order, cooked his
dinners, and tended his light, which, although only third-class,
shone and glittered under her daily care in the old square
tower which was founded by the Spaniards, heightened by
the English, and now finished and owned by the United
States, whose Lighthouse Board said to each other every now
and then that really they must put a first-class Fresnel on
Pelican Island and a good substantial tower instead of that
old-fashioned beacon. They did so a year or two later; and
a hideous barber's pole it remains to the present day. But
when Carrington and Keith landed there the square tower
still stood in its gray old age at the very edge of the ocean,
so that high tides swept the step of the keeper's house. It
was originally a lookout where the Spanish soldier stood and
fired his culverin when a vessel came in sight outside the reef;
then the British occupied the land, added a story, and placed
an iron grating on the top, where their coastguardsman lighted
a fire of pitch-pine knots that flared up against the sky, with
the tidings, "A sail! a sail!" Finally the United States
came into possession, ran up a third story, and put in a revolving light, one flash for the land and two for the sea—a
proportion unnecessarily generous now to the land, since nothing came in any more, and everything went by, the little
harbor being of no importance since the indigo culture had
failed. But ships still sailed by on their way to the Queen of
the Antilles, and to the far Windward and Leeward Islands,
and the old light went on revolving, presumably for their
benefit. The tower, gray and crumbling, and the keeper's
house, were surrounded by a high stone wall with angles
and loopholes—a small but regularly planned defensive
fortification built by the Spaniards; and odd enough it
looked there on that peaceful island, where there was nothing to defend. But it bore itself stoutly nevertheless, this
ancient little fortress, and kept a sharp lookout still over

the ocean for the damnable Huguenot sail of two centuries before.

The sea had encroached greatly on Pelican Island, and sooner or later it must sweep the keeper's house away; but now it was a not unpleasant sensation to hear the water wash against the step—to sit at the narrow little windows and watch the sea roll up, roll up, nearer and nearer, coming all the way landless in long surges from the distant African coast, only to never quite get at the foundations of that stubborn little dwelling, which held its own against them, and then triumphantly watched them roll back, roll back, departing inch by inch down the beach, until, behold! there was a magnificent parade-ground, broad enough for a thousand feet to tread—a floor more fresh and beautiful than the marble pavements of palaces. There were not a thousand feet to tread there, however; only six. For Melvyna had more than enough to do within the house, and Pedro never walked save across the island to the inlet once in two weeks or so, when he managed to row over to the village, and return with supplies, by taking two entire days for it, even Melvyna having given up the point, tacitly submitting to loitering she could not prevent, but recompensing herself by a general cleaning on those days of the entire premises, from the top of the lantern in the tower to the last step in front of the house.

You could not argue with Pedro. He only smiled back upon you as sweetly and as softly as molasses. Melvyna, endeavoring to urge him to energy, found herself in the position of an active ant wading through the downy recesses of a feather bed, which well represented his mind.

Pedro was six feet two inches in height, and amiable as a dove. His wife sensibly accepted him as he was, and he had his two days in town—a very mild dissipation, however, since the Minorcans are too indolent to do anything more than smoke, lie in the sun, and eat salads heavily dressed in oil. They said, " The serene and august wife of our friend is well, we trust ? " and, " The island—does it not remain lonely ? "

and then the salad was pressed upon him again. For they all considered Pedro a man of strange and varied experiences. Had he not married a woman of wonder—of an energy unfathomable? And he lived with her alone in a lighthouse, on an island; alone, mind you, without a friend or relation near!

The six feet that walked over the beautiful beach of the southern ocean were those of Keith, Carrington, and Sister St. Luke.

"Now go, Miss Luke," Melvyna had said, waving her energetically away with the skimmer as she stood irresolute at the kitchen door. "'Twill do you a power of good, and they're nice, quiet gentlemen who will see to you, and make things pleasant. Bless you, *I* know what they are. They ain't none of the miserable, good-for-nothing race about here! Your convent is fifty miles off, ain't it? And besides, you were brought over here half dead for me to cure up—now, warn't you?"

The Sister acknowledged that she was, and Melvyna went on:

"You see, things is different up North, and I understand 'em, but you don't. Now you jest go right along and hev a pleasant walk, and I'll hev a nice bowl of venison broth ready for you when you come back. Go right along now." The skimmer waved again, and the Sister went.

"Yes, she's taken the veil, and is a nun for good and all," explained Melvyna to her new guests the evening of their arrival, when the shy little Sister had retreated to her own room above. "They thought she was dying, and she was so long about it, and useless on their hands, that they sent her up here to the village for sea air, and to be red of her, I guess. 'Tany rate, there she was in one of them crowded, dirty old houses, and so—I jest brought her over here. To tell the truth, gentlemen—the real bottom of it—my baby died last year—and—and Miss Luke she was so good I'll never forget it. I ain't a Catholic—fur from it; I hate 'em. But she seen

us coming up from the boat with our little coffin, and she
came out and brought flowers to lay on it, and followed to
the grave, feeble as she was; and she even put in her little
black shawl, because the sand was wet—this miserable half-
afloat land, you know—and I couldn't bear to see the coffin
set down into it. And I said to myself then that I'd never
hate a Catholic again, gentlemen. I don't love 'em yet, and
don't know as I ever shell; but Miss Luke, she's different.
Consumption? Well, I hardly know. She's a sight better
than she was when she come. I'd like to make her well again,
and, someway, I can't help a-trying to, for I was a nurse by
trade once. But then what's the use? She'll only hev to go
back to that old convent!" And Melvyna clashed her pans
together in her vexation. " Is she a good Catholic, do you
say? Heavens and earth, yes! She's *that* religious—my!
I couldn't begin to tell! She believes every word of all that
rubbish those old nuns have told her. She thinks it's beautiful to be the bride of heaven; and, as far as that goes, I don't
know but she's right: 'tain't much the other kind is wuth,"
pursued Melvyna, with fine contempt for mankind in general.
" As to freedom, they've as good as shoved her off their hands,
haven't they? And I guess I can do as I like any way on my
own island. There wasn't any man about their old convent,
as I can learn, and so Miss Luke, she hain't been taught to
run away from 'em like most nuns. Of course, if they knew,
they would be sending over here after her; but they don't
know, and them priests in the village are too fat and lazy to
earn their salt, let alone caring what has become of her. I
guess, if they think of her at all, they think that she died, and
that they buried her in their crowded, sunken old graveyard.
They're so slow and sleepy that they forget half the time who
they're burying! But Miss Luke, she ought to go out in the
air, and she is so afraid of everything that it don't do her no
good to go alone. I haven't got the time to go; and so, if
you will let her walk along the beach with you once in a while,
it will do her a sight of good, and give her an appetite—al-

though what I want her to hev an appetite for I am sure I don't know; for, ef she gets well, of course she'll go back to the convent. Want to go? *That* she does. She loves the place, and feels lost and strange anywhere else. She was taken there when she was a baby, and it is all the home she has. *She* doesn't know they wanted to be red of her, and she wouldn't believe it ef I was to tell her forty times. She loves them all dearly, and prays every day to go back there. Spanish? Yes, I suppose so; she don't know herself what she is exactly. She speaks English well though, don't she? Yes, Sister St. Luke is her name; and a heathenish name it is for a woman, in my opinion. *I* call her Miss Luke. Convert her? Couldn't any more convert her than you could convert a white gull, and make a land-bird of him. It's his nature to ride on the water and be wet all the time. Towels couldn't dry him—not if you fetched a thousand!"

"Our good hostess is a woman of discrimination, and sorely perplexed, therefore, over her *protégée*," said Keith, as the two young men sought their room, a loft under the peaked roof, which was to be their abode for some weeks, when they were not afloat. "As a nurse she feels a professional pride in curing, while as a Calvinist she would almost rather kill than cure, if her patient is to go back to the popish convent. But the little Sister looks very fragile. She will probably save trouble all round by fading away."

"She is about as faded now as a woman can be," answered Carrington.

The two friends, or rather companions, plunged into all the phases of the southern ocean with a broad, inhaling, expanding delight which only a physique naturaily fine, or carefully trained, can feel. George Carrington was a vigorous young Saxon, tall and broad, feeling his life and strength in every vein and muscle. Each night he slept his eight hours dreamlessly, like a child, and each day he lived four hours in one, counting by the pallid hours of other men. Andrew Keith, on the other hand, represented the physique cultured and trained up to a high point by years of attention and care. He was a slight man, rather undersized, but his wiry strength was more than a match for Carrington's bulk, and his finely cut face, if you would but study it, stood out like a cameo by the side of a ruddy miniature in oils. The trouble is that but few people study cameos. He was older than his companion, and "one of those quiet fellows, you know," said the world. The two had never done or been anything remarkable in their lives. Keith had a little money, and lived as he pleased, while Carrington, off now on a vacation, was junior member of a firm in which family influence had placed him. Both were city men.

"You absolutely do not know how to walk, señora," said Keith. "I will be doctor now, and you must obey me. Never mind the crabs, and never mind the jelly-fish, but throw back your head and walk off briskly. Let the wind blow in your face, and try to stand more erect."

"You are doctor? They told me, could I but see one, well would I be," said the Sister. "At the convent we have only Sister Inez, with her small and old medicines."

"Yes, I think I may call myself doctor," answered Keith gravely. "What do you say, Carrington?"

"Knows no end, Miss, Miss—Miss Luke—I should say, Miss St. Luke. I am sure I do not know why I should stumble over it when St. John is a common enough name," answered Carrington, who generally did his thinking aloud.

"No end?" repeated the little Sister inquiringly. "But there is an end in this evil world to all things."

"Never mind what he says, señora," interrupted Keith, "but step out strongly and firmly, and throw back your head. There now, there are no crabs in sight, and the beach is hard as a floor. Try it with me: one, two; one, two."

So they treated her, partly as a child, partly as a gentle being of an inferior race. It was a new amusement, although a rather mild one Carrington said, to instruct this unformed, timid mind, to open the blinded eyes, and train the ignorant ears to listen to the melodies of nature.

3

"Do you not hear? It is like the roll of a grand organ," said Keith as they sat on the door-step one evening at sunset. The sky was dark; the wind had blown all day from the north to the south, and frightened the little Sister as she toiled at her lace-work, made on a cushion in the Spanish fashion, her lips mechanically repeating prayers meanwhile; for never had they such winds at the inland convent, embowered in its orange-trees. Now, as the deep, low roll of the waves sounded on the shore, Keith, who was listening to it with silent enjoyment, happened to look up and catch the pale, repressed nervousness of her face.

"Oh, not like an organ," she murmured. "This is a fearful sound; but an organ is sweet—soft and sweet. When Sister Teresa plays the evening hymn it is like the sighing of angels."

"But your organ is probably small, señora."

"We have not thought it small. It remains in our chapel, by the window of arches, and below we walk, at the hour of meditation, from the lime-tree to the white-rose bush, and back again, while the music sounds above. We have not thought it small, but large—yes, very large."

"Four feet long, probably," said Carrington, who was smoking an evening pipe, now listening to the talk awhile, now watching the movements of two white heron who were promenading down the beach. "I saw the one over in the village church. It was about as long as this step."

"Yes," said the Sister, surveying the step, "it is about as long as that. It is a very large organ.

"Walk with me down to the point," said Keith—"just once and back again."

The docile little Sister obeyed; she always did immediately whatever they told her to do.

"I want you to listen now; stand still and listen—listen to the sea," said Keith, when they had turned the point and stood alone on the shore. "Try to think only of the pure, deep, blue water, and count how regularly the sound rolls up in long, low chords, dying away and then growing louder, dying away and then growing louder, as regular as your own breath. Do you not hear it ? "

" Yes," said the little Sister timorously.

" Keep time, then, with your hand, and let me see whether you catch the measure."

So the small brown hand, nerveless and slender, tried to mark and measure the roar of the great ocean surges, and at last succeeded, urged on by the alternate praises and rebukes of Keith, who watched with some interest a faint color rise in the pale oval face, and an intent listening look come into the soft, unconscious eyes, as, for the first time, the mind caught the mighty rhythm of the sea. She listened, and listened, standing mute, with head slightly bent and parted lips.

" I want you to listen to it in that way every day," said Keith, as he led the way back. " It has different voices : sometimes a fresh, joyous song, sometimes a faint, loving whisper; but always something. You will learn in time to love it, and then it will sing to you all day long."

" Not at the dear convent ; there is no ocean there."

" You want to go back to the convent ? "

" Oh, could I go ! could I go ! " said the Sister, not impatiently, but with an intense yearning in her low voice. " Here, so lost, so strange am I, so wild is everything. But I must not murmur "; and she crossed her hands upon her breast and bowed her head.

The two young men led a riotous life ; they rioted with the ocean, with the winds, with the level island, with the sunshine and the racing clouds. They sailed over to the reef daily and plunged into the surf ; they walked for miles along the beach, and ran races over its white floor ; they hunted down the center of the island, and brought back the little brown deer who lived in the low thicket on each side of the island's backbone. The island was twenty miles long and a mile or two broad, with a central ridge of shell-formed rock about twenty feet in height, that seemed like an Appalachian chain on the level waste; below, in the little hollows on each side, spread a low tangled thicket, a few yards wide; and all the rest was barren sand, with movable hills here and there—hills a few feet in height, blown up by the wind, and changed in a night. The only vegetation besides the thicket was a rope-like vine that crept over the sand, with few leaves far apart, and now and then a dull purple blossom—a solitary tenacious vine of the desert, satisfied with little, its growth slow, its life monotonous; yet try to tear it from the surface of the sand, where its barren length seems to lie loosely like an old brown rope thrown down at random, and behold, it resists you stubbornly. You find a mile or two of it on your hands, clinging and pulling as the strong ivy clings to a stone wall; a giant could not conquer it, this seemingly dull and half-dead thing; and so you leave it there to creep on in its own way, over the damp, shell-strewn waste. One day Carrington came home in great glory; he had found a salt marsh. "Something besides this sand, you know—a stretch of saw-grass away to the south, the very place for fat ducks. And somebody has been there before us, too, for I saw the mast of a sail-boat some distance down, tipped up against the sky."

"That old boat is ourn, I guess," said Melvyna. "She drifted down there one high tide, and Pedro he never would go for her. She was a mighty nice little boat, too, ef she *was* cranky."

Pedro smiled amiably back upon his spouse, and helped himself to another hemisphere of pie. He liked the pies, although she was obliged to make them, she said, of such outlandish things as figs, dried oranges, and pomegranates. "If you could only see a pumpkin, Pedro," she often remarked, shaking her head. Pedro shook his back in sympathy; but, in the mean time, found the pies very good as they were.

"Let us go down after the boat," said Carrington. "You have only that old tub over at the inlet, Pedro, and you really need another boat." (Carrington always liked to imagine that he was a constant and profound help to the world at large.) "Suppose anything should happen to the one you have?" Pedro had not thought of that; he slowly put down his knife and fork to consider the subject.

"We will go this afternoon," said Keith, issuing his orders, "and you shall go with us, señora."

"And Pedro, too, to help you," said Melvyna. "I've always wanted that boat back, she was such a pretty little thing ; one sail, you know, and decked over in front; you sat on the bottom. I'd like right well to go along myself; but I suppose I'd better stay at home and cook a nice supper for you."

Pedro thought so, decidedly.

When the February sun had stopped blazing down directly overhead, and a few white afternoon clouds had floated over from the east to shade his shining, so that man could bear it, the four started inland toward the backbone ridge, on whose summit there ran an old trail southward, made by the fierce Creeks three centuries before. Right up into the dazzling light soared the great eagles—straight up, up to the sun, their unshrinking eyes fearlessly fixed full on his fiery ball.

"It would be grander if we did not know they had just stolen their dinners from the poor hungry fish-hawks over there on the inlet," said Carrington.

Sister St. Luke had learned to walk quite rapidly now. Her little black gown trailed lightly along the sand behind her, and she did her best to "step out boldly," as Keith directed; but it was not firmly, for she only succeeded in making a series of quick, uncertain little paces over the sand like bird-tracks. Once Keith had taken her back and made her look at her own uneven footsteps. "Look—no two the same distance apart," he said. The little Sister looked and was very much mortified. "Indeed, I *will* try with might to do better," she said. And she did try with might; they saw her counting noiselessly to herself as she walked, "One, two; one, two." But she had improved so much that Keith now devoted his energies to teaching her to throw back her head and look about her. " Do you not see those soft banks of clouds piled up in the west ? " he said, constantly directing her attention to óbjects above her. But this was a harder task, for the timid eyes had been trained from childhood to look down, and the head was habitually bent, like a pendant flower on its stem. Melvyna had deliberately laid hands upon the heavy veil and white band that formerly encircled the small face. " You can not breathe in them," she said. But the Sister still wore a light veil over the short dark hair, which would curl in little rings upon her temples in spite of her efforts to prevent it ; the cord and heavy beads and cross encircled her slight waist, while the wide sleeves of her nun's garb fell over her hands to the finger-tips.

" How do you suppose she would look dressed like other women ? " said Carrington one day. The two men were drifting in their small yacht, lying at ease on the cushions, and smoking.

" Well," answered Keith slowly, " if she was well dressed —very well, I mean, say in the French style—and if she had any spirit of her own, any vivacity, you might, with that dark face of hers and those eyes—you *might* call her piquant."

" Spirit ? She has not the spirit of a fly," said Carrington, knocking the ashes out of his pipe and fumbling in an embroidered velvet pouch, one of many offerings at his shrine, for a fresh supply of the strong aromatic tobacco he affected, Keith meanwhile smoking nothing but the most delicate cigarettes. " The other day I heard a wild scream ; and rushing down stairs I found her half fainting on the steps, all in a little heap. And what do you think it was ? She had been sitting there, lost in a dream—mystic, I suppose, like St. Agnes—

    Deep on the convent roof the snows
      Are sparkling to the moon :
    My breath to heaven like vapor goes.
      May my soul follow soon—

and that sort of thing."

"No," said Keith, "there is nothing mystical about the Luke maiden; she has never even dreamed of the ideal ecstasies of deeper minds. She says her little prayers simply, almost mechanically, so many every day, and dwells as it were content in the lowly valleys of religion."

"Well, whatever she was doing," continued Carrington, "a great sea crab had crawled up and taken hold of the toe of her little shoe. Grand tableau—crab and Luke maiden! And the crab had decidedly the better of it."

"She *is* absurdly timid," admitted Keith.

And absurdly timid she was now, when, having crossed the stretch of sand and wound in and out among the low hillocks, they came to the hollow where grew the dark green thicket, through which they must pass to reach the Appalachian range, the backbone of the island, where the trail gave them an easier way than over the sands. Carrington went first and hacked out a path with his knife; Keith followed, and held back the branches; the whole distance was not more than twelve feet; but its recesses looked dark and shadowy to the little Sister, and she hesitated.

"Come, said Carrington; "we shall never reach the salt marsh at this rate."

"There is nothing dangerous here, señora," said Keith. "Look, you can see for yourself. And there are three of us to help you."

"Yes," said Pedro—"three of us." And he swung his broad bulk into the gap.

Still she hesitated.

"Of what are you afraid?" called out Carrington impatiently.

"I know not, indeed," she answered, almost in tears over her own behavior, yet unable to stir. Keith came back, and saw that she was trembling—not violently, but in a subdued, helpless sort of way which was pathetic in its very causelessness.

"Take her up, Pedro," he ordered; and, before she could

object, the good-natured giant had borne her in three strides
through the dreaded region, and set her down safely upon
the ridge. She followed them humbly now, along the safe
path, trying to step firmly, and walk with her head up, as
Keith had directed. Carrington had already forgotten her
again, and even Keith was eagerly looking ahead for the first
glimpse of green.

"There is something singularly fascinating in the stretch
of a salt marsh," he said. "Its level has such a far sweep
as you stand and gaze across it, and you have a dreamy feeling that there is no end to it. The stiff, drenched grasses
hold the salt which the tide brings in twice a day, and you
inhale that fresh, strong, briny odor, the rank, salt, invigorat-
ing smell of the sea ; the breeze that blows across has a tang
to it like the snap of a whip-lash across your face, bringing
the blood to the surface, and rousing you to a quicker pace.

"Ha!" said Carrington ; "there it is. Don't you see the
green? A little farther on, you will see the mast of the
boat."

"That is all that is wanted," said Keith. "A salt marsh
is not complete without a boat tilted up aground somewhere,
with its slender dark mast outlined against the sky. A boat
sailing along in a commonplace way would blight the whole
thing ; what we want is an abandoned craft, aged and deserted, aground down the marsh with only its mast rising above
the waste."

"*Bien!* there it is," said Carrington ; "and now the question is, how to get to it."

"You two giants will have to go," said Keith, finding a
comfortable seat. "I see a mile or two of tall wading before us, and up to your shoulders is over my head. I went
duck-shooting with that man last year, señora. 'Come on,'
he cried—'splendid sport ahead, old fellow ; come on.'   .

"'Is it deep?' I asked from behind. I was already up
to my knees, and could not see bottom, the water was so
dark.

"'Oh, no, not at all; just right,' he answered, striding ahead. 'Come on.'

" I came; and went in up to my eyes."

But the señora did not smile.

" You know Carrington is taller than I am," explained Keith, amused by the novelty of seeing his own stories fall flat.

" Is he ? " said the Sister vaguely.

It was evident that she had not observed whether he was or not.

Carrington stopped short, and for an instant stared blankly at her. What every one noticed and admired all over the country wherever he went, this little silent creature had not even seen !

" He will never forgive you," said Keith laughing, as the two tall forms strode off into the marsh. Then, seeing that she did not comprehend in the ₁east, he made a seat for her by spreading his light coat on the Appalachian chain, and, leaning back on his elbow, began talking to her about the marsh. " Breathe in the strong salt," he said, " and let your eyes rest on the green, reedy expanse. Supposing you were painting a picture, now—does any one paint pictures at your convent ? "

" Ah, yes," said the little nun, rousing to animation at once. " Sister St. James paints pictures the most beautiful on earth. She painted for us Santa Inez with her lamb, and Santa Rufina of Sevilla, with her palms and earthen vases."

" And has she not taught you to paint also ? "

" Me! Oh, no. I am only a Sister young and of no gifts. Sister St. James is a great saint, and of age she has seventy years."

" Not requisites for painting, either of them, that I am aware," said Keith. " However, if you were painting this marsh, do you not see how the mast of that boat makes the feature of the landscape the one human element; and yet, even that abandoned, merged as it were in the desolate wildness of the scene ? "

The Sister looked over the green earnestly, as if trying to
see all that he suggested. Keith talked on. He knew that
he talked well, and he did not confuse her with more than
one subject, but dwelt upon the marsh; stories of men who
had been lost in them, of women who had floated down in
boats and never returned; descriptions clear as etchings;
studies of the monotone of hues before them—one subject
pictured over and over again, as, wishing to instruct a child,
he would have drawn with a chalk one letter of the alphabet
a hundred times, until the wandering eyes had learned at last
to recognize and know it.

"Do you see nothing at all, feel nothing at all?" he said.
"Tell me exactly."

Thus urged, the Sister replied that she thought she did
feel the salt breeze a little.

"Then take off that shroud and enjoy it," said Keith, extending his arm suddenly, and sweeping off the long veil by
the corner that was nearest to him.

"Oh!" said the little Sister—"oh!" and distressfully she
covered her head with her hands, as if trying to shield herself
from the terrible light of day. But the veil had gone down
into the thicket, whither she dared not follow. She stood irresolute.

"I will get it for you before the others come back," said
Keith. "It is gone now, however, and, what is more, you
could not help it; so sit down, like a sensible creature, and
enjoy the breeze."

The little nun sat down, and confusedly tried to be a sensible creature. Her head, with its short rings of dark hair,
rose childlike from the black gown she wore, and the breeze
swept freshly over her; but her eyes were full of tears, and
her face so pleading in its pale, silent distress, that at length
Keith went down and brought back the veil.

"See the cranes flying home," he said, as the long line
dotted the red of the west. "They always seem to be flying
right into the sunset, sensible birds!"

The little Sister had heard that word twice now; evidently the cranes were more sensible than she. She sighed as she fastened on the veil; there were a great many hard things out in the world, then, she thought. At the dear convent it was not expected that one should be as a crane.

The other two came back at length, wet and triumphant, with their prize. They had stopped to bail it out, plug its cracks, mend the old sail after a fashion, and nothing would do but that the three should sail home in it, Pedro, for whom there was no room, returning by the way they had come. Carrington, having worked hard, was determined to carry out his plan ; and said so.

" A fine plan to give us all a wetting," remarked Keith.

" You go down there and work an hour or two yourself, and see how *you* like it," answered the other, with the irrelevance produced by aching muscles and perspiration dripping from every pore.

This conversation had taken place at the edge of the marsh where they had brought the boat up through one of the numerous channels.

" Very well," said Keith. " But mind you, not a word about danger before the Sister. I shall have hard enough work to persuade her to come with us as it is."

He went back to the ridge, and carelessly suggested returning home by water.

" You will not have to go through the thicket then," he said.

Somewhat to his surprise, Sister St. Luke consented immediately, and followed without a word as he led the way. She was mortally afraid of the water, but, during his absence, she had been telling her beads, and thinking with contrition of two obstinacies in one day—that of the thicket and that of the veil—she could not, she would not have three. So, commending herself to all the saints, she embarked.

" Look here, Carrington, if ever you inveigle me into such danger again for a mere fool's fancy, I will show you what I think of it. You knew the condition of that boat, and I did not," said Keith, sternly, as the two men stood at last on the beach in front of the lighthouse. The Sister had gone within, glad to feel land underfoot once more. She had sat quietly in her place all the way, afraid of the water, of the wind, of everything, but entirely unconscious of the real danger that menaced them. For the little craft would not mind her helm; her mast slipped about erratically; the planking at the bow seemed about to give way altogether; and they were on a lee shore, with the tide coming in, and the surf beating roughly on the beach. They were both good sailors, but it had taken all they knew to bring the boat safely to the lighthouse.

"To tell the truth, I did not think she was so crippled," said Carrington. "She really is a good boat for her size."

"Very," said Keith sarcastically.

But the younger man clung to his opinion; and, in order to verify it, he set himself to work repairing the little craft. You would have supposed his daily bread depended upon her being made seaworthy, by the way he labored. She was made over from stem to stern: a new mast, a new sail; and, finally, scarlet and green paint were brought over from the village, and out she came as brilliant as a young paroquet. Then Carrington took to sailing in her. Proud of his handy work, he sailed up and down, over to the reef, and up the inlet, and even persuaded Melvyna to go with him once, accompanied by the meek little Sister.

"Why shouldn't you both learn how to manage her?" he said in his enthusiasm. "She's as easy to manage as a child—"

"And as easy to tip over," replied Melvyna, screwing up her lips tightly and shaking her head. "You don't catch me out in her again, sure's as my name's Sawyer."

For Melvyna always remained a Sawyer in her own mind, in spite of her spouse's name; she could not, indeed, be anything else—*noblesse oblige.* But the Sister, obedient as usual, bent her eyes in turn upon the ropes, the mast, the sail, and the helm, while Carrington, waxing eloquent over his favorite science, delivered a lecture upon their uses, and made her experiment a little to see if she comprehended. He used the simplest words for her benefit, words of one syllable, and unconsciously elevated his voice somewhat, as though that would make her understand better; her wits seemed to him always of the slowest. The Sister followed his directions, and imitated his motions with painstaking minuteness. She did very well until a large porpoise rolled up his dark, glistening back close alongside, when, dropping the sail-rope with a scream, she crouched down at Melvyna's feet and hid her face in her veil. Carrington from that day could get no more passengers for his paroquet boat. But he sailed up and down alone in his little craft, and, when that amusement palled, he took the remainder of the scarlet and green paint and adorned the shells of various sea-crabs and other crawling things, so that the little Sister was met one afternoon by a whole procession of unearthly creatures, strangely variegated, proceeding gravely in single file down the beach from the pen where they had been confined. Keith pointed out to her, however, the probability of their being much admired in their own circles as long as the hues lasted, and she was comforted.

They strolled down the beach now every afternoon, sometimes two, sometimes three, sometimes four when Melvyna had no cooking to watch, no bread to bake; for she rejected with scorn the omnipresent hot biscuit of the South, and kept her household supplied with light loaves in spite of the difficulties of yeast. Sister St. Luke had learned to endure the crabs, but she still fled from the fiddlers when they strayed over from their towns in the marsh; she still went carefully around the great jelly-fish sprawling on the beach, and regarded from a safe distance the beautiful blue Portuguese men-of-war, stranded unexpectedly on the dangerous shore, all their fair voyagings over. Keith collected for her the brilliant sea-weeds, little flecks of color on the white sand, and

showed her their beauties; he made her notice all the varieties
of shells, enormous conches for the tritons to blow, and beds
of wee pink ovals and cornucopias, plates and cups for the
little web-footed fairies. Once he came upon a sea-bean.

"It has drifted over from one of the West Indian islands,"
he said, polishing it with his handkerchief—"one of the
islands—let us say Miraprovos—a palmy tropical name, bringing up visions of a volcanic mountain, vast cliffs, a tangled
gorgeous forest, and the soft lapping wash of tropical seas.
Is it not so, señora?"

But the señora had never heard of the West Indian
Islands. Being told, she replied: "As you say it, it is so.
There is, then, much land in the world?"

"If you keep the sea-bean for ever, good will come," said
Keith, gravely presenting it; "but, if after having once accepted it you then lose it, evil will fall upon you."

The Sister received the amulet with believing reverence.
"I will lay it up before the shrine of Our Lady," she said,
carefully placing it in the little pocket over her heart, hidden
among the folds of her gown, where she kept her most precious treasures—a bead of a rosary that had belonged to some
saint who lived somewhere some time, a little faded prayer
copied in the handwriting of a young nun who had died some
years before and whom she had dearly loved, and a list of her
own most vicious faults, to be read over and lamented daily;
crying evils such as a perverse and insubordinate bearing, a
heart froward and evil, gluttonous desires of the flesh, and a
spirit of murderous rage. These were her own ideas of herself, written down at the convent. Had she not behaved herself perversely to the Sister Paula, with whom one should be
always mild on account of the affliction which had sharpened
her tongue? Had she not wrongfully coveted the cell of the
novice Felipa, because it looked out upon the orange walk?
Had she not gluttonously longed for more of the delectable
marmalade made by the aged Sanchita? And, worse than
all, had she not, in a spirit of murderous rage, beat the yellow

cat with a palm-branch for carrying off the young doves, her
especial charge ? " Ah, my sins are great indeed," she sighed
daily upon her knees, and smote her breast with tears.

Keith watched the sea-bean go into the little heart-pocket
almost with compunction. Many of these amulets of the
sea, gathered during his winter rambles, had he bestowed
with formal warning of their magic powers, and many a fair
hand had taken them, many a soft voice had promised to
keep them "for ever." But he well knew they would be mis-
laid and forgotten in a day. The fair ones well knew it too,
and each knew that the other knew, so no harm was done.
But this sea-bean, he thought, would have a different fate—
laid up in some little nook before the shrine, a witness to the
daily prayers of the simple-hearted little Sister. " I hope they
may do it good," he thought vaguely. Then, reflecting that
even the most depraved bean would not probably be much
affected by the prayers, he laughed off the fancy, yet did not
quite like to think, after all, that the prayers were of no use.
Keith's religion, however, was in the primary rocks.

Far down the beach they came upon a wreck, an old and
long hidden relic of the past. The low sand-bluff had caved
away suddenly and left a clean new side, where, imbedded in
the lower part, they saw a ponderous mast. " An old Spanish galleon," said Keith, stooping to examine the remains. " I
know it by the curious bolts. They ran ashore here, broad-
side on, in one of those sudden tornadoes they have along
this coast once in a while, I presume. Singular ! This was
my very place for lying in the sun and letting the blaze scorch
me with its clear scintillant splendor. I never imagined I was
lying on the bones of this old Spaniard."

" God rest the souls of the sailors ! " said the Sister, making the sign of the cross.

" They have been in—wherever they are, let us say, for
about three centuries now," observed Keith, " and must be
used to it, good or bad."

" Nay ; but purgatory, señor."

"True. I had forgotten that," said Keith.

One morning there came up a dense, soft, southern-sea fog, "The kind you can cut with a knife," Carrington said. It lasted for days, sweeping out to sea at night on the land breeze, and lying in a gray bank low down on the horizon, and then rolling in again in the morning enveloping the water and the island in a thick white cloud which was not mist and did not seem damp even, so freshly, softly salt was the feeling it gave to the faces that went abroad in it. Carrington and Keith, of course, must needs be out in it every moment of the time. They walked down the beach for miles, hearing the muffled sound of the near waves, but not seeing them. They sailed in it not knowing whither they went, and they drifted out at sunset and watched the land breeze lift it, roll it up, and carry it out to sea, where distant ships on the horizon line, bound southward, and nearer ones, sailing northward with the Gulf Stream, found themselves enveloped and bothered by their old and baffling foe. They went over to the reef every morning, these two, and bathed in the fog, coming back by sense of feeling, as it were, and landing not infrequently a mile below or above the lighthouse; then what appetites they had for breakfast! And, if it was not ready, they roamed about, roaring like young lions. At least that is what Melvyna said one morning when Carrington had put his curly head into her kitchen door six times in the course of one half hour.

The Sister shrank from the sea fog; she had never seen one before, and she said it was like a great soft white creature that came in on wings, and brooded over the earth. "Yes, beautiful, perhaps," she said in reply to Keith, "but it is so strange—and—and—I know not how to say it—but it seems like a place for spirits to walk, and not of the mortal kind."

They were wandering down the beach, where Keith had lured her to listen to the sound of the hidden waves. At that moment Carrington loomed into view coming toward them. He seemed of giant size as he appeared, passed them, and disappeared again into the cloud behind, his voice sounding muffled as he greeted them. The Sister shrank nearer to her companion as the figure had suddenly made itself visible. " Do you know it is a wonder to me how you have ever managed to live so far," said Keith smiling.

" But it was not far," said the little nun. " Nothing was ever far at the dear convent, but everything was near, and not of strangeness to make one afraid ; the garden wall was the end. There we go not outside, but our walk is always from the lime-tree to the white rose-bush and back again. Everything we know there—not roar of waves, not strong wind, not the thick, white air comes to give us fear, but all is still and at peace. At night I dream of the organ, and of the orange-trees, and of the doves. I wake, and hear only the sound of the great water below."

" You will go back," said Keith.

He had begun to pity her lately, for her longing was deeper than he had supposed. It had its roots in her very being. He had studied her and found it so.

" She will die of pure homesickness if she stays here much longer," he said to Carrington. " What do you think of our writing down to that old convent and offering—of course unknown to her—to pay the little she costs them, if they will take her back ? "

" All right," said Carrington. " Go ahead."

He was making a larger sail for his paroquet boat. " If none of you will go out in her, I might as well have all the sport I can," he said.

" Sport to consist in being swamped ? " Keith asked.

" By no means, croaker. Sport to consist in shooting over the water like a rocket ; I sitting on the tilted edge, watching the waves, the winds, and the clouds, and hearing the water sing as we rush along."

Keith took counsel with no one else, not even with Melvyna, but presently he wrote his letter and carried it himself over to the village to mail. He did good deeds like that once in a while, "to help humanity," he said. They were tangible always; like the primary rocks.

At length one evening the fog rolled out to sea for good and all, at least as far as that shore was concerned. In the morning there stood the lighthouse, and the island, and the reef, just the same as ever. They had almost expected to see them altered, melted a little.

"Let us go over to the reef, all of us, and spend the day," said Keith. "It will do us good to breathe the clear air, and feel the brilliant, dry, hot sunshine again."

"Hear the man!" said Melvyna laughing. "After trying to persuade us all those days that he liked that sticky fog too!"

"Mme. Gonsalvez, we like a lily; but is that any reason why we may not also like a rose?"

"Neither of 'em grows on this beach as I'm aware of," answered Melvyna dryly.

Then Carrington put in his voice, and carried the day. Women never resisted Carrington long, but yielded almost unconsciously to the influence of his height and his strength, and his strong, hearty will. A subtiler influence over them, however, would have waked resistance, and Carrington himself would have been conquered far sooner (and was conquered later) by one who remained unswayed by those influences, to which others paid involuntary obeisance.

Pedro had gone to the village for his supplies and his two days of mild Minorcan dissipation, and Melvyna, beguiled and cajoled by the chaffing of the two young men, at last consented, and not only packed the lunch-basket with careful hand, but even donned for the occasion her "best bonnet," a structure trimmed in Vermont seven years before by the experienced hand of Miss Althy Spears, the village milliner, who had adorned it with a durable green ribbon and a vigorous wreath of artificial flowers. Thus helmeted, Mme. Gonsalvez presided at the stern of the boat with great dignity. For they were in the safe, well-appointed little yacht belonging to the two gentlemen, the daring paroquet having been left at home tied to the last of a low heap of rocks that jutted out into the water in front of the lighthouse, the only remains of the old stone dock built by the Spaniards long before. Sister St. Luke was with them of course, gentle and frightened as usual. Her breath came quickly as they neared the reef, and Carrington with a sure hand guided the little craft outside into the surf, and, rounding a point, landed them safely in a miniature harbor he had noted there. Keith had counted the days, and felt sure that the answer from the convent would come soon. His offer—for he had made it his alone without Carrington's aid—had been liberal; there could be but one reply. The little Sister would soon go back to the lime-tree, the white rose-bush, the doves, the old organ that was "so large" —all the quiet routine of the life she loved so well; and they would see her small oval face and timid dark eyes no more. So he took her for a last walk down the reef, while Melvyna made coffee, and Carrington, having noticed a dark line floating on the water, immediately went out in his boat, of course, to see what it was.

The reef had its high backbone, like the island. Some day it would be the island, with another reef outside, and the lighthouse beach would belong to the mainland. Down the stretch of sand toward the sea the pelicans stood in rows, toeing a mark, solemn and heavy, by the hundreds—a countless number—for the reef was their gathering-place.

"They are holding a conclave," said Keith. "That old fellow has the floor. See him wag his head."

In and out among the pelicans, and paying no attention to them and their conclave, sped the sickle-bill curlews, actively probing everywhere with their long, grotesque, sickle-shaped bills; and woe be to the burrowing things that came in their way! The red-beaked oyster-bird flew by, and close down to the sea skimmed the razor-bill shear-water, with his head bent forward and his feet tilted up, just grazing the water with his open bill as he flew, and leaving a shining mark

behind, as though he held a pencil in his mouth and was running a line. The lazy gulls, who had no work to do, and
would not have done it if they had, rode at ease on the little
wavelets close in shore. The Sister, being asked, confessed
that she liked the lazy gulls best. Being pressed to say why, she
thought it was because they were more like the white doves
that sat on the old stone well-curb in the convent garden.

Keith had always maintained that he liked to talk to women. He said that the talk of any woman was more piquant
than the conversation of the most brilliant men. There was
only one obstacle: the absolute inability of the sex to be sin-
cere, or to tell the truth, for ten consecutive minutes. To-
day, however, as he wandered to and fro whither he would on
the reef, he also wandered to and fro whither he would in the
mind, and the absolutely truthful mind too, of a woman. Yet
he found it dull! He sighed to himself, but was obliged to
acknowledge that it *was* dull. The lime-tree, the organ, the
Sisters, the Sisters, the lime-tree, the organ; it grew monotonous after a while. Yet he held his post, for the sake of the
old theory, until the high voice of Melvyna called them back
to the little fire on the beach and the white cloth spread with
her best dainties. They saw Carrington sailing in with an
excited air, and presently he brought the boat into the cove
and dragged ashore his prize, towed behind—nothing less
than a large shark, wounded, dead, after a struggle with some
other marine monster, a sword-fish probably. "A man-
eater," announced the captor. "Look at him, will you?
Look at him, Miss Luke!"

But Miss Luke went far away, and would not look. In
truth he was an ugly creature; even Melvyna kept at a safe
distance. But the two men noted all his points; they measured him carefully; they turned him over, and discussed him
generally in that closely confined and exhaustive way which
marks the masculine mind. Set two women to discussing a
shark, or even the most lovely little brook-trout, if you please,
and see how far off they will be in five minutes!

But the lunch was tempting, and finally its discussion called them away even from that of the shark. And then they all sailed homeward over the green and blue water, while the white sand-hills shone silvery before them, and then turned red in the sunset. That night the moon was at its full. Keith went out and strolled up and down on the beach. Carrington was playing fox-and-goose with Mme. Gonsalvez on a board he had good-naturedly constructed for her entertainment when she confessed one day to a youthful fondness for that exciting game. Up stairs gleamed the little Sister's light. "Saying her prayers with her lips, but thinking all the time of that old convent," said the stroller to himself, half scornfully. And he said the truth.

The sea was still and radiant ; hardly more than a ripple broke at his feet ; the tide was out, and the broad beach silvery and fresh. "At home they are buried in snow," he thought, "and the wind is whistling around their double windows." And then he stretched himself on the sand, and lay looking upward into the deep blue of the night, bathed in the moonlight, and listening dreamily to the soft sound of the water as it returned slowly, slowly back from the African coast. He thought many thoughts, and deep ones too, and at last he was so far away on ideal heights, that, coming home after midnight, it was no wonder if, half unconsciously, he felt himself above the others ; especially when he passed the little Sister's closed door, and thought, smiling not unkindly, how simple she was.

The next morning the two men went off in their boat again for the day, this time alone. There were still a few more questions to settle about that shark, and, to tell the truth, they both liked a good day of unencumbered sailing better than anything else.

About four o'clock in the afternoon Melvyna, happening to look out of the door, saw a cloud no bigger than a man's hand low down on the horizon line of the sea. Something made her stand and watch it for a few moments. Then,

"Miss Luke! Miss Luke! Miss Luke! Miss Luke!" she called quickly. Down came the little Sister, startled at the cry, her lace-work still in her hand.

"Look!" said Melvyna.

The Sister looked, and this is what she saw : a line white as milk coming toward them on the water, and behind it a blackness.

"What is it?" she asked.

"A tornader," said Melvyna with white lips. "I've only seen one, and then I was over in the town; but it's awful! We must run back to the thicket." Seizing her companion's arm, the strong Northern woman hurried her across the sand, through the belt of sand-hills, and into the thicket, where they crouched on its far side close down under the projecting backbone. "The bushes will break the sand, and the ridge will keep us from being buried in it," she said. "I dursn't stay on the shore, for the water'll rise."

The words were hardly spoken before the tornado was upon them, and the air was filled with the flying sand, so that they could hardly breathe. Half choked, they beat with their hands before them to catch a breath. Then came a roar, and for an instant, distant as they were, they caught a glimpse of the crest of the great wave that followed the whirlwind. It seemed to them mountain-high, and ready to ingulf the entire land. With a rushing sound it plunged over the keeper's house, broke against the lower story of the tower, hissed across the sand, swallowed the sand-hills, and swept to their very feet, then sullenly receded with slow, angry muttering. A gale of wind came next, singularly enough from another direction, as if to restore the equipoise of the atmosphere. But the tornado had gone on inland, where there were trees to uproot, and houses to destroy, and much finer entertainment generally.

As soon as they could speak, "Where are the two out in the sail-boat?" asked the Sister.

"God knows!" answered Melvyna. "The last time I

noticed their sail they were about a mile outside of the reef."

"I will go and see."

"Go and see! Are you crazy? You can never get through that water."

"The saints would help me, I think," said the little Sister.

She had risen, and now stood regarding the watery waste with the usual timid look in her gentle eyes. Then she stepped forward with her uncertain tread, and before the woman by her side comprehended her purpose she was gone, ankle-deep in the tide, knee-deep, and finally wading across the sand up to her waist in water toward the lighthouse. The great wave was no deeper, however, even there. She waded to the door of the tower, opened it with difficulty, climbed the stairway, and gained the light-room, where the glass of the windows was all shattered, and the little chamber half full of the dead bodies of birds, swept along by the whirlwind and dashed against the tower, none of them falling to the ground or losing an inch of their level in the air as they sped onward, until they struck against some high object, which broke their mad and awful journey. Holding on by the shattered casement, Sister St. Luke gazed out to sea. The wind was blowing fiercely, and the waves were lashed to fury. The sky was inky black. The reef was under water, save one high knob of its backbone, and to that two dark objects were clinging. Farther down she saw the wreck of the boat driving before the gale. Pedro was over in the village; the tide was coming in over the high sea, and night was approaching. She walked quickly down the rough stone stairs, stepped into the water again, and waded across where the paroquet boat had been driven against the wall of the house, bailed it out with one of Melvyna's pans, and then, climbing in from the window of the sitting-room, she hoisted the sail, and in a moment was out on the dark sea.

Melvyna had ascended to the top of the ridge, and when the sail came into view beyond the house she fell down on her knees and began to pray aloud: "O Lord, save her; save the lamb! She don't know what's she is doing, Lord. She's as simple as a baby. Oh, save her, out on that roaring sea! Good Lord, good Lord, deliver her!" Fragments of prayers she had heard in her prayer-meeting days came confusedly back into her mind, and she repeated them all again and again, wringing her hands as she saw the little craft tilt far over under its all too large sail, so that several times, in the hollows of the waves, she thought it was gone. The wind was blowing hard but steadily, and in a direction that carried the boat straight toward the reef; no tacks were necessary, no change of course; the black-robed little figure simply held the sail-rope, and the paroquet drove on. The two clinging to the rock, bruised, exhausted, with the waves rising and falling around them, did not see the boat until it was close upon them.

"By the great heavens!" said Keith.

His face was pallid and rigid, and there was a ghastly cut across his forehead, the work of the sharp-edged rock. The next moment he was on board, brought the boat round just in time, and helped in Carrington, whose right arm was injured.

"You have saved our lives, señora," he said abruptly.

"By Jove, yes," said Carrington. "We could not have stood it long, and night was coming." Then they gave all their attention to the hazardous start.

Sister St. Luke remained unconscious of the fact that she had done anything remarkable. Her black gown was spoiled, which was a pity, and she knew of a balm which was easily compounded and which would heal their bruises. Did they think Melvyna had come back to the house yet? And did they know that all her dishes were broken—yes, even the cups with the red flowers on the border? Then she grew timorous again, and hid her face from the sight of the waves.

Keith said not a word, but sailed the boat, and it was a wild and dangerous voyage they made, tacking up and down in the gayly painted little craft, that seemed like a toy on that angry water. Once Carrington took the little Sister's hand in his, and pressed his lips fervently upon it. She had never had her hand kissed before, and looked at him, then at the place, with a vague surprise, which soon faded, however, into the old fear of the wind. It was night when at last they reached the lighthouse; but during the last two tacks they had a light from the window to guide them; and when nearly in they saw the lantern shining out from the shattered windows of the tower in a fitful, surprised sort of way, for Melvyna had returned, and, with the true spirit of a Yankee, had immediately gone to work at the ruins.

The only sign of emotion she gave was to Keith. " I saw it all," she said. " That child went right out after you, in that terrible wind, as natural and as quiet as if she was only going across the room. And she so timid a fly could frighten her! Mark my words, Mr. Keith, the good Lord helped her to do it! And I'll go to that new mission chapel over in the town every Sunday after this, as sure's my name is Sawyer!" She ceased abruptly, and, going into her kitchen, slammed the door behind her. Emotion with Melvyna took the form of roughness.

Sister St. Luke went joyfully back to her convent the next day, for Pedro, when he returned, brought the letter, written, as Keith had directed, in the style of an affectionate invitation. The little nun wept for happiness when she read it. " You see how they love me—love me as I love them," she repeated with innocent triumph again and again.

" It is all we can do," said Keith. " She could not be happy anywhere else, and with the money behind her she will not be neglected. Besides, I really believe they do love her. The sending her up here was probably the result of some outside dictation."

Carrington, however, was dissatisfied. " A pretty return we make for our saved lives!" he said. " I hate ingratitude." For Carrington was half disposed now to fall in love with his preserver.

4

But Keith stood firm.

"Addios," said the little Sister, as Pedro's boat received her. Her face had lighted so with joy and glad anticipation that they hardly knew her. "I wish you could to the convent go with me," she said earnestly to the two young men. "I am sure you would like it." Then, as the boat turned the point, "I am sure you would like it," she called back, crossing her hands on her breast. "It is very heavenly there—very heavenly."

That was the last they saw of her.

Carrington sent down the next winter from New York a large silver crucifix, superbly embossed and ornamented. It was placed on the high altar of the convent, and much admired and reverenced by all the nuns. Sister St. Luke admired it too. She spoke of the island occasionally, but she did not tell the story of the rescue. She never thought of it. Therefore, in the matter of the crucifix, the belief was that a special grace had touched the young man's heart. And prayers were ordered for him. Sister St. Luke tended her doves, and at the hour of meditation paced to and fro between the lime-tree and the bush of white roses. When she was thirty years old her cup was full, for then she was permitted to take lessons and play a little upon the old organ.

Melvyna went every Sunday to the bare, struggling little Presbyterian mission over in the town, and she remains to this day a Sawyer.

But Keith remembered. He bares his head silently in reverence to all womanhood, and curbs his cynicism as best he can, for the sake of the little Sister—the sweet little Sister St. Luke.

MISS ELISABETHA.

In yonder homestead, wreathed with bounteous vines,
A lonely woman dwells, whose wandering feet
Pause oft amid one chamber's calm retreat,
Where an old mirror from its quaint frame shines.
And here, soft wrought in memory's vague designs,
Dim semblances her wistful gaze will greet
Of lost ones that inthrall phantasmally sweet
The mirror's luminous quietude enshrines.

But unto her these dubious forms that pass
With shadowy majesty or dreamy grace,
Wear nothing of ghostliness in mien or guise.
The only ghost that haunts this glimmering glass
Carries the sad reality in its face
Of her own haggard cheeks and desolate eyes !

EDGAR FAWCETT.

OVERLOOKING the tide-water river stands an old house,
gleaming white in the soft moonlight ; the fragrance of tropic
flowers floats out to sea on the land-breeze, coming at sunset
over the pine-barrens to take the place of the ocean winds that
have blown all day long, bringing in the salt freshness to do
battle with the hot shafts of the sun and conquer them. The
side of the house toward the river shows stone arches, door-
less, opening into a hall; beyond is a large room, lighted by
two candles placed on an old-fashioned piano ; and full in
their yellow radiance sits Miss Elisabetha, playing, with clear,
measured touch, an old-time minuet. The light falls upon
her face, with its sharp, high-curved features, pale-blue eyes,
and the three thin curls of blonde hair on each side. She is
not young, our Elisabetha : the tall, spare form, stiffly erect,
the little wisp of hair behind ceremoniously braided and

adorned with a high comb, the long, thin hands, with the tell-tale wrist-bones prominent as she plays, and the fine network of wrinkles over her pellucid, colorless cheeks, tell this. But the boy who listens sees it not; to him she is a St. Cecilia, and the gates of heaven open as she plays. He leans his head against the piano, and his thoughts are lost in melody; they do not take the form of words, but sway to and fro with the swell and the ebb of the music. If you should ask him, he could not express what he feels, for his is no analytical mind; attempt to explain it to him, and very likely he would fall asleep before your eyes. Miss Elisabetha plays well—in a prim, old-fashioned way, but yet well; the ancient piano has lost its strength, but its tones are still sweet, and the mistress humors its failings. She tunes it herself, protects its strings from the sea-damps, dusts it carefully, and has embroidered for it a cover in cross-stitch, yellow tulips growing in straight rows out of a blue ground—an heirloom pattern brought from Holland. Yet entire happiness can not be ours in this world, and Miss Elisabetha sometimes catches herself thinking how delightful it would be to use E flat once more; but the piano's E flat is hopelessly gone.

"Is not that enough for this evening, Theodore?" said Miss Elisabetha, closing the manuscript music-book, whose delicate little pen-and-ink notes were fading away with age.

"Oh, no, dear aunt; sing for me, please, 'The Proud Ladye.'"

And so the piano sounded forth again in a prim melody, and the thin voice began the ballad of the knight, who, scorned by his lady-love, went to the wars with her veil bound on his heart; he dies on the field, but a dove bears back the veil to the Proud Ladye, who straightway falls "a-weeping and a-weeping till she weeps her life away." The boy who listens is a slender stripling, with brown eyes, and a mass of brown curls tossed back from a broad, low forehead; he has the outlines of a Greek, and a dark, silken fringe just borders his boyish mouth. He is dressed in a simple suit of dark-blue

cotton jacket and trousers, the broad white collar turned down,
revealing his round young throat ; on his slender feet he wears
snowy stockings, knitted by Miss Elisabetha's own hands, and
over them a low slipper of untanned leather. His brown
hands are clasped over one knee, the taper fingers and almond-
shaped nails betraying the artistic temperament—a sign which
is confirmed by the unusually long, slender line of the eyebrows, curving down almost to the cheeks.

"A-weeping and a-weeping till she weeps her life away,"
sang Miss Elisabetha, her voice in soft *diminuendo* to express
the mournful end of the Proud Ladye. Then, closing the
piano carefully, and adjusting the tulip-bordered cover, she
extinguished the candles, and the two went out under the
open arches, where chairs stood ready for them nightly. The
tide-water river—the Warra—flowed by, the moon-path shining goldenly across it ; up in the north palmettos stood in
little groups alongshore, with the single feathery pine-trees of
the barrens coming down to meet them ; in the south shone
the long lagoon, with its low islands, while opposite lay the
slender point of the mainland, fifteen miles in length, the
Warra on one side, and on the other the ocean ; its white
sand-ridges gleamed in the moonlight, and the two could hear
the sound of the waves on its outer beach.

"It is so beautiful," said the boy, his dreamy eyes following the silver line of the lagoon.

"Yes," replied Miss Elisabetha, "but we have no time to
waste, Theodore. Bring your guitar and let me hear you
sing that *romanza* again ; remember the pauses—three beats
to the measure."

Then sweetly sounded forth the soft tenor voice, singing
an old French *romanza*, full of little quavers, and falls, and
turns, which the boy involuntarily slurred into something like
naturalness, or gave *staccato* as the mocking-bird throws out
his shower of short, round notes. But Miss Elisabetha allowed no such license : had she not learned that very *romanza*
from Monsieur Vocard himself forty years before? and had

he not carefully taught her every one of those little turns and
quavers ? Taking the guitar from Theodore's hand, she executed all the flourishes slowly and precisely, making him follow her, note for note. Then he must sing it all over again
while she beat the time with her long, slender foot, incased
in a black-silk slipper of her own making. The ladies of the
Daarg family always wore slippers—the heavy-sounding modern boot they considered a structure suitable only for persons
of plebeian origin. A lady should not even step perceptibly;
she should glide.

" Miss 'Lisabeet, de toas' is ready. Bress de chile, how
sweet he sings to-night ! Mos' like de mock-bird's self, Mass'
Doro."

So spoke old Viny, the one servant of the house, a broad-
shouldered, jet-black, comfortable creature, with her gray
wool peeping from beneath a gay turban. She had belonged
to Doro's Spanish mother, but, when Miss Elisabetha came
South to take the house and care for the orphan-boy, she had
purchased the old woman, and set her free immediately.

" It don't make naw difference as I can see, Miss 'Lisabeet," said Viny, when the new mistress carefully explained
to her that she was a free agent from that time forth. " 'Pears
harnsome in you to do it, but it arn't likely I'll leabe my chile,
my Doro-boy, long as I lib—is it, now? When I die, he'll
have ole Viny burred nice, wid de priests, an' de candles, an'
de singing, an' all."

" Replace your guitar, Theodore," said Miss Elisabetha,
rising, " and then walk to and fro between here and the gate
ten times. Walk briskly, and keep your mouth shut; after
singing you should always guard against the damps."

The boy obeyed in his dreamy way, pacing down the white
path, made hard with pounded oyster-shells, to the high stone
wall. The old iron-clamped gate, which once hung between
the two pomegranate-topped pillars, was gone; for years it
had leaned tottering half across the entrance-way, threaten-
ing to brain every comer, but Miss Elisabetha had ordered its

removal in the twinkling of her Northern eye, and in its place
now hung a neat, incongruous little wicket, whose latch was
a standing bone of contention between the mistress and the
entire colored population of the small village.

"Go back and latch the gate," was her constantly repeated
order; "the cows might enter and injure the garden."

"But th' arn't no cows, Miss 'Lisabeet."

"There should be, then," the ancient maiden would reply,
severely. "Grass would grow with a little care and labor;
look at our pasture. You are much too indolent, good people!"

Theodore stood leaning over the little gate, his eyes fixed
on the white sand-hills across the Warra; he was listening to
the waves on the outer beach.

"Theodore, Theodore!" called Miss Elisabetha's voice,
"do not stand, but pace to and fro; and be sure and keep
your mouth closed."

Mechanically the boy obeyed, but his thoughts were following the sound of the water. Following a sound? Yes.
Sounds were to him a language, and he held converse with
the surf, the winds, the rustling marsh-grass, and the sighing
pines of the barrens. The tale of the steps completed, he re-
entered the house, and, following the light, went into a long,
narrow room, one of three which, built out behind the main
body of the house, formed with its back-wall a square, sur-
rounding a little courtyard, in whose center stood the well, a
ruined fountain, rose- and myrtle-bushes, and two ancient fig-
trees, dwarfed and gnarled. Miss Elisabetha was standing at
the head of the table; before her was a plate containing three
small slices of dry toast, crisp and brown, and a decanter of
orange-wine, made by her own hands. One slice of the toast
was for herself, two were for the boy, who was still supposed
to be growing; a Northerner would have said that he was
over twenty, but Spanish blood hastens life, and Teodoro in
years was actually not yet eighteen. In mind he was still
younger, thanks to Miss Elisabetha's care and strict control.

It had never even occurred to him that he need not so absolutely obey her; and, to tell the truth, neither had it occurred
to her. Doro ate his simple supper standing—the Daarg
family never sat down gluttonously to supper, but browsed
lightly on some delicate fragments, moving about and chatting
meanwhile as though half forgetting they were eating at all.
Then Miss Elisabetha refilled his little glass, watched him
drink the clear amber liquid to the last drop, and bade him
good night in her even voice. He turned at the door and
made her a formal bow, not without grace ; she had carefully
taught him this salutation, and required it of him every night.

" I wish you a blessed rest, Theodore," she said, courtesying in reply ; " do not keep the light burning."

Half an hour later, when the ancient maiden glided out of
her chamber, clad in a long frilled wrapper, the three curls in
papers on each side of her head, she saw no gleam from
under the low door of the little room across the hall ; she listened, but there was no sound, and, satisfied, she retired to
her high couch and closed the gayly flowered curtains around
her. But, out on the small balcony which hung like a cage
from his eastern window, Doro stood, leaning over the iron
railing and listening, listening to the far sound of the sea.

Such had been the life down in the old house for sixteen
long, winterless years, the only changes being more difficult
music and more toast, longer lessons in French, longer legs
to the little blue trousers, increased attention to sea-baths and
deportment, and always and ever a careful saving of every
copper penny and battered shilling. What became of these
coins old Viny did not know ; she only knew how patiently
they were collected, and how scrupulously saved. Miss Elisabetha attended to the orange-grove in person ; not one orange
was lost, and the annual waste of the other proprietors, an
ancient and matter-of-course waste, handed down from father
to son, represented in her purse not a few silver pieces. Pedro, the Minorcan, who brought her fish and sea-food, she
had drilled from boyhood in his own art by sheer force of

will, paying him by the day, and sending him into the town to
sell from door to door all she did not need herself, to the very
last clam. The lazy housewives soon grew into the habit of
expecting Pedro and his basket, and stood in their doorways
chatting in the sun and waiting for him, while the husbands
let their black dugouts lie idle, and lounged on the sea-wall,
smoking and discussing the last alligator they had shot, or the
last ship, a coasting-schooner out of water, which had sailed
up their crooked harbor six months before. Miss Elisabetha
had learned also to braid palmetto, and her long fingers, once
accustomed to the work, accomplished as much in a week as
Zanita Perez and both her apprentices accomplished in two;
she brought to the task also original ideas, original at least in
Beata, where the rude hats and baskets were fac-similes of
those braided there two hundred years before by the Spanish
women, who had learned the art from the Indians. Thus
Miss Elisabetha's wares found ready sale at increased prices,
little enough to Northern ideas—sixpence for a hat—one shilling for a basket; but all down the coast, and inland toward
the great river, there was a demand for her work, and the
lines hung in the garden were almost constantly covered with
the drying palmetto. Then she taught music. To whom, do
you ask? To the black-eyed daughters of the richer towns-
people, and to one or two demoiselles belonging to Spanish
families down the coast, sent up to Beata to be educated by
the nuns. The good Sisters did their best, but they knew
little, poor things, and were glad to call in Miss Elisabetha
with her trills and quavers; so the wiry organ in the little cathedral sounded out the ballads and *romanzas* of Monsieur
Vocard, and the demoiselles learned to sing them in their
broken French, no doubt greatly to the satisfaction of the
golden-skinned old fathers and mothers on the plantations
down the coast. The *padre* in charge of the parish had often
importuned Miss Elisabetha to play this organ on Sundays, as
the decorous celebration of high-mass suffered sadly, not to
say ludicrously, from the blunders of poor Sister Paula. But

Miss Elisabetha briefly refused; she must draw a line somewhere, and a pagan ceremonial she could not countenance. The Daarg family, while abhorring greatly the Puritanism of the New England colonies, had yet held themselves equally aloof from the image-worship of Rome; and they had always considered it one of the inscrutable mysteries of Providence that the French nation, so skilled in polite attitude, so versed in the singing of *romanzas*, should yet have been allowed to remain so long in ignorance of the correct religious mean.

The old house was managed with the nicest care. Its thick coquina-walls remained solid still, and the weak spots in the roof were mended with a thatch of palmetto and tar, applied monthly under the mistress's superintendence by Viny, who never ceased to regard the performance as a wonder of art, accustomed as she was to the Beata fashion of letting roofs leak when they wanted to, the family never interfering, but encamping on the far side of the flow with calm undisturbed. The few pieces of furniture were dusted and rubbed daily, and the kitchen department was under martial law; the three had enough to eat—indeed, an abundance—oysters, fish, and clams, sweet potatoes from the garden, and various Northern vegetables forced to grow under the vigilant nursing they received, but hating it, and coming up as spindling as they could. The one precious cow gave them milk and butter, the well-conducted hens gave them eggs; flour and meal, coffee and tea, hauled across the barrens from the great river, were paid for in palmetto-work. Yes, Miss Elisabetha's household, in fact, lived well, better perhaps than any in Beata; but so measured were her quantities, so exact her reckonings, so long her look ahead, that sometimes, when she was away, old Viny felt a sudden wild desire to toss up fritters in the middle of the afternoon, to throw away yesterday's tea-leaves, to hurl the soured milk into the road, or even to eat oranges without counting them, according to the fashions of the easy old days when Doro's Spanish grandmother held the reins, and everything went to ruin comfortably. Every morning after breakfast Miss Elisabetha went the rounds through the house and garden ; then English and French with Doro for two hours ; next a sea-bath for him, and sailing or walking as he pleased, when the sun was not too hot. Luncheon at noon, followed by a *siesta ;* then came a music-lesson, long and charming to both ; and, after that, he had his choice from among her few books. Dinner at five, a stroll along the beach, music in the evenings—at first the piano in the parlor, then the guitar under the arches ; last of all, the light supper, and good-night. Such was Doro's day. But Miss Elisabetha, meanwhile, had a hundred other duties which she never neglected, in spite of her attention to his welfare—first the boy, then his money, for it was earned and destined for him. Thus the years had passed, without change, without event, without misfortune ; the orange-trees had not failed, the palmetto-work had not waned, and the little store of money grew apace. Doro, fully employed, indulged by Viny, amused with his dogs, his parrot, his mocking-birds, and young owls, all the variety of pets the tropical land afforded, even to young alligators clandestinely kept in a sunken barrel up the marsh, knew no *ennui.* But, most of all, the music filled his life, rounding out every empty moment, and making an undercurrent, as it were, to all other occupations ; so that the French waltzed through his brain, the English went to marches, the sailing made for itself *gondelieds,* and even his plunges in the Warra were like crashes of fairy octaves, with *arpeggios* of pearly notes in showers coming after.

These were the *ante-bellum* days, before the war had opened the Southern country to winter visitors from the North ; invalids a few, tourists a few, came and went, but the great tide, which now sweeps annually down the Atlantic coast to Florida, was then unknown. Beata, lying by itself far down the peninsula, no more looked for winter visitors than it looked for angels ; but one day an angel arrived unawares, and Doro saw her.

Too simple-hearted to conceal, excited, longing for sympathy, he poured out his story to Miss Elisabetha, who sat copying from her music-book a certain ballad for the Demoiselle Xantez.

"It was over on the north beach, aunt, and I heard the music and hastened thither. She was sitting on a tiger-skin thrown down on the white sand; purple velvet flowed around her, and above, from embroideries like cream, rose her flower-face set on a throat so white, where gleamed a star of brilliancy; her hair was like gold—yellow gold—and it hung in curls over her shoulders, a mass of radiance; her eyes were blue as the deepest sky-color; and oh! so white her skin, I could scarcely believe her mortal. She was playing on a guitar, with her little hands so white, so soft, and singing—aunt, it was like what I have dreamed."

The boy stopped and covered his face with his hands. Miss Elisabetha had paused, pen in hand. What was this new talk of tiger-skins and golden hair? No one could sing in Beata save herself alone; the boy was dreaming!

"Theodore," she said, "fancy is permitted to us under certain restrictions, but no well-regulated mind will make to itself realities of fancies. I am sorry to be obliged to say it, but the romances must be immediately removed from the shelf."

These romances, three in number, selected and sanctioned by the governess of the Misses Daarg forty years before, still stood in Miss Elisabetha's mind as exemplars of the wildest flights of fancy.

"But this is not fancy, dear aunt," said Doro eagerly, his brown eyes velvet with moisture, and his brown cheeks flushed. "I saw it all this afternoon over on the beach; I could show you the very spot where the tiger-skin lay, and the print of her foot, which had a little shoe so odd—like this," and rapidly he drew the outline of a walking-boot in the extreme of the Paris fashion.

Miss Elisabetha put on her glasses.

" Heels," she said slowly ; " I have heard of them."

" There is nothing in all the world like her," pursued the excited boy, " for her hair is of pure gold, not like the people here ; and her eyes are so sweet, and her forehead so white ! I never knew such people lived—why have you not told me all these years ? "

" She is a blonde," replied Miss Elisabetha primly. " I, too, am a blonde, Theodore."

" But not like this, aunt. My lovely lady is like a rose."

" A subdued monotone of coloring has ever been a characteristic of our family, Theodore. But I do not quite understand your story. Who is this person, and was she alone on the beach ? "

" There were others, but I did not notice them ; I only looked at her."

" And she sang ? "

" O aunt, so heavenly sweet—so strange, so new her song, that I was carried away up into the blue sky as if on strong wings—I seemed to float in melody. But I can not talk of it ; it takes my breath away, even in thought ! "

Miss Elisabetha sat perplexed.

" Was it one of our *romanzas,* Theodore, or a ballad ? " she said, running over the list in her mind.

" It was something I never heard before," replied Doro, in a low voice ; " it was not like anything else—not even the mocking-bird, for, though it went on and on, the same strain floated back into it again and again ; and the mocking-bird, you know, has a light and fickle soul. Aunt, I can not tell you what it was like, but it seemed to tell me a new story of a new world."

" How many beats had it to the measure ? " asked Miss Elisabetha, after a pause.

" I do not know," replied the boy dreamily.

" You do not know ! All music is written in some set time, Theodore. At least, you can tell me about the words. Were they French ? "

"No."

"Nor English?"

"No."

"What then?"

"I know not; angel-words, perhaps.

"Did she speak to you?"

"Yes," replied Doro, clasping his hands fervently. "She asked me if I liked the song, and I said, 'Lady, it is of the angels.' Then she smiled, and asked my name, and I told her, 'Doro'—"

"You should have said, 'Theodore,'" interrupted Miss Elisabetha; "do I not always call you so?"

"And she said it was a lovely name; and could I sing? I took her guitar, and sang to her—"

"And she praised your method, I doubt not?"

"She said, 'Oh, what a lovely voice!' and she touched my hair with her little hands, and I—I thought I should die, aunt, but I only fell at her feet."

"And where—where is this person now?" said the perplexed maiden, catching at something definite.

"She has gone—gone! I stood and watched the little flag on the mast until I could see it no more. She has gone! Pity me, aunt, dear aunt. What shall I do? How shall I live?"

The boy broke into sobs, and would say no more. Miss Elisabetha was strangely stirred; here was a case beyond her rules; what should she do? Having no precedent to guide her, she fell back into her old beliefs gained from studies of the Daarg family, as developed in boys. Doro was excused from lessons, and the hours were made pleasant to him. She spent many a morning reading aloud to him; and old Viny stood amazed at the variety and extravagance of the dishes ordered for him.

"What! chickens ebery day, Miss 'Lisabeet? 'Pears like Mass' Doro hab eberyting now!"

"Theodore is ill, Lavinia," replied the mistress; and she really thought so.

Music, however, there was none; the old charmed afternoons and evenings were silent.

" I can not bear it," the boy had said, with trembling lips.

But one evening he did not return : the dinner waited for
him in vain ; the orange after-glow faded away over the pine-
barrens; and in the pale green of the evening sky arose the
star of the twilight; still he came not.

Miss Elisabetha could eat nothing.

" Keep up the fire, Lavinia," she said, rising from the table
at last.

" Keep up de fire, Miss 'Lisabeet !   Till when ? "

" Till Theodore comes ! " replied the mistress shortly.

" De worl' mus' be coming to de end," soliloquized the old
black woman, carrying out the dishes ; " sticks of wood no
account ! "

Late in the evening a light footstep sounded over the
white path, and the strained, watching eyes under the stone
arches saw at last the face of the missing one.

" O aunt, I have seen her—I have seen her ! I thought
her gone for ever. O aunt—dear, dear aunt, she has sung for
me again ! " said the boy, flinging himself down on the stones,
and laying his flushed face on her knee. " This time it was
over by the old lighthouse, aunt. I was sailing up and down
in the very worst breakers I could find, half hoping they
would swamp the boat, for I thought perhaps I could forget
her down there under the water—when I saw figures moving
over on the island-beach. Something in the outlines of one
made me tremble ; and I sailed over like the wind, the little
boat tilted on its side within a hair's-breadth of the water,
cutting it like a knife as it flew. It was she, aunt, and she
smiled ! ' What, my young Southern nightingale,' she said,
' is it you ? '   And she gave me her hand—her soft little
hand."

The thin fingers, hardened by much braiding of palmetto,
withdrew themselves instinctively from the boy's dark curls.
He did not notice it, but rushed on with his story unheeding :

"She let me walk with her, aunt, and hold her parasol, decked with lace, and she took off her hat and hung it on my arm, and it had a long, curling plume. She gave me sweet things—oh, so delicious! See, I kept some," said Doro, bringing out a little package of bonbons. "Some are of sugar, you see, and some have nuts in them; those are chocolate. Are they not beautiful?"

"Candies, I think," said Miss Elisabetha, touching them doubtfully with the end of her quill.

"And she sang for me, aunt, the same angel's music; and then, when I was afar in heaven, she brought me back with a song about three fishermen who sailed out into the west; and I wept to hear her, for her voice then was like the sea when it feels cruel. She saw the tears, and, bidding me sit by her side, she struck a few chords on her guitar and sang to me of a miller's daughter who grew so dear, so dear. Do you know it, aunt?"

"A miller's daughter? No; I have no acquaintance with any such person," said Miss Elisabetha, considering.

"Wait, I will sing it to you," said Doro, running to bring his guitar; "she taught it to me herself!"

And then the tenor voice rose in the night air, bearing on the lovely melody the impassioned words of the poet. Doro sang them with all his soul, and the ancient maiden felt her heart disquieted within her—why, she knew not. It seemed as though her boy was drifting away whither she could not follow.

"Is it not beautiful, aunt? I sang it after her line by line until I knew it all, and then I sang her all my songs; and she said I must come and see her the day after to-morrow, and she would give me her picture and something else. What do you suppose it is, aunt? She would not tell me, but she smiled and gave me her hand for good-by. And now I can live, for I am to see her at Martera's house, beyond the convent, the day after to-morrow, the day after to-morrow—oh, happy day, the day after to-morrow!"

"Come and eat your dinner, Theodore," said Miss Elisabetha, rising. Face to face with a new world, whose possibilities she but dimly understood, and whose language was to her an unknown tongue, she grasped blindly at the old anchors riveted in years of habit; the boy had always been something of an epicure in his fastidious way, and one of his favorite dishes was on the table.

"You may go, Lavinia," she said, as the old slave lingered to see if her darling enjoyed the dainties; she could not bear that even Viny's faithful eyes should notice the change, if change there was.

The boy ate nothing.

"I am not hungry, aunt," he said, "I had so many delicious things over on the beach. I do not know what they were, but they were not like our things at all." And, with a slight gesture of repugnance, he pushed aside his plate.

"You had better go to bed," said Miss Elisabetha, rising. In her perplexity this was the first thing which suggested itself to her; a good night's rest had been known to work wonders; she would say no more till morning. The boy went readily; but he must have taken his guitar with him, for long after Miss Elisabetha had retired to her couch she heard him softly singing again and again the romance of the miller's daughter. Several times she half rose as if to go and stop him; then a confused thought came to her that perhaps his unrest might work itself off in that way, and she sank back, listening meanwhile to the fanciful melody with feelings akin to horror. It seemed to have no regular time, and the harmony was new and strange to her old-fashioned ears. "Truly, it must be the work of a composer gone mad," said the poor old maid, after trying in vain for the fifth time to follow the wild air. There was not one trill or turn in all its length, and the accompaniment, instead of being the decorous one octave in the bass, followed by two or three chords according to the time, seemed to be but a general sweeping over the strings, with long pauses, and unexpected minor harmony introduced, turning the air suddenly upside down, and then back again before one had time to comprehend what was going on. "Heaven help me!" said Miss Elisabetha, as the melody began again for the sixth time, "but I fear I am sinful enough to hate that miller's daughter." And it was very remarkable, to say the least, that a person in her position "was possessed of a jewel to tremble in her ear," she added censoriously, "not even to speak of a necklace." But the comfort was cold, and, before she knew it, slow, troubled tears had dampened her pillow.

Early the next morning she was astir by candle-light, and, going into the detached kitchen, began preparing breakfast with her own hands, adding to the delicacies already ordered certain honey-cakes, an heirloom in the Daarg family. Viny could scarcely believe her eyes when, on coming down to her domain at the usual hour, she found the great fireplace glowing, and the air filled with the fragrance of spices; Christmas alone had heretofore seen these honey-cakes, and to-day was only a common day!

"I do not care for anything, aunt," said Doro, coming listlessly to the table when all was ready. He drank some coffee, broke a piece of bread, and then went back to his guitar; the honey-cakes he did not even notice.

One more effort remained. Going softly into the parlor during the morning, Miss Elisabetha opened the piano, and, playing over the prelude to "The Proud Ladye," began to sing in her very best style, giving the flourishes with elaborate art, scarcely a note without a little step down from the one next higher; these airy descents, like flights of fairy stairs, were considered very high art in the days of Monsieur Vocard. She was in the middle of "a-weeping and a-weeping," when Doro rushed into the room. "O aunt," he cried, "please, please do not sing! Indeed, I can not bear it. We have been all wrong about our music; I can not explain it, but I feel it—I know it. If you could only hear her! Come

with me to-morrow and hear her, dear aunt, and then you
will understand what I mean."

Left to herself again, Miss Elisabetha felt a great resolve
come to her. She herself would go and see this stranger, and
grind her to powder! She murmured these words over several times, and derived much comfort from them.

With firm hands she unlocked the cedar chest which had
come with her from the city seventeen years before; but the
ladies of the Daarg family had not been wont to change their
attire every passing fashion, and the robe she now drew forth
was made in the style of full twenty-five years previous—a
stiff drab brocade flowered in white, two narrow flounces
around the bottom of the scant skirt, cut half low in the neck
with a little bertha, the material wanting in the lower part
standing out resplendent in the broad leg-of-mutton sleeves,
stiffened with buckram. Never had the full daylight of Beata
seen this precious robe, and Miss Elisabetha herself considered it for a moment with some misgivings as to its being
too fine for such an occasion. But had not Doro spoken of
"velvet" and "embroideries"? So, with solemnity, she ar-
rayed herself, adding a certain Canton-crape scarf of a delicate
salmon color, and a Leghorn bonnet with crown and cape,
which loomed out beyond her face so that the three curls
slanted forward over the full ruche to get outside, somewhat
like blinders. Thus clad, with her slippers, her bag on her
arm, and lace mits on her hands, Miss Elisabetha surveyed
herself in the glass. In the bag were her handkerchief, an
ancient smelling-bottle, and a card, yellow indeed, but still a
veritable engraved card, with these words upon it :

"Miss ELISABETHA DAARG,

DAARG'S BAY."

The survey was satisfactory. "Certainly I look the gen-
tlewoman," she thought, with calm pride, "and this person,
whoever she is, can not fail to at once recognize me as such.

It has never been our custom to visit indiscriminately; but in
this case I do it for the boy's sake." So she sallied forth, going out by a side-door to escape observation, and walked toward the town, revolving in her mind the words she should
use when face to face with the person. "I shall request her
—with courtesy, of course—still I shall feel obliged to request
her to leave the neighborhood," she thought. "I shall express to her—with kindness, but also with dignity—my opinion of the meretricious music she has taught my boy, and I
shall say to her frankly that I really can not permit her to see
him again. Coming from me, these words will, of course,
have weight, and—"

"Oh, see Miss 'Lisabeet!" sang out a child's voice.
"Nita, do but come and see how fine she is!"

Nita came, saw, and followed, as did other children—girls
carrying plump babies, olive-skinned boys keeping close together, little blacks of all ages, with go-carts made of turtle-
shells. · It was not so much the splendor—though that was
great, too—as it was the fact that Miss Elisabetha wore it.
Had they not all known her two cotton gowns as far back as
they could remember? Reaching the Martera house at last,
her accustomed glide somewhat quickened by the presence of
her escort (for, although she had often scolded them over her
own gate, it was different now when they assumed the pro-
portions of a body-guard), she gave her card to little Inez, a
daughter of the household, and one of her pupils.

"Bear this card to the person you have staying with you,
my child, and ask her if she will receive me."

"But there is more than one person, señora," replied Inez,
lost in wonder over the brocade.

"The one who sings, then."

"They all sing, Miss 'Lisabeet."

"Well, then, I mean the person who—who wears purple
velvet and—and embroideries," said the visitor, bringing out
these items reluctantly.

"Ah! you mean the beautiful lady," cried Inez. "I run,

I run, señora"; and in a few minutes Miss Elisabetha was ushered up the stairs, and found herself face to face with "the person."

"To whom have I the honor of speaking?" said a languid voice from the sofa.

"Madame, my card—"

"Oh, was that a card? Pray excuse me.—Lucille, my glasses." Then, as a French maid brought the little, gold-rimmed toy, the person scanned the name. "Ma'm'selle Dag?" she said inquiringly.

"Daarg, madame," replied Miss Elisabetha. "If you have resided in New York at all, you are probably familiar with the name"; and majestically she smoothed down the folds of the salmon-colored scarf.

"I have resided in New York, and I am not familiar with the name," said the person, throwing her head back indolently among the cushions.

She wore a long, full robe of sea-green silk, opening over a mist of lace-trimmed skirts, beneath whose filmy borders peeped little feet incased in green-silk slippers, with heels of grotesque height; a cord and tassels confined the robe to her round waist; the hanging sleeves, open to the shoulders, revealed superb white arms; and the mass of golden hair was gathered loosely up behind, with a mere *soupçon* of a cap perched on top, a knot of green ribbon contrasting with the low-down golden ripples over the forehead. Miss Elisabetha surveyed the attitude and the attire with disfavor; in her young days no lady in health wore a wrapper, or lolled on sofas. But the person, who was the pet prima donna of the day, English, with a world-wide experience and glory, knew nothing of such traditions.

"I have called, madame," began the visitor, ignoring the slight with calm dignity (after all, how should "a person" know anything of the name of Daarg?), "on account of my— my ward, Theodore Oesterand."

"Never heard of him," replied the diva. It was her hour

for *siesta*, and any infringement of her rules told upon the
carefully tended, luxuriant beauty.

"I beg your pardon," said Miss Elisabetha, with increased
accentuation of her vowels. "Theodore has had the honor
of seeing you twice, and he has also sung for you."

"What! you mean my little bird of the tropics, my Southern nightingale!" exclaimed the singer, raising herself from
the cushions.—"Lucille, why have you not placed a chair for
this lady?—I assure you, I take the greatest interest in the
boy, Miss Dag."

"Daarg," replied Miss Elisabetha; and then, with dignity,
she took the chair, and, seating herself, crossed one slipper
over the other, in the attitude number one of her youth.
Number one had signified "repose," but little repose felt she
now; there was something in the attire of this person, something in her yellow hair and white arms, something in the
very air of the room, heavy with perfumes, that seemed to
hurt and confuse her.

"I have never heard a tenor of more promise, never in my
life; and consider how much that implies, ma'm'selle! You
probably know who I am?"

"I have not that pleasure."

"*Bien*, I will tell you. I am Kernadi."

Miss Elisabetha bowed, and inhaled salts from her smelling-bottle, her little finger elegantly separated from the others.

"You do not mean to say that you have never heard of
Kernadi—Cécile Kernadi?" said the diva, sitting fairly erect
now in her astonishment.

"Never," replied the maiden, not without a proud satisfaction in the plain truth of her statement.

"Where have you lived, ma'm'selle?"

"Here, Mistress Kernadi."

The singer gazed at the figure before her in its ancient
dress, and gradually a smile broke over her beautiful face.

"Ma'm'selle," she said, dismissing herself and her fame
with a wave of her white hand, "you have a treasure in Doro,

a voice rare in a century; and, in the name of the world, I ask you for him."

Miss Elisabetha sat speechless; she was never quick with words, and now she was struck dumb.

"I will take him with me when I go in a few days," pursued Kernadi; "and I promise you he shall have the very best instructors. His method now is bad—insufferably bad. The poor boy has had, of course, no opportunities; but he is still young, and can unlearn as well as learn. Give him to me. I will relieve you of all expenses, so sure do I feel that he will do me credit in the end. I will even pass my word that he shall appear with me upon either the London or the Vienna stage before two years are out."

Miss Elisabetha had found her words at last.

"Madame," she said, "do you wish to make an operasinger of the son of Petrus Oesterand?"

"I wish to make an opera-singer of this pretty Doro; and, if this good Petrus is his father, he will, no doubt, give his consent."

"Woman, he is dead."

"So much the better; he will not interfere with our plans, then," replied the diva, gayly.

Miss Elisabetha rose; her tall form shook perceptibly.

"I have the honor to bid you good day," she said, courtesying formally.

The woman on the sofa sprang to her feet.

"You are offended?" she asked; "and why?"

"That you, a person of no name, of no antecedents, a public singer, should presume to ask for my boy, an Oesterand —should dare to speak of degrading him to your level!"

Kernadi listened to these words in profound astonishment. Princes had bowed at her feet, blood-royal had watched for her smile. Who was this ancient creature, with her scarf and bag? Perhaps, poor thing! she did not comprehend! The diva was not bad-hearted, and so, gently enough, she went over her offer a second time, dwelling upon and explaining its advantages. "That he will succeed, I do not doubt," she said; "but in any case he shall not want."

Miss Elisabetha was still standing.

"Want?" she repeated; "Theodore want? I should think not."

"He shall have the best instructors," pursued Kernadi, all unheeding. To do her justice, she meant all she said. It is ever a fancy of singers to discover singers—provided they sing other *rôles*.

"Madame, I have the honor of instructing him myself."

"Ah, indeed. Very kind of you, I am sure; but—but no doubt you will be glad to give up the task. And he shall see all the great cities of Europe, and hear their music. I am down here merely for a short change—having taken cold in your miserable New York climate; but I have my usual engagements in London, St. Petersburg, Vienna, and Paris, you know."

"No, madame, I do not know," was the stiff reply.

Kernadi opened her fine eyes still wider. It was true, then, and not a pretense. People really lived—white people, too—who knew nothing of her and her movements! She thought, in her vague way, that she really must give something to the missionaries; and then she went back to Doro.

"It will be a great advantage to him to see artist-life abroad—" she began.

"I intend him to see it," replied Miss Elisabetha.

"But he should have the right companions—advisers—"

"*I* shall be with him, madame."

The diva surveyed the figure before her, and amusement shone in her eyes.

"But you will find it fatiguing," she said—"so much journeying, so much change! Nay, ma'm'selle, remain at home in your peaceful quiet, and trust the boy to me." She had sunk back upon her cushions, and, catching a glimpse of her face in the mirror, she added, smiling: "One thing more.

You need not fear lest I should trifle with his young heart. I assure you I will not; I shall be to him like a sister."

"You could scarcely be anything else, unless it was an aunt," replied the ancient maiden; "I should judge you fifteen years his senior, madame."

Which was so nearly accurate that the beauty started, and for the first time turned really angry.

"Will you give me the boy?" she said, shortly. "If he were here I might show you how easily— But, *ciel!* you could never understand such things; let it pass. Will you give me the boy—yes or no?"

"No."

There was a silence. The diva lolled back on her cushions, and yawned.

"You must be a very selfish woman—I think the most selfish I have ever known," she said coolly, tapping the floor with her little slippered feet, as if keeping time to a waltz.

"I—selfish?"

"Yes, you—selfish. And, by the by, what right have you to keep the boy at all? Certainly, he resembles you in nothing. What relation does he hold to you?"

"He is—he is my ward," answered Miss Elisabetha, nervously rearranging her scarf. "I bid you, madame, good day."

"Ward!" pursued Kernadi; "that means nothing. Was his mother your sister?"

"Nay; his mother was a Spanish lady," replied the troubled one, who knew not how to evade or lie.

"And the father—you spoke of him—was he a relative?"

A sudden and painful blush dyed the thin old face, creeping up to the very temples.

"Ah," said the singer, with scornful amusement in her voice, "if that is all, I shall take the boy without more ado"; and, lifting her glasses, she fixed her eyes full on the poor face before her, as though it was some rare variety of animal.

"You shall not have him; I say you shall not!" cried the

5

elder woman, rousing to the contest like a tigress defending her young.

"Will you let him choose?" said Kernadi, with her mocking laugh. "See! I dare you to let him choose"; and, springing to her feet, she wheeled her visitor around suddenly, so that they stood side by side before the mirror. It was a cruel deed. Never before had the old eyes realized that their mild blue had faded; that the curls, once so soft, had grown gray and thin; that the figure, once sylph-like, was now but angles; and the throat, once so fair, yellow and sinewed. It came upon her suddenly—the face, the coloring, and the dress; a veil was torn away, and she saw it all. At the same instant gleamed the golden beauty of the other, the folds of her flowing robe, the mists of her laces. It was too much. With ashen face the stricken woman turned away, and sought the door-knob; she could not speak; a sob choked all utterance. Doro would choose.

But Cécile Kernadi rushed forward; her better nature was touched.

"No, no," she said impulsively, "you shall not go so. See! I will promise; you shall keep the boy, and I will let him go. He is all you have, perhaps, and I—I have so much! Do you not believe me? I will go away this very day and leave no trace behind. He will pine, but it will pass—a boy's first fancy. I promised him my picture, but you shall take it. There! Now go, go, before I regret what I do. He has such a voice!—but never mind, you shall not be robbed by me. Farewell, poor lady; I, too, may grow old some day. But hear one little word of advice from my lips: The boy has waked up to life; he will never be again the child you have known. Though I go, another will come; take heed!"

That night, in the silence of her own room, Miss Elisabetha prayed a little prayer, and then, with firm hand, burned the bright picture to ashes.

Wild was the grief of the boy; but the fair enchantress was gone. He wept, he pined; but she was gone. He fell

ill, and lay feverish upon his narrow bed; but she was none
the less gone, and nothing brought her back. Miss Elisabetha
tended him with a great patience, and spoke no word. When
he raved of golden hair, she never said, "I have seen it";
when he cried, "Her voice, her angel-voice!" she never said,
"I have heard it." But one day she dropped these words:
"Was she not a false woman, Theodore, who went away not
caring, although under promise to see you, and to give you
her picture?" And then she walked quietly to her own
room, and barred the door, and wept; for the first time in
her pure life she had burdened her soul with falsehood—yet
would she have done it ten times over to save the boy.

Time and youth work wonders; it is not that youth for-
gets so soon; but this—time is then so long. Doro recovered,
almost in spite of himself, and the days grew calm again.
Harder than ever worked Miss Elisabetha, giving herself
hardly time to eat or sleep. Doro studied a little listlessly,
but he no longer cared for his old amusements. He had freed
his pets: the mocking-birds had flown back to the barrens,
and the young alligators, who had lived in the sunken barrel,
found themselves unexpectedly obliged to earn their own
living along the marshes and lagoons. But of music he would
have none; the piano stood silent, and his guitar had disappeared.

"It is wearing itself away," thought the old maid; "then
he will come back to me." But nightly she counted her secret
store, and, angered at its smallness, worked harder and harder,
worked until her shoulders ached and her hands grew knotted.
"One more year, only one more year," she thought; "then
he shall go!" And through all the weary toil these words
echoed like a chant—"One more year—only one more!"

Two months passed, and then the spring came to the
winterless land—came with the yellow jasmine. "But four
months now, and he shall go," said Miss Elisabetha, in her
silent musings over the bag of coin. "I have shortened the
time by double tasks." Lightly she stepped about the house,

counted her orange-buds, and reckoned up the fish. She played the cathedral organ now on Sundays, making inward protest after every note, and sitting rigidly with her back toward the altar in the little high-up gallery during the sermon, as much as to say: " It is only my body which is here. Behold ! I do not even bow down in the house of Rimmon." Thus laboring early and late, with heart, and hand, and strength, she saw but little of Doro, save at meals and through his one hour of listless study; but the hidden hope was a comforter, and she worked and trusted on. There was one little gleam of light : he had begun to play again on his guitar, softly, furtively, and as it were in secret. But she heard him, and was cheered.

One evening, toiling home through the white sand after a late music-lesson, laden with a bag of flour which she would not trust Viny to buy, she heard a girl's voice singing. It was a plaintive, monotonous air that she sang, simple as a Gregorian chant ; but her voice was a velvet contralto, as full of rich tones as a peach is full of lusciousness. The contralto voice is like the violoncello.

" The voice is not bad," thought Miss Elisabetha, listening critically, " but there is a certain element of the *sauvage* in it. No lady, no person of culture, would permit herself to sing in that way ; it must be one of the Minorcans."

Still, in spite of prejudices, the music in her turned her steps toward the voice ; her slippers made no sound, and she found it. A young girl, a Minorcan, sat under a bower of jasmine, leaning back against her lover's breast ; her dark eyes were fixed on the evening star, and she sang as the bird sings, naturally, unconsciously, for the pure pleasure of singing. She was a pretty child. Miss Elisabetha knew her well —Catalina, one of a thriftless, olive-skinned family down in the town. " Not fourteen, and a lover already," thought the old maid with horror. " Would it be of any use, I wonder, if I spoke to her mother ? " Here the lover—the Paul of this Virginia—moved, and the shadows slid off his face ; it was Doro !

Alone in her chamber sat Miss Elisabetha. Days had passed, but of no avail. Even now the boy was gone to the tumble-down house in the village where Catalina's little brothers and sisters swarmed out of doors and windows, and the brown, broad mother bade him welcome with a hearty slap on the shoulder. She had tried everything—argument, entreaty, anger, grief—and failed ; there remained now only the secret, the secret of years, of much toil and many pains. The money was not yet sufficient for two ; so be it. She would stay herself, and work on ; but he should go. Before long she would hear his step, perhaps not until late, for those people had no settled hours (here a remembrance of all their ways made her shudder), but come he would in time ; this was still his home. At midnight she heard the footfall, and opening the door called gently, " Theodore, Theodore." The youth came, but slowly. Many times had she called him lately, and he was weary of the strife. Had he not told her all—the girl singing as she passed, her voice haunting him, his search for her, and her smile ; their meetings in the *chaparral*, where she sang to him by the hour, and then, naturally as the bud opens, their love ? It seemed to him an all-sufficient story, and he could not understand the long debates.

" And the golden-haired woman," Miss Elisabetha had said ; " she sang to you too, Theodore."

" I had forgotten her, aunt," replied the youth simply.

So he came but slowly. This time, however, the voice was gentle, and there was no anger in the waiting eyes. She told him all as he sat there : the story of his father, who was once her friend, she said with a little quiver in her voice, the death of the young widowed mother, her own coming to this far Southern land, and her long labors for him. Then she drew a picture of the bright future opening before him, and bringing forth the bag showed him its contents, the savings and earnings of seventeen years, tied in packages with the contents noted on their labels. " All is for you, dear child," she said, " for you are still but a child. Take it and go. I had planned to accompany you, but I give that up for the present. I will remain and see to the sale of everything here, and then I will join you—that is, if you wish it, dear. Perhaps you will enjoy traveling alone, and—and I have plenty of friends to whom I can go, and shall be quite content, dear —quite content."

"Where is it that you wish me to go, aunt?" asked Doro coldly. They were going over the same ground, then, after all.

"Abroad, dear—abroad, to all the great cities of the world," said the aunt, faltering a little as she met his eyes. "You are well educated, Theodore; I have taught you myself. You are a gentleman's son, and I have planned for you a life suited to your descent. I have written to my cousins in Amsterdam; they have never seen me, but for the sake of the name they will—O my boy, my darling, tell me that you will go!" she burst forth, breaking into entreaty as she read his face.

But Doro shook off her hands. "Aunt," he said, rising, "why will you distress yourself thus? I shall marry Catalina, and you know it; have I not told you so? Let us speak no more on the subject. As to the money, I care not for it; keep it." And he turned toward the door as if to end the discussion. But Miss Elisabetha followed and threw herself on her knees before him.

"Child!" she cried, "give me, give yourself a little delay; only that, a little delay. Take the money—go; and if at the end of the year your mind is still the same, I will say not one word, no, not one, against it. She is but young, too young to marry. O my boy, for whom I have labored, for whom I have planned, for whom I have prayed, will you too forsake me?"

"Of course not, aunt," replied Doro; "I mean you to live with us always"; and with his strong young arms he half led, half carried her back to her arm-chair. She sat speechless. To live with them always—with *them!* Words surged to her lips in a flood—then, as she met his gaze, surged back to her heart again. There was that in the expression of his face which told her all words were vain; the placid, far-away look, unmoved in spite of her trouble, silenced argument and killed hope. As well attack a creamy summer cloud with axes; as well attempt to dip up the ocean with a cup. She saw it all in a flash, as one sees years of past life in the moment before drowning; and she was drowning, poor soul! Yet Doro saw nothing, felt nothing, save that his aunt was growing into an old woman with foolish fancies, and that he himself was sleepy. And then he fell to thinking of his love, and all her enchanting ways—her little angers and quick repentances, the shoulder turned away in pretended scorn, and the sudden waves of tenderness that swept him into paradise. So he stood dreaming, while tearless, silent Miss Elisabetha sat before her broken hopes. At last Doro, coming back to reality, murmured, "Aunt, you will like her when you know her better, and she will take good care of you."

But the aunt only shuddered.

"Theodore, Theodore!" she cried, "will you break my heart? Shall the son of Petrus Oesterand marry so?"

"I do not know what you mean by 'so,' aunt. All men marry, and why not I? I never knew my father; but, if he were here, I feel sure he would see Catalina with my eyes. Certainly, in all my life, I have never seen a face so fair, or eyes so lustrous."

"Child, you have seen nothing—nothing. But I intended, Heaven knows I intended—"

"It makes no difference now, aunt; do not distress yourself about it."

"Theodore, I have loved you long—your youth has not been an unhappy one; will you, for my sake, go for this one year?" she pleaded, with quivering lips.

The young man shook his head with a half smile.

"Dear aunt," he said gently, "pray say no more. I do not care to see the world; I am satisfied here. As to Catalina, I love her. Is not that enough?" He bent and kissed her cold forehead, and then went away to his happy dreams; and, if he thought of her at all as he lingered in the soft twilight that comes before sleep, it was only to wonder over her distress—a wonder soon indolently comforted by the belief that she would be calm and reasonable in the morning. But, across the hall, a gray old woman sat, her money beside her, and the hands that had earned it idle in her lap. God keep us from such a vigil!

And did she leave him? No; not even when the "him" became "them."

The careless young wife, knowing nothing save how to love, queened it right royally over the old house, and the little brown brothers and sisters ran riot through every room. The piano was soon broken by the ignorant hands that sounded its chords at random; but only Doro played on it now, and nothing pleased him so well as to improvise melodies from the plaintive Minorcan songs the little wife sang in her velvet voice. Years passed; the money was all spent, and the house full—a careless, idle, ignorant, happy brood, asking for nothing, planning not at all, working not at all, but loving each other in their own way, contented to sit in the sunshine, and laugh, and eat, and sing, all the day long. The tall, gaunt figure that came and went among them, laboring ceaselessly, striving always against the current, they regarded with tolerating eyes as a species differing from theirs, but good in its way, especially for work. The children loved the still silent old woman, and generously allowed her to take care of them until she tried to teach them; then away they flew like wild birds of the forest, and not one learned more than the alphabet.

Doro died first, a middle-aged man; gently he passed away without pain, without a care. "You have been very good to me, aunt; my life has been a happy one; I have had nothing to wish for," he murmured, as she bent to catch the last look from his dying eyes.

He was gone; and she bore on the burden he had left to her. I saw her last year—an old, old woman, but working still.

OLD GARDISTON.

One by one they died—
    Last of all their race ;
Nothing left but pride,
    Lace and buckled hose ;
Their quietus made,
    On their dwelling-place
Ruthless hands are laid :
    Down the old house goes !

Many a bride has stood
    In yon spacious room ;
Here her hand was wooed
    Underneath the rose ;
O'er that sill the dead
    Reached the family tomb ;
All that were have fled—
    Down the old house goes !

EDMUND CLARENCE STEDMAN.

OLD GARDISTON was a manor-house down in the rice-
lands, six miles from a Southern seaport. It had been
called Old Gardiston for sixty or seventy years, which
showed that it must have belonged to colonial days, since
no age under that of a century could have earned for it
that honorable title in a neighborhood where the Declara-
tion of Independence was still considered an event of comparatively modern times. The war was over, and the mistress of the house, Miss Margaretta Gardiston, lay buried in
St. Mark's churchyard, near by. The little old church had
long been closed ; the very road to its low stone doorway
was overgrown, and a second forest had grown up around
it ; but the churchyard was still open to those of the dead

who had a right there; and certainly Miss Margaretta had
this right, seeing that father, grandfather, and great-grand-
father all lay buried there, and their memorial tablets, quaint-
ly emblazoned, formed a principal part of the decorations of
the ancient little sanctuary in the wilderness. There was no
one left at Old Gardiston now save Cousin Copeland and
Gardis Duke, a girl of seventeen years, Miss Margaretta's
niece and heir. Poor little Gardis, having been born a girl
when she should have been a boy, was christened with the
family name—a practice not uncommon in some parts of the
South, where English customs of two centuries ago still retain
their hold with singular tenacity; but the three syllables were
soon abbreviated to two for common use, and the child grew
up with the quaint name of Gardis.

They were at breakfast now, the two remaining members
of the family, in the marble-floored dining-room. The latticed
windows were open; birds were singing outside, and roses
blooming; a flood of sunshine lit up every corner of the apartment, showing its massive Chinese vases, its carved ivory
ornaments, its hanging lamp of curious shape, and its spindle-
legged sideboard, covered with dark-colored plates and plat-
ters ornamented with dark-blue dragons going out to walk,
and crocodiles circling around fantastically roofed temples as
though they were waiting for the worshipers to come out in
order to make a meal of them. But, in spite of these accessories, the poor old room was but a forlorn place : the marble
flooring was sunken and defaced, portions were broken into
very traps for unwary feet, and its ancient enemy, the pene-
trating dampness, had finally conquered the last resisting
mosaic, and climbed the walls, showing in blue and yellow
streaks on the old-fashioned moldings. There had been no
fire in the tiled fireplace for many years; Miss Margaretta
did not approve of fires, and wood was costly : this last reason, however, was never mentioned; and Gardis had grown
into a girl of sixteen before she knew the comfort of the
sparkling little fires that shine on the hearths morning and

evening during the short winters in well-appointed Southern homes. At that time she had spent a few days in the city with some family friends who had come out of the war with less impoverishment than their neighbors. (Miss Margaretta did not approve of them exactly; it was understood that all Southerners of "our class" were "impoverished.") She did not refuse the cordial invitation *in toto,* but she sent for Gardis sooner than was expected, and set about carefully removing from the girl's mind any wrong ideas that might have made a lodgment there. And Gardis, warmly loving her aunt, and imbued with all the family pride from her birth, immediately cast from her the bright little comforts she had met in the city as plebeian, and, going up stairs to the old drawing-room, dusted the relics enshrined there with a new reverence for them, glorifying herself in their undoubted antiquity. Fires, indeed ! Certainly not.

The breakfast-table was spread with snowy damask, worn thin almost to gossamer, and fairly embroidered with delicate darning; the cups and plates belonged to the crocodile set, and the meager repast was at least daintily served. Cousin Copeland had his egg, and Gardis satisfied her young appetite with fish caught in the river behind the house by Pompey, and a fair amount of Dinah's corn-bread. The two old slaves had refused to leave Gardiston House. They had been trained all their lives by Miss Margaretta; and now that she was gone, they took pride in keeping the expenses of the table, as she had kept them, reduced to as small a sum as possible, knowing better than poor Gardis herself the pitiful smallness of the family income, derived solely from the rent of an old ware-house in the city. For the war had not impoverished Gardiston House; it was impoverished long before. Acre by acre the land had gone, until nothing was left save a small corn-field and the flower-garden; piece by piece the silver had vanished, until nothing was left save three teaspoons, three tablespoons, and four forks. The old warehouse had brought in little rent during those four long years, and they had fared

hardly at Gardiston. Still, in their isolated situation away
from the main roads, their well-known poverty a safeguard,
they had not so much as heard a drum or seen a uniform,
blue or gray, and this was a rare and fortunate exemption in
those troublous times; and when the war was at last ended,
Miss Margaretta found herself no poorer than she was before,
with this great advantage added, that now everybody was
poor, and, indeed, it was despicable to be anything else. She
bloomed out into a new cheerfulness under this congenial
state of things, and even invited one or two contemporaries
still remaining on the old plantations in the neighborhood to
spend several days at Gardiston. Two ancient dames accepted
the invitation, and the state the three kept together in the old
drawing-room under the family portraits, the sweep of their
narrow-skirted, old-fashioned silk gowns on the inlaid stair-
case when they went down to dinner, the supreme uncon-
sciousness of the break-neck condition of the marble flooring
and the mold-streaked walls, the airy way in which they drank
their tea out of the crocodile cups, and told little stories of
fifty years before, filled Gardis with admiring respect. She
sat, as it were, in the shadow of their greatness, and obediently ate only of those dishes that required a fork, since the three
spoons were, of course, in use. During this memorable visit
Cousin Copeland was always "engaged in his study" at
meal-times; but in the evening he appeared, radiant and
smiling, and then the four played whist together on the Chinese table, and the ladies fanned themselves with stately
grace, while Cousin Copeland dealt not only the cards,
but compliments also—both equally old-fashioned and well
preserved.

But within this first year of peace Miss Margaretta had died
—an old lady of seventy-five, but bright and strong as a winter
apple. Gardis and Cousin Copeland, left alone, moved on in
the same way: it was the only way they knew. Cousin Copeland lived only in the past, Gardis in the present; and indeed
the future, so anxiously considered always by the busy, rest-

less Northern mind, has never been lifted into the place of
supreme importance at the South.

When breakfast was over, Gardis went up stairs into the
drawing-room. Cousin Copeland, remarking, in his busy
little way, that he had important work awaiting him, retired
to his study—a round room in the tower, where, at an old
desk with high back full of pigeon-holes, he had been accustomed for years to labor during a portion of the day over
family documents a century or two old, recopying them with
minute care, adding foot-notes, and references leading back
by means of red-ink stars to other documents, and appending
elaborately phrased little comments neatly signed in flourishes
with his initials and the date, such as " Truly a doughty deed.
C. B. G. 1852."—" ' Worthy,' quotha ? Nay, it seemeth unto
my poor comprehension a *marvelous* kindness ! C. B. G.
1856."—" May we all profit by this ! C. B. G. 1858."

This morning, as usual, Gardis donned her gloves, threw
open the heavy wooden shutters, and, while the summer
morning sunshine flooded the room, she moved from piece to
piece of the old furniture, carefully dusting it all. The room
was large and lofty ; there was no carpet on the inlaid floor,
but a tapestry rug lay under the table in the center of the
apartment ; everything was spindle-legged, chairs, tables, the
old piano, two cabinets, a sofa, a card-table, and two little
tabourets embroidered in Scriptural scenes, reduced now to
shadows, Joseph and his wicked brethren having faded to the
same dull yellow hue, which Gardis used to think was not the
discrimination that should have been shown between the just
and the unjust. The old cabinets were crowded with curious
little Chinese images and vases, and on the high mantel were
candelabra with more crocodiles on them, and a large mirror
which had so long been veiled in gauze that Gardis had never
fairly seen the fat, gilt cherubs that surrounded it. A few
inches of wax-candle still remained in the candelabra, but
they were never lighted, a tallow substitute on the table serving as a nucleus during the eight months of warm weather

when the evenings were spent in the drawing-room. When it was really cold, a fire was kindled in the boudoir—a narrow chamber in the center of the large rambling old mansion, where, with closed doors and curtained windows, the three sat together, Cousin Copeland reading aloud, generally from the " Spectator," often pausing to jot down little notes as they occurred to him in his orderly memorandum-book—" mere outlines of phrases, but sufficiently full to recall the desired train of thought," he observed. The ladies embroidered, Miss Margaretta sitting before the large frame she had used when a girl. They did all the sewing for the household (very little new material, and much repairing of old), but these domestic labors were strictly confined to the privacy of their own apartments ; in the drawing-room or boudoir they always embroidered. Gardis remembered this with sadness as she removed the cover from the large frame, and glanced at " Moses in the Bulrushes," which her inexperienced hand could never hope to finish ; she was thinking of her aunt, but any one else would have thought of the bulrushes, which were now pink, now saffron, and now blue, after some mediæval system of floss-silk vegetation.

Having gone all around the apartment and dusted everything, Chinese images and all, Gardis opened the old piano and gently played a little tune. Miss Margaretta had been her only teacher, and the young girl's songs were old-fashioned ; but the voice was sweet and full, and before she knew it she was filling the house with her melody.

> " Little Cupid one day in a myrtle-bough strayed,
> And among the sweet blossoms he playfully played,
> Plucking many a sweet from the boughs of the tree,
> Till he felt that his finger was stung by a bee,"

sang Gardis, and went on blithely through the whole, giving Mother Venus's advice archly, and adding a shower of improvised trills at the end.

"Bravo!" said a voice from the garden below.

Rushing to the casement, Miss Duke beheld, first with astonishment, then dismay, two officers in the uniform of the United States army standing at the front door. They bowed courteously, and one of them said, "Can I see the lady of the house?"

"I—I am the lady," replied Gardis, confusedly; then drawing back, with the sudden remembrance that she should not have shown herself at all, she ran swiftly up to the study for Cousin Copeland. But Cousin Copeland was not there, and the little mistress remembered with dismay that old Dinah was out in the corn-field, and that Pompey had gone fishing. There was nothing for it, then, but to go down and face the strangers. Summoning all her self-possession, Miss Duke descended. She would have preferred to hold parley from the window over the doorway, like the ladies of olden time, but she feared it would not be dignified, seeing that the times were no longer olden, and therefore she went down to the entrance where the two were awaiting her. "Shall I ask them in?" she thought. "What would Aunt Margaretta have done?" The Gardiston spirit was hospitable to the core; but these—these were the Vandals, the despots, under whose presence the whole fair land was groaning. No; she would not ask them in.

The elder officer, a grave young man of thirty, was spokesman. "Do I address Miss Gardiston?" he said.

"I am Miss Duke. My aunt, Miss Gardiston, is not living," replied Gardis.

"Word having been received that the yellow fever has appeared on the coast, we have been ordered to take the troops a few miles inland and go into camp immediately, Miss Duke. The grove west of this house, on the bank of the river, having been selected as camping-ground for a portion of the command, we have called to say that you need feel no alarm at the proximity of the soldiers; they will be under strict orders not to trespass upon your grounds."

"Thanks," said Gardis mechanically; but she was alarmed; they both saw that.

"I assure you, Miss Duke, that there is not the slightest cause for nervousness," said the younger officer, bowing as he spoke.

"And your servants will not be enticed away, either," added the other.

"We have only two, and they—would not go," replied Gardis, not aggressively, but merely stating her facts.

The glimmer of a smile crossed the face of the younger officer, but the other remained unmoved.

"My name, madam, is Newell—David Newell, captain commanding the company that will be encamped here. I beg you to send me word immediately if anything occurs to disturb your quiet," he said.

Then the two saluted the little mistress with formal courtesy, and departed, walking down the path together with a quick step and soldierly bearing, as though they were on parade.

"Ought I to have asked them in?" thought Gardis; and she went slowly up to the drawing-room again and closed the piano. "I wonder who said 'bravo'? The younger one, I presume." And she presumed correctly.

At lunch (corn-bread and milk) Cousin Copeland's old-young face appeared promptly at the dining-room door. Cousin Copeland, Miss Margaretta's cousin, was a little old bachelor, whose thin dark hair had not turned gray, and whose small bright eyes needed no spectacles; he dressed always in black, with low shoes on his small feet, and his clothes seemed never to wear out, perhaps because his little frame hardly touched them anywhere; the cloth certainly was not strained. Everything he wore was so old-fashioned, however, that he looked like the pictures of the high-collared, solemn little men who, accompanied by ladies all bonnet, are depicted in English Sunday-school books following funeral processions, generally of the good children who die young.

"O Cousin Copeland, where were you this morning when I went up to your study?" began Gardis, full of the event of the morning.

"You may well ask where I was, my child," replied the bachelor, cutting his toasted corn-bread into squares with mathematical precision. "A most interesting discovery—most interesting. Not being thoroughly satisfied as to the exact identity of the first wife of one of the second cousins of our grandfather, a lady who died young and left no descendants, yet none the less a Gardiston, at least by marriage, the happy idea occurred to me to investigate more fully the contents of the papers in barrel number two on the east side of the central garret—documents that I myself classified in 1849, as collateral merely, not relating to the main line. I assure you, my child, that I have spent there, over that barrel, a most delightful morning—most delightful. I had not realized that there was so much interesting matter in store for me when I shall have finished the main line, which will be, I think, in about a year and a half—a year and a half. And I have good hopes of finding there, too, valuable information respecting this first wife of one of the second cousins of our respected grandfather, a lady whose memory, by some strange neglect, has been suffered to fall into oblivion. I shall be proud to constitute myself the one to rescue it for the benefit of posterity," continued the little man, with chivalrous enthusiasm, as he took up his spoon. (There was one spoon to spare now; Gardis often thought of this with a saddened heart.) Miss Duke had not interrupted her cousin by so much as an impatient glance; trained to regard him with implicit respect, and to listen always to his gentle, busy little stream of talk, she waited until he had finished all he had to say about this "first wife of one of the second cousins of our grandfather" (who, according to the French phrase-books, she could not help thinking, should have inquired immediately for the green shoe of her aunt's brother-in-law's wife) before she told her story. Cousin Copeland shook his head many times during the recital. He had not the bitter feelings of Miss Margaretta concerning the late war; in fact, he had never come down much farther than the Revolution, having merely skirmished a little, as it were, with the war of 1812; but he knew his cousin's opinions, and respected their memory. So he "earnestly hoped" that some other site would be selected for the camp. Upon being told that the blue army-wagons had already arrived, he then "earnestly hoped" that the encampment would not be of long continuance. Cousin Copeland had hoped a great many things during his life; his capacity for hoping was cheering and unlimited; a hope carefully worded and delivered seemed to him almost the same thing as reality; he made you a present of it, and rubbed his little hands cheerfully afterward, as though now all had been said.

"Do you think I should have asked them in?" said Gardis, hesitatingly.

"Most certainly, most certainly. Hospitality has ever been one of our characteristics as a family," said Cousin Copeland, finishing the last spoonful of milk, which had come out exactly even with the last little square of corn-bread.

"But I did not ask them."

"Do I hear you aright? You did not ask them, Cousin Gardiston?" said the little bachelor, pausing gravely by the table, one hand resting on its shining mahogany, the other extended in the attitude of surprise.

"Yes, Cousin Copeland, you do. But these are officers of the United States army, and you know Aunt Margaretta's feelings regarding them."

"True," said Cousin Copeland, dropping his arm; "you are right; I had forgotten. But it is a very sad state of things, my dear—very sad. It was not so in the old days at Gardiston House: then we should have invited them to dinner."

"We could not do that," said Gardis thoughtfully, "on account of forks and spoons; there would not be enough to go— But I would not invite them anyway," she added, the color rising in her cheeks, and her eyes flashing. "Are they not our enemies, and the enemies of our country? Vandals? Despots?"

"Certainly," said Cousin Copeland, escaping from these signs of feminine disturbance with gentle haste. Long before, he was accustomed to remark to a bachelor friend that an atmosphere of repose was best adapted to his constitution and to his work. He therefore now retired to the first wife of the second cousin of his grandfather, and speedily forgot all about the camp and the officers. Not so Gardis. Putting on her straw hat, she went out into the garden to attend to her flowers and work off her annoyance. Was it annoyance, or excitement merely? She did not know. But she did know that the grove was full of men and tents, and she could see several of the blue-coats fishing in the river. "Very well," she said to herself hotly; "we shall have no dinner, then!" But the river was not hers, and so she went on clipping the roses, and tying back the vines all the long bright afternoon, until old Dinah came to call her to dinner. As she went, the bugle sounded from the grove, and she seemed to be obeying its summons; instantly she sat down on a bench to wait until its last echo had died away. "I foresee that I shall hate that bugle," she said to herself.

The blue-coats were encamped in the grove three long months. Captain Newell and the lieutenant, Roger Saxton, made no more visits at Gardiston House; but, when they passed by and saw the little mistress in the garden or at the window, they saluted her with formal courtesy. And the lieutenant looked back; yes, there was no doubt of that—the lieutenant certainly looked back. Saxton was a handsome youth; tall and finely formed, he looked well in his uniform, and knew it. Captain Newell was not so tall—a gray-eyed, quiet young man. "Commonplace," said Miss Gardis. The bugle still gave forth its silvery summons. "It is insupportable," said the little mistress daily; and daily Cousin Copeland replied, "Certainly." But the bugle sounded on all the same.

One day a deeper wrath came. Miss Duke discovered Dinah in the act of taking cakes to the camp to sell to the soldiers !

"Well, Miss Gardis, dey pays me well for it, and we's next to not'ing laid up for de winter," replied the old woman anxiously, as the irate little mistress forbade the sale of so much as "one kernel of corn."

"Dey don't want de corn, but dey pays well for de cakes, dearie Miss Gardis. Yer see, yer don't know not'ing about it; it's only ole Dinah makin' a little money for herself and Pomp," pleaded the faithful creature, who would have given her last crumb for the family, and died content. But Gardis sternly forbade all dealings with the camp from that time forth, and then she went up to her room and cried like a child. "They knew it, of course," she thought; "no doubt they have had many a laugh over the bakery so quietly carried on at Gardiston House. They are capable of supposing even that *I* sanctioned it." And with angry tears she fell to planning how she could best inform them of their mistake, and overwhelm them with her scorn. She prepared several crushing little speeches, and held them in reserve for use; but the officers never came to Gardiston House, and of course she never went to the camp—no, nor so much as looked that way; so there was no good opportunity for delivering them. One night, however, the officers did come to Gardiston House— not only the officers, but all the men; and Miss Duke was very glad to see them.

It happened in this way. The unhappy State had fallen into the hands of double-faced, conscienceless whites, who used the newly enfranchised blacks as tools for their evil purposes. These leaders were sometimes emigrant Northerners, sometimes renegade Southerners, but always rascals. In the present case they had inflamed their ignorant followers to riotous proceedings in the city, and the poor blacks, fancying that the year of jubilee had come, when each man was to have a plantation, naturally began by ejecting the resident owners before the grand division of spoils. At least this was their idea. During the previous year, when the armies were still marching through the land, they had gone out now and then in a motiveless sort of way and burned the fine planta- tion residences near the city ; and now, chance having brought Gardiston to their minds, out they came, inconsequent and reasonless as ever, to burn Gardiston. But they did not know the United States troops were there.

There was a siege of ten minutes, two or three volleys from the soldiers, and then a disorderly retreat; one or two wounded were left on the battle-field (Miss Duke's flower- garden), and the dining-room windows were broken. Beyond this there was no slaughter, and the victors drew off their forces in good order to the camp, leaving the officers to re- ceive the thanks of the household—Cousin Copeland, envel- oped in a mammoth dressing-gown that had belonged to his grandfather, and Gardis, looking distractingly pretty in a has- tily donned short skirt and a little white sack (she had no dressing-gown), with her brown hair waving over her shoul- ders, and her cheeks scarlet from excitement. Roger Saxton fell into love on the spot : hitherto he had only hovered, as it were, on the border.

" Had you any idea she was so exquisitely beautiful ? " he exclaimed, as they left the old house in the gray light of dawn.

" Miss Duke is not exquisitely beautiful; she is not even beautiful," replied the slow-voiced Newell. " She has the true Southern colorless, or rather cream-colored, complexion, and her features are quite irregular."

" Colorless ! I never saw more beautiful coloring in my life than she had to-night," exclaimed Saxton.

" To-night, yes ; I grant that. But it took a good-sized riot to bring it to the surface," replied the impassive captain.

A guard was placed around the house at night and pickets sent down the road for some time after this occurrence. Gar- dis, a prey to conflicting feelings, deserted her usual haunts

and shut herself up in her own room, thinking, thinking what
she ought to do. In the mean time, beyond a formal note of
inquiry delivered daily by a wooden-faced son of Mars, the
two officers made no effort toward a further acquaintance;
the lieutenant was on fire to attempt it, but the captain held
him back. " It is her place to make the advances now," he
said. It was ; and Gardis knew it.

One morning she emerged from her retreat, and with a
decided step sought Cousin Copeland in his study. The little
man had been disquieted by the night attack; it had come to
him vaguely once or twice since then that perhaps there
might be other things to do in the world besides copying
family documents ; but the nebula—it was not even a definite
thought—had faded, and now he was at work again with
more ardor than ever.

" Cousin Copeland," said Gardis, appearing at the door of
the study, " I have decided at last to yield to your wishes, and
—and invite the officers to dinner."

" By all means," said Cousin Copeland, putting down his
pen and waving his hands with a hearty little air of acquies-
cence—" by all means." It was not until long afterward that
he remembered he had never expressed any wish upon the
subject whatever. But it suited Gardis to imagine that he
had done so ; so she imagined it.

" We have little to work with," continued the little mistress of the house; " but Dinah is an excellent cook, and—
and—O cousin, I do not wish to do it ; I can not bear the
mere thought of it ; but oh ! we must, we must." Tears
stood in her eyes as she concluded.

" They are going soon," suggested Cousin Copeland, hesitatingly, biting the end of his quill.

" That is the very reason. They are going soon, and we
have done nothing to acknowledge their aid, their courtesy—
we Gardistons, both of us. They have saved our home, perhaps our lives ; and we—we let them go without a word !
O cousin, it must not be. Something we must do ; *noblesse*

oblige! I have thought and thought, and really there is nothing but this: we must invite them to dinner," said Miss Duke, tragically.

"I—I always liked little dinners," said Cousin Copeland, in a gentle, assenting murmur.

Thus it happened that the officers received two formal little notes with the compliments of Miss Gardiston Duke inclosed, and an invitation to dinner. "Hurrah!" cried Saxton "At last!"

The day appointed was at the end of the next week; Gardis had decided that that would be more ceremonious. "And they are to understand," she said proudly, "that it is a mere dinner of ceremony, and not of friendship."

"Certainly," said Cousin Copeland.

Old Dinah was delighted. Gardis brought out some of the half-year rent money, and a dinner was planned, of few dishes truly, but each would be a marvel of good cooking, as the old family servants of the South used to cook when time was nothing to them. It is not much to them now; but they have heard that it ought to be, and that troubles the perfection of their pie-crust. There was a little wine left in the wine-room—a queer little recess like a secret chamber; and there was always the crocodile china and the few pieces of cut glass. The four forks would be enough, and Gardis would take no jelly, so that the spoons would serve also; in fact, the dinner was planned to accommodate the silver. So far, so good. But now as to dress; here the poor little mistress was sadly pinched. She knew this; but she hoped to make use of a certain well-worn changeable silk that had belonged to Miss Margaretta, in hue a dull green and purple. But, alas! upon inspection she discovered that the faithful garment had given way at last, after years of patient service, and now there was nothing left but mildew and shreds. The invitation had been formally accepted; the dinner was in course of preparation: what should she do? She had absolutely nothing, poor child, save the two faded old lawns which she wore ordinarily, and the one shabby woolen dress for cooler weather. "If they were anything but what they are," she said to herself, after she had again and again turned over the contents of her three bureau drawers, "I would wear my every-day dress without a moment's thought or trouble. But I will not allow these men, belonging to the despot army of the North, these aliens forced upon us by a strong hand and a hard fate, to smile at the shabby attire of a Southern lady."

She crossed the hall to Miss Margaretta's closed room: she would search every corner; possibly there was something she did not at the moment recall. But, alas! only too well did she know the contents of the closet and the chest of drawers, the chest of drawers and the closet; had she not been familiar with every fold and hue from her earliest childhood ? Was there nothing else ? There was the cedar chamber, a little cedar cupboard in the wall, where Miss Margaretta kept several stately old satin bonnets, elaborate structures of a past age. Mechanically Gardis mounted the steps, and opened the little door half-way up the wall. The bonnets were there, and with them several packages; these she took down and opened. Among various useless relics of finery appeared, at last, one whole dress; narrow-skirted, short, with a scantily fashioned waist, it was still a complete robe of its kind, in color a delicate blue, the material clinging and soft like Canton crape. Folded with the dress were blue kid slippers and a silk belt with a broad buckle. The package bore a label with this inscription, " The gown within belonged to my respected mother, Pamela Gardiston," in the handwriting of Miss Margaretta; and Gardis remembered that she had seen the blue skirt once, long ago, in her childhood. But Miss Margaretta allowed no prying, and her niece had been trained to ask permission always before entering her apartment, and to refrain from touching anything, unless asked to do so while there. Now the poverty-stricken little hostess carried the relics carefully across to her own room, and, locking the door, attired herself, and anxiously surveyed the effect. The old-fashioned gown left her shoulders and arms bare, the broad belt could not lengthen the short waist, and the skirt hardly covered her ankles. " I can wear my old muslin cape, but my arms will have to show, and my feet too," she thought, with nervous distress. The creased blue kid slippers were full of little holes and somewhat mildewed, but the girl mended them bravely ; she said to herself that she need only walk down to the dining-room and back ; and, besides, the rooms would not be brightly lighted. If she had had any- thing to work with, even so much as one yard of material, she would have made over the old gown ; but she had absolutely nothing, and so she determined to overcome her necessities by sheer force of will.

" How do I look, cousin ? " she said, appearing at the study-door on the afternoon of the fatal day. See spoke ner- vously, and yet proudly, as though defying criticism. But Cousin Copeland had no thought of criticism.

" My child," he said, with pleased surprise, " you look charming. I am very glad you have a new gown, dear, very glad."

" Men are all alike," thought Gardis exultingly. " The others will think it is new also."

Cousin Copeland possessed but one suit of clothes; con- sequently he had not been able to honor the occasion by a change of costume ; but he wore a ruffled shirt and a flower in his buttonhole, and his countenance was sedately illumined by the thought of the festal board below. He was not at work, but merely dabbling a little on the outer edges—mak- ing flourishes at the ends of the chapters, numbering pages, and so forth. Gardis had gone to the drawing-room ; she longed to see herself from head to foot, but, with the excep- tion of the glasses in two old pier-tables, there was no large mirror save the gauze-veiled one in the drawing-room. Should she do it ? Eve listened to the tempter, and fell. Likewise Gardis. A scissors, a chair, a snip, and lo ! it was done. There she was, a little figure in a quaint blue gown,

6

the thick muslin cape hiding the neck, but the dimpled arms
bare almost to the shoulder, since the sleeve was but a narrow
puff ; the brown hair of this little image was braided around
the head like a coronet ; the wistful face was colorless and
sad ; in truth, there seemed to be tears in the brown eyes.
" I will not cry," said Gardis, jumping down from her chair,
" but I *do* look odd ; there is no doubt of that." Then she
remembered that she should not have jumped, on account of
the slippers, and looked anxiously down ; but the kid still
held its place over the little feet, and, going to the piano, the
young mistress of the manor began playing a gay little love-
song, as if to defy her own sadness. Before it was finished,
old Pompey, his every-day attire made majestic by a large,
stiffly starched collar, announced the guests, and the solem-
nities began.

Everything moved smoothly, however. Cousin Copeland's
conversation was in its most flowing vein, the simple little
dinner was well cooked and served, Pompey was statuesque,
and the two guests agreeable. They remained at the table
some time, according to the old Gardiston custom, and then,
the ends of wax-candles having been lighted in the drawing-
room, coffee was served there in the crocodile cups, and Miss
Duke sang one or two songs. Soon after the officers took
leave. Captain Newell bowed as he said farewell, but Roger
Saxton, younger and more impulsive, extended his hand.
Miss Duke made a stately courtesy, with downcast eyes, as
though she had not observed it ; but by her heightened color
the elder guest suspected the truth, and smiled inwardly at
the proud little reservation. " The *hand* of Douglas is his
own," he said to himself.

The dreaded dinner was over, and the girl had judged
correctly : the two visitors had no suspicion of the antiquity
of the blue gown.

" Did you ever see such a sweet little picture, from the
pink rose in the hair down to the blue slipper ! " said Saxton
enthusiastically.

"She looked well," replied Newell; "but as for cordiality—"

"I'll win that yet. I like her all the better for her little ways," said the lieutenant. "I suppose it is only natural that Southern girls should cherish bitterness against us; although, of course, *she* is far too young to have lost a lover in the war —far too young."

"Which is a comfort," said Newell dryly.

"A great comfort, old man. Don't he bearish, now, but just wait a while and see."

"Precisely what I intend to do," said Newell.

In the mean time Gardis, in the privacy of her own room, was making a solemn funeral pyre on the hearth, composed of the blue gown, the slippers, and the pink rose, and watching the flame as it did its work. "So perish also the enemies of my country!" she said to herself. (She did not mean exactly that they should be burned on funeral pyres, but merely consigned them on this, as on all occasions, to a general perdition.) The old dress was but a rag, and the slippers were worthless; but, had they been new and costly, she would have done the same. Had they not been desecrated? Let them die!

It was, of course, proper that the guests should call at Gardiston House within a day or two; and Roger Saxton, ignoring the coldness of his reception, came again and again. He even sought out Cousin Copeland in his study, and won the heart of the old bachelor by listening a whole morning to extracts from the documents. Gardis found that her reserve was of no avail against this bold young soldier, who followed her into all her little retreats, and paid no attention to her stinging little speeches. Emboldened and also angered by what she deemed his callousness, she every day grew more and more open in her tone, until you might have said that she, as a unit, poured out upon his head the whole bitterness of the South. Saxton made no answer until the time came for the camp to break up, the soldiers being ordered back to the city. Then he came to see her one afternoon, and sat for some time in silence; the conversation of the little mistress was the same as usual.

"I forgive this, and all the bitter things you have said to me, Gardis," he remarked abruptly.

"Forgive! And by what right, sir—"

"Only this: I love you, dear." And then he poured out all the tide of his young ardor, and laid his heart and his life at her feet.

But the young girl, drawing her slight figure up to its full height, dismissed him with haughty composure. She no longer spoke angrily, but simply said, "That you, a Northerner and a soldier, should presume to ask for the hand of a Southern lady, shows, sir, that you have not the least comprehension of us or of our country." Then she made him a courtesy and left the room. The transformation was complete; it was no longer the hot-tempered girl flashing out in biting little speeches, but the woman uttering the belief of her life. Saxton rode off into town that same night, dejected and forlorn.

Captain Newell took his leave a day later in a different fashion; he told Miss Duke that he would leave a guard on the premises if she wished it.

"I do not think it will be necessary," answered the lady.

"Nor do I; indeed, I feel sure that there will be no further trouble, for we have placed the whole district under military rule since the last disturbance. But I thought possibly you might feel timid."

"I am not timid, Captain Newell."

The grave captain stroked his mustache to conceal a smile, and then, as he rose to go, he said: "Miss Duke, I wish to say to you one thing. You know nothing of us, of course, but I trust you will accept my word when I say that Mr. Saxton is of good family, that he is well educated, and that he is heir to a fair fortune. What he is personally you have seen for yourself—a frank, kind-hearted, manly young fellow."

" Did you come here to plead his cause ? " said the girl scornfully.

" No ; I came here to offer you a guard, Miss Duke, for the protection of your property. But at the same time I thought it only my duty to make you aware of the real value of the gift laid at your feet."

" How did you know—" began Gardis.

" Roger tells me everything," replied the officer. " If it were not so, I—" Here he paused ; and then, as though he had concluded to say no more, he bowed and took leave.

That night Gardiston House was left to itself in the forest stillness. " I am glad that bugle is silenced for ever," said Gardis.

" And yet it was a silvern sound," said Cousin Copeland.

The rains began, and there was no more walking abroad ; the excitement of the summer and the camp gone, in its place came the old cares which had been half forgotten. (Care always waits for a cold or a rainy day.) Could the little household manage to live—live with their meager comforts—until the next payment of rent came in ? That was the question.

Bitterly, bitterly poor was the whole Southern country in those dreary days after the war. The second year was worse than the first ; for the hopes that had buoyed up the broken fortunes soon disappeared, and nothing was left. There was no one to help Gardis Duke, or the hundreds of other women in like desolate positions. Some of the furniture and ornaments of the old house might have been sold, could they have been properly brought forward in New York City, where there were people with purses to buy such things ; but in the South no one wanted Chinese images, and there was nothing of intrinsic value. So the little household lived along, in a spare, pinched way, until, suddenly, final disaster overtook them : the tenant of the warehouse gave up his lease, declaring that the old building was too ruinous for use ; and, as no one succeeded him, Gardiston House beheld itself face to face with starvation.

" If we wasn't so old, Pomp and me, Miss Gardis, we could

work for yer," said Dinah, with great tears rolling down her
wrinkled cheeks; "but we's just good for not'ing now."

Cousin Copeland left his manuscripts and wandered aimlessly around the garden for a day or two; then the little man
rose early one morning and walked into the city, with the
hopeful idea of obtaining employment as a clerk. "My handwriting is more than ordinarily ornate, I think," he said to
himself, with proud confidence.

Reaching the town at last, he walked past the stores several times and looked timidly within; he thought perhaps
some one would see him, and come out. But no one came;
and at last he ventured into a clothing-store, through a grove
of ticketed coats and suspended trousers. The proprietor of
the establishment, a Northern Hebrew whose venture had not
paid very well, heard his modest request, and asked what he
could do.

"I can write," said Cousin Copeland, with quiet pride;
and in answer to a sign he climbed up on a tall stool and pro-
ceeded to cover half a sheet of paper in his best style. As he
could not for the moment think of anything else, he wrote
out several paragraphs from the last family document.

"Richard, the fourth of the name, a descendant on the
maternal side from the most respected and valorous family—"

"Oh, we don't care for that kind of writing; it's old-fashioned," said Mr. Ottenheimer, throwing down the paper, and
waving the applicant toward the door with his fat hand. "I
don't want my books frescoed."

Cousin Copeland retired to the streets again with a new
sensation in his heart. Old-fashioned? Was it old-fashioned? And even if so, was it any the less a rarely attained
and delicately ornate style of writing? He could not understand it. Weary with the unaccustomed exercise, he sat
down at last on the steps of a church—an old structure whose
spire bore the marks of bomb-shells sent in from the block-
ading fleet outside the bar during those months of dreary
siege—and thought he would refresh himself with some fur-

tive mouthfuls of the corn-bread hidden in his pocket for lunch.

" Good morning, sir," said a voice, just as he had drawn forth his little parcel and was opening it behind the skirt of his coat. " When did you come in from Gardiston ? "

It was Captain Newell. With the rare courtesy which comes from a kind heart, he asked no questions regarding the fatigue and the dust-powdered clothes of the little bachelor, and took a seat beside him as though a church-step on a city street was a customary place of meeting.

" I was about to—to eat a portion of this corn-bread," said Cousin Copeland, hesitatingly; " will you taste it also ? "

The young officer accepted a share of the repast gravely, and then Cousin Copeland told his story. He was a simple soul. Miss Margaretta would have made the soldier believe she had come to town merely for her own lofty amusement or to buy jewels. It ended, however, in the comfortable eating of a good dinner at the hotel, and a cigar in Captain Newell's own room, which was adorned with various personal appliances for comfort that astonished the eyes of the careful little bachelor, and left him in a maze of vague wonderings. Young men lived in that way, then, nowadays ? They could do so, and yet not be persons of—of irregular habits ?

David Newell persuaded his guest to abandon, for the present, all idea of obtaining employment in the city. " These shopkeepers are not capable of appreciating qualifications such as yours, sir," he said. " Would it not be better to set about obtaining a new tenant for the warehouse ? "

Cousin Copeland thought it would ; but repairs were needed, and—

" Will you give me the charge of it ? I am in the city all the time, and I have acquaintances among the Northerners who are beginning to come down here with a view of engaging in business."

Cousin Copeland gladly relinquished the warehouse, and then, after an hour's rest, he rode gallantly back to Gardiston

House on one of the captain's horses; he explained at some
length that he had been quite a man of mettle in his youth as
regards horse-flesh—"often riding, sir, ten and fifteen miles a
day."

"I will go in for a moment, I think," said the young officer, as they arrived at the old gate.

"Most certainly," said Cousin Copeland cordially; "Gardis will be delighted to see you."

"Will she ? " said the captain.

Clouds had gathered, a raw wind from the ocean swept
over the land, and fine rain was beginning to fall. The house
seemed dark and damp as the two entered it. Gardis listened
to Cousin Copeland's detailed little narrative in silence, and
made no comments while he was present; but when he left
the room for a moment she said abruptly:

"Sir, you will make no repairs, and you will take no steps
toward procuring a tenant for our property in the city. I will
not allow it."

"And why may I not do it as well as any other person ? "
said Captain Newell.

"You are not 'any other person,' and you know it," said
Gardis, with flushed cheeks. "I do not choose to receive a
favor from your hands."

"It is a mere business transaction, Miss Duke."

"It is not. You know you intend to make the repairs
yourself," cried the girl passionately.

"And if I do so intend ? It will only be advancing the
money, and you can pay me interest if you like. The city
will certainly regain her old position in time; my venture is a
sure one. But I *wish* to assist you, Miss Duke; I do not
deny it."

"And I—will not allow it ! "

"What will you do, then ? "

"God knows," said Gardis. "But I would rather starve
than accept assistance from you." Her eyes were full of tears
as she spoke, but she held her head proudly erect.

"And from Saxton? He has gone North, but he would be so proud to help you."

"From him least of all."

"Because of his love for you?"

Gardis was silent.

"Miss Duke, let me ask you one question. If you had loved Roger Saxton, would you have married him?"

"Never!"

"You would have sacrificed your whole life, then, for the sake of—"

"My country, sir."

"We have a common country, Gardis," answered the young man gravely. Then, as he rose, "Child," he said, "I shall not relinquish the charge of your property, given into my hands by Mr. Copeland Gardiston, and, for your own sake, I beg you to be more patient, more gentle, as becomes a woman. A few weeks will no doubt see you released from even your slight obligation to me: you will have but a short time to wait."

Poor Gardis! Her proud scorn went for nothing, then? She was overridden as though she had been a child, and even rebuked for want of gentleness. The drawing-room was cheerless and damp in the rainy twilight; the girl wore a faded lawn dress, and her cheeks were pale; the old house was chilly through and through, and even the soldier, strong as he was, felt himself shivering. At this instant enter Cousin Copeland. "Of course you will spend the night here," he said heartily. "It is raining, and I must insist upon your staying over until to-morrow—must really insist."

Gardis looked up quickly; her dismayed face said plainly, "Oh no, no." Thereupon the young officer immediately accepted Cousin Copeland's invitation, and took his seat again with quiet deliberation. Gardis sank down upon the sofa. "Very well," she thought desperately, "this time it is hopeless. Nothing can be done."

And hopeless it was. Pompey brought in a candle, and

placed it upon the table, where its dim light made the large apartment more dismal than before; the rain poured down outside, and the rising wind rattled the loose shutters. Dinner was announced—one small fish, potatoes, and corn-bread. Pale Gardis sat like a statue at the head of the table, and made no effort to entertain the guest; but Cousin Copeland threw himself bravely into the breach, and, by way of diversion, related the whole story of the unchronicled "wife of one of our grandfather's second cousins," who had turned out to be a most remarkable personage of Welsh descent, her golden harp having once stood in the very room in which they were now seated.

"Do you not think, my child, that a—a little fire in your aunt Margaretta's boudoir would—would be conducive to our comfort?" suggested the little bachelor, as they rose from the table.

"As you please," said Gardis.

So the three repaired thither, and when the old red curtains were drawn, and the fire lighted, the little room had at least a semblance of comfort, whatever may have been in the hearts of its occupants. Gardis embroidered, Cousin Copeland chatted on in a steady little stream, and the guest listened. "I will step up stairs to my study, and bring down that file of documents," said the bachelor, rising. He was gone, and left only silence behind him. Gardis did not raise her head, but went steadily on with the embroidered robe of the Queen of Sheba.

"I am thinking," began David Newell, breaking the long pause at last, "how comfortable you would be, Miss Duke, as the wife of Roger Saxton. He would take you North, away from this old house, and he would be so proud and so fond of you."

No answer.

"The place could be put in order if you did not care to sell it, and your cousin Copeland could live on here as usual; indeed, I could scarcely imagine him in any other home."

" Nor myself."

" Oh yes, Miss Duke ; I can easily imagine you in New York, Paris, or Vienna. I can easily imagine you at the opera, in the picture-galleries, or carrying out to the full your exquisite taste in dress."

Down went the embroidery. " Sir, do you mean to insult me ? " said the pale, cotton-robed little hostess.

" By no means."

" Why do you come here ? Why do you sneer at my poor clothes ? Why—" Her voice trembled, and she stopped abruptly.

" I was not aware that they were poor or old, Miss Duke. I have never seen a more exquisite costume than yours on the evening when we dined here by invitation ; it has been like a picture in my memory ever since."

" An old robe that belonged to my grandmother, and I burned it, every shred, as soon as you had gone," said Gardis hotly.

Far from being impressed as she had intended he should be, David Newell merely bowed ; the girl saw that he set the act down as " temper."

" I suppose your Northern ladies never do such things ? " she said bitterly.

" You are right ; they do not," he answered.

" Why do you come here ? " pursued Gardis. " Why do you speak to me of Mr. Saxton ? Though he had the fortune of a prince, he is nothing to me."

" Roger's fortune is comfortable, but not princely, Miss Duke—by no means princely. We are not princely at the North," added Newell, with a slight smile, " and neither are we 'knightly.' We must, I fear, yield all claim to those prized words of yours."

" I am not aware that I have used the words," said Miss Duke, with lofty indifference.

" Oh, I did not mean you alone—you personally—but all Southern women. However, to return to our subject :

Saxton loves you, and has gone away with a saddened
heart."

This was said gravely. "As though," Miss Duke remarked to herself—"really as though a heart was of consequence!"

"I presume he will soon forget," she said carelessly, as
she took up her embroidery again.

"Yes, no doubt," replied Captain Newell. "I remember
once on Staten Island, and again out in Mississippi, when he
was even more— Yes, as you say, he will soon forget."

"Then why do you so continually speak of him?" said
Miss Duke sharply. Such prompt corroboration was not,
after all, as agreeable as it should have been to a well-regulated mind.

"I speak of him, Miss Duke, because I wish to know
whether it is only your Southern girlish pride that speaks, or
whether you really, as would be most natural, love him as he
loves you; for, in the latter case, you would be able, I think,
to fix and retain his somewhat fickle fancy. He is a fine
fellow, and, as I said before, it would be but natural, Miss
Duke, that you should love him."

"I do not love him," said Gardis, quickly and angrily, putting in her stitches all wrong. Who was this person, daring
to assume what would or would not be natural for her to do?

"Very well; I believe you. And now that I know the
truth, I will tell you why I come here: you have asked me
several times. I too love you, Miss Duke."

Gardis had risen. "You?" she said—"you?"

"Yes, I; I too."

He was standing also, and they gazed at each other a
moment in silence.

"I will never marry you," said the girl at last—"never!
never! You do not, can not, understand the hearts of Southern women, sir."

"I have not asked you to marry me, Miss Duke," said the
young soldier composedly; "and the hearts of Southern wo-

men are much like those of other women, I presume." Then,
as the girl opened the door to escape, "You may go away
if you like, Gardis," he said, "but I shall love you all the
same, dear."

She disappeared, and in a few moments Cousin Copeland
reëntered, with apologies for his lengthened absence. "I
found several other documents I thought you might like to
see," he said eagerly. "They will occupy the remainder of
our evening delightfully."

They did. But Gardis did not return; neither did she appear at the breakfast-table the next morning. Captain Newell
rode back to the city without seeing her.

Not long afterward Cousin Copeland received a formal
letter from a city lawyer. The warehouse had found a tenant,
and he, the lawyer, acting for the agent, Captain Newell, had
the honor to inclose the first installment of rent-money, and
remained an obedient servant, and so forth. Cousin Copeland was exultant. Gardis said to herself, "He is taking
advantage of our poverty," and, going to her room, she sat
down to plan some way of release. "I might be a governess,"
she thought. But no one at the South wanted a governess
now, and how could she go North? She was not aware how
old-fashioned were her little accomplishments—her music, her
embroidery, her ideas of literature, her prim drawings, and
even her deportment. No one made courtesies at the North
any more, save perhaps in the Lancers. As to chemistry,
trigonometry, physiology, and geology, the ordinary studies
of a Northern girl, she knew hardly more than their names.
"We might sell the place," she thought at last, "and go away
somewhere and live in the woods."

This, indeed, seemed the only way open to her. The
house was an actual fact; it was there; it was also her own.
A few days later an advertisement appeared in the city newspaper: "For sale, the residence known as Gardiston House,
situated six miles from the city, on Green River. Apply by
letter, or on the premises, to Miss Gardiston Duke." Three

days passed, and no one came. The fourth day an applicant appeared, and was ushered into the dining-room. He sent up no name; but Miss Duke descended hopefully to confer with him, and found—Captain Newell.

"You!" she said, paling and flushing. Her voice faltered; she was sorely disappointed.

"It will always be myself, Gardis," said the young man gravely. "So you wish to sell the old house? I should not have supposed it."

"I wish to sell it in order to be freed from obligations forced upon us, sir."

"Very well. But if *I* buy it, then what?"

"You will not buy it, for the simple reason that I will not sell it to you. You do not wish the place; you would only buy it to assist us."

"That is true."

"Then there is nothing more to be said, I believe," said Miss Duke, rising.

"*Is* there nothing more, Gardis?"

"Nothing, Captain Newell."

And then, without another word, the soldier bowed, and rode back to town.

The dreary little advertisement remained in a corner of the newspaper a month longer, but no purchaser appeared. The winter was rainy, with raw east winds from the ocean, and the old house leaked in many places. If they had lived in one or two of the smaller rooms, which were in better condition and warmer than the large apartments, they might have escaped; but no habit was changed, and three times a day the table was spread in the damp dining-room, where the atmosphere was like that of a tomb, and where no fire was ever made. The long evenings were spent in the somber drawing-room by the light of the one candle, and the rain beat against the old shutters so loudly that Cousin Copeland was obliged to elevate his gentle little voice as he read aloud to his silent companion. But one evening he found himself forced to pause; his voice had failed. Four days afterward he died, gentle and placid to the last. He was an old man, although no one had ever thought so.

The funeral notice appeared in the city paper, and a few old family friends came out to Gardiston House to follow the last Gardiston to his resting-place in St. Mark's forest churchyard. They were all sad-faced people, clad in mourning much the worse for wear. Accustomed to sorrow, they followed to the grave quietly, not a heart there that had not its own dead. They all returned to Gardiston House, sat a while in the drawing-room, spoke a few words each in turn to the desolate little mistress, and then took leave. Gardis was left alone.

Captain Newell did not come to the funeral; he could not come into such a company in his uniform, and he would not come without it. He had his own ideas of duty, and his own pride. But he sent a wreath of beautiful flowers, which must have come from some city where there was a hot-house. Miss Duke would not place the wreath upon the coffin, neither would she leave it in the drawing-room; she stood a while with it in her hand, and then she stole up stairs and laid it on Cousin Copeland's open desk, where daily he had worked so patiently and steadily through so many long years. Uselessly? Who among us shall dare to say that?

A week later, at twilight, old Dinah brought up the young officer's card.

"Say that I see no one," replied Miss Duke.

A little note came back, written on a slip of paper: "I beg you to see me, if only for a moment; it is a business matter that has brought me here to-day." And certainly it was a very forlorn day for a pleasure ride: the wind howled through the trees, and the roads were almost impassable with deep mire. Miss Duke went down to the dining-room. She wore no mourning garments; she had none. She had not worn mourning for her aunt, and for the same reason. Pale and silent, she stood before the young officer waiting to hear

his errand. It was this : some one wished to purchase Gardiston House—a real purchaser this time, a stranger. Captain Newell did not say that it was the wife of an army contractor, a Northern woman, who had taken a fancy for an old
family residence, and intended to be herself an old family in
future; he merely stated the price offered for the house and
its furniture, and in a few words placed the business clearly
before the listener.

Her face lighted with pleasure.

"At last!" she said.

"Yes, at last, Miss Duke." There was a shade of sadness in his tone, but he spoke no word of entreaty. "You
accept?"

"I do," said Gardis.

"I must ride back to the city," said David Newell, taking
up his cap, "before it is entirely dark, for the roads are very
heavy. I came out as soon as I heard of the offer, Miss
Duke, for I knew you would be glad, very glad."

"Yes," said Gardis, "I am glad ; very glad." Her cheeks
were flushed now, and she smiled as she returned the young
officer's bow. "Some time, Captain Newell—some time I
trust I shall feel like thanking you for what was undoubtedly
intended, on your part, as kindness," she said.

"It was never intended for kindness at all," said Newell
bluntly. "It was never but one thing, Gardis, and you know
it; and that one thing is, and always will be, love. Not 'always will be,' though; I should not say that. A man can
conquer an unworthy love if he chooses."

"Unworthy?" said Gardis involuntarily.

"Yes, unworthy; like this of mine for you. A woman
should be gentle, should be loving ; a woman should have a
womanly nature. But you—you—you do not seem to have
anything in you but a foolish pride. I verily believe, Gardis
Duke, that, if you loved me enough to die for me, you would
still let me go out of that door without a word, so deep, so
deadly is that pride of yours. What do I want with such a

wife? No. My wife must love me—love me ardently, as I shall love her. Farewell, Miss Duke; I shall not see you again, probably. I will send a lawyer out to complete the sale."

He was gone, and Gardis stood alone in the darkening room. Gardiston House, where she had spent her life—Gardiston House, full of the memories and associations of two centuries—Gardiston House, the living reminder and the constant support of that family pride in which she had been nurtured, her one possession in the land which she had so loved, the beautiful, desolate South—would soon be hers no longer. She began to sob, and then when the sound came back to her, echoing through the still room, she stopped suddenly, as though ashamed. "I will go abroad," she said; "there will be a great deal to amuse me over there." But the comfort was dreary; and, as if she must do something, she took a candle, and slowly visited every room in the old mansion, many of them long unused. From garret to cellar she went, touching every piece of the antique furniture, folding back the old curtains, standing by the dismantled beds, and softly pausing by the empty chairs; she was saying farewell. On Cousin Copeland's desk the wreath still lay; in that room she cried from sheer desolation. Then, going down to the dining-room, she found her solitary repast awaiting her, and, not to distress old Dinah, sat down in her accustomed place. Presently she perceived smoke, then a sound, then a hiss and a roar. She flew up stairs; the house was on fire. Somewhere her candle must have started the flame; she remembered the loose papers in Cousin Copeland's study, and the wind blowing through the broken window-pane; it was there that she had cried so bitterly, forgetting everything save her own loneliness.

Nothing could be done; there was no house within several miles—no one to help. The old servants were infirm, and the fire had obtained strong headway; then the high wind rushed in, and sent the flames up through the roof and over the tops of the trees. When the whole upper story was one sheet of red and yellow, some one rode furiously up the road and into the garden, where Gardis stood alone, her little figure illumined by the glare; nearer the house the two old servants were at work, trying to save some of the furniture from the lower rooms.

"I saw the light and hurried back, Miss Duke," began Captain Newell. Then, as he saw the wan desolation of the girl's face: "O Gardis! why will you resist me longer?" he cried passionately. "You shall be anything you like, think anything you like—only love me, dear, as I love you."

And Gardis burst into tears. "I can not help it," she sobbed; " everything is against me. The very house is burning before my eyes. O David, David! it is all wrong; everything is wrong. But what can I do when—when you hold me so, and when— Oh, do not ask me any more."

"But I shall," said Newell, his face flushing with deep happiness. "When what, dear?"

"When I—"

"Love me?" said Newell. He would have it spoken.

"Yes," whispered Gardis, hanging her head.

"And I have adored the very shoe-tie of my proud little love ever since I first saw her sweet face at the drawing-room window," said Newell, holding her close and closer, and gazing down into her eyes with the deep gaze of the quiet heart that loves but once.

And the old house burned on, burned as though it knew a contractor's wife was waiting for it. "I see our Gardis is provided for," said the old house. "She never was a real Gardiston—only a Duke; so it is just as well. As for that contractor's wife, she shall have nothing; not a Chinese image, not a spindle-legged chair, not one crocodile cup—no, not even one stone upon another."

It kept its word: in the morning there was nothing left. Old Gardiston was gone!

THE SOUTH DEVIL.

The trees that lean'd in their love unto trees,
    That lock'd in their loves, and were made so strong,
Stronger than armies ; ay, stronger than seas
    That rush from their caves in a storm of song.

The cockatoo swung in the vines below,
    And muttering hung on a golden thread,
Or moved on the moss'd bough to and fro,
    In plumes of gold and array'd in red.

The serpent that hung from the sycamore bough,
    And sway'd his head in a crescent above,
Had folded his head to the white limb now,
    And fondled it close like a great black love.
                              JOAQUIN MILLER.

ON the afternoon of the 23d of December, the thermometer marked eighty-six degrees in the shade on the outside
wall of Mark Deal's house. Mark Deal's brother, lying on
the white sand, his head within the line of shadow cast by a
live-oak, but all the remainder of his body full in the hot sunshine, basked liked a chameleon, and enjoyed the heat. Mark
Deal's brother spent much of his time basking. He always
took the live-oak for a head-protector ; but gave himself variety by trying new radiations around the tree, his crossed legs
and feet stretching from it in a slightly different direction each
day, as the spokes of a wheel radiate from the hub. The
live-oak was a symmetrical old tree, standing by itself ; having always had sufficient space, its great arms were straight,
stretching out evenly all around, densely covered with the
small, dark, leathery leaves, unnotched and uncut, which are
as unlike the Northern oak-leaf as the leaf of the willow is

unlike that of the sycamore. Behind the live-oak, two tall, ruined chimneys and a heap of white stones marked where the mansion-house had been. The old tree had watched its foundations laid ; had shaded its blank, white front and little hanging balcony above ; had witnessed its destruction, fifty years before, by the Indians ; and had mounted guard over its remains ever since, alone as far as man was concerned, until this year, when a tenant had arrived, Mark Deal, and, somewhat later, Mark Deal's brother.

The ancient tree was Spanish to the core ; it would have resented the sacrilege to the tips of its small acorns, if the new-comer had laid hands upon the dignified old ruin it guarded. The new-comer, however, entertained no such intention ; a small out-building, roofless, but otherwise in good condition, on the opposite side of the circular space, attracted his attention, and became mentally his residence, as soon as his eyes fell upon it, he meanwhile standing with his hands in his pockets, surveying the place critically. It was the old Monteano plantation, and he had taken it for a year.

The venerable little out-building was now firmly roofed with new, green boards ; its square windows, destitute of sash or glass, possessed new wooden shutters hung by strips of deer's hide ; new steps led up to its two rooms, elevated four feet above the ground. But for a door it had only a red cotton curtain, now drawn forward and thrown carelessly over a peg on the outside wall, a spot of vivid color on its white. Underneath the windows hung flimsy strips of bark covered with brightly-hued flowers.

" They won't live," said Mark Deal.

" Oh, I shall put in fresh ones every day or two," answered his brother. It was he who had wanted the red curtain.

As he basked, motionless, in the sunshine, it could be noted that this brother was a slender youth, with long, pale-yellow hair—hair fine, thin, and dry, the kind that crackles if the comb is passed rapidly through it. His face in sleep was

pale and wizened, with deep purple shadows under the closed
eyes; his long hands were stretched out on the white, hot
sand in the blaze of the sunshine, which, however, could not
alter their look of blue-white cold. The sunken chest and
blanched temples told of illness; but, if cure were possible, it
would be gained from this soft, balmy, fragrant air, now
soothing his sore lungs. He slept on in peace; and an old
green chameleon came down from the tree, climbed up on the
sleeve of his brown sack-coat, occupied himself for a moment
in changing his own miniature hide to match the cloth, swelled
out his scarlet throat, caught a fly or two, and then, pleasant-
ly established, went to sleep also in company. Butterflies, in
troops of twenty or thirty, danced in the golden air; there
was no sound. Everything was hot and soft and brightly
colored. Winter? Who knew of winter here? Labor?
What was labor? This was the land and the sky and the
air of never-ending rest.

Yet one man was working there, and working hard, namely, Mark Deal. His little central plaza, embracing perhaps
an acre, was surrounded when he first arrived by a wall of
green, twenty feet high. The sweet orange-trees, crape-myr-
tles, oleanders, guavas, and limes planted by the Spaniards
had been, during the fifty years, conquered and partially en-
slaved by a wilder growth—andromedas, dahoons, bayberries,
and the old field loblollies, the whole bound together by the
tangled vines of the jessamine and armed smilax, with bear-
grass and the dwarf palmetto below. Climbing the central
live-oak, Deal had found, as he expected, traces of the six
paths which had once led from this little plaza to the various
fields and the sugar plantation, their course still marked by
the tops of the bitter-sweet orange-trees, which showed themselves glossily, in regular lines, amid the duller foliage around
them. He took their bearings and cut them out slowly, one
by one. Now the low-arched aisles, eighty feet in length,
were clear, with the thick leaves interlacing overhead, and
the daylight shining through at their far ends, golden against

the green. Here, where the north path terminated, Deal was now working.

He was a man slightly below middle height, broad-shouldered, and muscular, with the outlines which are called thickset. He appeared forty-five, and was not quite thirty-five. Although weather-beaten and bronzed, there was yet a pinched look in his face, which was peculiar. He was working in an old field, preparing it for sweet potatoes—those omnipresent, monotonous vegetables of Florida which will grow anywhere, and which at last, with their ugly, gray-mottled skins, are regarded with absolute aversion by the Northern visitor.

The furrows of half a century before were still visible in the field. No frost had disturbed the winterless earth; no atom had changed its place, save where the gopher had burrowed beneath, or the snake left its waving trail above in the sand which constitutes the strange, white, desolate soil, wherever there is what may be called by comparison solid ground, in the lake-dotted, sieve-like land. There are many such traces of former cultivation in Florida: we come suddenly upon old tracks, furrows, and drains in what we thought primeval forest; rose-bushes run wild, and distorted old fig-trees meet us in a jungle where we supposed no white man's foot had ever before penetrated; the ruins of a chimney gleam whitely through a waste of thorny *chaparral.* It is all natural enough, if one stops to remember that fifty years before the first settlement was made in Virginia, and sixty-three before the Mayflower touched the shores of the New World, there were flourishing Spanish plantations on this Southern coast—more flourishing, apparently, than any the indolent peninsula has since known. But one does not stop to remember it; the belief is imbedded in all our Northern hearts that, because the narrow, sun-bathed State is far away and wild and empty, it is also new and virgin, like the lands of the West; whereas it is old—the only gray-haired corner our country holds.

Mark Deal worked hard. Perspiration beaded his fore-head and cheeks, and rolled from his short, thick, red-brown hair. He worked in this way every day from daylight until dusk, and was probably the only white man in the State who did. When his task was finished, he made a circuit around the belt of thicket through which the six paths ran to his orange-grove on the opposite side. On the way he skirted an edge of the sugar-plantation, now a wide, empty waste, with the old elevated causeway still running across it. On its far edge loomed the great cypresses of South Devil, a swamp forty miles long; there was a sister, West Devil, not far away, equally beautiful, dark, and deadly. Beyond the sugar waste were the indigo-fields, still fenced by their old ditches. Then came the orange-grove; luxuriant, shady word—the orange-grove !

It was a space of level white sand, sixty feet square, ferti-lized a century before with pounded oyster-shells, in the Span-ish fashion. Planted in even rows across it, tied to stakes, were slips of green stem, each with three leaves—forlorn little plants, five or six inches in height. But the stakes were new and square and strong, and rose to Deal's shoulder; they were excellent stakes, and made quite a grove of themselves, firm, if somewhat bare.

Deal worked in his grove until sunset; then he shouldered his tools and went homeward through one of the arched aisles to the little plaza within, where stood his two-roomed house with its red cotton door. His brother was still sleeping on the sand, at least, his eyes were closed. Deal put his tools in a rack behind the house, and then crossed to where he lay.

"You should not sleep here after sunset, Carl," he said, somewhat roughly. "You know better; why do you do it?"

"I'm not asleep," answered the other, sitting up, and then slowly getting on his feet. "Heigh-ho! What are you going to have for dinner?"

"You are tired, Carl; and I see the reason. You have been in the swamp." Deal's eyes as he spoke were fixed upon the younger man's shoes, where traces of the ink-black soil of South Devil were plainly visible.

Carl laughed. " Can't keep anything from your Yankee eyes, can I, Mark ? " he said. " But I only went a little way."

" It isn't the distance, it's the folly," said Mark, shortly, going toward the house.

" I never pretended to be wise," answered Carl, slouching along behind him, with his hands wrapped in his blue cotton handkerchief, arranged like a muff.

Although Deal worked hard in his fields all day, he did not cook. In a third out-building lived a gray-headed old negro with one eye, who cooked for the new tenant—and cooked well. His name was Scipio, but Carl called him Africanus ; he said it was equally appropriate, and sounded more impressive. Scip's kitchen was out-of-doors—simply an old Spanish chimney. His kettle and few dishes, when not in use, hung on the sides of this chimney, which now, all alone in the white sand, like an obelisk, cooked solemnly the old negro's messes, as half a century before it had cooked the more dignified repasts of the dead hidalgos. The brothers ate in the open air also, sitting at a rough board table which Mark had made behind the house. They had breakfast soon after daylight, and at sunset dinner ; in the middle of the day they took only fruit and bread.

" Day after to-morrow will be Christmas," said Carl, leaving the table and lighting his long pipe. " What are you going to do ? "

" I had not thought of doing anything in particular."

" Well, at least don't work on Christmas day."

" What would you have me do ? "

Carl took his pipe from his mouth, and gazed at his brother in silence for a moment. " Go into the swamp with me," he urged, with sudden vehemence. " Come—for the whole day ! "

Deal was smoking, too, a short clay pipe, very different from the huge, fantastic, carved bowl with long stem which weighed down Carl's thin mouth. " I don't know what to do with you, boy. You are mad about the swamp," he said, smoking on calmly.

They were sitting in front of the house now, in two chairs tilted back against its wall. The dark, odorous earth looked up to the myriad stars, but was not lighted by them; a soft, languorous gloom lay over the land. Carl brushed away the ashes from his pipe impatiently.

" It's because you can't understand," he said. " The swamp haunts me. I *must* see it once; you will be wise to let me see it once. We might go through in a canoe together by the branch; the branch goes through."

" The water goes, no doubt, but a canoe couldn't."

" Yes, it could, with an axe. It has been done. They used to go up to San Miguel that way sometimes from here; it shortens the distance more than half."

" Who told you all this—Scip ? What does he know about it ? "

" Oh, Africanus has seen several centuries; the Spaniards were living here only fifty years ago, you know, and that's nothing to him. He remembers the Indian attack."

" Ponce de Leon, too, I suppose; or, to go back to the old country, Cleopatra. But you must give up the swamp, Carl. I positively forbid it. The air inside is thick and deadly, to say nothing of the other dangers. How do you suppose it gained its name ? "

" Diabolus is common enough as a title among Spaniards and Italians; it don't mean anything. The prince of darkness never lives in the places called by his name; he likes baptized cities better."

" Death lives there, however; and I brought you down here to cure you."

" I'm all right. See how much stronger I am ! I shall soon be quite well again, old man," answered Carl, with the strange, sanguine faith of the consumptive.

The next day Deal worked very hard. He had a curious,

7

inflexible, possibly narrow kind of conscience, which required
him to do double duty to-day in order to make up for the
holiday granted to Carl to-morrow.   There was no task-
master over him ; even the seasons were not task-masters
here.   But so immovable were his own rules for himself that
nothing could have induced him to abate one jot of the task he
had laid out in his own mind when he started afield at dawn.

When he returned home at sunset, somewhat later than
usual, Carl was absent.   Old Scipio could give no information ; he had not seen "young marse" since early morning.
Deal put up his tools, ate something, and then, with a flask
in his pocket, a fagot of light-wood torches bound on his
back, and one of these brilliant, natural flambeaux in his hand,
he started away on his search, going down one of the orange-
aisles, the light gleaming back through the arch till he reached
the far end, when it disappeared.   He crossed an old indigo-
field, and pushed his way through its hedge of Spanish-bayo-
nets, while the cacti sown along the hedge—small, flat green
plates with white spines, like hideous tufted insects—fastened
themselves viciously on the strong leather of his high boots.
Then, reaching the sugar waste, he advanced a short distance
on the old causeway, knelt down, and in the light of the torch
examined its narrow, sandy level.   Yes, there were the footprints he had feared to find.   Carl had gone again into the
poisonous swamp—the beautiful, deadly South Devil.   And
this time he had not come back.

The elder brother rose, and with the torch held downward
slowly traced the footmarks.   There was a path, or rather
trail, leading in a short distance.   The footprints followed it
as far as it went, and the brother followed the footprints, the
red glare of the torch foreshortening each swollen, gray-white
cypress-trunk, and giving to the dark, hidden pools below
bright gleamings which they never had by day.   He soon
came to the end of the trail ; here he stopped and shouted
loudly several times, with pauses between for answer.   No
answer came.

"But I know the trick of this thick air," he said to himself. "One can't hear anything in a cypress-swamp."

He was now obliged to search closely for the footprints, pausing at each one, having no idea in which direction the next would tend. The soil did not hold the impressions well; it was not mud or mire, but wet, spongy, fibrous, black earth, thinly spread over the hard roots of trees, which protruded in distorted shapes in every direction. He traced what seemed footmarks across an open space, and then lost them on the brink of a dark pool. If Carl had kept on, he must have crossed this pool; but how? On the sharp cypress-knees standing sullenly in the claret-colored water? He went all around the open space again, seeking for footmarks elsewhere; but no, they ended at the edge of the pool. Cutting a long stick, he made his way across by its aid, stepping from knee-point to knee-point. On the other side he renewed his search for the trail, and after some labor found it, and went on again.

He toiled forward slowly in this way a long time, his course changing often; Carl's advance seemed to have been aimless. Then, suddenly, the footprints ceased. There was not another one visible anywhere, though he searched in all directions again and again. He looked at his watch; it was midnight. He hallooed; no reply. What could have become of the lad? He now began to feel his own fatigue; after the long day of toil in the hot sun, these hours of laboring over the ground in a bent position, examining it inch by inch, brought on pains in his shoulders and back. Planting the torch he was carrying in the soft soil of a little knoll, he placed another one near it, and sat down between the two flames to rest for a minute or two, pouring out for himself a little brandy in the bottom of the cup belonging to his flask. He kept strict watch as he did this. Venomous things, large and small, filled the vines above, and might drop at any moment upon him. But he had quick eyes and ears, and no intention of dying in the South Devil; so, while he watched keenly, he took

the time to swallow the brandy. After a moment or two he
was startled by a weak human voice saying, with faint decision, " *That's* brandy ! "

" I should say it was," called Deal, springing to his feet.
" Where are you, then ? "

" Here."

The rescuer followed the sound, and, after one or two
errors, came upon the body of his brother lying on a dank
mat of water-leaves and ground-vines at the edge of a pool.
In the red light of the torch he looked as though he was dead ;
his eyes only were alive.

" Brandy," he said again, faintly, as Deal appeared.

After he had swallowed a small quantity of the stimulant,
he revived with unexpected swiftness.

" I have been shouting for you not fifty feet away," said
Deal ; " how is it that you did not hear ? " Then in the same
breath, in a soft undertone, he added, " Ah-h-h-h ! " and without stirring a hair's breadth from where he stood, or making
an unnecessary motion, he slowly drew forth his pistol, took
careful aim, and fired. He was behind his brother, who lay
with closed eyes, not noticing the action.

" What have you killed ? " asked Carl languidly. " I 've
seen nothing but birds ; and the most beautiful ones, too."

" A moccasin, that's all," said Deal, kicking the dead creature into the pool. He did not add that the snake was coiled
for a spring. " Let us get back to the little knoll where I was,
Carl ; it's drier there."

" I don't think I can walk, old man. I fell from the vines
up there, and something's the matter with my ankles."

" Well, I can carry you that distance," said Deal. " Put
your arms around my neck, and raise yourself as I lift you—
so."

The burning flambeau on the knoll served as a guide, and,
after one or two pauses, owing to the treacherous footing, the
elder brother succeeded in carrying the other thither. He
then took off the light woolen coat he had put on before en-

tering the swamp, spread it over the driest part of the little
knoll, and laid Carl upon it.

"If you can not walk," he said, "we shall have to wait
here until daylight. I could not carry you and the torch also;
and the footing is bad—there are twenty pools to cross, or go
around. Fortunately, we have light-wood enough to burn all
night."

He lit fresh torches and arranged them at the four corners
of their little knoll; then he began to pace slowly to and fro,
like a picket walking his beat.

"What were you doing up among those vines?" he asked.
He knew that it would be better for them both if they could
keep themselves awake; those who fell asleep in the night air
of South Devil generally awoke the next morning in another
world.

"I climbed up a ladder of vines to gather some of the
great red blossoms swinging in the air; and, once up, I went
along on the mat to see what I could find. It's beautiful
there—fairy-land. You can't see anything down below, but
above the long moss hangs in fine, silvery lines like spray from
ever so high up, and mixed with it air-plants, sheafs, and bells
of scarlet and cream-colored blossoms. I sat there a long
time looking, and I suppose I must have dozed; for I don't
know when I fell."

"You did not hear me shout?"

"No. The first consciousness I had was the odor of
brandy."

"The odor reached you, and the sound did not; that is
one of the tricks of such air as this! You must have climbed
up, I suppose, at the place where I lost the trail. What time
did you come in?"

"I don't know," murmured Carl drowsily.

"Look here! you *must* keep awake!"

"I can't," answered the other.

Deal shook him, but could not rouse him even to anger.
He only opened his blue eyes and looked reproachfully at his

brother, but as though he was a long distance off.   Then Deal
lifted him up, uncorked the flask, and put it to his lips.

"Drink!" he said, loudly and sternly; and mechanically
Carl obeyed.   Once or twice his head moved aside, as if refusing more; but Deal again said, "Drink!" and without
pity made the sleeper swallow every drop the flask contained.
Then he laid him down upon the coat again, and covered his
face and head with his own broad-brimmed palmetto hat,
Carl's hat having been lost.   He had done all he could—
changed the lethargy of the South Devil into the sleep of
drunkenness, the last named at least a human slumber.   He
was now left to keep the watch alone.

During the first half hour a dozen red and green things,
of the centipede and scorpion kind, stupefied by the glare of
the torches, fell from the trees; and he dispatched them.
Next, enormous grayish-white spiders, in color exactly like
the bark, moved slowly one furred leg into view, and then another, on the trunks of the cypresses near by, gradually coming wholly into the light—creatures covering a circumference
as large as that of a plate.   At length the cypresses all
around the knoll were covered with them; and they all seemed
to be watching him.   He was not watching the spiders, however; he cared very little for the spiders.   His eyes were
upon the ground all the time, moving along the borders of his
little knoll-fort.   It was bounded on two sides by pools, in
whose dark depths he knew moccasins were awake, watching
the light, too, with whatever of curiosity belongs to a snake's
cold brain.   His torches aroused them; and yet darkness would
have been worse.   In the light he could at least see them, if
they glided forth and tried to ascend the brilliant knoll.   After
a while they began to rise to the surface; he could distinguish
portions of their bodies in waving lines, moving noiselessly
hither and thither, appearing and disappearing suddenly, until
the pools around seemed alive with them.   There was not a
sound; the soaked forest stood motionless.   The absolute
stillness made the quick gliding motions of the moccasins

even more horrible. Yet Deal had no instinctive dread of snakes. The terrible "coach-whip," the deadly and grotesque spread-adder, the rattlesnake of the barrens, and these great moccasins of the pools were endowed with no imaginary horrors in his eyes. He accepted them as nature made them, and not as man's fancy painted them ; it was only their poison-fangs he feared.

"If the sea-crab could sting, how hideous we should think him ! If the lobster had a deadly venom, how devilish his shape would seem to us ! " he said.

But now no imagination was required to make the moccasins terrible. His revolver carried six balls ; and he had already used one of them. Four hours must pass before dawn ; there could be no unnecessary shooting. The creatures might even come out and move along the edge of his knoll ; only when they showed an intention of coming up the slope must their gliding life be ended. The moccasin is not a timorous or quick-nerved snake ; in a place like the South Devil, when a human foot or boat approaches, generally he does not stir. His great body, sometimes over six feet in length, and thick and fat in the middle, lies on a log or at the edge of a pool, seemingly too lazy to move. But none the less, when roused, is his coil sudden and his long spring sure ; his venom is deadly. After a time one of the creatures did come out and glide along the edge of the knoll. He went back into the water ; but a second came out on the other side. During the night Deal killed three ; he was an excellent marksman, and picked them off easily as they crossed his dead-line.

"Fortunately they come one by one," he said to himself. "If there was any concert of action among them, I couldn't hold the place a minute."

As the last hour began, the long hour before dawn, he felt the swamp lethargy stealing into his own brain ; he saw the trees and torches doubled. He walked to and fro more quickly, and sang to keep himself awake. He knew only a few old-

fashioned songs, and the South Devil heard that night, probably for the first time in its tropical life, the ancient Northern
strains of " Gayly the Troubadour touched his Guitar." Deal
was no troubadour, and he had no guitar. But he sang on
bravely, touching that stringed instrument, vocally at least,
and bringing himself " home from the war " over and over
again, until at last faint dawn penetrated from above down to
the knoll where the four torches were burning. They were
the last torches, and Deal was going through his sixtieth
rehearsal of the " Troubadour " ; but, instead of " Lady-love,
lady-lo-o-o-ve," whom he apostrophized, a large moccasin
rose from the pool, as if in answer. She might have been the
queen of the moccasins, and beautiful—to moccasin eyes ;
but to Deal she was simply the largest and most hideous of
all the snake-visions of the night. He gave her his fifth ball,
full in her mistaken brain ; and, if she had admired him (or
the " Troubadour "), she paid for it with her life.

This was the last. Daylight appeared. The watchman
put out his torches and roused the sleeper. " Carl! Carl!
It's daylight. Let us get out of this confounded crawling
hole, and have a breath of fresh air."

Carl stirred, and opened his eyes; they were heavy and
dull. His brother lifted him, told him to hold on tightly, and
started with his burden toward home. The snakes had disappeared, the gray spiders had vanished; he could see his
way now, and he followed his own trail, which he had taken
care to make distinct when he came in the night before.
But, loaded down as he was, and obliged to rest frequently,
and also to go around all the pools, hours passed before he
reached the last cypresses and came out on the old causeway
across the sugar-waste.

It was Christmas morning ; the thermometer stood at
eighty-eight.

Carl slept off his enforced drunkenness in his hammock.
Mark, having bandaged his brother's strained ankles, threw
himself upon his rude couch, and fell into a heavy slumber

also. He slept until sunset; then he rose, plunged his head into a tub of the limpid, pure, but never cold water of Florida, drawn from his shallow well, and went out to the chimney to see about dinner. The chimney was doing finely: a fiery plume of sparks waved from its white top, a red bed of coals glowed below. Scip moved about with as much equanimity as though he had a row of kitchen-tables upon which to arrange his pans and dishes, instead of ruined blocks of stone, under the open sky. The dinner was good. Carl, awake at last, was carried out to the table to enjoy it, and then brought back to his chair in front of the house to smoke his evening pipe.

"I must make you a pair of crutches," said Deal.

"One will do; my right ankle is not much hurt, I think."

The fall, the air of the swamp, and the inward drenching of brandy had left Carl looking much as usual; the tenacious disease that held him swallowed the lesser ills. But for the time, at least, his wandering footsteps were staid.

"I suppose there is no use in my asking, Carl, *why* you went in there?" said Deal, after a while.

"No, there isn't. I'm haunted—that's all."

"But what is it that haunts you?"

"Sounds. *You* couldn't understand, though, if I was to talk all night."

"Perhaps I could; perhaps I can understand more than you imagine. I'll tell you a story presently; but first you must explain to me, at least as well as you can, what it is that attracts you in South Devil."

"Oh—well," said Carl, with a long, impatient sigh, closing his eyes wearily. "I am a musician, you know, a musician *manqué;* a musician who can't play. Something's the matter; I *hear* music, but can not bring it out. And I know so well what it ought to be, ought to be and isn't, that I've broken my violin in pieces a dozen times in my rages about it. Now, other fellows in orchestras, who *don't* know, get along very well. But I couldn't. I've thought at times that, although I can not sound what I hear with my own hands, perhaps I could *write* it out so that other men could sound it. The idea has never come to anything definite yet—that is, what *you* would call definite; but it haunts me persistently, and *now* it has got into that swamp. The wish," here Carl laid down his great pipe, and pressed his hand eagerly upon his brother's knee—" the wish that haunts me—drives me—is to write out the beautiful music of the South Devil, the sounds one hears in there "—

" But there are no sounds."

" No sounds? You must be deaf! The air fairly reeks with sounds, with harmonies. But there—I told you you couldn't understand." He leaned back against the wall again, and took up the great pipe, which looked as though it must consume whatever small store of strength remained to him.

" Is it what is called an opera you want to write, like—like the 'Creation,' for instance?" asked Deal. The " Creation " was the only long piece of music he had ever heard.

Carl groaned. " Oh, *don't* talk of it!" he said; then added, irritably, " It's a song, that's all—the song of a Southern swamp."

"Call it by it's real name, Devil," said the elder brother, grimly.

" I would, if I was rich enough to have a picture painted —the Spirit of the Swamp—a beautiful woman, falsely called a devil by cowards, dark, languorous, mystical, sleeping among the vines I saw up there, with the great red blossoms dropping around her."

" And the great mottled snakes coiling over her?"

" *I* didn't see any snakes."

" Well," said Mark, refilling his pipe, " now I'm going to tell you *my* story. When I met you on that windy pier at Exton, and proposed that you should come down here with me, I was coming myself, in any case, wasn't I? And why? I wanted to get to a place where I could be warm—warm, hot, baked; warm through and through; warm all the time.

I wanted to get to a place where the very ground was warm. And *now*—I'll tell you why."

He rose from his seat, laid down his pipe, and, extending his hand, spoke for about fifteen minutes without pause. Then he turned, went back hastily to the old chimney, where red coals still lingered, and sat down close to the glow, leaving Carl wonder-struck in his tilted chair. The elder man leaned over the fire and held his hands close to the coals; Carl watched him. It was nine o'clock, and the thermometer marked eighty.

For nearly a month after Christmas, life on the old plantation went on without event or disaster. Carl, with his crutch and cane, could not walk far; his fancy now was to limp through the east orange-aisle to the place of tombs, and sit there for hours, playing softly, what might be called crooning, on his violin. The place of tombs was a small, circular space surrounded by wild orange-trees in a close, even row, like a hedge; here were four tombs, massive, oblong blocks of the white conglomerate of the coast, too coarse-grained to hold inscription or mark of any kind. Who the old Spaniards were whose bones lay beneath, and what names they bore in the flesh, no one knew; all record was lost. Outside in the wild thicket was a tomb still more ancient, and of different construction: four slabs of stone, uncovered, about three feet high, rudely but firmly placed, as though inclosing a coffin. In the earth between these low walls grew a venerable cedar; but, old as it was, it must have been planted by chance or by hand after the human body beneath had been laid in its place.

"Why do you come here?" said Deal, pausing and looking into the place of tombs, one morning, on his way to the orange-grove. "There are plenty of pleasanter spots about."

"No; I like this better," answered Carl, without stopping the low chant of his violin. "Besides, they like it too."

"Who?"

"The old fellows down below. The chap outside there, who must have been an Aztec, I suppose, and the original proprietor, catches a little of it; but I generally limp over and give him a tune to himself before going home. I have to imagine the Aztec style."

Mark gave a short laugh, and went on to his work. But he knew the real reason for Carl's fancy for the place; between the slim, clean trunks of the orange-trees, the long green line of South Devil bounded the horizon, the flat tops of the cypresses far above against the sky, and the vines and silver moss filling the space below—a luxuriant wall across the broad, thinly-treed expanses of the pine barrens.

One evening in January Deal came homeward as usual at sunset, and found a visitor. Carl introduced him. "My friend Schwartz," he said. Schwartz merited his name; he was dark in complexion, hair, and eyes, and if he had any aims they were dark also. He was full of anecdotes and jests, and Carl laughed heartily; Mark had never heard him laugh in that way before. The elder brother ordered a good supper, and played the host as well as he could; but, in spite of the anecdotes, he did not altogether like friend Schwartz. Early the next morning, while the visitor was still asleep, he called Carl outside, and asked in an undertone who he was.

"Oh, I met him first in Berlin, and afterward I knew him in New York," said Carl. "All the orchestra fellows know Schwartz."

"Is he a musician, then?"

"Not exactly; but he used to be always around, you know."

"How comes he down here?"

"Just chance. He had an offer from a sort of a—of a restaurant, up in San Miguel, a new place recently opened. The other day he happened to find out that I was here, and so came down to see me."

"How did he find out?"

"I suppose you gave our names to the agent when you took the place, didn't you?"

"I gave mine; and—yes, I think I mentioned you."

" If you didn't, I mentioned myself. I was at San Miguel, two weeks you remember, while you were making ready down here; and I venture to say almost everybody remembers Carl Brenner."

Mark smiled. Carl's fixed, assured self-conceit in the face of the utter failure he had made of his life did not annoy, but rather amused him; it seemed part of the lad's nature.

" I don't want to grudge you your amusement, Carl," he said ; " but I don't much like this Schwartz of yours."

" He won't stay; he has to go back to-day. He came in a cart with a man from San Miguel, who, by some rare chance, had an errand down this forgotten, God-forsaken, dead-alive old road. The man will pass by on his way home this afternoon, and Schwartz is to meet him at the edge of the barren."

" Have an early dinner, then ; there are birds and venison, and there is lettuce enough for a salad. Scip can make you some coffee."

But, although he thus proffered his best, none the less did the elder brother take with him the key of the little chest which contained his small store of brandy and the two or three bottles of orange wine which he had brought down with him from San Miguel.

After he had gone, Schwartz and Carl strolled around the plantation in the sunshine. Schwartz did not care to sit down among Carl's tombs; he said they made him feel moldy. Carl argued the point with him in vain, and then gave it up, and took him around to the causeway across the sugar-waste, where they stretched themselves out in the shade cast by the ruined wall of the old mill.

" What brought this brother of yours away down here ? " asked the visitor, watching a chameleon on the wall near by. " See that little beggar swelling out his neck ! "

" He's catching flies. In a storm they will come and hang themselves by one paw on our windows, and the wind will blow them out like dead leaves, and rattle them about, and they'll never move. But, when the sun shines out, there they are all alive again."

"But about your brother?"

"He isn't my brother."

"What?"

"My mother, a widow, named Brenner, with one son, Carl, married his father, a widower, named Deal, with one son, Mark. There you have the whole."

"He is a great deal older than you. I suppose he has been in the habit of assisting you?"

"Never saw him in my life until this last October, when, one windy day, he found me coughing on the Exton pier; and, soon afterward, he brought me down here."

"Came, then, on your account?"

"By no means; he was coming himself. It's a queer story; I'll tell it to you. It seems he went with the Kenton Arctic expedition—you remember it? Two of the ships were lost; his was one. But I'll have to get up and say it as he did." Here Carl rose, put down his pipe, extended one hand stiffly in a fixed position, and went on speaking, his very voice, by force of the natural powers of mimicry he possessed, sounding like Mark's:

"We were a company of eight when we started away from the frozen hulk, which would never see clear water under her bows again. Once before we had started, thirty-five strong, and had come back thirteen. Five had died in the old ship, and now the last survivors were again starting forth. We drew a sledge behind us, carrying our provisions and the farcical records of the expedition which had ended in death, as they must all end. We soon lose sight of the vessel. It was our only shelter, and we look back; then, at each other. 'Cheer up!' says one. 'Take this extra skin, Mark; I am stronger than you.' It's Proctor's voice that speaks. Ten days go by. There are only five of us now, and we are walking on doggedly across the ice, the numbing ice, the killing ice, the never-ending, gleaming, taunting, devilish ice. We have left the sledge behind. No trouble now for each to carry his share of food, it is so light. Now we walk together for a while ; now we separate, sick of seeing one another's pinched faces, but we keep within call. On the eleventh day a wind rises ; bergs come sailing into view. One moves down upon us. Its peak shining in the sunshine far above is nothing to the great mass that moves on under the water. Our ice-field breaks into a thousand pieces. We leap from block to block ; we cry aloud in our despair ; we call to each other, and curse, and pray. But the strips of dark water widen between us ; our ice-islands grow smaller ; and a current bears us onward. We can no longer keep in motion, and freeze as we stand. Two float near each other as darkness falls ; ' Cheer up, Mark, cheer up !' cries one, and throws his flask across the gap between. Again it is Proctor's voice that speaks.

"In the morning only one is left alive. The others are blocks of ice, and float around in the slow eddy, each solemnly staring, one foot advanced, as if still keeping up the poor cramped steps with which he had fought off death. The one who is still alive floats around and around, with these dead men standing stiffly on their islands, all day, sometimes so near them that the air about him is stirred by their icy forms as they pass. At evening his cake drifts away through an opening toward the south, and he sees them no more, save that after him follows his dead friend, Proctor, at some distance behind. As night comes, the figure seems to wave its rigid hand in the distance, and cry from its icy throat, ' Cheer up, Mark, and good-by !' "

Here Carl stopped, rubbed his hands, shivered, and looked to see how his visitor took the narrative.

"It's a pretty cold story," said Schwartz, "even in this broiling sun. So he came down here to get a good, full warm, did he ? He's got the cash, I suppose, to pay for his fancies."

" I don't call that a fancy, exactly," said Carl, seating himself on the hot white sand in the sunshine, with his thin hands clasped around his knees. "As to cash—I don't know. He works very hard."

"He works because he likes it," said Schwartz, contemptuously; "he looks like that sort of a man. But, at any rate, he don't make *you* work much!"

"He *is* awfully good to me," admitted Carl.

"It isn't on account of your beauty."

"Oh, I'm good looking enough in my way," replied the youth. "I acknowledge it isn't a common way; like yours, for instance." As he spoke, he passed his hand through his thin light hair, drew the ends of the long locks forward, and examined them admiringly.

"As he never saw you before, it couldn't have been brotherly love," pursued the other. "I suppose it was pity."

"No, it wasn't pity, either, you old blockhead," said Carl, laughing. "He *likes* to have me with him; he *likes* me."

"I see that myself, and that's exactly the point. Why should he? You haven't any inheritance to will to him, have you?"

"My violin, and the clothes on my back. I believe that's all," answered Carl, lightly. He took off his palmetto hat, made a pillow of it, and stretched himself out at full length, closing his eyes.

"Well, give *me* a brother with cash, and I'll go to sleep, too," said Schwartz. When Deal came home at sunset, the dark-skinned visitor was gone.

But he came again; and this time stayed three days. Mark allowed it, for Carl's sake. All he said was, "He can not be of much use in the restaurant up there. What is he? Cook? Or waiter?"

"Oh, Schwartz isn't a servant, old fellow. He helps entertain the guests."

"Sings, I suppose."

Carl did not reply, and Deal set Schwartz down as a lager-beer-hall ballad-singer, borne southward on the tide of winter travel to Florida. One advantage at least was gained—when Schwartz was there, Carl was less tempted by the swamp.

And now, a third time, the guest came. During the first evening of this third visit, he was so good-tempered, so frankly lazy and amusing, that even Deal was disarmed. "He's a good-for-nothing, probably; but there's no active harm in him," he said to himself.

The second evening was a repetition of the first.

When he came home at sunset on the third evening, Carl was lying coiled up close to the wall of the house, his face hidden in his arms.

"What are you doing there?" said Deal, as he passed by, on his way to put up the tools.

No answer. But Carl had all kinds of whims, and Deal was used to them. He went across to Scip's chimney.

"Awful time, cap'en," said the old negro, in a low voice. "Soon's you's gone, dat man make young marse drink, and bot' begin to holler and fight."

"Drink? They had no liquor."

"Yes, dey hab. Mus' hab brought 'em 'long."

"Where is the man?"

"Oh, he gone long ago—gone at noon."

Deal went to his brother. "Carl," he said, "get up. Dinner is ready." But the coiled form did not stir.

"Don't be a fool," continued Deal. "I know you've been drinking; Scip told me. It's a pity. But no reason why you should not eat."

Carl did not move. Deal went off to his dinner, and sent some to Carl. But the food remained untasted. Then Deal passed into the house to get some tobacco for his pipe. Then a loud cry was heard. The hiding-place which his Yankee fingers had skillfully fashioned in the old wall had been rifled; all his money was gone. No one knew the secret of the spot but Carl.

"Did he overpower you and take it?" he asked, kneeling down and lifting Carl by force, so that he could see his face.

"No; I gave it to him," Carl answered, thickly and slowly.

"You *gave* it to him ? "

" I lost it—at cards."

" *Cards !* "

Deal had never thought of that. All at once the whole flashed upon him : the gambler who was always "around " with the "orchestra fellows "; the "restaurant" at San Miguel where he helped "entertain " the guests; the probability that business was slack in the ancient little town, unaccustomed to such luxuries; and the treasure-trove of an old acquaintance within a day's journey—an old acquaintance like Carl, who had come also into happy possession of a rich brother. A rich brother !—probably that was what Schwartz called him !

At any rate, rich or poor, Schwartz had it all. With the exception of one hundred dollars which he had left at San Miguel as a deposit, he had now only five dollars in the world ; Carl had gambled away his all.

It was a hard blow.

He lifted his brother in his arms and carried him in to his hammock. A few minutes later, staff in hand, he started down the live-oak avenue toward the old road which led northward to San Miguel. The moonlight was brilliant ; he walked all night. At dawn he was searching the little city.

Yes, the man was known there. He frequented the Esmeralda Parlors. The Esmeralda Parlors, however, represented by an attendant, a Northern mulatto, with straight features, long, narrow eyes, and pale-golden skin, a bronze piece of insolence, who was also more faultlessly dressed than any one else in San Miguel, suavely replied that Schwartz was no longer one of their "guests "; he had severed his connection with the Parlors several days before. Where was he ? The Parlors had no idea.

But the men about the docks knew. Schwartz had been seen the previous evening negotiating passage at the last moment on a coasting schooner bound South—one of those nondescript little craft engaged in smuggling and illegal trading, with which the waters of the West Indies are infested. The schooner had made her way out of the harbor by moonlight. Although ostensibly bound for Key West, no one could say with any certainty that she would touch there; bribed by Schwartz, with all the harbors, inlets, and lagoons of the West Indies open to her, pursuit would be worse than hopeless. Deal realized this. He ate the food he had brought with him, drank a cup of coffee, called for his deposit, and then walked back to the plantation.

When he came into the little plaza, Carl was sitting on the steps of their small house. His head was clear again; he looked pale and wasted.

" It's all right,"—said Deal. " I've traced him. In the mean time, don't worry, Carl. If I don't mind it, why should you ? "

Without saying more, he went inside, changed his shoes, then came out, ordered dinner, talked to Scip, and when the meal was ready called Carl, and took his place at the table as though nothing had happened. Carl scarcely spoke ; Deal approved his silence. He felt so intensely for the lad, realized so strongly what he must be feeling—suffering and feeling— that conversation on the subject would have been at that early moment unendurable. But waking during the night, and hearing him stirring, uneasy, and apparently feverish, he went across to the hammock.

" You are worrying about it, Carl, and you are not strong enough to stand worry. Look here—I have forgiven you; I would forgive you twice as much. Have you no idea why I brought you down here with me ? "

" Because you're kind-hearted. And perhaps, too, you thought it would be lonely," answered Carl.

" No, I'm not kind-hearted, and I never was lonely in my life. I didn't intend to tell you, but—you *must not* worry. It is your name, Carl, and—and your blue eyes. I was fond of Eliza."

"Fond of Leeza—Leeza Brenner? Then why on earth
didn't you marry her?" said Carl, sitting up in his hammock,
and trying to see his step-brother's face in the moonlight
that came through the chinks in the shutters.

Mark's face was in shadow. "She liked some one else
better," he said.

"Who?"

"Never mind. But—yes, I will tell you—Graves."

"John Graves? That dunce? No, she didn't."

"As it happens, I know she did. But we won't talk
about it. I only told you to show you why I cared for
you."

"*I* wouldn't care about a girl that didn't care for me,"
said Carl, still peering curiously through the checkered darkness. The wizened young violin-player fancied himself an
omnipotent power among women. But Deal had gone to his
bed, and would say no more.

Carl had heard something now which deeply astonished
him. He had not been much troubled about the lost money;
it was not in his nature to be much troubled about money at
any time. He was sorry; but what was gone was gone;
why waste thought upon it? This he called philosophy.
Mark, out of regard for Carl's supposed distress, had forbid-
den conversation on the subject; but he was not shutting out,
as he thought, torrents of shame, remorse, and self-condemna-
tion. Carl kept silence willingly enough; but, even if the bar
had been removed, he would have had little to say. During
the night his head had ached, and he had had some fever;
but it was more the effect of the fiery, rank liquor pressed
upon him by Schwartz than of remorse. But *now* he had
heard what really interested and aroused him. Mark in love!
—hard-working, steady, dull old Mark, whom he had thought
endowed with no fancies at all, save perhaps that of being
thoroughly warmed after his arctic freezing. Old Mark fond
of Leeza—in love with Leeza!

Leeza wasn't much. Carl did not even think his cousin

pretty ; his fancy was for something large and Oriental. But, pretty or not, she had evidently fascinated Mark Deal, coming, a poor little orphan maid, with her aunt, Carl's mother, to brighten old Abner Deal's farm-house, one mile from the windy Exton pier. Carl's mother could not hope to keep her German son in this new home ; but she kept little Leeza, or Eliza, as the neighbors called her. And Mark, a shy, awkward boy, had learned to love the child, who had sweet blue eyes, and thick braids of flaxen hair fastened across the back of her head.

"To care all that for Leeza!" thought Carl, laughing silently in his hammock. "And then to fancy that she liked that Graves! And then to leave her, and come away off down here, just on the suspicion!"

But Carl was mistaken. A man, be he never so awkward and silent, will generally make at least one effort to get the woman he loves. Mark had made two, and failed. After his first, he had gone North ; after his second, he had come South, bringing Leeza's cousin with him.

In the morning a new life began on the old plantation. First, Scipio was dismissed ; then the hunter who had kept the open-air larder supplied with game, an old man of unknown, or rather mixed descent, having probably Spanish, African, and Seminole blood in his veins, was told that his services were required no more.

"But are you going to starve us, then?" asked Carl, with a comical grimace.

"I am a good shot, myself," replied Deal ; "and a fair cook, too."

"But *why* do you do it?" pursued the other. He had forgotten all about the money.

The elder man looked at his brother. Could it be possible that he had forgotten? And, if he had, was it not necessary, in their altered circumstances, that the truth should be brought plainly before his careless eyes?

"I am obliged to do it," he answered, gravely. "We

must be very saving, Carl. Things will be easier, I hope,
when the fields begin to yield."

"Good heavens, you don't mean to say I took all you
had!" said Carl, with an intonation showing that the fact that
the abstracted sum was "all" was impressing him more than
any agency of his own in the matter.

"I told you I did not mind it," answered Mark, going off
with his gun and game-bag.

"But *I* do, by Jove!" said Carl to himself, watching him
disappear.

Musicians, in this world's knowledge and wisdom, are
often fools, or rather they remain always children. The beautiful gift, the divine gift, the gift which is the nearest to heaven,
is accompanied by lacks of another sort. Carl Brenner, like
a child, could not appreciate poverty unless his dinner was
curtailed, his tobacco gone. The petty changes now made
in the small routine of each day touched him acutely, and
roused him at last to the effort of connected, almost practical
thought. Old Mark was troubled—poor. The cook was going, the hunter discharged; the dinners would be good no
longer. This was because he, Carl, had taken the money.
There was no especial harm in the act *per se;* but, as the
sum happened to be all old Mark had, it was unfortunate.
Under the circumstances, what could he, Carl, do to help old
Mark?

Mark loved that light-headed little Leeza. Mark had
brought him down here and taken care of him on Leeza's
account. Mark, therefore, should have Leeza. He, Carl,
would bring it about. He set to work at once to be special
providence in Mark's affairs. He sat down, wrote a long letter, sealed it with a stern air, and then laid it on the table,
got up, and surveyed it with decision. There it was—done!
Gone! But no; not "gone" yet. And how could it go?
He was now confronted by the difficulty of mailing it without
Mark's knowledge. San Miguel was the nearest post-office;
and San Miguel was miles away. Africanus was half crip-

pled; the old hunter would come no more; he himself could
not walk half the distance. Then an idea came to him: Africanus, although dismissed, was not yet gone. He went out
to find him.

Mark came home at night with a few birds. "They will
last us over one day," he said, throwing down the spoil.
"You still here, Scip? I thought I sent you off."

"He's going to-morrow," interposed Carl. Scip sat up
all night cooking.

"What in the world has got into him?" said Deal, as the
light from the old chimney made their sleeping-room bright.

"He wants to leave us well supplied, I suppose," said
Carl, from his hammock. "Things keep better down here
when they're cooked, you know." This was true; but it was
unusual for Carl to interest himself in such matters.

The next morning Deal started on a hunting expedition,
intending to be absent two days. Game was plenty in the
high lands farther west. He had good luck, and came back
at the end of the second day loaded, having left also several
caches behind to be visited on the morrow. But there was
no one in the house, or on the plantation; both Scip and Carl
were gone.

A slip of paper was pinned to the red cotton door. It
contained these words: "It's all right, old fellow. If I'm
not back at the end of three days, counting this as one, come
into South Devil after me. You'll find a trail."

"Confound the boy!" said Deal, in high vexation. "He's
crazy." He took a torch, went to the causeway, and there
saw from the foot-prints that two had crossed. "Scip went
with him," he thought, somewhat comforted. "The old
black rascal used to declare that he knew every inch of the
swamp." He went back, cooked his supper, and slept. In
the matter of provisions, there was little left save what he
kept under lock and key. Scipio had started with a good
supply. At dawn he rose, made a fire under the old chimney,
cooked some venison, baked some corn-bread, and, placing

them in his bag, started into South Devil, a bundle of torches slung on his back as before, his gun in his hand, his revolver and knife in his belt. "They have already been gone two days," he said to himself; "they must be coming toward home, now." He thought Carl was carrying out his cherished design of exploring the swamp. There was a trail— hatchet marks on the trees, and broken boughs. "That's old Scip. Carl would never have been so systematic," he thought.

He went on until noon, and then suddenly found himself on the bank of a sluggish stream. "The Branch," he said— "South Devil Branch. It joins West Devil, and the two make the San Juan Bautista (a queer origin for a saint!) three miles below Miguel. But where does the trail go now?" It went nowhere. He searched and searched, and could not find it. It ended at the Branch. Standing there in perplexity, he happened to raise his eyes. Small attention had he hitherto paid to the tangled vines and blossoms swinging above him. He hated the beauty of South Devil. But now he saw a slip of paper hanging from a vine, and, seizing it, he read as follows: "We take boat here; wait for me if not returned."

Mark stood, the paper in his hand, thinking. There was only one boat in the neighborhood, a canoe belonging to the mongrel old hunter, who occasionally went into the swamp. Carl must have obtained this in some way; probably the mongrel had brought it in by the Branch, or one of its tributaries, and this was the rendezvous. One comfort—the old hunter must then be of the party, too. But why should he, Mark, wait, if Carl had two persons with him? Still, the boy had asked. It ended in his waiting.

He began to prepare for the night. There was a knoll near by, and here he made a camp-fire, spending the time before sunset in gathering the wood by the slow process of climbing the trees and vines, and breaking off dead twigs and branches; everything near the ground was wet and sogged.

He planted his four torches, ate his supper, examined his gun and revolver, and then, as darkness fell, having nothing else to do, he made a plot on the ground with twigs and long splinters of light-wood, and played, one hand against the other, a swamp game of fox-and-geese. He played standing (his fox-and-geese were two feet high), so that he could keep a lookout for every sort of creature. There were wild-cats and bears in the interior of South Devil, and in the Branch, alligators. He did not fear the large creatures, however; his especial guard, as before, was against the silent snakes. He lighted the fire and torches early, so that whatever uncanny inhabitants there might be in the near trees could have an opportunity of coming down and seeking night-quarters elsewhere. He played game after game of fox-and-geese; and this time he sang "Sweet Afton." He felt that he had exhausted the "Troubadour" on the previous occasion. He shot five snakes, and saw (or rather it seemed to him that he saw) five thousand others coiling and gliding over the roots of the cypresses all around. He made a rule not to look at them if he could help it, as long as they did not approach. "Otherwise," he thought, "I shall lose my senses, and think the very trees are squirming."

It was a long, long night. The knoll was dented all over with holes made by the long splinters representing his fox-and-geese. Dizziness was creeping over him at intervals. His voice, singing "Sweet Afton," had become hoarse and broken, and his steps uneven, as he moved to and fro, still playing the game dully, when at last dawn came. But, although the flat tops of the great cypresses far above were bathed in the golden sunshine, it was long before the radiance penetrated to the dark glades below. The dank, watery aisles were still in gray shadow, when the watcher heard a sound—a real sound now, not an imaginary one—and at the same moment his glazed eyes saw a boat coming up the Branch. It was a white canoe, and paddled by a wraith; at least, the creature who sat within looked so grayly pale, and

8

its eyes in its still, white face so large and unearthly, that it
seemed like a shade returned from the halls of death.

"Why, Carl!" said Mark, in a loud, unsteady voice, breaking through his own lethargy by main force. "It's you, Carl,
isn't it?"

He tramped down to the water's edge, each step seeming
to him a rod long, and now a valley, and now a hill. The
canoe touched the bank, and Carl fell forward; not with vio-
lence, but softly, and without strength. What little consciousness he had kept was now gone.

Dawn was coming down from above; the air was slightly
stirred. The elder man's head grew more steady, as he lifted
his step-brother, gave him brandy, rubbed his temples and
chest, and then, as he came slowly back to life again, stood
thinking what he should do. They were a half-day's journey
from home, and Carl could not walk. If he attempted to
carry him, he was fearful that they should not reach pure air
outside before darkness fell again, and a second night in the
thick air might be death for both of them; but there was the
boat. It had come into South Devil in some way; by that
way it should go out again. He laid Carl in one end, putting
his own coat under his head for a pillow, and then stepped
in himself, took the paddle, and moved off. Of course he
must ascend the Branch; as long as there were no tributaries, he could not err. But presently he came to an everglade
—a broadening of the stream with apparently twenty different
outlets, all equally dark and tangled. He paddled around the
border, looking first at one, then at another. The matted
water-vines caught at his boat like hundreds of hands; the
great lily-leaves slowly sank and let the light bow glide over
them. Carl slept; there was no use trying to rouse him; but
probably he would remember nothing, even if awake. The
elder brother took out his compass, and had decided by it
which outlet to take, when his eye rested upon the skin of a
moccasin nailed to a cypress on the other side of the pond.
It was the mongrel's way of making a guide-post. Without

hesitation, although the direction was the exact opposite of the one he had selected, Deal pushed the canoe across and entered the stream thus indicated. At the next pool he found another snake-skin; and so on out of the swamp. Twenty-five snakes had died in the cause. He came to firm land at noon, two miles from the plantation. Carl was awake now, but weak and wandering. Deal lifted him on shore, built a fire, heated some meat, toasted corn-bread, and made him eat. Then, leaning upon his brother's arm, walking slowly, and often pausing to rest, the blue-eyed ghost reached home at sunset—two miles in five hours.

Ten days now passed; the mind of the young violin player did not regain its poise. He rose and dressed himself each morning, and slept in the sunshine as before. He went to the place of tombs, carrying his violin, but forgot to play. Instead, he sat looking dreamily at the swamp. He said little, and that little was disconnected. The only sentence which seemed to have meaning, and to be spoken earnestly, was, "It's all right, old fellow. Just you wait fifteen days—fifteen days!" But, when Mark questioned him, he could get no definite reply, only a repetition of the exhortation to "wait fifteen days."

Deal went over to one of the mongrel's haunts, and, by good luck, found him at home. The mongrel had a number of camps, which he occupied according to convenience. The old man acknowledged that he had lent his canoe, and that he had accompanied Carl and Scip part of the way through South Devil. But only part of the way; then he left them, and struck across to the west. Where were they going? Why, straight to San Miguel; the Branch brought them to the King's Road crossing, and the rest of the way they went on foot. What were they going to do in San Miguel? The mongrel had no idea; he had not many ideas. Scip was to stay up there; Brenner was to return alone in the canoe, they having made a trail all the way.

Deal returned to the plantation. He still thought that Carl's idea had been merely to explore the swamp.

Twelve days had passed, and had grown to fourteen; Carl was no stronger. He was very gentle now, like a sick child. Deal was seized with a fear that this soft quiet was the peace that often comes before the last to the poor racked frame of the consumptive. He gave up all but the necessary work, and stayed with Carl all day. The blue-eyed ghost smiled, but said little; into its clouded mind penetrated but one ray—"Wait fifteen days." Mark had decided that the sentence meant nothing but some wandering fancy. Spring in all her superb luxuriance was now wreathing Florida with flowers; the spring flowers met the old flowers, the spring leaves met the old leaves. The yellow jessamine climbed over miles of thicket; the myriad purple balls of the sensitive-plant starred the ground; the atamasco lilies grew whitely, each one shining all alone, in the wet woods; chocolate-hued orchids nodded, and the rose-colored ones rang their bells, at the edge of the barren. The old causeway across the sugar waste was blue with violets, and Mark carried Carl thither; he would lie there contentedly in the sunshine for hours, his pale fingers toying with the blue blossoms, his eyes lifted to the green line of South Devil across the sapphire sky.

One afternoon he fell asleep there, and Mark left him, to cook their dinner. When he came back, his step-brother's eyes had reason in them once more, or rather remembrance.

"Old fellow," he said, as Mark, surprised and somewhat alarmed at the change, sat down beside him, "you got me out of the swamp, I suppose? I don't remember getting myself out. Now I want to ask something. I'm going to leave this world in a few days, and try it in another; better luck next time, you know. What I want to ask is that you'll take me up and bury me at San Miguel in a little old burying-ground they have there, on a knoll overlooking the ocean. I don't want to lie here with the Dons and the Aztecs; and, besides, I particularly want to be carried through the swamp. Take me through in the canoe, as I went the last time; it's the easiest way, and there's a trail. And I want to go. And do not cover my face, either; I want to see. Promise."

Mark promised, and Carl closed his eyes. Then he roused himself again.

"Inquire at the post-office in San Miguel for a letter," he said drowsily. "Promise." Again Mark promised. He seemed to sleep for some minutes; then he spoke again.

"I heard that music, you know—heard it all out plainly and clearly," he said, looking quietly at his brother. "I know the whole, and have sung it over to myself a thousand times since. I can not write it down *now*. But it will not be lost."

"Music is never lost, I suppose," answered Mark, somewhat at random.

"Certainly not," said Carl, with decision. "My song will be heard some time. I'm sure of that. And it will be much admired."

"I hope so."

"You try to be kind always, don't you, old fellow, whether you comprehend or not?" said the boy, with his old superior smile—the smile of the artist, who, although he be a failure and a pauper, yet always pities the wise. Then he slept again. At dawn, peacefully and with a smile, he died.

It should not have been expected, perhaps, that he could live. But in some way Mark had expected it.

A few hours later a canoe was floating down the Branch through South Devil. One man was paddling at the stern; another was stretched on a couch, with his head on a pillow placed at the bow, where he could see the blossoming network above through his closed eyes. As Carl had said, Scipio had left a trail all the way—a broken branch, a bent reed, or a shred of cloth tied to the lily-leaves. All through the still day they glided on, the canoe moving without a sound on the bosom of the dark stream. They passed under the gray and solemn cypresses, rising without branches to an enormous height, their far foliage hidden by the moss, which hung down thickly in long flakes, diffusing the sunshine and making it silvery like mist ; in the silver swung the air-plants, great cream-colored disks, and wands of scarlet, crowded with little buds, blossoms that looked like butterflies, and blossoms that looked like humming-birds, and little dragon-heads with grinning faces. Then they came to the region of the palms ; these shot up, slender and graceful, and leaned over the stream, the great auréum-ferns growing on their trunks high in the air. Beneath was a firmer soil than in the domain of the cypresses, and here grew a mat of little flowers, each less than a quarter of an inch wide, close together, pink, blue, scarlet, yellow, purple, but never white, producing a hue singularly rich, owing to the absence of that colorless color which man ever mingles with his floral combinations, and strangely makes sacred alike to the bridal and to death. Great vines ran up the palms, knotted themselves, and came down again, hand over hand, wreathed in little fresh leaves of exquisite green. Birds with plumage of blush-rose pink flew slowly by ; also some with scarlet wings, and the jeweled paroquets. The great Savannah cranes stood on the shore, and did not stir as the boat moved by. And, as the spring was now in its prime, the alligators showed their horny heads above water, and climbed awkwardly out on the bank; or else, swimming by the side of the canoe, accompanied it long distances, no doubt moved by dull curiosity concerning its means of locomotion, and its ideas as to choice morsels of food. The air was absolutely still; no breeze reached these blossoming aisles ; each leaf hung motionless. The atmosphere was hot, and heavy with perfumes. It was the heart of the swamp, a riot of intoxicating, steaming, swarming, fragrant, beautiful, tropical life, without man to make or mar it. All the world was once so, before man was made.

Did Deal appreciate this beauty? He looked at it, because he could not get over the feeling that Carl was looking at it too; but he did not admire it. The old New England spirit was rising within him again at last, after the crushing palsy of the polar ice, and the icy looks of a certain blue-eyed woman.

He came out of the swamp an hour before sunset, and, landing, lifted his brother in his arms, and started northward toward San Miguel. The little city was near; but the weight of a dead body grown cold is strange and mighty, and it was late evening before he entered the gate, carrying his motionless burden. He crossed the little plaza, and went into the ancient cathedral, laying it down on the chancel-step before the high altar. It was the only place he could think of; and he was not repelled. A hanging lamp of silver burned dimly; in a few moments kind hands came to help him. And thus Carl, who never went to church in life, went there in death, and, with tapers burning at his head and feet, rested all night under the picture of the Madonna, with nuns keeping watch and murmuring their gentle prayers beside him.

The next morning he was buried in the dry little burial-ground on the knoll overlooking the blue Southern ocean.

When all was over, Deal, feeling strangely lonely, remembered his promise, and turned toward the post-office. He expected nothing; it was only one of the poor lad's fancies; still, he would keep his word. There was nothing for him.

He went out. Then an impulse made him turn back and ask if there was a letter for Carl. "For Carl Brenner," he said, and thought how strange it was that there was now no Carl. There was a letter; he put it into his pocket and left the town, going homeward by the King's Road on foot; the South Devil should see *him* no more. He slept part of the night by the roadside, and reached home the next morning; everything was as he had left it. He made a fire and boiled some coffee; then he set the little house in order, loaded his gun, and went out mechanically after game. The routine of daily life had begun again.

"It's a pleasant old place," he said to himself, as he went through one of the orange-aisles and saw the wild oranges dotting the ground with their golden color. "It's a pleasant

old place," he repeated, as he went out into the hot, still sunshine beyond. He filled his game-bag, and sat down to rest
a while before returning. Then for the first time he remembered the letter, and drew it forth. This was the letter Carl
meant; Carl asked him to get it after he was dead; he must
have intended, then, that he, Mark, should read it. He
opened it, and looked at the small, slanting handwriting without recognizing it. Then from the inside a photograph fell
out, and he took it up; it was Leeza. On the margin was
written, "For Mark."

She had written; but, womanlike, not, as Carl expected,
to Mark. Instead, she had written to Carl, and commissioned
him to tell Mark—what? Oh, a long story, such as girls tell,
but with the point that, after all, she "liked" (liked?) Mark
best. Carl's letter had been blunt, worded with unflattering
frankness. Leeza was tired of her own coquetries, lonely, and
poor; she wrote her foolish little apologizing, confessing letter
with tears in her blue eyes—those blue eyes that sober, reticent Mark Deal could not forget.

Carl had gone to San Miguel, then, to mail a letter—a
letter which had brought this answer! Mark, with his face
in his hands, thanked God that he had not spoken one harsh
word to the boy for what had seemed obstinate disobedience,
but had tended him gently to the last.

Then he rose, stretched his arms, drew a long breath, and
looked around. Everything seemed altered. The sky was
brassy, the air an oven. He remembered the uplands where
the oats grew, near Exton; and his white sand-furrows
seemed a ghastly mockery of fields. He went homeward and
drew water from his well to quench his burning thirst; it was
tepid, and he threw it away, recalling as he did so the spring
under the cool, brown rocks where he drank when a boy. A
sudden repugnance came over him when his eyes fell on the
wild oranges lying on the ground, over-ripe with rich, pulpy
decay; he spurned them aside with his foot, and thought of
the firm apples in the old orchard, a fruit cool and reticent, a

little hard, too, not giving itself to the first comer. Then there came over him the hue of Northern forests in spring, the late, reluctant spring of Exton ; and the changeless olive-green of the pine barrens grew hideous in his eyes. But, most of all, there seized him a horror of the swamp—a horror of its hot steaming air, and its intoxicating perfume, which reached him faintly even where he stood ; it seemed to him that if he staid long within their reach his brain would be affected as Carl's had been, and that he should wander within and die. For there would be no one to rescue *him.*

So strong was this new feeling, like a giant full armed, that he started that very night, carrying his gun and Carl's violin, and a knapsack of clothes on his back, and leaving his other possessions behind. Their value was not great, but they made a princely home for the mongrel, who came over after he had departed, looked around stealthily, stole several small articles, and hastened away; came back again after a day or two, and stole a little more ; and finally, finding the place deserted, brought back all his spoil and established himself there permanently, knowing full well that it would be long before Monteano's would find another tenant from the North.

As Mark Deal passed across the King's Road Bridge over the Branch (now soon to be sainted), he paused, and looked down into the north border of South Devil. Then he laid aside his gun and the violin, went off that way, and gathered a large bunch of swamp blossoms. Coming into San Miguel, he passed through the town and out to the little burial-ground beyond. Here he found the new-made grave, and laid the flowers upon it.

" He will like them because they come from *there,*" was his thought.

Then, with a buoyant step, he started up the long, low, white peninsula, set with its olive-woods in a sapphire sea ; and his face was turned northward.

IN THE COTTON COUNTRY.

The loveliest land that smiles beneath the sky,
The coast-land of our western Italy.
I view the waters quivering; quaff the breeze,
Whose briny raciness keeps an under taste
Of flavorous tropic sweets, perchance swept home
From Cuba's perfumed groves and garden spiceries.
                                    PAUL HAMILTON HAYNE.

Call on thy children of the hill,
Wake swamp and river, coast and rill,
Rouse all thy strength, and all thy skill,
                        Carolina!
Tell how the patriot's soul was tried,
And what his dauntless breast defied;
How Rutledge ruled and Laurens died,
                        Carolina!
                                    HENRY TIMROD.

Do you know the cotton country—the country of broad
levels open to the sun, where the ungainly, ragged bushes
stand in long rows, bearing the clothing of a nation on their
backs? Not on their backs either, for the white wool is scattered over the branches and twigs, looking, not as if it grew
there, but as if it had been blown that way, and had caught
and clung at random. When I first came to the cotton country, I used to stand with my chin on the top-rail of the fences,
trying to rid my eyes of that first impression. I saw the fields
only when the cotton was white, when there were no green
leaves left, and the fleecy down did not seem to me a vege-
table at all. Starved cows passed through the half-plucked
rows untempted, and I said to myself: "Of course. Cows
do not eat cotton any more than they eat wool; but what

bush is there at the North that they would not nibble if starving?" Accustomed to the trim, soldierly ranks of the Western corn-fields, or the billowy grace of the wheat, I could think of nothing save a parade of sturdy beggarmen unwillingly drawn up in line, when I gazed upon the stubborn, uneven branches, and generally lop-sided appearance of these plants—plants, nevertheless, of wealth, usefulness, and historic importance in the annals of our land. But after a while I grew accustomed to their contrary ways, and I even began to like their defiant wildness, as a contrast, perhaps, to the languorous sky above, the true sky of the cotton country, with its soft heat, its hazy air, and its divine twilight that lingers so long. I always walked abroad at sunset, and it is in the sunset-light that I always see the fields now when far away. No doubt there was plenty of busy, prosaic reality down there in the mornings, but I never saw it; I only saw the beauty and the fancies that come with the soft after-glow and the shadows of the night.

Down in the cotton country the sun shines steadily all day long, and the earth is hot under your feet. There are few birds, but at nightfall the crows begin to fly home in a long line, going down into the red west as though they had important messages to deliver to some imprisoned princess on the edge of the horizon. One day I followed the crows. I said to myself: "The princess is a *ruse;* they probably light not far from here, and I am going to find their place. The crows at home—that would be something worth seeing." Turning from the path, I went westward. "What!" said a country-woman, meeting Wordsworth on the road, "are ye stepping westward, sir?" I, too, stepped westward.

Field after field I crossed; at last the fences ceased, and only old half-filled ditches marked the boundary-lines. The land sloped downward slightly, and after a while the ridge behind me seemed like a line of heights, the old cotton-plants on its top standing out as distinctly as single pine-trees on a mountain-summit outlined against the sky; so comparative is height. The crows still flew westward as I came out upon a second level lower down than the first, and caught a golden gleam through the fringe of bushes in the middle of the plain. I had unwittingly found the river at last, that broad, brown river that I knew was down there somewhere, although I had not seen it with my bodily eyes. I had full knowledge of what it was, though, farther south toward the ocean; I knew the long trestles over the swamps and dark canebrakes that stretched out for miles on each side of the actual stream—trestles over which the trains passed cautiously every day, the Northern passengers looking nervously down at the quaking, spongy surface below, and prophesying accidents as certain some time—when they were not on board. Up here in the cotton country, however, the river was more docile; there were no tides to come up and destroy the banks, and with the exception of freshets the habits of the stream were orderly. The levels on each side might have been, should have been, rich with plenty. Instead, they were uncultivated and desolate. Here and there a wild, outlawed cotton-bush reared its head, and I could trace the old line of the cart-road and cross-tracks; but the soil was spongy and disintegrated, and for a long time evidently no care had been bestowed upon it. I crossed over to the river, and found that the earth-bank which had protected the field was broken down and washed away in many places; the low trees and bushes on shore still held the straws and driftwood that showed the last freshet's high-water mark.

The river made an irregular bend a short distance below, and I strolled that way, walking now on the thick masses of lespedeza that carpeted the old road-track, and now on the singularly porous soil of the level, a soil which even my inexperienced eyes recognized as worthless, all its good particles having been drained out of it and borne away on the triumphant tide of the freshets. The crows still evaded me, crossing the river in a straight line and flying on toward the west, and, in that arbitrary way in which solitary pedestrians make compacts with themselves, I said, " I will go to that tree at the exact turn of the bend, and not one step farther." I went to that tree at the exact turn of the bend, and then I went—farther; for I found there one solemn, lonely old house. Now, if there had been two, I should not have gone on; I should not have broken my compact. Two houses are sociable and commonplace; but one all alone on a desolate waste like that inspired me with—let us call it interest, and I went forward.

It was a lodge rather than a house; in its best day it could never have been more than a very plain abode, and now, in its worst, it seemed to have fallen into the hands of Giant Despair. " Forlorn " was written over its lintels, and " without hope " along its low roof-edge. Raised high above the ground, in the Southern fashion, on wooden supports, it seemed even more unstable than usual to Northern eyes, because the lattice-work, the valance, as it were, which generally conceals the bare, stilt-like underpinning, was gone, and a thin calf and some melancholy chickens were walking about underneath, as though the place was an arbor. There was a little patch of garden, but no grass, no flowers; everything was gray, the unpainted house, the sand of the garden-beds, and the barren waste stretching away on all sides. At first I thought the place was uninhabited, but as I drew nearer a thin smoke from one of the chimneys told of life within, and I said to myself that the life would be black-skinned life, of course. For I was quite accustomed now to finding the families of the freedmen crowded into just such old houses as this, hidden away in unexpected places; for the freedmen hardly ever live up on the even ground in the broad sunshine as though they had a right there, but down in the hollows or out into the fringes of wood, where their low-roofed cabins, numerous though they may be, are scarcely visible to the passer-by. There was no fence around this house; it stood at large on the waste as though it belonged there. Take away the fence from a house, and you take away its respecta-

bility; it becomes at once an outlaw. I ascended the crazy,
sunken steps that led to the front door, and lifted the knocker
that hung there as if in mockery; who ever knocked there
now save perhaps a river-god with his wet fingers as he hurried by, mounted on the foaming freshet, to ravage and lay
waste again the poor, desolate fields? But no spirit came to
the door, neither came the swarm of funny little black faces I
had expected; instead, I saw before me a white woman, tall,
thin, and gray-haired. Silently she stood there, her great,
dark eyes, still and sad, looking at me as much as to say,
" By what right are you here? "

" Excuse me, madam," was my involuntary beginning;
then I somewhat stupidly asked for a glass of water.

" I would not advise you to drink the water we have here;
it is not good," replied the woman. I knew it was not; the
water is never good down on the levels. But I was very stu-
pid that day.

" I should like to rest a while," was my next attempt. It
brought out a wooden chair, but no cordiality. I tried everything I could think of in the way of subjects for conversation,
but elicited no replies beyond monosyllables. I could not
very well say, " Who are you, and how came you here? " and
yet that was exactly what I wanted to know. The woman's
face baffled me, and I do not like to be baffled. It was a face
that was old and at the same time young; it had deep lines,
it was colorless, and the heavy hair was gray; and still I felt
that it was not old in years, but that it was like the peaches
we find sometimes on the ground, old, wrinkled, and withered,
yet showing here and there traces of that evanescent bloom
which comes before the ripeness. The eyes haunted me;
they haunt me now, the dry, still eyes of immovable, hopeless
grief. I thought, " Oh, if I could only help her!" but all I
said was, " I fear I am keeping you standing"; for that is the
senseless way we human creatures talk to each other.

Her answer was not encouraging.

" Yes," she replied, in her brief way, and said no more.

I felt myself obliged to go.

But the next afternoon I wandered that way again, and the next, and the next. I used to wait impatiently for the hour when I could enter into the presence of her great silence. How still she was! If she had wept, if she had raved, if she had worked with nervous energy, or been resolutely, doggedly idle, if she had seemed reckless, or callous, or even pious; but no, she was none of these. Her old-young face was ever the same, and she went about her few household tasks in a steady, nerveless manner, as though she could go on doing them for countless ages, and yet never with the least increase of energy. She swept the room, for instance, every day, never thoroughly, but in a gentle, incompetent sort of way peculiarly her own; yet she always swept it and never neglected it, and she took as much time to do it as though the task was to be performed with microscopic exactness.

She lived in her old house alone save for the presence of one child, a boy of six or seven years—a quiet, grave-eyed little fellow, who played all by himself hour after hour with two little wooden soldiers and an empty spool. He seldom went out of the house; he did not seem to care for the sunshine or the open air as other children care, but gravely amused himself in-doors in his own quiet way. He did not make his wooden soldiers talk or demolish each other triumphantly, according to the manner of boys; but he marshaled them to and fro with slow consideration, and the only sound was the click of their little muskets as he moved them about. He seemed never to speak of his own accord; he was strangely silent always. I used to wonder if the two ever talked together playfully as mother and child should talk; and one day, emboldened by a welcome, not warmer, for it was never warm, but not quite so cold perhaps, I said:

"Your little son is very quiet, madam."

"He is not my son."

"Ah!" I replied, somewhat disconcerted. "He is a pretty child; what is his name?"

"His name is John."

The child heard us in his barren corner, but did not look up or speak; he made his two soldiers advance solemnly upon the spool in silence, with a flank movement. I have called the corner barren, because it seemed doubly so when the boy sat there. The poorest place generally puts on something of a homelike air when a little child is in it; but the two bare walls and angle of bare floor remained hopelessly empty and desolate. The room was large, but there was nothing in it save the two wooden chairs and a table; there was no womanly attempt at a rag-carpet, curtains for the windows, or newspaper pictures for the walls—none of those little contrivances for comfort with which women generally adorn even the most miserable abiding-places, showing a kind of courage which is often pathetic· in its hopefulness. Here, however, there was nothing. A back-room held a few dishes, some boxes and barrels, and showed on its cavernous hearth the ashes of a recent fire. " I suppose they sleep in a third bare room somewhere, with their two beds, no doubt, standing all alone in the center of the chamber; for it would be too human, of course, to put them up snugly against the wall, as anybody else would do," I said to myself.

In time I succeeded in building up a sort of friendship with this solitary woman of the waste, and in time she told me her story. Let me tell it to you. I have written stories of imagination, but this is a story of fact, and I want you to believe it. It is true, every word of it, save the names given, and, when you read it, you whose eyes are now upon these lines, stop and reflect that it is only one of many life-stories like unto it. " War is cruelty," said our great general. It is. It must be so. But shall we not, we women, like Sisters of Charity, go over the field when the battle is done, bearing balm and wine and oil for those who suffer?

" Down here in the cotton country we were rich once, madam ; we were richer than Northerners ever are, for we toiled not for our money, neither took thought for it ; it came

and we spent it ; that was all. My father was Clayton Cotes-
worth, and our home was twenty miles from here, at the
Sand Hills. Our cotton-lands were down on these river-
levels; this was one of our fields, and this house was built
for the overseer; the negro-quarters that stood around it have
been carried off piecemeal by the freedmen." (Impossible to
put on paper her accentuation of this title.) "My father was
an old man; he could not go to battle himself, but he gave
first his eldest son, my brother James. James went away
from earth at Fredericksburg. It was in the winter, and very
cold. How often have I thought of that passage, ' And pray
ye that your flight be not in the winter,' when picturing his
sufferings before his spirit took flight ! Yes, it was very cold
for our Southern boys; the river was full of floating ice, and
the raw wind swept over them as they tried to throw up in-
trenchments on the heights. They had no spades, only pointed
sticks, and the ground was frozen hard. Their old uniforms,
worn thin by hard usage, hung in tatters, and many of them
had no shoes ; the skin of their poor feet shone blue, or glistening white, like a dead man's skin, through the coverings of
rags they made for themselves as best they could. They say
it was a pitiful sight to see the poor fellows sitting down in
the mornings, trying to adjust these rag-wrappings so that
they would stay in place, and fastening them elaborately with
their carefully saved bits of string. He was an honored man
who invented a new way. My brother was one of the shoe-
less ; at the last, too, it seems that he had no blanket, only a
thin counterpane. When night came, hungry and tired as he
was, he could only wrap himself in that and lie down on the
cold ground to wait for morning. When we heard all this
afterward, we said, ' Blessed be the bullet that put him out of
his misery !' for poor James was a delicate boy, and had been
accustomed to loving, watchful care all his life. Yet, oh, if I
could only know that he was warm once, just once, before he
died ! They told us he said nothing after he was shot save
' How cold ! How cold !' They put his poor, stiff body has-

tily down under the sod, and then the brigade moved on; 'no
man knoweth his sepulchre unto this day.'

"Next John went, my second brother. He said good-by,
and marched away northward—northward, northward, always
northward—to cold, corpse-strewed Virginia, who cried aloud
to us continually, 'More! more!' Her roads are marked
with death from her Peaks of Otter to the sea, and her great
valley ran red. We went to her from all over the South, from
Alabama, Florida, and Georgia, and from our own Carolina.
We died there by thousands, and by tens of thousands. O
Virginia, our dead lie thick in thy tidewater plains, in thy
tangled Wilderness, and along thy river-shores, with faces up-
turned, and hearts still for ever.

"John came back to us once, and wedded the fair girl to
whom he was betrothed. It was a sad bridal, although we
made it as gay as we could; for we had come to the times of
determined gayety then. The tone of society was like the
determinedly gay quicksteps which the regimental bands play
when returning from a funeral, as much as to say, 'Le roi est
mort, vive le roi!' So we turned our old silk dresses, and made
a brave appearance; if our shoes were shabby, we hid them
under our skirts as well as we could, and held our heads the
higher. Maum Sally made a big wedding-cake, as of old,
and we went without meat to pay for the spices in it; such
luxuries we obtained from the blockade-runners now and then,
but they were worth almost their weight in gold. Then John,
too, left us. In four months he also was taken—killed by
guerrillas, it is supposed, as he rode through a lonely moun-
tain-defile. He was not found for weeks; the snow fell and
covered him, mercifully giving the burial the frozen earth de-
nied. After a while the tidings came to us, and poor Mabel
slowly wept herself into the grave. She was a loving-hearted
little creature, and her life was crushed. She looked at her
baby once, called his name John, and then died. The child,
that boy yonder, seems to have inherited her grief. He sheds
no tears, however; his girl-mother shed them all, both for

him and for herself, before ever he saw the light. My turn
came next.

"You have been married, madam? Did you love, too? I
do not mean regard, or even calm affection; I do not mean
sense of duty, self-sacrifice, or religious goodness. I mean
love—love that absorbs the entire being. Some women love
so; I do not say they are the happiest women. I do not say
they are the best. I am one of them. But God made us all;
he gave us our hearts—we did not choose them. Let no woman take credit to herself for her even life, simply because it
has been even. Doubtless, if he had put her out in the
breakers, she would have swayed too. Perhaps she would
have drifted from her moorings also, as I have drifted. I go
to no church; I can not pray. But do not think I am defiant;
no, I am only dead. I seek not the old friends, few and ruined,
who remain still above-ground; I have no hope, I might almost say no wish. Torpidly I draw my breath through day
and night, nor care if the rain falls or the sun shines. You
Northern women would work; I can not. Neither have I
the courage to take the child and die. I live on as the palsied
animal lives, and if some day the spring fails, and the few
herbs within his reach, he dies. Nor do I think he grieves
much about it; he only eats from habit. So I.

"It was in the third year of the war that I met Ralph
Kinsolving. I was just eighteen. Our courtship was short;
indeed, I hardly knew that I loved him until he spoke and
asked me to give him myself. 'Marry me, Judith,' he pleaded
ardently; 'marry me before I go; let it be my wife I leave
behind me, and not my sweetheart. For sweethearts, dear,
can not come to us in camp when we send, as we shall surely
send soon, that you may all see our last grand review.' So
spoke Rafe, and with all his heart he believed it. We all believed it. Never for a moment did we doubt the final triumph
of our arms. We were so sure we were right!

"'Our last grand review,' said Rafe; but he did not dream
of that last review at Appomattox, when eight thousand hun-

gry, exhausted men stacked their muskets in the presence of
the enemy, whose glittering ranks, eighty thousand strong,
were drawn up in line before them, while in the rear their
well-filled wagons stood — wagons whose generous plenty
brought tears to the eyes of many a poor fellow that day,
thinking, even while he eagerly ate, of his desolated land, and
his own empty fields at home.

"I did marry my soldier, and, although it was in haste, I
had my wedding-dress, my snowy veil; lace and gauze were
not needed at the hospitals! But we went without the
wedding-cake this time, and my satin slippers were made at
home, looking very like a pair of white moccasins when finished.

"In the middle of the ceremony there was an alarm; the
slaves had risen at Latto's down the river, and were coming
to the village armed with clubs, and, worse still, infuriated
with liquor they had found. Even our good old rector paused.
There were but few white men at home. It seemed indeed a
time for pausing. But Rafe said, quietly, 'Go on!' and, un-
sheathing his sword, he laid it ready on the chancel-rail. 'To
have and to hold, from this day forward, for better for worse,
for richer for poorer, in sickness and in health, to love and to
cherish, till death us do part,' repeated Rafe, holding my hand
in his firm clasp, and looking down into my frightened face so
tenderly that I forgot my alarm—everything, indeed, save his
love. But when the last word was spoken, and the blessing
pronounced over our bowed heads, the shining sword seeming
a silent witness, Rafe left me like a flash. The little church
was empty when I rose from my knees; the women had hurried home with blanched faces to bar their doors and barri-
cade their windows, and the men had gone for their horses
and guns; only my old father waited to give me his blessing,
and then we, too, hastened homeward. Our little band of
defenders assembled in the main street, and rode gallantly
out to meet the negroes, who were as fifty to their one. Rafe
was the leader, by virtue of his uniform, and he waved his

hand to me as he rode by. 'Cheer up, Judith,' he cried; 'I will soon return.'

" I never saw him again.

" They dispersed the negroes without much difficulty; Latto's slaves had been badly treated for months, they had not the strength to fight long. But Rafe rode to the next town with the prisoners under his charge, and there he met an imploring summons to the coast; the Federal ships had appeared unexpectedly off the harbor, and the little coast-city lay exposed and helpless at the mouth of the river. All good men and true within reach were summoned to the defense. So my soldier went, sending back word to me a second time, ' I will soon return.' But the siege was long, long—one of those bitterly contested little sieges of minor importance, with but small forces engaged on each side, which were so numerous during the middle times of the war—those middle times after the first high hopes had been disappointed, and before the policy of concentration had been adopted by the North— that slow, dogged North of yours that kept going back and beginning over again, until at last it found out how to do it. This little siege was long and weary, and when at last the Federal vessels went suddenly out beyond the bar again, and the town, unconquered, but crippled and suffering, lay exhausted on the shore, there was not much cause for rejoicing. Still I rejoiced; for I thought that Rafe would come. I did not know that his precious furlough had expired while he was shut up in the beleaguered city, and that his colonel had sent an imperative summons, twice repeated. Honor, loyalty, commanded him to go, and go immediately. He went.

" The next tidings that came to me brought word that he loved me and was well; the next, that he loved me and was well; the next, that he loved me and was—dead. Madam, my husband, Ralph Kinsolving, was shot—as a spy!

"You start—you question—you doubt. But spies were shot in those days, were they not? That is a matter of history. Very well; you are face to face now with the wife of one of them.

"You did not expect such an ending, did you? You have always thought of spies as outcasts, degraded wretches, and, if you remembered their wives at all, it was with the idea that they had not much feeling, probably, being so low down in the scale of humanity. But, madam, in those bitter, hurrying days men were shot as spies who were no spies. Nay, let me finish; I know quite well that the shooting was not confined to one side; I acknowledge that; but it was done, and mistakes were made. Now and then chance brings a case to light, so unmistakable in its proof that those who hear it shudder—as now and then also chance brings a coffin to light whose occupant was buried alive, and came to himself when it was too late. But what of the cases that chance does *not* bring to light?

"My husband was no spy; but it had been a trying time for the Northern commanders: suspicion lurked everywhere; the whole North clamored to them to advance, and yet their plans, as fast as they made them, were betrayed in some way to the enemy. An example was needed—my husband fell in the way.

"He explained the suspicious circumstances of his case, but a cloud of witnesses rose up against him, and he proudly closed his lips. They gave him short shrift; that same day he was led out and met his death in the presence of thousands. They told me that he was quite calm, and held himself proudly; at the last he turned his face to the south, as if he were gazing down, down, into the very heart of that land for whose sake he was about to die. I think he saw the cotton-fields then, and our home; I think he saw me, also, for the last time.

"By the end of that year, madam, my black hair was gray, as you see it now; I was an old woman at nineteen.

"My father and I and that grave-eyed baby lived on in the old house. Our servants had left us, all save one, old

Cassy, who had been my nurse or 'maumee,' as we called her. We suffered, of course. We lived as very poor people live. The poorest slaves in the old time had more than we had then. But we did not murmur; the greater griefs had swallowed up the less. I said, 'Is there any sorrow like unto my sorrow?' But the end was not yet.

"You have heard the story of the great march, the march to the sea? But there was another march after that, a march of which your own writers have said that its route was marked by a pillar of smoke by day and of flame by night—the march through South Carolina. The Northern soldiers shouted when they came to the yellow tide of the Savannah, and looked across and knew that the other shore was South Carolina soil. They crossed, and Carolina was bowed to the dust. Those were the days we cried in the morning, 'O God, that it were night!' and in the night, 'O God, that it were morning!' Retribution, do you say? It may be so. But love for our State seemed loyalty to us; and slavery was the sin of our fathers, not ours. Surely we have expiated it now.

"'Chile, chile, dey is come!' cried old Cassy, bursting into my room one afternoon, her withered black face grayly pale with fear. I went out. Cavalrymen were sweeping the village of all it contained, the meager little that was left to us in our penury. My father was asleep; how I prayed that he might not waken! Although an old man, he was fiery as a boy, and proudly, passionately rebellious against the fate which had come upon us. Our house was some distance back from the road, and broad grounds separated us from the neighboring residences. Cassy and I softly piled our pillows and cushions against the doors and windows that opened from his room to the piazza, hoping to deaden the sounds outside, for some of our people were resisting, and now and then I heard shouts and oaths. But it was of no use. My dear old father woke, heard the sounds, and rushed out into the street sword in hand; for he had been a soldier too, serving with honor through the Mexican War. Made desperate

by my fears for him, I followed. There was a *mêlée* in the
road before our house; a high wind blew the thick dust in
my eyes and half blinded me, so that I only saw struggling
forms on foot and on horseback, and could not distinguish
friend or foe. Into this group my father rushed. I never knew
the cause of the contest; probably it was an ill-advised attack
by some of our people, fiery and reasonless always. But,
whatever it was, at length there came one, two, three shots,
and then the group broke apart. I rushed forward and received my old father in my arms, dying—dead. His head lay
on my shoulder as I knelt in the white road, and his silver
hair was dabbled with blood; he had been shot through the
head and breast, and lived but a moment.

"We carried him back to the house, old Cassy and I,
slowly, and with little regard for the bullets which now
whistled through the air; for the first shots had brought together the scattered cavalrymen, who now rode through the
streets firing right and left, more at random, I think, than
with direct aim, yet still determined to 'frighten the rebels,'
and avenge the soldier, one of their number, who had been
killed at the beginning of the fray. We laid my father down
in the center of the hall, and prepared him for his long sleep.
No one came to help us; no one came to sorrow with us;
each household gathered its own together and waited with
bated breath for what was still to come. I watched alone
beside my dead that night, the house-doors stood wide open,
and lights burned at the head and foot of the couch. I said
to myself, 'Let them come now and take their fill.' But no
one disturbed me, and I kept my vigil from midnight until
dawn; then there came a sound of many feet, and when the
sun rose our streets were full of blue-coated soldiers, thousands upon thousands; one wing of the great army was marching through. There was still hot anger against us for our
resistance, and when the commanding officers arrived they
ordered guards to be stationed at every house, with orders to
shoot any man or boy who showed himself outside of his

doorway. All day and night the Federal soldiers would be passing through, and the guards gave notice that if another man was injured twenty rebel lives should answer for it.

" ' We must bury my father, you and I together, Cassy,' I said ; ' there is no one to help us. Come ! '

" The old woman followed me without a word. Had I bidden her go alone, even as far as the door-step, she would have cowered at my feet in abject terror ; but, following me, she would have gone unquestioning to the world's end. The family burial-place was on our own grounds, according to the common custom of the South ; thither we turned our steps, and in silence hollowed out a grave as best we could.. The guard near by watched us with curiosity for some time ; at last he approached :

" ' What are you two women doing there ? '

" ' Digging a grave.'

" ' For whom ? '

" ' For my father, who lies dead in the house.'

" He withdrew a short distance, but still watched us closely, and when all was ready, and we returned to the house for our burden, I saw him signal the next guard. ' They will not interrupt us,' I said ; ' we are only two women and a dead man.'

" I wrapped my dear father in his cloak, and covered his face ; then we bore the lounge on which he lay out into the sunshine down toward the open grave. The weight of this poor frame of ours when dead is marvelous, and we moved slowly ; but at length we reached the spot. I had lined the grave with coverlids and a fine linen sheet, and now, with the aid of blankets, we lowered the clay to its last resting-place. Then, opening my prayer-book, I read aloud the service for the burial of the dead, slowly, and without tears, for I was thinking of the meeting above of the old father and his two boys : ' Lord, thou hast been our refuge from one generation to another. Before the mountains were brought forth, or ever the earth and the world were made, thou art God from

9

everlasting.' I took a clod and cast it upon the shrouded breast below. 'Earth to earth, ashes to ashes, dust to dust,' I said, and old Cassy, kneeling opposite, broke forth into low wailing, and rocked her body to and fro. Then we filled the grave. I remember that I worked with feverish strength; if it was not done quickly, I knew I could never do it at all. Can you realize what it would be to stand and shovel the earth with your own hands upon your dead?—to hear the gravel fall and strike?—to see the last shrouded outline disappear under the stifling, heavy clods? All this it was mine to do. When it was over I turned to go, and for the first time lifted my eyes. There at the fence-corner stood a row of Federal soldiers, silent, attentive, and with bared heads; my father was buried with military honors after all.

"During all that day and night the blue-coated ranks marched by; there seemed to be no end to the line of glittering muskets. I watched them passively, holding the orphan-boy on my knee; I felt as though I should never move or speak again. But after the army came the army-followers and stragglers, carrion-birds who flew behind the conquerors and devoured what they had left. They swept the town clean of food and raiment; many houses they wantonly burned; what they could not carry with them they destroyed. My own home did not escape: rude men ransacked every closet and drawer, and cut in ribbons the old portraits on the wall. A German, coming in from the smoke-house, dripping with bacon-juice, wiped his hands upon my wedding-veil, which had been discovered and taken from its box by a former intruder. It was a little thing; but, oh, how it hurt me! At length the last straggler left us, and we remained in the ashes. We could not sit down and weep for ourselves and for our dead; the care of finding wherewithal to eat thrust its coarse necessity upon us, and forced us to our feet. I had thought that all the rest of my life would be but a bowed figure at the door of a sepulchre; but the camp-followers came by, took the bowed figure by the arm, and forced it back to every-day life. We could no longer taste the luxury of tears. For days our people lived on the refuse left by the army, the bits of meat and bread they had thrown aside from their plenty; we picked up the corn with which they had fed their horses, kernel by kernel, and boiled it for our dinner; we groped in the ashes of their camp-fires; little children learned the sagacity of dogs seeking for bones, and quarreled over their findings. The fortune of war, do you say? Yes, the fortune of war! But it is one thing to say, and another thing to feel!

"We came away, madam, for our home was in ashes—old Cassy, the child, and I; we came on foot to this place, and here we have staid. No, the fields are never cultivated now. The dike has been broken down in too many places, and freshets have drained all the good out of the soil; the land is worthless. It was once my father's richest field. Yes, Cassy is dead. She was buried by her own people, who forgave her at the last for having been so spiritless as to stay with 'young missis,' when she might have tasted the glories of freedom over in the crowded hollow where the blacks were enjoying themselves and dying by the score. In six months half of them were gone. They had their freedom—oh, yes, plenty of it; they were quite free—to die! For, you see, madam, their masters, those villainous old masters of theirs, were no longer there to feed and clothe them. Oh! it was a great deliverance for the enfranchised people! Bitter, am I? Put yourself in my place.

"What am I going to do? Nothing. The boy? He must take his chances. Let him grow up under the new *régime;* I have told him nothing of the old. It may be that he will prosper; people do prosper, they tell me. It seems we were wrong, all wrong; then we must be very right now, for the blacks are our judges, councilors, postmasters, representatives, and law-makers. That is as it should be, isn't it? What! not so? But how can it be otherwise? Ah, you think that a new king will arise who knows not Joseph—that is, that a new generation will come to whom these questions

will be things of the past. It may be so ; I do not know. I
do not know anything certainly any more, for my world has
been torn asunder, and I am uprooted and lost. No, you can
not help me, no one can help me. I can not adjust myself to
the new order of things ; I can not fit myself in new soil ; the
fibers are broken. Leave me alone, and give your help to the
young ; they can profit by it. The child ? Well, if—if you
really wish it, I will not oppose you. Take him, and bring
him up in your rich, prosperous North ; the South has no
place for him. Go, and God speed you ! But, as for me, I
will abide in mine own country. It will not be until such as
I have gone from earth that the new blood can come to her.
Let us alone ; we will watch the old life out with her, and
when her new dawning comes we shall have joined our dead,
and all of us, our errors, our sins, and our sufferings will be
forgotten."

FELIPA.

Glooms of the live-oaks, beautiful-braided and woven
With intricate shades of the vines that, myriad cloven,
Clamber the forks of the multiform boughs.
    . . . . Green colonnades
Of the dim sweet woods, of the dear dark woods,
Of the heavenly woods and glades,
That run to the radiant marginal sand-beach within
  The wide sea-marshes of Glynn.
    . . . . Free
By a world of marsh that borders a world of sea.
Sinuous southward and sinuous northward the shimmering band
Of the sand-beach fastens the fringe of the marsh to the folds of the land.

Inward and outward to northward and southward the beach-lines linger and
  curl
As a silver-wrought garment that clings to and follows the firm, sweet limbs of
  a girl.
A league and a league of marsh-grass, waist-high, broad in the blade,
Green, and all of a height, and unflecked with a light or a shade.
          SIDNEY LANIER.

CHRISTINE and I found her there. She was a small, dark-skinned, yellow-eyed child, the offspring of the ocean and the heats, tawny, lithe and wild, shy yet fearless—not unlike one of the little brown deer that bounded through the open reaches of the pine-barren behind the house. She did not come to us—we came to her; we loomed into her life like genii from another world, and she was partly afraid and partly proud of us. For were we not her guests? proud thought! and, better still, were we not women? "I have only seen three women in all my life," said Felipa, inspecting us gravely, "and I like women. I am a woman too, although these clothes of the son of Pedro make me appear as a boy; I wear them on

account of the boat and the hauling in of the fish. The son
of Pedro being dead at a convenient age, and his clothes fitting me, what would you have? It was a chance not to be
despised. But when I am grown I shall wear robes long and
beautiful like the señora's." The little creature was dressed
in a boy's suit of dark-blue linen, much the worse for wear,
and torn.

"If you are a girl, why do you not mend your clothes?"
I said.

"Do you mend, señora?"

"Certainly : all women sew and mend."

"The other lady?"

Christine laughed as she lay at ease upon the brown carpet of pine-needles, warm and aromatic after the tropic day's
sunshine. "The child has divined me already, Catherine,"
she said.

Christine was a tall, lissome maid, with an unusually long
stretch of arm, long sloping shoulders, and a long fair throat ;
her straight hair fell to her knees when unbound, and its clear
flaxen hue had not one shade of gold, as her clear gray eyes
had not one shade of blue. Her small, straight, rose-leaf lips
parted over small, dazzlingly white teeth, and the outline of
her face in profile reminded you of an etching in its distinct-
ness, although it was by no means perfect according to the
rules of art.   Still, what a comfort it was, after the blurred outlines and smudged profiles many of us possess—seen to best
advantage, I think, in church on Sundays, crowned with flower-
decked bonnets, listening calmly serene to favorite ministers,
unconscious of noses! When Christine had finished her
laugh—and she never hurried anything—she stretched out
her arm carelessly and patted Felipa's curly head. The child
caught the descending hand and kissed the long white fingers.

It was a wild place where we were, yet not new or crude—
the coast of Florida, that old-new land, with its deserted plantations, its skies of Paradise, and its broad wastes open to the
changeless sunshine. The old house stood on the edge of the

dry land, where the pine-barren ended and the salt-marsh began; in front curved the tide-water river that seemed ever trying to come up close to the barren and make its acquaintance, but could not quite succeed, since it must always turn and flee at a fixed hour, like Cinderella at the ball, leaving not a silver slipper behind, but purple driftwood and bright sea-weeds, brought in from the Gulf Stream outside. A planked platform ran out into the marsh from the edge of the barren, and at its end the boats were moored; for, although at high tide the river was at our feet, at low tide it was far away out in the green waste somewhere, and if we wanted it we must go and seek it. We did not want it, however; we let it glide up to us twice a day with its fresh salt odors and flotsam of the ocean, and the rest of the time we wandered over the barrens or lay under the trees looking up into the wonderful blue above, listening to the winds as they rushed across from sea to sea. I was an artist, poor and painstaking. Christine was my kind friend. She had brought me South because my cough was troublesome, and here because Edward Bowne recommended the place. He and three fellow sportsmen were down at the Madre Lagoon, farther south; I thought it probable we should see him, without his three fellow sportsmen, before very long.

"Who were the three women you have seen, Felipa?" said Christine.

"The grandmother, an Indian woman of the Seminoles who comes sometimes with baskets, and the wife of Miguel of the island. But they are all old, and their skins are curled: I like better the silver skin of the señora."

Poor little Felipa lived on the edge of the great salt-marsh alone with her grandparents, for her mother was dead. The yellow old couple were slow-witted Minorcans, part pagan, part Catholic, and wholly ignorant; their minds rarely rose above the level of their orange-trees and their fish-nets. Felipa's father was a Spanish sailor, and, as he had died only the year before, the child's Spanish was fairly correct, and we could converse with her readily, although we were slow to comprehend the patois of the old people, which seemed to borrow as much from the Italian tongue and the Greek as from its mother Spanish. " I know a great deal," Felipa remarked confidently, " for my father taught me. He had sailed on the ocean out of sight of land, and he knew many things. These he taught to me. Do the gracious ladies think there is anything else to know ? "

One of the gracious ladies thought not, decidedly. In answer to my remonstrance, expressed in English, she said, " Teach a child like that, and you ruin her."

" Ruin her ? "

" Ruin her happiness—the same thing."

Felipa had a dog, a second self—a great gaunt yellow creature of unknown breed, with crooked legs, big feet, and the name Drollo. What Drollo meant, or whether it was an abbreviation, we never knew; but there was a certain satisfaction in it, for the dog was droll : the fact that the Minorcan title, whatever it was, meant nothing of that sort, made it all the better. We never saw Felipa without Drollo. " They look a good deal alike," observed Christine—" the same coloring."

" For shame ! " I said.

But it was true. The child's bronzed yellow skin and soft eyes were not unlike the dog's, but her head was crowned with a mass of short black curls, while Drollo had only his two great flapping ears and his low smooth head. Give him an inch or two more of skull, and what a creature a dog would be ! For love and faithfulness even now what man can match him ? But, although ugly, Felipa was a picturesque little object always, whether attired in boy's clothes or in her own forlorn bodice and skirt. Olive-hued and meager-faced, lithe and thin, she flew over the pine-barrens like a creature of air, laughing to feel her short curls toss and her thin childish arms buoyed up on the breeze as she ran, with Drollo barking behind. For she loved the winds, and always knew

when they were coming—whether down from the north, in
from the ocean, or across from the Gulf of Mexico : she
watched for them, sitting in the doorway, where she could
feel their first breath, and she taught us the signs of the
clouds. She was a queer little thing : we used to find her
sometimes dancing alone out on the barren in a circle she had
marked out with pine-cones, and once she confided to us that
she talked to the trees. " They hear," she said in a whisper ;
" you should see how knowing they look, and how their leaves
listen."

Once we came upon her most secret lair in a dense thicket
of thorn-myrtle and wild smilax—a little bower she had
made, where was hidden a horrible-looking image formed of
the rough pieces of saw-palmetto grubbed up by old Bartolo
from his garden. She must have dragged these fragments
thither one by one, and with infinite pains bound them together with her rude withes of strong marsh-grass, until at
last she had formed a rough trunk with crooked arms and a
sort of a head, the red hairy surface of the palmetto looking
not unlike the skin of some beast, and making the creature
all the more grotesque. This fetich was kept crowned with
flowers, and after this we often saw the child stealing away
with Drollo to carry to it portions of her meals or a new-found
treasure—a sea-shell, a broken saucer, or a fragment of ribbon. The food always mysteriously disappeared, and my
suspicion is that Drollo used to go back secretly in the night
and devour it, asking no questions and telling no lies : it fitted
in nicely, however, Drollo merely performing the ancient
part of the priests of Jupiter, men who have been much admired. " What a little pagan she is ! " I said.

"Oh, no, it is only her doll," replied Christine.

I tried several times to paint Felipa during these first
weeks, but those eyes of hers always evaded me. They were,
as I have said before, yellow—that is, they were brown with
yellow lights—and they stared at you with the most inflexible
openness. The child had the full-curved, half-open mouth of

the tropics, and a low Greek forehead. "Why isn't she
pretty ? " I said.

"She is hideous," replied Christine; "look at her elbows."

Now Felipa's arms *were* unpleasant: they were brown
and lean, scratched and stained, and they terminated in a
pair of determined little paws that could hold on like grim
Death. I shall never forget coming upon a tableau one day
out on the barren—a little Florida cow and Felipa, she holding on by the horns, and the beast with its small fore feet
stubbornly set in the sand; girl pulling one way, cow the
other; both silent and determined. It was a hard contest,
but the girl won.

"And if you pass over her elbows, there are her feet,"
continued Christine languidly. For she was a sybaritic lover
of the fine linens of life, that friend of mine—a pre-Raphaelite
lady with clinging draperies and a mediæval clasp on her belt.
Her whole being rebelled against ugliness, and the mere sight
of a sharp-nosed, light-eyed woman on a cold day made her
uncomfortable.

"Have we not feet too ? " I replied sharply.

But I knew what she meant. Bare feet are not pleasant
to the eye nowadays, whatever they may have been in the
days of the ancient Greeks; and Felipa's little brown insteps
were half the time torn or bruised by the thorns of the chaparral. Besides, there was always the disagreeable idea that
she might step upon something cold and squirming when she
prowled through the thickets knee-deep in the matted grasses.
Snakes abounded, although we never saw them; but Felipa
went up to their very doors, as it were, and rang the bell defiantly.

One day old Grandfather Bartolo took the child with him
down to the coast : she was always wild to go to the beach,
where she could gather shells and sea-beans, and chase the
little ocean-birds that ran along close to the waves with that
swift gliding motion of theirs, and where she could listen to
the roar of the breakers. We were several miles up the salt-

marsh, and to go down to the ocean was quite a voyage to Felipa. She bade us good-by joyously; then ran back to hug Christine a second time, then to the boat again; then back.

" I thought you wanted to go, child ? " I said, a little impatiently; for I was reading aloud, and these small irruptions were disturbing.

" Yes," said Felipa, " I want to go ; and still— Perhaps if the gracious señora would kiss me again—"

Christine only patted her cheek and told her to run away : she obeyed, but there was a wistful look in her eyes, and, even after the boat had started, her face, watching us from the stern, haunted me.

" Now that the little monkey has gone, I may be able at last to catch and fix a likeness of her," I said ; " in this case a recollection is better than the changing quicksilver reality."

" You take it as a study of ugliness ? "

" Do not be hard upon the child, Christine."

" Hard ? Why, she adores me," said my friend, going off to her hammock under the tree.

Several days passed, and the boat returned not. I accomplished a fine amount of work, and Christine a fine amount of swinging in the hammock and dreaming. At length one afternoon I gave my final touch, and carried my sketch over to the pre-Raphaelite lady for criticism. " What do you see ? " I said.

" I see a wild-looking child with yellow eyes, a mat of curly black hair, a lank little bodice, her two thin brown arms embracing a gaunt old dog with crooked legs, big feet, and turned-in toes."

" Is that all ? "

" All."

" You do not see latent beauty, courage, and a possible great gulf of love in that poor wild little face ? "

" Nothing of the kind," replied Christine decidedly. " I see an ugly little girl ; that is all."

The next day the boat returned, and brought back five persons, the old grandfather, Felipa, Drollo, Miguel of the island, and—Edward Bowne.

"Already?" I said.

"Tired of the Madre, Kitty; thought I would come up here and see you for a while. I knew you must be pining for me."

"Certainly," I replied; "do you not see how I have wasted away?"

He drew my arm through his and raced me down the plank-walk toward the shore, where I arrived laughing and out of breath.

"Where is Christine?" he asked.

I came back into the traces at once. "Over there in the hammock. You wish to go to the house first, I suppose?"

"Of course not."

"But she did not come to meet you, Edward, although she knew you had landed."

"Of course not, also."

"I do not understand you two."

"And of course not, a third time," said Edward, looking down at me with a smile. "What do peaceful little artists know about war?"

"Is it war?"

"Something very like it, Kitty. What is that you are carrying?"

"Oh! my new sketch. What do you think of it?"

"Good, very good. Some little girl about here, I suppose?

"Why, it is Felipa!"

"And who is Felipa? Seems to me I have seen that old dog, though."

"Of course you have; he was in the boat with you, and so was Felipa; but she was dressed in boy's clothes, and that gives her a different look."

"Oh! that boy? I remember him. His name is Philip. He is a funny little fellow," said Edward calmly.

"Her name is Felipa, and she is not a boy or a funny little fellow at all," I replied.

"Isn't she? I thought she was both," replied Ned carelessly; and then he went off toward the hammock. I turned away, after noting Christine's cool greeting, and went back to the boat.

Felipa came bounding to meet me. "What is his name?" she demanded.

"Bowne."

"Buon—Buona; I can not say it."

"Bowne, child—Edward Bowne."

"Oh! Eduardo; I know that. Eduardo—Eduardo—a name of honey."

She flew off singing the name, followed by Drollo carrying his mistress's palmetto basket in his big patient mouth; but when I passed the house a few moments afterward she was singing, or rather talking volubly of, another name—"Miguel," and "the wife of Miguel," who were apparently important personages on the canvas of her life. As it happened, I never really saw that wife of Miguel, who seemingly had no name of her own; but I imagined her. She lived on a sand-bar in the ocean not far from the mouth of our salt-marsh; she drove pelicans like ducks with a long switch, and she had a tame eagle; she had an old horse also, who dragged the driftwood across the sand on a sledge, and this old horse seemed like a giant horse always, outlined as he was against the flat bar and the sky. She went out at dawn, and she went out at sunset, but during the middle of the burning day she sat at home and polished sea-beans, for which she obtained untold sums; she was very tall, she was very yellow, and she had but one eye. These items, one by one, had been dropped by Felipa at various times, and it was with curiosity that I gazed upon the original Miguel, the possessor of this remarkable spouse. He was a grave-eyed, yellow man, who said little and thought less, applying *cui bono?* to mental much as the city man applies it to bodily exertion, and therefore achieving, I think, a finer degree of inanition. The tame eagle, the pelicans, were nothing to him ; and, when I saw his lethargic, gentle countenance, my own curiosity about them seemed to die away in haze, as though I had breathed in an invisible opiate. He came, he went, and that was all ; exit Miguel.

Felipa was constantly with us now. She and Drollo followed the three of us wherever we went—followed the two also whenever I staid behind to sketch, as I often staid, for in those days I was trying to catch the secret of the salt-marsh ; a hopeless effort—I know it now. "Stay with me, Felipa," I said ; for it was natural to suppose that the lovers might like to be alone. (I call them lovers for want of a better name, but they were more like haters ; however, in such cases it is nearly the same thing.) And then Christine, hearing this, would immediately call "Felipa!" and the child would dart after them, happy as a bird. She wore her boy's suit now all the time, because the señora had said she "looked well in it." What the señora really said was, that in boy's clothes she looked less like a grasshopper. But this had been translated as above by Edward Bowne when Felipa suddenly descended upon him one day and demanded to be instantly told what the gracious lady was saying about her ; for she seemed to know by intuition when we spoke of her, although we talked in English and mentioned no names. When told, her small face beamed, and she kissed Christine's hand joyfully and bounded away. Christine took out her handkerchief and wiped the spot.

"Christine," I said, "do you remember the fate of the proud girl who walked upon bread?"

"You think that I may starve for kisses some time?" said my friend, going on with the wiping.

"Not while I am alive," called out Edward from behind. His style of courtship *was* of the sledge-hammer sort sometimes. But he did not get much for it on that day ; only lofty tolerance, which seemed to amuse him greatly.

Edward played with Felipa very much as if she was a

rubber toy or a little trapeze performer. He held her out at arm's length in mid-air, he poised her on his shoulder, he tossed her up into the low myrtle-trees, and dangled her by her little belt over the claret-colored pools on the barren; but he could not frighten her; she only laughed and grew wilder and wilder, like a squirrel. "She has muscles and nerves of steel," he said admiringly.

"Do put her down; she is too excitable for such games." I said in French, for Felipa seemed to divine our English now. "See the color she has."

For there was a trail of dark red over the child's thin oval cheeks which made her look unlike herself. As she caught our eyes fixed upon her, she suddenly stopped her climbing and came and sat at Christine's feet. "Some day I shall wear robes like the señora's," she said, passing her hand over the soft fabric; "and I think," she added after some slow consideration, "that my face will be like the señora's too."

Edward burst out laughing. The little creature stopped abruptly and scanned his face.

"Do not tease her," I said.

Quick as a flash she veered around upon me. "He does not tease me," she said angrily in Spanish; "and, besides, what if he does? I like it." She looked at me with gleaming eyes and stamped her foot.

"What a little tempest!" said Christine.

Then Edward, man-like, began to explain. "You could not look much like this lady, Felipa," he said, "because you are so dark, you know."

"Am I dark?"

"Very dark; but many people are dark, of course; and for my part I always liked dark eyes," said this mendacious person.

"Do you like my eyes?" asked Felipa anxiously.

"Indeed I do: they are like the eyes of a dear little calf I once owned when I was a boy."

The child was satisfied, and went back to her place beside

Christine. "Yes, I shall wear robes like this," she said
dreamily, drawing the flowing drapery over her knees clad in
the little linen trousers, and scanning the effect; "they would
trail behind me—so." Her bare feet peeped out below the
hem, and again we all laughed, the little brown toes looked
so comical coming out from the silk and the snowy embroideries. She came down to reality again, looked at us, looked
at herself, and for the first time seemed to comprehend the
difference. Then suddenly she threw herself down on the
ground like a little animal, and buried her head in her arms.
She would not speak, she would not look up: she only re-
laxed one arm a little to take in Drollo, and then lay motionless. Drollo looked at us out of one eye solemnly from
his uncomfortable position, as much as to say: "No use;
leave her to me." So after a while we went away and left
them there.

That evening I heard a low knock at my door. "Come
in," I said, and Felipa entered. I hardly knew her. She was
dressed in a flowered muslin gown which had probably belonged to her mother, and she wore her grandmother's stockings and large baggy slippers; on her mat of curly hair was
perched a high-crowned, stiff white cap adorned with a ribbon streamer; and her lank little neck, coming out of the big
gown, was decked with a chain of large sea-beans, like ex-
aggerated lockets. She carried a Cuban fan in her hand
which was as large as a parasol, and Drollo, walking behind,
fairly clanked with the chain of sea-shells which she had
wound around him from head to tail. The droll tableau and
the supreme pride on Felipa's countenance overcame me, and
I laughed aloud. A sudden cloud of rage and disappointment came over the poor child's face: she threw her cap on
the floor and stamped on it; she tore off her necklace and
writhed herself out of her big flowered gown, and, running to
Drollo, nearly strangled him in her fierce efforts to drag off
his shell chains. Then, a half-dressed, wild little phantom,
she seized me by the skirts and dragged me toward the look-

ing-glass. "You are not pretty either," she cried. "Look at yourself! look at yourself!"

"I did not mean to laugh at you, Felipa," I said gently; "I would not laugh at any one; and it is true I am not pretty, as you say. I can never be pretty, child; but, if you will try to be more gentle, I could teach you how to dress yourself so that no one would laugh at you again. I could make you a little bright-barred skirt and a scarlet bodice : you could help, and that would teach you to sew. But a little girl who wants all this done for her must be quiet and good."

"I am good," said Felipa; "as good as everything."

The tears still stood in her eyes, but her anger was forgotten : she improvised a sort of dance around my room, followed by Drollo dragging his twisted chain, stepping on it with his big feet, and finally winding himself up into a knot around the chair-legs.

"Couldn't we make Drollo something too? dear old Drollo!" said Felipa, going to him and squeezing him in an enthusiastic embrace. I used to wonder how his poor ribs stood it : Felipa used him as a safety-valve for her impetuous feelings.

She kissed me good night, and then asked for "the other lady."

"Go to bed, child," I said; "I will give her your good night."

"But I want to kiss her too," said Felipa.

She lingered at the door and would not go; she played with the latch, and made me nervous with its clicking; at last I ordered her out. But on opening my door half an hour afterward there she was sitting on the floor outside in the darkness, she and Drollo, patiently waiting. Annoyed, but unable to reprove her, I wrapped the child in my shawl and carried her out into the moonlight, where Christine and Edward were strolling to and fro under the pines. "She will not go to bed, Christine, without kissing you," I explained.

"Funny little monkey!" said my friend, passively allowing the embrace.

"Me too," said Edward, bending down. Then I carried my bundle back satisfied.

The next day Felipa and I in secret began our labors: hers consisted in worrying me out of my life and spoiling material — mine in keeping my temper and trying to sew. The result, however, was satisfactory, never mind how we got there. I led Christine out one afternoon: Edward followed. "Do you like tableaux?" I said. "There is one I have arranged for you."

Felipa sat on the edge of the low, square-curbed Spanish well, and Drollo stood behind her, his great yellow body and solemn head serving as a background. She wore a brown petticoat barred with bright colors, and a little scarlet bodice fitting her slender waist closely; a chemisette of soft cream-color with loose sleeves covered her neck and arms, and set off the dark hues of her cheeks and eyes; and around her curly hair a red scarf was twisted, its fringed edges forming a drapery at the back of the head, which, more than anything else, seemed to bring out the latent character of her face. Brown moccasins, red stockings, and a quantity of bright beads completed her costume.

"By Jove!" cried Edward, "the little thing is almost pretty."

Felipa understood this, and a great light came into her face: forgetting her pose, she bounded forward to Christine's side. "I am pretty, then?" she said with exultation; "I *am* pretty, then, after all? For now you yourself have said it—have said it."

"No, Felipa," I interposed, "the gentleman said it." For the child had a curious habit of confounding the two identities which puzzled me then as now. But this afternoon, this happy afternoon, she was content, for she was allowed to sit at Christine's feet and look up into her fair face unmolested. I was forgotten, as usual.

"It is always so," I said to myself. But cynicism, as Mr. Aldrich says, is a small brass field-piece that eventually bursts and kills the artilleryman. I knew this, having been blown up myself more than once; so I went back to my painting and forgot the world. Our world down there on the edge of the salt-marsh, however, was a small one : when two persons went out of it there was a vacuum.

One morning Felipa came sadly to my side. "They have gone away," she said.

"Yes, child."

"Down to the beach to spend all the day."

"Yes, I know it."

"And without me !"

This was the climax. I looked up. Her eyes were dry, but there was a hollow look of disappointment in her face that made her seem old ; it was as though for an instant you caught what her old-woman face would be half a century on.

"Why did they not take me ? " she said. "I am pretty now : she herself said it."

"They can not always take you, Felipa," I replied, giving up the point as to who had said it.

"Why not ? I am pretty now : she herself said it," persisted the child. "In these clothes, you know : she herself said it. The clothes of the son of Pedro you will never see more : they are burned."

"Burned ? "

"Yes, burned," replied Felipa composedly. "I carried them out on the barren and burned them. Drollo singed his paw. They burned quite nicely. But they are gone, and I am pretty now, and yet they did not take me ! What shall I do ? "

"Take these colors and make me a picture," I suggested. Generally, this was a prized privilege, but to-day it did not attract ; she turned away, and a few moments after I saw her going down to the end of the plank-walk, where she stood gazing wistfully toward the ocean. There she staid all day,

going into camp with Drollo, and refusing to come to dinner
in spite of old Dominga's calls and beckonings. At last the
patient old grandmother went down herself to the end of the
long walk where they were, with some bread and venison on
a plate. Felipa ate but little, but Drollo, after waiting politely
until she had finished, devoured everything that was left in
his calmly hungry way, and then sat back on his haunches
with one paw on the plate, as though for the sake of memory.
Drollo's hunger was of the chronic kind; it seemed impossible either to assuage it or to fill him. There was a gaunt
leanness about him which I am satisfied no amount of food
could ever fatten. I think he knew it too, and that accounted
for his resignation. At length, just before sunset, the boat
returned, floating up the marsh with the tide, old Bartolo
steering and managing the brown sails. Felipa sprang up
joyfully; I thought she would spring into the boat in her
eagerness. What did she receive for her long vigil? A short
word or two; that was all. Christine and Edward had quarreled.

How do lovers quarrel ordinarily? But I should not ask
that, for these were no ordinary lovers: they were extraordinary.

"You should not submit to her caprices so readily," I said
the next day while strolling on the barren with Edward. (He
was not so much cast down, however, as he might have
been.)

"I adore the very ground her foot touches, Kitty."

"I know it. But how will it end?"

"I will tell you: some of these days I shall win her, and
then—she will adore me."

Here Felipa came running after us, and Edward immediately challenged her to a race: a game of romps began. If
Christine had been looking from her window she might have
thought he was not especially disconsolate over her absence;
but she was not looking. She was never looking out of anything or for anybody. She was always serenely content where

she was. Edward and Felipa strayed off among the pine-trees, and gradually I lost sight of them. But as I sat sketching an hour afterward Edward came into view, carrying the child in his arms. I hurried to meet them.

"I shall never forgive myself," he said; "the little thing has fallen and injured her foot badly, I fear."

"I do not care at all," said Felipa; "I like to have it hurt. It is *my* foot, isn't it?"

These remarks she threw at me defiantly, as though I had laid claim to the member in question. I could not help laughing.

"The other lady will not laugh," said the child proudly. And in truth Christine, most unexpectedly, took up the *rôle* of nurse. She carried Felipa to her own room—for we each had a little cell opening out of the main apartment—and as white-robed Charity she shone with new radiance, "Shone" is the proper word; for through the open door of the dim cell, with the dark little face of Felipa on her shoulder, her white robe and skin seemed fairly to shine, as white lilies shine on a dark night. The old grandmother left the child in our care and watched our proceedings wistfully, very much as a dog watches the human hands that extract the thorn from the swollen foot of her puppy. She was grateful and asked no questions; in fact, thought was not one of her mental processes. She did not think much; she felt. As for Felipa, the child lived in rapture during those days in spite of her suffering. She scarcely slept at all—she was too happy: I heard her voice rippling on through the night, and Christine's low replies. She adored her beautiful nurse.

The fourth day came: Edward Bowne walked into the cell. "Go out and breathe the fresh air for an hour or two," he said in the tone more of a command than a request.

"The child will never consent," replied Christine sweetly.

"Oh, yes, she will; I will stay with her," said the young man, lifting the feverish little head on his arm and passing his hand softly over the bright eyes.

"Felipa, do you not want me?" said Christine, bending down.

"He stays; it is all the same," murmured the child.

"So it is.—Go, Christine," said Edward with a little smile of triumph.

Without a word Christine left the cell. But she did not go to walk; she came to my room, and, throwing herself on my bed, fell in a moment into a deep sleep, the reaction after her three nights of wakefulness. When she awoke it was long after dark, and I had relieved Edward in his watch.

"You will have to give it up," he said as our lily came forth at last with sleep-flushed cheeks and starry eyes shielded from the light. "The spell is broken; we have all been taking care of Felipa, and she likes one as well as the other."

Which was not true, in my case at least, since Felipa had openly derided my small strength when I lifted her, and beat off the sponge with which I attempted to bathe her hot face, "They" used no sponges, she said, only their nice cool hands; and she wished "they" would come and take care of her again. But Christine had resigned *in toto.* If Felipa did not prefer her to all others, then Felipa should not have her; she was not a common nurse. And indeed she was not. Her fair face, ideal grace, cooing voice, and the strength of her long arms and flexible hands, were like magic to the sick, and—distraction to the well; the well in this case being Edward Bowne looking in at the door.

"You love them very much, do you not, Felipa?" I said one day when the child was sitting up for the first time in a cushioned chair.

"Ah, yes; it is so strong when they carry me," she replied. But it was Edward who carried her.

"He is very strong," I said.

"Yes; and their long soft hair, with the smell of roses in it too," said Felipa dreamily. But the hair was Christine's.

"I shall love them for ever, and they will love me for ever," continued the child. "Drollo too." She patted the dog's head as she spoke, and then concluded to kiss him on his little inch of forehead; next she offered him all her medicines and lotions in turn, and he smelled at them grimly. "He likes to know what I am taking," she explained.

I went on: "You love them, Felipa, and they are fond of you. They will always remember you, no doubt."

"Remember!" cried Felipa, starting up from her cushions like a Jack-in-the box. "They are not going away? Never! never!"

"But of course they must go some time, for—"

But Felipa was gone. Before I could divine her intent she had flung herself out of her chair down on the floor, and was crawling on her hands and knees toward the outer room. I ran after her, but she reached the door before me, and, dragging her bandaged foot behind her, drew herself toward Christine. "You are *not* going away! You are not! you are not!" she sobbed, clinging to her skirts.

Christine was reading tranquilly; Edward stood at the outer door mending his fishing-tackle. The coolness between them remained, unwarmed by so much as a breath. "Run away, child; you disturb me," said Christine, turning over a leaf. She did not even look at the pathetic little bundle at her feet. Pathetic little bundles must be taught some time what ingratitude deserves.

"How can she run, lame as she is?" said Edward from the doorway.

"You are not going away, are you? Tell me you are not," sobbed Felipa in a passion of tears, beating on the floor with one hand, and with the other clinging to Christine.

"I am not going," said Edward. "Do not sob so, you poor little thing!"

She crawled to him, and he took her up in his arms and soothed her into stillness again; then he carried her out on the barren for a breath of fresh air.

"It is a most extraordinary thing how that child confounds

you two," I said. " It is a case of color-blindness, as it were
—supposing you two were colors."

" Which we are not," replied Christine carelessly. " Do
not stray off into mysticism, Catherine."

" It is not mysticism ; it is a study of character—"

" Where there is no character," replied my friend.

I gave it up, but I said to myself : " Fate, in the next
world make me one of those long, lithe, light-haired women,
will you ? I want to see how it feels."

Felipa's foot was well again, and spring had come. Soon
we must leave our lodge on the edge of the pine-barren, our
outlook over the salt-marsh, with the river sweeping up twice a
day, bringing in the briny odors of the ocean ; soon we should
see no more the eagles far above us or hear the night-cry of
the great owls, and we must go without the little fairy flowers
of the barren, so small that a hundred of them scarcely made
a tangible bouquet, yet what beauty ! what sweetness ! In
my portfolio were sketches and studies of the salt-marsh, and
in my heart were hopes. Somebody says somewhere : " Hope
is more than a blessing ; it is a duty and a virtue." But I fail
to appreciate preserved hope—hope put up in cans and served
out in seasons of depression. I like it fresh from the tree.
And so when I hope it *is* hope, and not that well-dried, monotonous cheerfulness which makes one long to throw the persistent smilers out of the window. Felipa danced no more
on the barrens ; her illness had toned her down ; she seemed
content to sit at our feet while we talked, looking up dreamily
into our faces, but no longer eagerly endeavoring to comprehend. We were there ; that was enough.

"She is growing like a reed," I said ; "her illness has left
her weak."

" -Minded," suggested Christine.

At this moment Felipa stroked the lady's white hand tenderly and laid her brown cheek against it.

" Do you not feel reproached ? " I said.

" Why ? Must we give our love to whoever loves us ? A

fine parcel of paupers we should all be, wasting our inheritance in pitiful small change! Shall I give a thousand beggars a half hour's happiness, or shall I make one soul rich his whole life long?"

"The latter," remarked Edward, who had come up unobserved.

They gazed at each other unflinchingly. They had come to open battle during those last days, and I knew that the end was near. Their words had been cold as ice, cutting as steel, and I said to myself, "At any moment." There would be a deadly struggle, and then Christine would yield. Even I comprehended something of what that yielding would be.

"Why do they hate each other so?" Felipa said to me sadly.

"Do they hate each other?"

"Yes, for I feel it here," she answered, touching her breast with a dramatic little gesture.

"Nonsense! Go and play with your doll, child." For I had made her a respectable, orderly doll to take the place of the ungainly fetich out on the barren.

Felipa gave me a look and walked away. A moment afterward she brought the doll out of the house before my very eyes, and, going down to the end of the dock, deliberately threw it into the water; the tide was flowing out, and away went my toy-woman out of sight, out to sea.

"Well!" I said to myself. "What next?"

I had not told Felipa we were going; I thought it best to let it take her by surprise. I had various small articles of finery ready as farewell gifts, which should act as sponges to absorb her tears. But Fate took the whole matter out of my hands. This is how it happened: One evening in the jasmine arbor, in the fragrant darkness of the warm spring night, the end came; Christine was won. She glided in like a wraith, and I, divining at once what had happened, followed her into her little room, where I found her lying on her bed, her hands clasped on her breast, her eyes open and veiled in soft shad-

10

ows, her white robe drenched with dew. I kissed her fondly —I never could help loving her then or now—and next I went out to find Edward. He had been kind to me all my poor gray life; should I not go to him now? He was still in the arbor, and I sat down by his side quietly; I knew that the words would come in time. They came; what a flood! English was not enough for him. He poured forth his love in the rich-voweled Spanish tongue also; it has sounded doubly sweet to me ever since.

> " Have you felt the wool of the beaver?
>   Or swan's down ever?
>   Or have smelt the bud o' the brier?
>   Or the nard in the fire?
>   Or ha' tasted the bag o' the bee?
>   Oh so white, oh so soft, oh so sweet is she !"

said the young lover; and I, listening there in the dark fragrant night, with the dew heavy upon me, felt glad that the old simple-hearted love was not entirely gone from our tired metallic world.

It was late when we returned to the house. After reaching my room I found that I had left my cloak in the arbor. It was a strong fabric; the dew could not hurt it, but it could hurt my sketching materials and various trifles in the wide inside pockets—*objets de luxe* to me, souvenirs of happy times, little artistic properties that I hang on the walls of my poor studio when in the city. I went softly out into the darkness again and sought the arbor; groping on the ground I found, not the cloak, but—Felipa! She was crouched under the foliage, face downward; she would not move or answer.

"What is the matter, child?" I said, but she would not speak. I tried to draw her from her lair, but she tangled herself stubbornly still farther among the thorny vines, and I could not move her. I touched her neck; it was cold. Frightened, I ran back to the house for a candle.

"Go away," she said in a low hoarse voice when I flashed

the light over her. "I know all, and I am going to die. I have eaten the poison things in your box, and just now a snake came on my neck and I let him. He has bitten me, and I am glad. Go away; I am going to die."

I looked around; there was my color-case rifled and empty, and the other articles were scattered on the ground. "Good Heavens, child!" I cried, "what have you eaten?"

"Enough," replied Felipa gloomily. "I knew they were poisons; you told me so. And I let the snake stay."

By this time the household, aroused by my hurried exit with the candle, came toward the arbor. The moment Edward appeared Felipa rolled herself up like a hedgehog again and refused to speak. But the old grandmother knelt down and drew the little crouching figure into her arms with gentle tenderness, smoothing its hair and murmuring loving words in her soft dialect.

"What is it?" said Edward; but even then his eyes were devouring Christine, who stood in the dark vine-wreathed doorway like a picture in a frame. I explained.

Christine smiled. "Jealousy," she said in a low voice. "I am not surprised."

But at the first sound of her voice Felipa had started up, and, wrenching herself free from old Dominga's arms, threw herself at Christine's feet. "Look at *me* so," she cried—"me too; do not look at him. He has forgotten poor Felipa; he does not love her any more. But *you* do not forget, señora; *you* love me—*you* love me. Say you do, or I shall die!"

We were all shocked by the pallor and the wild, hungry look of her uplifted face. Edward bent down and tried to lift her in his arms; but when she saw him a sudden fierceness came into her eyes; they shot out yellow light and seemed to narrow to a point of flame. Before we knew it she had turned, seized something, and plunged it into his encircling arm. It was my little Venetian dagger.

We sprang forward; our dresses were spotted with the fast-flowing blood; but Edward did not relax his hold on the writhing, wild little body he held until it lay exhausted in his arms. "I am glad I did it," said the child, looking up into his face with her inflexible eyes. "Put me down—put me down, I say, by the gracious señora, that I may die with the trailing of her white robe over me." And the old grandmother with trembling hands received her and laid her down mutely at Christine's feet.

Ah, well! Felipa did not die. The poisons racked but did not kill her, and the snake must have spared the little thin brown neck so despairingly offered to him. We went away; there was nothing for us to do but to go away as quickly as possible and leave her to her kind. To the silent old grandfather I said: "It will pass; she is but a child."

"She is nearly twelve, señora. Her mother was married at thirteen."

"But she loved them both alike, Bartolo. It is nothing; she does not know."

"You are right, lady; she does not know," replied the old man slowly; "but *I* know. It was two loves, and the stronger thrust the knife."

"B R O."

To him that hath, we are told,
Shall be given. Yes, by the Cross!
To the rich man Fate sends gold,
To the poor man loss on loss.

THOMAS BAILEY ALDRICH.

TWO houses, a saw-mill, and a tide-water marsh, with a railroad-track crossing it from northeast to southwest; on the other side the sea. One of the houses was near the drawbridge, and there the keeper lived, old Mr. Vickery. Not at all despised was old Mr. Vickery on account of his lowly occupation: the Vickerys had always lived on Vickery Island, and, although they were poor now, they had once been rich, and their name was still as well known as the sun in Port Wilbarger, and all Wilbarger district. Fine sea-island cotton was theirs once, and black hands to sow and gather it; salt-air made the old house pleasant. The air was still there, but not the cotton or the hands; and, when a keeper was wanted for the drawbridge of the new railroad, what more natural than that one should be selected who lived on the spot rather than a resident of Port Wilbarger, two miles away?

The other house was on Wilbarger Island, at the edge of the town, and, in itself uninteresting and unimportant, was yet accepted, like the plain member of a handsome family, because of its associations; for here lived Mrs. Manning and her daughter Marion.

The saw-mill was on the one point of solid mainland which ran down into the water cleanly and boldly, without

any fringe of marsh ; the river-channel was narrow here, and
a row-boat brought the saw-miller across to the Manning
cottage opposite three times each day.   His name was
Cranch, Ambrose Cranch, but everybody called him "Bro."
He took his meals at the cottage, and had taken them there
for years.   New-comers at Wilbarger, and those persons who
never have anything straight in their minds, supposed he was
a relative ; but he was not—only a friend.   Mrs. Manning
was a widow, fat, inefficient, and amiable.   Her daughter
Marion was a slender, erect young person of twenty-five
years of age, with straight eyebrows, gray eyes, a clearly cut,
delicate profile, and the calmness of perfect but unobtrusive
health.   She was often spoken of as an unmoved sort of girl,
and certainly there were few surface-ripples ; but there is a
proverb about still waters which sometimes came to the minds
of those who noticed physiognomy when they looked at her,
although it is but fair to add that those who noticed anything
in particular were rare in Wilbarger, where people were either
too indolent or too good-natured to make those conscientious
studies of their neighbors which are demanded by the code
of morals prevailing on the coast farther north.

Port Wilbarger was a very small seaport, situated on the
inland side of a narrow island ; the coastwise steamers going
north and south touched there, coming in around the water-
corner, passing the Old Town, the mile-long foot-bridge, and
stopping at the New Town for a few moments ; then. back-
ing around with floundering and splashing, and going away
again.   The small inside steamers, which came down from
the last city in the line of sea-cities south of New York by
an anomalous route advertised as "strictly inland all the way,"
also touched there, as if to take a free breath before plunging
again into the narrow, grassy channels, and turning curves
by the process of climbing the bank with the bow and letting
the stern swing round, while men with poles pushed off again.
It was the channel of this inside route which the railroad-
drawbridge crossed in the midst of a broad, sea-green prairie

below the town. As there was but one locomotive, and, when
it had gone down the road in the morning, nothing could
cross again until it came back at night, one would suppose
that the keeper might have left the bridge turned for the
steamers all day. But no: the superintendent was a man
of spirit, and conducted his railroad on the principle of
what it should be rather than what it was. He had a hand-
car of his own, and came rolling along the track at all hours,
sitting with dignity in an arm-chair while two red-shirted negroes worked at the crank. There were several drawbridges
on his route, and it was his pleasure that they should all be
exactly in place, save when a steamer was actually passing
through; he would not even allow the keepers to turn the
bridges a moment before it was necessary, and timed himself
sometimes so as to pass over on his hand-car when the bow
of the incoming boat was not ten yards distant.

But, even with its steamers, its railroad, and railroad superintendent of the spirit above described, Port Wilbarger
was but a sleepy, half-alive little town. Over toward the sea
it had a lighthouse and a broad, hard, silver-white beach,
which would have made the fortune of a Northern village;
but when a Northern visitor once exclaimed, enthusiastically,
"Why, I understand that you can walk for twenty miles
down that beach!" a Wilbarger citizen looked at him slowly,
and answered, "Yes, you can—if you *want* to." There was,
in fact, a kind of cold, creeping east wind, which did not rise
high enough to stir the tops of the trees to and fro, but
which, nevertheless, counted for a good deal over on that
beach.

Mrs. Manning was poor; but everybody was poor at
Wilbarger, and nobody minded it much. Marion was the
housekeeper and house-provider, and everything went on like
clock-work. Marion was like her father, it was said; but
nobody remembered him very clearly. He was a Northerner,
who had come southward seeking health, and finding none.
But he found Miss Forsythe instead, and married her. How

it happened that Ambrose Cranch, not a relative but a nondescript, should be living in a household presided over by
Forsythe blood, was as follows: First, he had put out years
before a fire in Mrs. Manning's kitchen which would otherwise have burned the wooden house to the ground ; that began the acquaintance. Second, learning that her small property was in danger of being swept away entirely, owing to
unpaid taxes and mismanagement, he made a journey to the
capital of the State in her behalf, and succeeded after much
trouble in saving a part of it for her. It was pure kindness
on his part in a time of general distress, and from another
man would have been called remarkable ; but nothing could
be called remarkable in Ambrose Cranch : he had never been
of any consequence in Wilbarger or his life. Mrs. Manning
liked him, and, after a while, asked him to come and take his
meals at the cottage : the saw-mill was directly opposite, and
it would be neighborly. Ambrose, who had always eaten his
dinners at the old Wilbarger Hotel, in the dark, crooked dining-room, which had an air of mystery not borne out by anything, unless it might be its soups, gladly accepted, and trans-
ferred his life to the mainland point and the cottage opposite,
with the row-boat as a ferry between. He was so inoffensive
and willing, and so skillful with his hands, that he was soon
as much a part of the household as old Dinah herself ; he
mended and repaired, praised the good dishes, watered the
flowers, and was an excellent listener. It would be amusing
to know how much the fact of being, or securing, a good
listener has to do with our lives. Mrs. Manning, fond of
reminiscence and long narratives which were apt to run off at
random, so that, whereas you began with the Browns, you
ended with something about the Smiths, and never heard the
Brown story at all, actually retained Ambrose Cranch at her
table for eleven years because he listened well. But she did
not realize it ; neither did he. A simpler, more unplotting
soul never existed than that in the saw-miller's body. A
word now as to that body: it had a good deal to do with its

owner's life, and our story. (O brothers and sisters, if Justice
holds the balance, how handsome some of us are going to be
in the next life!) Ambrose Cranch was tall and thin, what is
called rawboned; all his joints were large and prominent,
from his knuckles to his ankles. He had large, long feet and
hands, and large, long ears; his feet shambled when he
walked, his arms dangled from the shoulders like the arms of
a wooden doll, and he had a long, sinewed throat, which no
cravat or collar could hide, though he wore them up to his
ears. Not that he did so wear them, however: he had no
idea that his throat was ugly; he never thought about it at
all. He had a long face, small, mild blue eyes, thin, lank
brown hair, a large mouth, and long, narrow nose; he was, also,
the most awkward man in the world. Was there no redeem-
ing point? Hardly. His fingers were nicely finished at the
ends, and sometimes he had rather a sweet smile. But in the
contemplation of his joints, shoulders, elbows, wrists, and
knuckles, even the student of anatomy hardly got as far as
his finger-ends; and as to the smile, nobody saw it but the
Mannings, who did not care about it. In origin he was, as
before mentioned, a nondescript, having come from the up-
country, where Southern ways shade off into mountain roughness; which again gives place to the river-people, and they,
farther on, to the Hoosiers and Buckeyes, who are felicitously
designated by the expressive title of "Western Yankees."
He had inherited the saw-mill from an uncle, who had tried
to make something of it, failed, and died. Ambrose, being a
patient man, and one of smallest possible personal expendi-
ture, managed to live, and even to save a little money—but
only a little. He had been there twelve years, and was now
thirty-eight years old. All this the whole town of Wilbarger
knew, or might have known; it was no secret. But the saw-
mill had a secret of its own, besides. Up stairs, in the back
part, was a small room with a lock on the door, and windows
with red cloth nailed over them in place of glass. Here Ambrose spent many moments of his day, and all of his even-

ings, quite alone. His red lights shone across the marsh, and could be seen from Vickery Island and the drawbridge; but they were not visible on the Wilbarger side, and attracted, therefore, no attention. However, it is doubtful whether they would have attracted attention anyway. Wilbarger people did not throw away their somewhat rarely excited interest upon Ambrose Cranch, who represented to them the flattest commonplace. They knew when his logs came, they knew the quantity and quality of his boards, they saw him superintending the loading of the schooner that bore them away, and that was all. Even the two negroes who worked in the mill—one bright, young, and yellow; the other old, slow, and black—felt no curiosity about the locked room and Cranch's absences; it was but a part of his way.

What was in this room, then? Nothing finished as yet, save dreams. Cranch had that strong and singular bias of mind which makes, whether successful or unsuccessful, the inventor.

It was a part of his unconsequence in every way that all persons called him " Bro "—even his negro helpers at the mill. When he first came to live with Mrs. Manning, she had tried hard to speak of him as " Mr. Cranch," and had taught her daughter to use the title; but, as time wore on, she had dropped into Bro again, and so had Marion. But, now that Marion was twenty-five and her own mistress, she had taken up the custom of calling him " Ambrose," the only person in the whole of Wilbarger who used, or indeed knew, the name. This she did, not on his account at all, but on her own; she disliked nicknames, and did not consider it dignified to use them. Cranch enjoyed her " Ambrose " greatly, and felt an inward pride every time she spoke it; but he said nothing,

There was a seminary at Wilbarger—a forlorn, ill-supported institution, under the charge of the Episcopal Church of the diocese. But the Episcopal Church of the diocese was, for the time being, extremely poor, and its missions and

schools were founded more in a spirit of hope than in any
certainty of support ; with much the same faith, indeed, which
its young deacons show when they enter (as they all do at the
earliest possible moment) into the responsibilities of matrimony. But in this seminary was, by chance, an excellent
though melancholy-minded teacher—a Miss Drough, equally
given to tears and arithmetic. Miss Drough was an adept at
figures, and, taking a fancy to Marion Manning, she taught
her all she knew up to trigonometry, with chess problems and
some astronomy thrown in. Marion had no especial liking
for mathematics in the beginning, but her clear mind had followed her ardent teacher willingly : at twenty-five she was
a skilled arithmetician, passably well educated in ordinary
branches, well read in strictly old-fashioned literature, and
not very pious, because she had never liked the reverend gentleman in charge of the seminary and the small church—a
thin man who called himself "a worm," and always ate all
the best bits of meat, pressing, meanwhile, with great cordiality, the pale, watery sweet-potatoes upon the hungry
schoolgirls. She was also exceedingly contemptuous in manner as to anything approaching flirtation with the few cavaliers of Wilbarger. It is rather hard to call them cavaliers,
since they no longer had any good horses ; but they came
from a race of cavaliers, the true "armed horsemen" of
America, if ever we had any. The old-time Southerners
went about on horseback much more than on foot or in carriages ; and they went armed.

"Bro, will you mend the gate-latch ? " said Mrs. Manning
at the breakfast-table. They did not breakfast early ; Mrs.
Manning had never been accustomed to early breakfasts : the
work at the saw-mill began and went on for three hours before the saw-miller broke his fast. Bro mended the latch,
and then, after a survey of the garden, went up to the open
window of the dining-room and said :

"Shall I water the flowers, Miss Marion ? They look
sadly this morning."

"Yes, if you please, Ambrose," replied the erect young person within, who was washing the cups, and the few old spoons and forks she called " the silver." The flowers were a link between them ; they would not grow, and everybody told her they would not save Bro, who believed in them to the last, and watched even their dying struggles with unfailing hope. The trouble was that she set her mind upon flowers not suited to the soil ; she sent regularly for seeds and slips, and would have it that they must grow whether they wished to or not. Whatever their wishes were, floral intentions necessarily escaping our grosser senses, one thing was certain— grow they did not, in spite of Bro's care. He now watered the consumptives of the day tenderly ; he coaxed straggling branches and gently tied up weak ones, saw with concern that the latest balsam was gone, and, after looking at it for a while, thought it his duty to tell its mistress.

"I am sorry, Miss Marion," he said, going to the window-sill, " but the pink balsam is dead again."

"What can you mean by 'dead again'"? said a vexed but clear voice within. " It can not be dead but once, of course."

"We have had a good many balsams," replied Bro apologetically, " and even a good many pink ones, like this ; I forget sometimes."

"That is because you have no *real* love for flowers," said the irate young mistress from her dish-pan : she was provoked at the loss of the balsam—it was her last one.

Bro, who could not see her from where he stood, waited a moment or two, shuffled his feet to and fro on the sand, and noiselessly drummed on the sill with his long fingers ; then he went slowly down to the shore, where his boat was drawn up, and rowed himself across to the saw-mill. He felt a sort of guilt about that pink balsam, as though he had not perhaps taken enough care of it ; but, in truth, he had watched every hair's-breadth of its limp, reluctant growth, knew its moist veining accurately, and even the habits and opinions, as it were, of two minute green inhabitants, with six legs, of the size, taken both together, of a pin's point, who considered the stalk quite a prairie.

When she was eighteen and nineteen years old, Marion Manning had refused several suitors, giving as a reason to her mother that they were all detestable; since then, she had not been troubled with suitors to refuse. There were girls with more coloring and brighter eyes in Wilbarger, and girls with warmer hearts: so said the gossips. And, certainly, the calm reserve, the incisive words, and clear gray eyes that looked straight at you of Marion Manning were not calculated to encourage the embarrassed but at the same time decidedly favor-conferring attentions of the youths of the town. Mrs. Manning, in the course of the years they had been together, had gradually taken Bro as a humble confidant: he knew of the offers and refusals; he knew of the succeeding suitorless period which Mrs. Manning, a stanch believer in love and romance, bewailed as wasted time. "*I* could never have resisted young Echols," she said, " sitting there on the door-step as he used to, with the sun shining on his curly hair. But there! I always had a fancy for curls." Bro received these confidences with strict attention, as valuable items. But one peculiarity of his mind was that he never generalized; and thus, for instance, instead of taking in the fact that curly hair plays a part in winning a heart, he only understood that Mrs. Manning, for some reason or other, liked kinks and twists in the covering of the head; as some persons liked hempen shoestrings, others leathern.

" But Miss Marion is happy," he said once, when the suitorless period was two years old, and the mother lamenting.

" Yes; but we can not live our lives more than once, Bro, and these years will never come back to her. What keeps *me* up through all the privations I have suffered but the memory of the short but happy time of my own courtship and marriage?" Here Mrs. Manning shed tears. The memory

must, indeed, have been a strong one, the unregenerated humorist would have thought, to "keep up" such a weight as
hers. But Bro was not a humorist: that Mrs. Manning was
fat was no more to him than that he himself was lean. He
had the most implicit belief in the romance of her life, upon
which she often expatiated; he knew all about the first time
she saw him, and how she felt; he knew every detail of the
courtship. This was only when Marion was absent, however; the mother, voluble as she was, said but little on that
subject when her daughter was in the room.

"But Miss Marion is happy," again said Bro, when the
suitorless period was now five years old.

"No, she is not," replied the mother this time. "She be-
gins to feel that her life is colorless and blank; I can see she
does. She is not an ordinary girl, and needlework and house-
keeping do not content her. If she had an orphan asylum to
manage, now, or something of that kind— But, dear me!
what would suit her best, I do believe, would be drilling a
regiment," added Mrs. Manning, her comfortable amplitude
heaving with laughter. "She is as straight as a ramrod always, for all her delicate, small bones. What she would like
best of all, I suppose, would be keeping accounts; she will
do a sum now rather than any kind of embroidery, and a
page of figures is fairly meat and drink to her. That Miss
Drough has, I fear, done her more harm than good: you can
not make life exactly even, like arithmetic, nor balance quantities, try as you may. And, whatever variety men may succeed in getting, we women have to put up with a pretty
steady course of subtraction, I notice."

"I am sorry you do not think she is happy," said Bro
thoughtfully.

"There you go!" said Mrs. Manning. "I do not mean
that she is exactly *un*happy; but you never understand
things, Bro."

"I know it; I have had so little experience," said the
other. But Bro's experience, large or small, was a matter of

no interest to Mrs. Manning, who rambled on about her daughter.

"The Mannings were always slow to develop, Edward used to say : I sometimes think Marion is not older now at heart than most girls of eighteen. She has always been more like the best scholar, the clear-headed girl at the top of the class, than a woman with a woman's feelings. She will be bitterly miserable if she falls in love at last, and all in vain. An old maid in love is a desperate sight."

"What do you call an old maid ? " asked Bro.

" Any unmarried woman over—well, I used to say twenty-five, but Marion is that, and not much faded yet — say twenty-eight," replied Mrs. Manning, decisively, having to the full the Southern ideas on the subject.

" Then Miss Marion has three years more ? "

" Yes ; but, dear me ! there is no one here she will look at. What I am afraid of is, that, after I am dead and gone, poor Marion, all thin and peaked (for she does not take after me in flesh), with spectacles on her nose, and little wrinkles at the corners of her eyes, will be falling in love with some one who will not care for her at all. I should say a clergyman," pursued Mrs. Manning meditatively, " only Marion hates clergymen ; a professor, then, or something of the kind. If I only had money enough to take her away and give her a change ! She might see somebody then who would not wind his legs around his chair."

" Around his chair ? "

"Yes," said Mrs. Manning, beginning on another knitting-needle. " Have you not noticed how all the young men about here twist their feet around the legs of their chairs, especially when telling a long story or at table ? Sometimes it is one foot, sometimes the other, and sometimes both, which I acknowledge *is* awkward. What pleasure they find in it I can not imagine ; *I* should think it would be dislocating. Young Harding, now, poor fellow ! had almost no fault but that."

" And Miss Marion dislikes it ? I hope *I* do not do it
then," said Bro simply.

" Well, no," replied Mrs. Manning.   " You see, your feet
are rather long, Bro."

They were ; it would have taken a giant's chair to give
them space enough to twist.

So Bro's life went on : the saw-mill to give him bread and
clothes, Mrs. Manning to listen to, the flowers to water, and,
at every other leisure moment night and day, his inventions.
For there were several, all uncompleted : a valve for a steam-
engine, an idea for a self-register, and, incidentally, a screw.
He had most confidence in the valve ; when completed, it
would regenerate the steam-engines of the world.   The self-
register gave him more trouble ; it haunted him, but would
not come quite right.   He covered pages of paper with calculations concerning it.   He had spent about twenty thousand
hours, all told, over that valve and register during his eleven
years at the saw-mill, and had not once been tired.   He had
not yet applied for patents, although the screw was complete.
That was a trifle : he would wait for his more important
works.

One day old Mr. Vickery, having watched the superintendent roll safely past down the road on his way to Bridge No.
2, left his charge in the care of old Julius for the time being,
and walked up the track toward Wilbarger.   It was the
shortest road to the village—indeed, the only road ; but one
could go by water.   Before the days of the railroad, the
Vickerys always went by water, in a wide-cushioned row-
boat, with four pairs of arms to row.   It was a great day, of
course, when the first locomotive came over Vickery Marsh ;
but old Mr. Vickery was lamentably old-fashioned, and preferred the small days of the past, with the winding, silver
channels and the row-boat, and the sense of wide possession
and isolation produced by the treeless, green expanse which
separated him from the town.   To-day, however, he did not
stop to think of these things, but hastened on as fast as his

short legs could carry him. Mrs. Manning was an old friend
of his; to her house he was hurrying.

"You are both—you are both," he gasped, bursting into
the sitting-room and sinking into a chair—"you are both—
ah, ugh! ugh!"

He choked, gurgled, and turned from red to purple. Mrs.
Manning seized a palm-leaf fan, and fanned him vigorously.

"Why *did* you walk so fast, Mr. Vickery?" she said reproachfully. "You know your short breath can not stand it."

"You would, too, Nannie," articulated the old man, "if—
if *your* boy had come home!"

"What, Lawrence? You do not mean it!" she exclaimed,
sinking into a chair in her turn, and fanning herself now. "I
congratulate you, Mr. Vickery; I do, indeed. How long is it
since you have seen him?"

"Thirteen years; thir—teen years! He was fifteen when
he went away, you know," whispered the old man, still giving
out but the husky form of words without any voice to support
them. "Under age, but would go. Since then he has been
wandering over the ocean and all about, the bold boy!"

"Dear me!" said Mrs. Manning; "how glad I shall be to
see him! I was very fond of his mother."

"Yes; Sally was a sweet little woman, and Lawrence
takes after his mother more than after his father, I see. My
son was a true Vickery; yes, a true Vickery. But what I
came to say was, that you and Marion must both come over
to-morrow and spend the day. We must kill the fatted calf,
Nannie—indeed we must."

Then, with his first free breath, the old man was obliged
to go, lest the superintendent should return unexpectedly and
find him absent. There was also the fatted calf to be provided: Julius must go across to the mainland and hunt down
a wild turkey.

At dinner Mrs. Manning had this great news to tell her
listener—two now, since Marion had returned.

"Who do you think has come home?" she said, enjoying

her words as she spoke them.   " Who but old Mr. Vickery's
grandson, Lawrence, his only living grandchild! He went
away thirteen years ago, and one of the sweetest boys I ever
knew he was then.—You remember him, Marion."

" I remember a boy," answered Marion briefly.   " He
never would finish any game, no matter what it was, but
always wanted to try something new."

" Like his mother," said Mrs. Manning, heaving a reminis-
cent sigh, and then laughing.   "Sally Telfair used to change
about the things in her work-basket and on her table every
day of her life.   Let me see—Lawrence must be twenty-eight
now."

" He has come back, I suppose, to take care of his grandfather in his old age," said Bro, who was eating his dinner in
large, slow mouthfuls, in a manner which might have been
called ruminative if ruminating animals were not generally
fat.

" Yes, of course," replied Mrs. Manning, with her comfortable belief in everybody's good motives.

When Marion and her mother returned home the next
day at dusk a third person was with them as they walked
along the track, their figures outlined clearly against the orange
after-glow in the west. Bro, who had come across for his tea,
saw them, and supposed it was young Vickery. He supposed
correctly. Young Vickery came in, staid to tea, and spent
the evening. Bro, as usual, went over to the mill. The next
day young Vickery came again, and the next; the third day
the Mannings went over to the island. Then it began over
again.

" I do hope, Bro, that your dinners have been attended to
properly," said Mrs. Manning, during the second week of
these visitations.

" Oh, yes, certainly," replied Bro, who would have eaten
broiled rhinoceros unnoticingly.

" You see Mr. Vickery has the old-time ideas about company and visiting to celebrate a great occasion, and Lawrence's

return is, of course, that. It is a perfect marvel to hear where, or rather where not, that young man has been."

" Where ? " said Bro, obediently asking the usual question which connected Mrs. Manning's narratives, and gave them a reason for being.

" Everywhere. All over the wide world, I should say."

" Oh, no, mother; he was in Germany most of the time," said Marion.

" He saw the Alps, Marion."

" The Bavarian Alps."

" And he saw France."

" From the banks of the Moselle."

" And Russia, and Holland, and Bohemia," pursued Mrs. Manning. " You will never make me believe that one can see all *those* countries from Germany, Marion. Germany was never of so much importance in *my* day. And to think, too, that he has lived in Bohemia ! I must ask him about it. I have never understood where it was, exactly; but I *have* heard persons called Bohemians who had not a foreign look at all."

" He did not *live* in Bohemia, mother."

" Oh, yes, he did, child; I am sure I heard him say so."

" You are thinking of Bavaria."

" Marion ! Marion ! how can you tell what I am thinking of ? " said Mrs. Manning oracularly. " There is no rule of arithmetic that can tell you that. But here is Lawrence himself at the door.—You *have* lived in Bohemia, have you not ? " she asked, as the young man entered : he came in and out now like one of the family. " Marion says you have not."

" Pray, don't give it up, but stick to that opinion, Miss Marion," said the young man, with a merry glint in his eyes. Ah ! yes, young Vickery had wandered, there was no doubt of it ; he used contractions, and such words as " stick." Mrs. Manning and Marion had never said " don't " or " can't " in their lives.

" I do not know what you mean," replied Marion, a slight

color rising in her cheeks. "It is not a matter of opinion one
way or the other, but of fact. You either have lived in Bohemia, or you have not."

"Well, then, I have," said Vickery, laughing.

"There! Marion," exclaimed Mrs. Manning triumphantly.

Vickery, overcome by mirth, turned to Bro, as if for relief; Bro was at least a man.

But Bro returned his gaze mildly, comprehending nothing.

"Going over to the mill?" said Vickery. "I'll go with
you, and have a look about."

They went off together, and Vickery examined the mill
from top to bottom; he measured the logs, inspected the engine, chaffed the negroes, climbed out on the roof, put his
head into Bro's cell-like bedroom, and came at last to the
locked door.

"What have we here?" he asked.

"Only a little workshop of mine, which I keep locked,"
replied Bro.

"So I see. But what's inside?"

"Nothing of much consequence—as yet," replied the other,
unable to resist adding the adverb.

"You must let me in," said Vickery, shaking the door.
"I never could abide a secret. Come, Bro; I won't tell. Let
me in, or I shall climb up at night and break in," he added
gayly.

Bro stood looking at him in silence. Eleven years had he
labored there alone, too humble to speak voluntarily of his
labors; too insignificant, apparently, for questions from others.
Although for the most part happy over his work, there were
times when he longed for a friendly ear to talk to, for other
eyes to criticise, the sympathy of other minds, the help of
other hands. At these moments he felt drearily lonely over
his valve and register; they even seemed to mock him. He
was not imaginative, yet occasionally they acted as if moved
by human motives, and, worse still, became fairly devilish in
their crooked perverseness. Nobody had ever asked before

to go into that room. Should he? Should he not? Should
he? Then he did.

Lawrence, at home everywhere, sat on a high stool, and
looked on with curiosity while the inventor brought out his
inventions and explained them. It was a high day for Bro :
new life was in him ; he talked rapidly ; a dark color burned
in his thin cheeks. He talked for one hour without stopping,
the buzz of the great saw below keeping up an accompaniment ; then he paused.

" How do they seem to you ? " he asked feverishly.

" Well, I have an idea that self-registers are about all they
can be now ; I have seen them in use in several places at the
North," said Lawrence. " As to the steam-valve, I don't
know ; there may be something in it. But there is no doubt
about that screw : for some uses it is perfect, better than anything we have, I should say."

" Oh, the screw ? " said the other man, in a slow, disappointed voice. " Yes, it is a good screw ; but the valve—"

" Yes, as you say, the valve," said Lawrence, jumping
down from his stool, and looking at this and that carelessly
on his way to the door. " I don't comprehend enough of the
matter, Bro, to judge. But you send up that screw to Washington at once and get a patent out on it ; you will make
money, I know."

He was gone ; there was nothing more to see in the saw-
mill, so he paddled across, and went down toward the dock.
The smoke of a steamer coming in from the ocean could be
seen ; perhaps there would be something going on down
there.

" He is certainly a remarkably active young fellow,' said
Mrs. Manning, as she saw the top of his head passing, the
path along-shore being below the level of the cottage. " He
has seen more in Wilbarger already than I have ever seen
here in all my life."

" We are, perhaps, a little old-fashioned, mother," replied
Marion.

"Perhaps we are, child. Fashions always were a long
time in reaching Wilbarger. But there! what did it matter?
We had them sooner or later, though generally later. Still,
bonnets came quite regularly. But I have never cared much
about bonnets," pursued Mrs. Manning reflectively, "since
capes went out, and those sweet ruches in front, full of little
rose-buds. There is no such thing now as a majestic bonnet."

Bro came over to tea as usual. He appeared changed.
This was remarkable; there had never been any change in
him before, as far back as they could remember.

"You are surely not going to have a fever?" asked Mrs.
Manning anxiously, skilled in fever symptoms, as are all
dwellers on that shore.

"No; I have been a little overturned in mind this afternoon, that is all," replied Bro. Then, with a shadow of importance, "I am obliged to write to Washington."

"What *do* you mean?" asked Mrs. Manning, for once
assuming the position of questioner.

"I have invented a—screw," he answered, hesitatingly—
"a screw, which young Mr. Vickery thinks a good one. I
am going to apply for a patent on it."

"Dear me! Apply for a patent? Do you know how?"

"Yes, I know how," replied the inventor quietly.

Marion was looking at him in surprise.

"You *invented* the screw, Ambrose?"

"Yes, Miss Marion." Then, unable to keep down his
feelings any longer—"But there is a valve also," he added
with pride, "which seems to *me* more important; and there
is a self-register."

"Lawrence was over there this evening, was he not?
And you showed him your inventions then?"

"Yes, Miss Marion, I did."

"But why in the world, Bro, have you not told *us*, or, indeed, any one, about them all these years?" interposed Mrs.
Manning, surveying her listener with new eyes.

"You did not ask; nobody has ever asked. Mr. Vickery is the only one."

" Then it was Lawrence who advised you to write to Washington ? " said Marion.

" Yes."

" You will take me over to the mill immediately," said the girl, rising; "I wish to see everything.—And, mother, will you come, too? "

"Certainly," replied Mrs. Manning, with a determination to go in spite of her avoirdupois, the darkness, the row-boat, and the steep mill-stairs. She was devoured by curiosity, and performed the journey without flinching. When they reached the work-room at last, Bro, in his excitement, lighted all the lamps he had in the mill and brought them in, so that the small place was brilliant. Mrs. Manning wondered and ejaculated, tried not to knock over small articles, listened, comprehended nothing, and finally took refuge mentally with the screw and physically in an old arm-chair; these two things at least she understood. Marion studied the valve a long time, listening attentively to Bro's eager explanations. " I can make nothing of it," she said at last, in a vexed tone.

" Neither could Mr. Vickery," said Bro.

She next turned to the register, and, before long, caught its idea.

" It is not *quite* right yet, for some reason," explained the inventor, apologetically.

She looked over his figures.

" It is plain enough why it is not right," she said, after a moment, in her schoolmistress tone. " Your calculations are wrong. Give me a pencil." She went to work at once, and soon had a whole sheet covered. " It will take me some time," she said, glancing up at the end of a quarter of an hour. " If you are tired, mother, you had better go back."

" I think I will," said Mrs. Manning, whose mind was now on the darkness and the row-boat. Bro went with her, and then returned. The mother no more thought of asking her

daughter to leave a column of unfinished figures than of asking a child to leave an unfinished cake.

"Do not interrupt me now, but sit down and wait," said
Marion, without looking up, when Bro came back. He
obeyed, and did not stir; instead, he fell to noticing the effect
of her profile against the red cloth over the window. It took
Marion longer than she expected to finish the calculation;
her cheeks glowed over the work. "There!" she said at
last, throwing down the pencil and pushing the paper toward
him. She had succeeded; the difficulty was practically at an
end. Bro looked at the paper and at her with admiring pride.

"It is your invention now," he said.

"Oh, no; I only did the sum for you. Astronomers often
have somebody to do the sums for them."

"I shall apply for patents on all three now," said Bro;
"and the register *is* yours, Miss Marion. In eleven years I
have not succeeded in doing what you have just done in an
hour."

"So much the worse for you, Ambrose," replied Marion
lightly. She was quite accustomed to his praise, she had had
it steadily from childhood. If not always gracefully expressed,
at least it was always earnest; but, like Ambrose, of no consequence.

Bro made his application in due form. Young Vickery
volunteered to write to an acquaintance in Washington, a
young lawyer, who aspired to "patent business," asking him,
as he expressed it, to "see Bro through." "No sharp practice in this case, Dan," he wrote privately. "Cranch is poor,
and a friend of friends of mine; do your best for him."

But, although he thus good-naturedly assisted the man, he
laughed at the woman for her part in the figures, which Bro
had related with pride.

"What will you do next?" he said. "Build a stone wall
—or vote? Imagine a girl taking light recreation in equa-
tions, and letting her mind wander hilariously among groves
of triangles on a rainy day!"

Marion colored highly, but said nothing. Her incisiveness seemed to fail her when with Lawrence Vickery. And, as he was never more than half in earnest, it was as hard to use real weapons against him as to fence with the summer wind. The young man seemed to have taken a fancy to Bro ; he spent an hour or two at the saw-mill almost every day, and Cæsar had become quite accustomed to his voice shouting for the boat. But the old negro liked him, and came across cheerfully, even giving him voluntarily the title " marse," which the blacks withheld whenever they pleased now, and tenaciously. Vickery took Bro over to see his grandfather, the old house, and the wastes which were once their cotton-fields. He had no pride about the old gentleman's lowly office ; he had roamed about the world too much for that. And, when Bro suggested that he should take the position himself and relieve his grandfather, he answered carelessly that his grandfather did not want to be relieved, which was true—old Mr. Vickery deriving the only amusement of his life now in plans for outwitting, in various small ways, the spirited superintendent.

" However," said Lawrence, " I could not in any case ; I have plans of importance waiting for me."

" Where ? " asked Bro.

" Well—abroad. I don't mind telling *you*," said Vickery ; " but it is a secret at present."

" Then you do not intend to stay here ? "

" Here ? Bless you, no ! The place is a howling, one-horse desert. I only came back awhile to see the old man."

The " while " lasted all winter. Young Vickery exhausted the town, the island, and the whole district ; he was " hail fellow " with everybody, made acquaintance with the light-house-keeper, knew the captains of all the schooners, and even rode on the hand-car and was admitted to the friendship of the superintendent. But, in the way of real intimacy, the cottage and the saw-mill were his favorite haunts. He was with Marion a part of every day ; he teased her, laughed at her flowers, mimicked her precise pronunciation, made cari-

11

catures of her friend Miss Drough, and occasionally walked
by with Nannie Barr, the most consummate little flirt in the
town.   Marion changed—that is, inwardly.   She was too
proud to alter her life outwardly, and, beyond putting away
the chess-problem book, and walking with Miss Drough in
quiet paths through the andromeda and smilax thickets, or
out on the barrens among the saw-palmettoes, rather than
through the streets of the town, what she *did* was the same
as usual.   But she was not what she had been.   She seemed
to have become timid, almost irresolute; she raised her eyes
quickly and dropped them as quickly: the old calm, steady
gaze was gone; her color came and went.   She was still erect
as ever : she could not change that; but she seemed disposed
to sit more in the shadow, or half behind the curtain, or to
withdraw to her own room, where the bolt was now often
used which had formerly rusted in its place.   Bro noticed all
this.   Marion's ways had not been changeable like those of
most girls, and he had grown into knowing them exactly :
being a creature of precise habit himself, he now felt uncomfortable and restless because she was so.   At last he spoke to
her mother.   " She is certainly changed : do you think there
is any danger of fever ? " he asked uneasily.   But Mrs. Manning only blinked and nodded smilingly back in answer, holding up her finger to signify that Marion was within hearing.
Supposing that he had comprehended her, of course, and glad
to have a confidant, she now blinked and nodded at him from
all sides—from behind doors, from over Marion's head, from
out of the windows, even throwing her confidential delight to
him across the river as he stood in the saw-mill doorway.
Marion, then, was going through something—something not
to be mentioned, but only mysteriously nodded—which was
beneficial to her; what could it be ?   She had taken to going
very frequently to church lately, in spite of her dislike to "the
worm," who still occupied the pulpit.   Bro went back to the
experience of his youth in the up-country, the only experience
he had to go back to, and decided that she must be having

what they used to call there " a change of heart." Upon
mentioning this in a furtive tone to Mrs. Manning, she
laughed heartily, rather to his surprise, for he was a reverent
sort of non-churchgoing pagan, and said, " Very good, Bro—
very good, indeed ! "

He decided that he had guessed rightly; the Episcopalian
was, he had heard, a very cheerful kind of religion, tears and
groaning not being required of its neophytes.

But his eyes were to be opened. The last trump could
not have startled him more than something he saw with his
own eyes one day. It happened in this way : There was an
accident on the wharf ; a young man was crushed between
the end of the dock and the side of the steamer; some one
came running to the cottage and said it was Lawrence Vickery. Mrs. Manning, the hands at the mill, and even old Dinah, started off at once ; the whole town was hurrying to the
scene. Bro, shut up in his workroom, going over his beloved
valve again, did not hear or see them. It was nearly dinner-
time, and, when he came out and found no boat, he was surprised ; but he paddled himself across on a rude raft he had,
and went up to the cottage. The doors stood open all over
the house as the hasty departures had left them, and he heard
Marion walking up and down in her room up stairs, sobbing
aloud and wildly. He had never heard her sob before ; even
as a child she had been reticent and self-controlled. He
stood appalled at the sound. What could it betoken ? He
stole to the foot of the stairs and listened. She was moaning
Lawrence's name over and over to herself — " Lawrence !
Lawrence ! Lawrence ! " He started up the stairs, hardly
knowing what he was doing. Her grief was dreadful to him :
he wanted to comfort her, but did not know how. He hardly
realized what the cry meant. But it was to come to him.
The heart-broken girl, who neither saw nor heard him, although he was now just outside the door, drew a locket from
her bosom and kissed it passionately with a flood of despairing, loving words. Then, as if at the end of her strength,

with a sigh like death, she sank to the floor lifeless; she had
fainted.

After a moment the man entered. He seemed to himself
to have been standing outside that door for a limitless period
of time ; like those rare, strange sensations we feel of having
done the same thing or spoken the same words before in
some other and unknown period of existence. He lifted Marion carefully and laid her on a lounge. As he moved her,
the locket swung loose against her belt on the long ribbon
which was fastened underneath her dress around her throat.
It was a clumsy, old-fashioned locket, with an open face, and
into its small frame she herself had inserted a photograph of
Lawrence Vickery, cut from a *carte de visite*. Bro saw it :
the open face of the locket was toward him, and he could not
help seeing. It occurred to him then vaguely that, as she had
worn it concealed, it should be again hidden before other eyes
saw it—before she could know that even his had rested upon
it. With shaking fingers he took out his knife, and, opening
its smallest blade, he gently severed the ribbon, took off the
locket, and put it into her pocket. It was surprising to see
how skillfully his large, rough hands did this. Then, with an
afterthought, he found a worn place in the ribbon's end, and
severed it again by pulling it apart, taking the cut portion
away with him. His idea was, that she would think the ribbon had parted of itself at the worn spot, and she did think
so. It was a pretty, slender little ribbon, of bright rose-color.
When all was finished, he went to seek assistance. He knew
no more what to do for her physically than he would have
known what to do for an angel. Although there was not the
faintest sign of consciousness, he had carefully refrained from
even touching her unnecessarily in the slightest degree : it
seemed to him profanation. But there was no one in the
house. He went to the gate, and there caught sight of Mrs.
Manning hurrying homeward across the sandy waste.

" It is all a mistake," she panted, with the tears still dropping on her crimson cheeks. " It was not Lawrence at all,

but young Harding. Lawrence has gone down the road with the superintendent ; but poor young Harding is, I fear, fatally injured."

Even then automatic memory brought to Bro's mind only the idea, " He will never twist his feet around chair-legs any more ! It was almost the only fault he had, poor fellow ! "

" Miss Marion is not quite well, I think," he said. " I heard her crying a little up stairs as I came in."

" Of course," said the mother, " poor child ! But it is all over now.—It was not Lawrence at all, Marion," she cried loudly, hurrying up the path to the doorway ; " it was only young Harding."

Love has ears, even in semi-death, and it heard that cry. When Mrs. Manning, breathless, reached her daughter's room, she found her on the lounge still, but with recovered consciousness, and even palely smiling. The picture was safely in her pocket ; she supposed, when she found it, that she must have placed it there herself. She never had any suspicion of Bro's presence or his action.

The saw-miller had disappeared. Mrs. Manning supposed that he, in his turn, had gone to the dock or to the Harding cottage.

When he came in to tea that night he looked strangely, but was able to account for it.

" Letters from Washington," he said. Then he paused ; they looked at him expectantly. " The idea of the register is not a new one," he added slowly ; " it has already been patented."

" My inheritance is gone, then," said Marion gayly.

She spoke without reflection, being so happy now in the reaction of her great relief that she was very near talking nonsense, a feminine safety-valve which she hardly ever before had had occasion to seek.

" Yes," said Bro, a pained quiver crossing his face for an instant. " The valve also is pronounced worthless," he added in a monotonous voice.

Mother and daughter noticed his tone and his lifeless look; they attributed it to his deep, bitter disappointment, and felt sorry for him.

"But the screw, Bro?" said Mrs. Manning.

"That is successful, I believe; the patent is granted."

"I knew it," she replied triumphantly. "Even *I* could see the great merits it had. I congratulate you, Bro."

"So do I," said Marion. She would have congratulated anybody that evening.

"The valve is a disappointment to me," said the man, speaking steadily, although dully. "I had worked over it so long that I counted upon it as certain."

Then he rose and went over to the mill.

In the mean time Lawrence Vickery was riding homeward comfortably on the hand-car, and had no idea that he was supposed to be dead. But he learned it; and learned something else also from Marion's sensitive, tremulous face, delicate as a flower. A warm-hearted, impulsive fellow, he was touched by her expression, and went further than he intended. That is to say, that, having an opportunity, thanks to Mrs. Manning, who went up stairs, purposely leaving them alone together, he began by taking Marion's hand reassuringly, and looking into her eyes, and ended by having her in his arms and continuing to look into her eyes, but at a much nearer range. In short, he put himself under as firm betrothal bonds as ever a man did in the whole history of betrothals.

In the mean time the soft-hearted mother, sitting in the darkness up stairs, was shedding tears tenderly, and thinking of her own betrothal. That Lawrence was poor was a small matter to her, compared with the fact that Marion was loved at last, and happy. Lawrence was a Vickery, and the son of her old friend; besides, to her, as to most Southern women, the world is very well lost for the sake of love.

And Bro, over at the saw-mill?

His red lights shone across the marsh as usual, and he was in his work-room; in his hand was the model of his valve. He had made it tell a lie that night; he had used it as a mask. He gazed at it, the creature of his brain, his companion through long years, and he felt that he no longer cared whether it was good for anything or not! Then he remembered listlessly that it *was* good for nothing; the highest authorities had said so. But, gone from him now was the comprehension of their reasons, and this he began to realize. He muttered over a formula, began a calculation, both well known to him; he could do neither. His mind strayed from its duty idly, as a loose bough sways in the wind. He put his hands to his head and sat down. He sat there motionless all night.

But oh, how happy Marion was! Not effusively, not spokenly, but internally; the soft light shining out from her heart, however, as it does through a delicate porcelain shade. Old Mr. Vickery was delighted too, and a new series of invitations followed in honor of the betrothal; even the superintendent was invited, and came on his hand-car. Bro was included also, but he excused himself. His excuses were accepted without insistence, because it was understood that he was almost heart-broken by his disappointments. Joy and sorrow meet. When the engagement had lasted five weeks, and Marion had had thirty-five days of her new happiness, the old grandfather died, rather suddenly, but peacefully, and without pain. Through a long, soft April day he lay quietly looking at them all, speechless but content; and then at sunset he passed away. Mrs. Manning wept heartily, and Marion too; even Lawrence was not ashamed of the drops on his cheeks as he surveyed the kind old face, now for ever still. Everybody came to the funeral, and everybody testified respect; then another morning broke, and life went on again. The sun shines just the same, no matter who has been laid in the earth, and the flowers bloom. This seems to the mourner a strange thing, and a hard. In this case, however, there was no one to suffer the extreme pain of violent separation, for all the old man's companions and contemporaries were already gone; he was the last.

Another month went by, and another; the dead heats of summer were upon them. Marion minded them not; scorching air and arctic snows were alike to her when Lawrence was with her. Poor girl! she had the intense, late-coming love of her peculiar temperament: to please him she would have continued smiling on the rack itself until she died. But why, after all, call her "poor"? Is not such love, even if unreturned, great riches?

Bro looked at her, and looked at her, and looked at her. He had fallen back into his old way of life again, and nobody noticed anything unusual in him save what was attributed to his disappointment.

"You see he had shut himself up there, and worked over that valve for years," explained Mrs. Manning; "and, not letting anybody know about it either, he had come to think too much of it, and reckon upon it as certain. He was always an odd, lonely sort of man, you know, and this has told upon him heavily."

By and by it became evident that Lawrence was restless. He had sold off what he could of his inheritance, but that was only the old furniture; no one wanted the sidling, unrepaired house, which was now little better than a shell, or the deserted cotton-fields, whose dikes were all down. He had a scheme for going abroad again; he could do better there, he said; he had friends who would help him.

"Shall you take Miss Marion?" asked Bro, speaking unexpectedly, and, for him, markedly. They were all present.

"Oh, no," said Lawrence, "not now. How could I? But I shall come back for her soon." He looked across at his betrothed with a smile. But Marion had paled suddenly, and Bro had seen it.

The next event was a conversation at the mill.

Young Vickery wandered over there a few days later. He was beginning to feel despondent and weary: everything at Wilbarger was at its summer ebb, and the climate, too, affected him. Having become really fond of Marion now, and accustomed to all the sweetness of her affection, he hated to think of leaving her; yet he must. He leaned against the window-sill, and let out disjointed sentences of discontent to Bro; it even seemed a part of his luck that it should be dead low water outside as he glanced down, and all the silver channels slimy.

"That saw makes a fearful noise," he said.

"Come into my room," said Bro; "you will not hear it so plainly there." It was not the work-room, but the bedroom. The work-room was not mentioned now, out of kindness to Bro. Lawrence threw himself down on the narrow bed, and dropped his straw hat on the floor. "The world's a miserable hole," he said, with unction.

Bro sat down on a three-legged stool, the only approach to a chair in the room, and looked at him; one hand, in the pocket of his old, shrunk linen coat, was touching a letter.

"Bah!" said Lawrence, clasping his hands under his head and stretching himself out to his full length on the bed, "how in the world *can* I leave her, Bro? Poor little thing!"

Now to Bro, to whom Marion had always seemed a cross between a heavenly goddess and an earthly queen, this epithet was startling; however, it was, after all, but a part of the whole.

"It is a pity that you *should* leave her," he replied slowly. "It would be much better to take her with you."

"Yes, I know it would. I am a fickle sort of fellow, too, and have all sorts of old entanglements over there, besides. They might take hold of me again."

Bro felt a new and strange misgiving, which went through three distinct phases, with the strength and depth of an ocean, in less than three seconds: first, bewilderment at the new idea that anybody *could* be false to Marion; second, a wild, darting hope for himself; third, the returning iron conviction that it could never be, and that, if Lawrence deserted Marion, she would die.

"If you had money, what would you do?" he asked, coming back to the present heavily.

"Depends upon how much it was."

"Five thousand dollars?"

"Well—I'd marry on that, but not very hilariously, old fellow."

"Ten?"

"That would do better."

Nothing has as yet been said of Lawrence Vickery's appearance. It will be described now, and will, perhaps, throw light backward over this narration.

Imagine a young man, five feet eleven inches in height, straight, strong, but slender still, in spite of his broad shoulders; imagine, in addition, a spirited head and face, bright, steel-blue eyes, a bold profile, and beautiful mouth, shaded by a golden mustache; add to this, gleaming white teeth, a dimple in the cleft, strongly molded chin, a merry laugh, and a thoroughly manly air; and you have Lawrence Broughton Vickery at twenty-eight.

When at last he took himself off, and went over to see Marion and be more miserable still, Bro drew the letter from his pocket, and read it for the sixth or seventh time. During these months his screw had become known, having been pushed persistently by the enterprising young lawyer who aspired to patent business in the beginning, and having held its own since by sheer force of merit. The enterprising young lawyer had, however, recently forsaken law for politics; he had gone out to one of the Territories with the intention of returning some day as senator when the Territory should be a State (it is but fair to add that his chance is excellent). But he had, of course, no further knowledge of the screw, and Bro now managed the business himself. This letter was from a firm largely engaged in the manufacture of machinery, and it contained an offer for the screw and patent outright—ten thousand dollars.

"I shall never invent anything more," thought Bro, the

words of the letter writing themselves vacantly on his brain.
"Something has gone wrong inside my head in some way,
and the saw-mill will be all I shall ever attend to again."

Then he paused.

"It would be worth more money in the end if I could keep
it," he said to himself. "But even a larger sum might not
serve so well later, perhaps." It was all to be Marion's in
either case—which would be best? Then he remembered
her sudden pallor, and that decided him. "He shall have it
now," he said. "How lucky that he was content with ten!"

Some men would have given the money also in the same
circumstances; but they would have given it to Marion. It
was characteristic of Bro's deep and minute knowledge of the
girl, and what would be for her happiness, that he planned to
give the money to the man, and thus weight down and steady
the lighter nature.

He dwelt a long time upon ways and means; he was several days in making up his mind. At last he decided what to
do; and did it.

Three weeks afterward a letter came to Wilbarger, directed in a clear handwriting to "Mr. Lawrence Broughton
Vickery." It was from a Northern lawyer, acting for another
party, and contained an offer for Vickery Island with its
house, cotton-fields, and marsh; price offered, ten thousand
dollars. The lawyer seemed to be acquainted with the size
of the island, the condition of the fields and out-buildings;
he mentioned that the purchase was made with the idea of
reviving the cotton-culture immediately, similar attempts on
the part of Rhode Island manufacturers, who wished to raise
their own cotton, having succeeded on the sea-islands farther
north. Lawrence, in a whirl of delight, read the letter aloud
in a cottage-parlor, tossed it over gayly to Mrs. Manning, and
clasped Marion in his arms.

"Well, little wife," he said happily, stroking her soft hair,
"we shall go over the ocean together now."

And Bro looked on.

The wedding took place in the early autumn. Although comparatively quiet, on account of old Mr. Vickery's death, all Wilbarger came to the church, and crowded into the cottage afterward. By a happy chance, "the worm" was at the North, soliciting aid for his "fold," and Marion was married by a gentle little missionary, who traversed the watery coast-district in a boat instead of on horseback, visiting all the sea-islands, seeing many sad, closed little churches, and encountering not infrequently almost pure paganism and fetich-worship among the neglected blacks. Bro gave the bride away. It was the proudest moment of his life—and the saddest.

"Somebody must do it," Mrs. Manning had said; "and why not Bro? He has lived in our house for twelve years, and, after all, now that old Mr. Vickery is gone, he is in one way our nearest friend.—Do let me ask him, Marion."

"Very well," assented the bride, caring but little for anything now but to be with Lawrence every instant.

She did, however, notice Bro during the crowded although informal reception which followed the ceremony. In truth, he was noticeable. In honor of the occasion, he had ordered from Savannah a suit of black, and had sent the measurements himself; the result was remarkable, the coat and vest being as much too short for him as the pantaloons were too long. He wore a white cravat, white-cotton gloves so large that he looked all hands, and his button-hole was decked with flowers, as many as it could hold. In this garb he certainly was an extraordinary object, and his serious face appearing at the top made the effect all the more grotesque. Marion was too good-hearted to smile; but she did say a word or two in an undertone to Lawrence, and the two young people had their own private amusement over his appearance.

But Bro was unconscious of it, or of anything save the task he had set for himself. It was remarked afterward that "really Bro Cranch talked almost like other people, joked and laughed, too, if you will believe it, at that Manning wedding."

Lawrence promised to bring his wife home at the end of a

year to see her mother, and perhaps, if all went well, to take
the mother back with them. Mrs. Manning, happy and sad
together, cried and smiled in a breath. But Marion was radiant as a diamond; her gray eyes flashed light. Not even
when saying good-by could she pretend to be anything but
supremely happy, even for a moment. By chance Bro had
her last look as the carriage rolled away; he went over to the
mill carrying it with him, and returned no more that night.

Wilbarger began to wonder after a while when that Rhode
Island capitalist would begin work in his cotton-fields; they
are wondering still. In course of time, and through the
roundabout way he had chosen, Bro received the deeds of
sale; he made his will, and left them to Marion. Once Mrs.
Manning asked him about the screw.

"I have heard nothing of it for some time," he replied;
and she said no more, thinking it had also, like the valve,
proved a failure. In the course of the winter the little work-
room was dismantled and the partitions taken down; there is
nothing there now but the plain wall of the mill. The red
lights no longer shine across the marsh to Vickery Island, and
there is no one there to see them. The new keeper lives in a
cabin at the bridge, and plays no tricks on the superintendent,
who, a man of spirit still, but not quite so sanguine as to the
future of Wilbarger, still rolls by on his hand-car from northeast to southeast.

Bro has grown old; he is very patient with everybody.
Not that he ever was impatient, but that patience seems now
his principal characteristic. He often asks to hear portions of
Marion's letters read aloud, and always makes gently the final
comment: "Yes, yes; she *is* happy!"

It is whispered around Wilbarger that he "has had a
stroke"; Mrs. Manning herself thinks so.

Well, in a certain sense, perhaps she is right.

KING DAVID.

I met a traveler on the road ;
His face was wan, his feet were weary ;
Yet he unresting went with such
A strange, still, patient mien—a look
Set forward in the empty air,
As he were reading an unseen book.

RICHARD WATSON GILDER.

THE scholars were dismissed. Out they trooped—big
boys, little boys, and full-grown men. Then what antics—
what linked lines of scuffling ; what double shuffles, leaps,
and somersaults ; what rolling laughter, interspersed with
short yelps and guttural cries, as wild and free as the sounds
the mustangs make, gamboling on the plains ! For King
David's scholars were black—black as the ace of spades. He
did not say that ; he knew very little about the ace. He said
simply that his scholars were "colored" ; and sometimes he
called them "the Children of Ham." But so many mistakes
were made over this title, in spite of his careful explanations
(the Children having an undoubted taste for bacon), that he
finally abandoned it, and fell back upon the national name of
"freedmen," a title both good and true. He even tried to
make it noble, speaking to them often of their wonderful lot
as the emancipated teachers and helpers of their race ; laying
before them their mission in the future, which was to go over
to Africa, and wake out of their long sloth and slumber the
thousands of souls there. But Cassius and Pompey had only
a mythic idea of Africa ; they looked at the globe as it was
turned around, they saw it there on the other side, and then

their attention wandered off to an adventurous ant who was making the tour of Soodan and crossing the mountains of Kong as though they were nothing.

Lessons over, the scholars went home. The schoolmaster went home too, wiping his forehead as he went. He was a grave young man, tall and thin, somewhat narrow-chested, with the diffident air of a country student. And yet this country student was here, far down in the South, hundreds of miles away from the New Hampshire village where he had thought to spend his life as teacher of the district school. Extreme near-sightedness and an inherited delicacy of constitution which he bore silently had kept him out of the field during the days of the war. "I should be only an encumbrance," he thought. But, when the war was over, the fire which had burned within burst forth in the thought, "The freedmen!" There was work fitted to his hand; that one thing he could do. "My turn has come at last," he said. "I feel the call to go." Nobody cared much because he was leaving. "Going down to teach the blacks?" said the farmers. "I don't see as you're called, David. We've paid dear enough to set 'em free, goodness knows, and now they ought to look out for themselves."

"But they must first be taught," said the schoolmaster. "Our responsibility is great; our task is only just begun."

"Stuff!" said the farmers. What with the graves down in the South, and the taxes up in the North, they were not prepared to hear any talk about beginning. Beginning, indeed! They called it ending. The slaves were freed, and it was right they should be freed; but Ethan and Abner were gone, and their households were left unto them desolate. Let the blacks take care of themselves.

So, all alone, down came David King, with such aid and instruction as the Freedman's Bureau could give him, to this little settlement among the pines, where the freedmen had built some cabins in a careless way, and then seated themselves to wait for fortune. Freedmen! Yes; a glorious

idea! But how will it work its way out into practical life?
What are you going to do with tens of thousands of ignorant,
childish, irresponsible souls thrown suddenly upon your hands;
souls that will not long stay childish, and that have in them
also all the capacities for evil that you yourselves have—you
with your safeguards of generations of conscious responsibility
and self-government, and yet—so many lapses! This is what
David King thought. He did not see his way exactly; no,
nor the nation's way. But he said to himself: "I can at least
begin; if I am wrong, I shall find it out in time. But now it
seems to me that our first duty is to educate them." So he
began at "a, b, and c"; "You must not steal"; "You must
not fight"; "You must wash your faces"; which may be
called, I think, the first working out of the emancipation
problem.

Jubilee Town was the name of the settlement; and when
the schoolmaster announced his own, David King, the title
struck the imitative minds of the scholars, and, turning it
around, they made "King David" of it, and kept it so. Delighted with the novelty, the Jubilee freedmen came to school
in such numbers that the master was obliged to classify them;
boys and men in the mornings and afternoons; the old people
in the evenings; the young women and girls by themselves
for an hour in the early morning. "I can not do full justice
to all," he thought, "and in the men lies the danger, in the
boys the hope; the women can not vote. Would to God the
men could not either, until they have learned to read and to
write, and to maintain themselves respectably!" For, abolitionist as he was, David King would have given years of his
life for the power to restrict the suffrage. Not having this
power, however, he worked at the problem in the only way
left open: "Take two apples from four apples, Julius—how
many will be left?" "What is this I hear, Cæsar, about
stolen bacon?"

On this day the master went home, tired and dispirited;
the novelty was over on both sides. He had been five months

at Jubilee, and his scholars were more of a puzzle to him than
ever. They learned, some of them, readily; but they forgot
as readily. They had a vast capacity for parrot-like repetition, and caught his long words so quickly, and repeated them
so volubly, with but slight comprehension of their meaning,
that his sensitive conscience shrank from using them, and he
was forced back upon a rude plainness of speech which was
a pain to his pedagogic ears. Where he had once said,
"Demean yourselves with sobriety," he now said, "Don't get
drunk." He would have fared better if he had learned to
say "uncle" and "aunty," or "maumer," in the familiar
Southern fashion. But he had no knowledge of the customs;
how could he have? He could only blunder on in his slow
Northern way.

His cabin stood in the pine forest, at a little distance from
the settlement; he had allowed himself that grace. There
was a garden around it, where Northern flowers came up
after a while—a little pale, perhaps, like English ladies in In-
dia, but doubly beautiful and dear to exiled eyes. The schoolmaster had cherished from the first a wish for a cotton-field
—a cotton-field of his own. To him a cotton-field represented the South—a cotton-field in the hot sunshine, with a
gang of slaves toiling under the lash of an overseer. This
might have been a fancy picture, and it might not. At any
rate, it was real to him. There was, however, no overseer
now, and no lash; no slaves and very little toil. The negroes
would work only when they pleased, and that was generally
not at all. There was no doubt but that they were almost
hopelessly improvident and lazy. "Entirely so," said the
planters. "Not quite," said the Northern schoolmaster. And
therein lay the difference between them.

David lighted his fire of pitch-pine, spread his little table,
and began to cook his supper carefully. When it was nearly
ready, he heard a knock at his gate. Two representative
specimens of his scholars were waiting without—Jim, a field-
hand, and a woman named Esther, who had been a house-

servant in a planter's family. Jim had come "to borry an axe," and Esther to ask for medicine for a sick child.

"Where is your own axe, Jim?" said the schoolmaster.

"Somehow et's rusty, sah. Dey gets rusty mighty quick."

"Of course, because you always leave them out in the rain. When will you learn to take care of your axes?"

"Don' know, mars."

"I have told you not to call me master," said David. "I am not your master."

"You's schoolmars, I reckon," answered Jim, grinning at his repartee.

"Well, Jim," said the schoolmaster, relaxing into a smile, "you have the best of it this time; but you know quite well what I mean. You can take the axe; but bring it back to-night. And you must see about getting a new one immediately; there is something to begin with.—Now, Esther, what is it? Your boy sick? Probably it is because you let him drink the water out of that swampy pool. I warned you."

"Yes, sah," said the woman impassively.

She was a slow, dull-witted creature, who had executed her tasks marvelously well in the planter's family, never varying by a hair's breadth either in time or method during long years. Freed, she was lost at once; if she had not been swept along by her companions, she would have sat down dumbly by the wayside, and died. The schoolmaster offered supper to both of his guests. Jim took a seat at the table at once, nothing loath, and ate and drank, talking all the time with occasional flashes of wit, and an unconscious suggestion of ferocity in the way he hacked and tore the meat with his clasp-knife and his strong white teeth. Esther stood; nothing could induce her to sit in the master's presence. She ate and drank quietly, and dropped a courtesy whenever he spoke to her, not from any especial respect or gratitude, however, but from habit. "I may possibly teach the man something," thought the schoolmaster; "but what a terrible crea-

ture to turn loose in the world, with power in his hand!
Hundreds of these men will die, nay, must die violent deaths
before their people can learn what freedom means, and what
it does not mean. As for the woman, it is hopeless; she can
not learn. But her child can. In truth, our hope is in the
children."

And then he threw away every atom of the food, washed
his dishes, made up the fire, and went back to the beginning
again and cooked a second supper. For he still shrank from
personal contact with the other race. A Southerner would
have found it impossible to comprehend the fortitude it required for the New-Englander to go through his daily rounds
among them. He did his best; but it was duty, not liking.
Supper over, he went to the schoolhouse again: in the evenings he taught the old people. It was an odd sight to note
them as they followed the letters with a big, crooked forefin-
ger, slowly spelling out words of three letters. They spelled
with their whole bodies, stooping over the books which lay
before them until their old grizzled heads and gay turbans
looked as if they were set on the table by the chins in a
long row. Patiently the master taught them; they had gone
no further then "cat" in five long months. He made the
letters for them on the blackboard again and again, but the
treat of the evening was the making of these letters on the
board by the different scholars in turn. "Now, Dinah—B."
And old Dinah would hobble up proudly, and, with much
screwing of her mouth and tongue, and many long hesita-
tions, produce something which looked like a figure eight
gone mad. Joe had his turn next, and he would make, perhaps, an H for a D. The master would go back and explain
to him carefully the difference, only to find at the end of ten
minutes that the whole class was hopelessly confused: Joe's
mistake had routed them all. There was one pair of spectacles among the old people: these were passed from hand
to hand as the turn came, not from necessity always, but as
an adjunct to the dignity of reading.

"Never mind the glasses, Tom. Surely you can spell 'bag' without them."

"Dey helps, Mars King David," replied old Tom with solemn importance. He then adorned himself with the spectacles, and spelled it—"g, a, b."

But the old people enjoyed their lesson immensely; no laughter, no joking broke the solemnity of the scene, and they never failed to make an especial toilet—much shirt-collar for the old men, and clean turbans for the old women. They seemed to be generally half-crippled, poor old creatures; slow in their movements as tortoises, and often unwieldy; their shoes were curiosities of patches, rags, strings, and carpeting. But sometimes a fine old black face was lifted from the slow-moving bulk, and from under wrinkled eyelids keen sharp eyes met the master's, as intelligent as his own.

There was no church proper in Jubilee. On Sundays, the people, who were generally Baptists, assembled in the school-room, where services were conducted by a brother who had "de gif' ob preachin'," and who poured forth a flood of Scripture phrases with a volubility, incoherence, and earnestness alike extraordinary. Presbyterian David attended these services, not only for the sake of example, but also because he steadfastly believed in "the public assembling of ourselves together for the worship of Almighty God."

"Perhaps they understand him," he thought, noting the rapt black faces, "and I, at least, have no right to judge them—I, who, with all the lights I have had, still find myself unable to grasp the great doctrine of Election." For David had been bred in Calvinism, and many a night, when younger and more hopeful of arriving at finalities, had he wrestled with its problems. He was not so sure, now, of arriving at finalities either in belief or in daily life; but he thought the fault lay with himself, and deplored it.

The Yankee schoolmaster was, of course, debarred from intercourse with those of his own color in the neighborhood.

There were no " poor whites " there; he was spared the sight
of their long, clay-colored faces, lank yellow hair, and half-
open mouths ; he was not brought into contact with the ignorance and dense self-conceit of this singular class. The
whites of the neighborhood were planters, and they regarded
the schoolmaster as an interloper, a fanatic, a knave, or a
fool, according to their various degrees of bitterness. The
phantom of a cotton-field still haunted the master, and he
often walked by the abandoned fields of these planters, and
noted them carefully. In addition to his fancy, there was
now another motive. Things were not going well at Jubilee,
and he was anxious to try whether the men would not work
for good wages, paid regularly, and for their Northern teacher
and friend. Thus it happened that Harnett Ammerton, retired planter, one afternoon perceived a stranger walking up
the avenue that led to his dilapidated mansion ; and as he
was near-sighted, and as any visitor was, besides, a welcome
interruption in his dull day, he went out upon the piazza to
meet him ; and not until he had offered a chair did he recognize his guest. He said nothing ; for he was in his own
house ; but a gentleman can freeze the atmosphere around
him even in his own house, and this he did. The schoolmaster stated his errand simply : he wished to rent one of the
abandoned cotton-fields for a year. The planter could have
answered with satisfaction that his fields might lie for ever
untilled before Yankee hands should touch them ; but he was
a poor man now, and money was money. He endured his visit-
or, and he rented his field ; and, with the perplexed feelings of
his class, he asked himself how it was, how it could be, that a
man like that—yes, like that—had money, while he himself had
none ! David had but little money—a mere handful to throw
away in a day, the planter would have thought in the lavish
old times ; but David had the New England thrift.

    " I am hoping that the unemployed hands over at Jubilee
will cultivate this field for me," he said—" for fair wages, of
course. I know nothing of cotton myself."

"You will be disappointed," said the planter.

"But they must live; they must lay up something for the winter."

"They do not know enough to live. They might exist, perhaps, in Africa, as the rest of their race exists; but here, in this colder climate, they must be taken care of, worked, and fed, as we work and feed our horses—precisely in the same way."

"I can not agree with you," replied David, a color rising in his thin face. "They are idle and shiftless, I acknowledge that; but is it not the natural result of generations of servitude and ignorance?"

"They have not capacity for anything save ignorance."

"You do not know then, perhaps, that I—that I am trying to educate those who are over at Jubilee," said David. There was no aggressive confidence in his voice; he knew that he had accomplished little as yet. He looked wistfully at his host as he spoke.

Harnett Ammerton was a born patrician. Poor, homely, awkward David felt this in every nerve as he sat there; for he loved beauty in spite of himself, and in spite of his belief that it was a tendency of the old Adam. (Old Adam has such nice things to bother his descendants with; almost a monopoly, if we are to believe some creeds.) So now David tried not to be influenced by the fine face before him, and steadfastly went on to sow a little seed, if possible, even upon this prejudiced ground.

"I have a school over there," he said.

"I have heard something of the kind, I believe," replied the old planter, as though Jubilee Town were a thousand miles away, instead of a blot upon his own border. "May I ask how you are succeeding?"

There was a fine irony in the question. David felt it, but replied courageously that success, he hoped, would come in time.

"And I, young man, hope that it will never come! The

negro with power in his hand, which you have given him, with a little smattering of knowledge in his shallow, crafty brain—a knowledge which you and your kind are now striving to give him—will become an element of more danger in this land than it has ever known before. You Northerners do not understand the blacks. They are an inferior race by nature; God made them so. And God forgive those (although I never can) who have placed them over us—yes, virtually over us, their former masters—poor ignorant creatures!"

At this instant an old negro came up the steps with an armful of wood, and the eye of the Northerner noted (was forced to note) the contrast. There sat the planter, his head crowned with silver hair, his finely chiseled face glowing with the warmth of his indignant words; and there passed the old slave, bent and black, his low forehead and broad animal features seeming to typify scarcely more intelligence than that of the dog that followed him. The planter spoke to the servant in his kindly way as he passed, and the old black face lighted with pleasure. This, too, the schoolmaster's sensitive mind noted: none of his pupils looked at him with anything like that affection. "But it *is* right they should be freed—it *is* right," he said to himself as he walked back to Jubilee; "and to that belief will I cling as long as I have my being. It *is* right." And then he came into Jubilee, and found three of his freedmen drunk and quarreling in the street.

Heretofore the settlement, poor and forlorn as it was, had escaped the curse of drunkenness. No liquor was sold in the vicinity, and David had succeeded in keeping his scholars from wandering aimlessly about the country from place to place—often the first use the blacks made of their freedom. Jubilee did not go to the liquor; but, at last, the liquor had come to Jubilee. Shall they not have all rights and privileges, these new-born citizens of ours? The bringer of these doctrines, and of the fluids to moisten them, was a white man, one of that class which has gone down on the page of American history, knighted with the initials C. B. "The Captain" the negroes called him; and he was highly popular already, three hours of the Captain being worth three weeks of David, as far as familiarity went. The man was a glib-tongued, smartly dressed fellow, well supplied with money; and his errand was, of course, to influence the votes at the next election. David, meanwhile, had so carefully kept all talk of politics from his scholars that they hardly knew that an election was near. It became now a contest between the two higher intelligences. If the schoolmaster had but won the easily won and strong affections of his pupils! But, in all those months, he had gained only a dutiful attention. They did not even respect him as they had respected their old masters, and the cause (poor David !) was that very thrift and industry which he relied upon an an example.

"Ole Mars Ammerton wouldn't wash his dishes ef dey was nebber washed," confided Maum June to Elsy, as they caught sight of David's shining pans.

The schoolmaster could have had a retinue of servants for a small price, or no price at all; but, to tell a truth which he never told, he could not endure them about him.

"I must have one spot to myself," he said feverishly, after he had labored all day among them, teaching, correcting untidy ways, administering simple medicines, or binding up a bruised foot. But he never dreamed that this very isolation of his personality, this very thrift, were daily robbing him of the influence which he so earnestly longed to possess. In New England every man's house was his castle, and every man's hands were thrifty. He forgot the easy familiarity, the lordly ways, the crowded households, and the royal carelessness to which the slaves had always been accustomed in their old masters' homes.

At first the Captain attempted intimacy.

"No reason why you and me shouldn't work together," he said with a confidential wink. "This thing's being done all over the South, and easy done, too. Now's the time for

smart chaps like us—'transition,'you know. The old Southerners are mad, and won't come forward, so we'll just sail in
and have a few years of it. When they're ready to come
back—why, we'll give 'em up the place again, of course, if
our pockets are well lined. Come, now, just acknowledge
that the negroes have got to have somebody to lead 'em."

"It shall not be such as you," said David indignantly.
"See those two men quarreling; that is the work of the liquor
you have given them!"

"They've as good a right to their liquor as other men
have," replied the Captain carelessly; "and that's what I tell
'em; they ain't slaves now—they're free. Well, boss, sorry
you don't like my idees, but can't help it; must go ahead.
Remember, I offered you a chance, and you would not take it.
Morning."

The five months had grown into six and seven, and Jubilee Town was known far and wide as a dangerous and disorderly neighborhood. The old people and the children still
came to school, but the young men and boys had deserted in
a body. The schoolmaster's cotton-field was neglected; he
did a little there himself every day, but the work was novel,
and his attempts were awkward and slow. One afternoon
Harnett Ammerton rode by on horseback; the road passed
near the angle of the field where the schoolmaster was at
work.

"How is your experiment succeeding?" said the planter,
with a little smile of amused scorn as he saw the lonely
figure.

"Not very well," replied David.

He paused and looked up earnestly into the planter's face.
Here was a man who had lived among the blacks all his life,
and knew them: if he would but give honest advice! The
schoolmaster was sorely troubled that afternoon. Should he
speak? He would at least try.

"Mr. Ammerton," he said, "do you intend to vote at the
approaching election?"

12

"No," replied the planter; "nor any person of my acquaintance."

"Then incompetent, and, I fear, evil-minded men will be put into office."

"Of course—the certain result of negro voting."

"But if you, sir, and the class to which you belong, would exert yourselves, I am inclined to think much might be done. The breach will only grow broader every year; act now, while you have still influence left."

"Then you think that we have influence?" said the planter.

He was curious concerning the ideas of this man, who, although not like the typical Yankee exactly, was yet plainly a fanatic; while as to dress and air—why, Zip, his old valet, had more polish.

"I know at least that I have none," said David. Then he came a step nearer. "Do you think, sir," he began slowly, "that I have gone to work in the wrong way? Would it have been wiser to have obtained some post of authority over them—the office of justice of the peace, for instance, with power of arrest?"

"I know nothing about it," said the planter curtly, touching his horse with his whip and riding on. He had no intention of stopping to discuss ways and means with an abolition schoolmaster!

Things grew from bad to worse at Jubilee. Most of the men had been field-hands; there was but little intelligence among them. The few bright minds among David's pupils caught the specious arguments of the Captain, and repeated them to the others. The Captain explained how much power they held; the Captain laid before them glittering plans; the Captain said that by good rights each family ought to have a plantation to repay them for their years of enforced labor; the Captain promised them a four-story brick college for their boys, which was more than King David had ever promised, teacher though he was. They found out that they were tired

of King David and his narrow talk; and they went over to
Hildore Corners, where a new store had been opened, which
contained, among other novelties, a bar. This was one of
the Captain's benefactions. "If you pay your money for it,
you've as good a right to your liquor as any one, I guess," he
observed. "Not that it's anything to me, of course; but I
allow I like to see fair play!"

It was something to him, however: the new store had a
silent partner; and this was but one of many small and silent
enterprises in which he was engaged throughout the neighborhood.

The women of Jubilee, more faithful than the men, still
sent their children to school; but they did it with discouraged
hearts, poor things! Often now they were seen with bandaged heads and bruised bodies, the result of drunken blows
from husband or brother; and, left alone, they were obliged
to labor all day to get the poor food they ate, and to keep
clothes on their children. Patient by nature, they lived along
as best they could, and toiled in their small fields like horses;
but the little prides, the vague, grotesque aspirations and
hopes that had come to them with their freedom, gradually
faded away. "A blue-painted front do'," "a black-silk apron
with red ribbons," "to make a minister of little Job," and "a
real crock'ry pitcher," were wishes unspoken now. The thing
was only how to live from day to day, and keep the patched
clothes together. In the mean while trashy finery was sold
at the new store, and the younger girls wore gilt ear-rings.

The master, toiling on at his vain task, was at his wit's
end. "They will not work; before long they must steal," he
said. He brooded and thought, and at last one morning he
came to a decision. The same day in the afternoon he set
out for Hildore Corners. He had thought of a plan. As he
was walking rapidly through the pine-woods Harnett Ammerton on horseback passed him. This time the Northerner
had no questions to ask—nay, he almost hung his head, so
ashamed was he of the reputation that had attached itself to

the field of his labors. But the planter reined in his horse when he saw who it was : he was the questioner now.

"Schoolmaster," he began, "in the name of all the white families about here, I really must ask if you can do nothing to keep in order those miserable, drinking, ruffianly negroes of yours over at Jubilee? Why, we shall all be murdered in our beds before long! Are you aware of the dangerous spirit they have manifested lately?"

"Only too well," said David.

"What are you going to do? How will it end?"

"God knows."

"God knows! Is that all you have to say? Of course he knows; but the question is, Do you know? You have brought the whole trouble down upon our heads by your confounded insurrectionary school! Just as I told you, your negroes, with the little smattering of knowledge you have given them, are now the most dangerous, riotous, thieving, murdering rascals in the district."

"They are bad; but it is not the work of the school, I hope."

"Yes, it is," said the planter angrily.

"They have been led astray lately, Mr. Ammerton; a person has come among them—"

"Another Northerner."

"Yes," said David, a flush rising in his cheek; "but not all Northerners are like this man, I trust."

"Pretty much all we see are. Look at the State."

"Yes, I know it; I suppose time alone can help matters," said the troubled teacher.

"Give up your school, and come and join us," said the planter abruptly. "You, at least, are honest in your mistakes. We are going to form an association for our own protection; join with us. You can teach my grandsons if you like, provided you do not put any of your—your fanaticism into them."

This was an enormous concession for Harnett Ammerton

to make; something in the schoolmaster's worn face had drawn it out.

"Thank you," said David slowly; "it is kindly meant, sir. But I can not give up my work. I came down to help the freedmen, and—"

"Then stay with them," said the planter, doubly angry for the very kindness of the moment before. "I thought you were a decent-living white man, according to your fashion, but I see I was mistaken. Dark days are coming, and you turn your back upon those of your own color and side with the slaves! Go and herd with your negroes. But, look you, sir, we are prepared. We will shoot down any one found upon our premises after dark—shoot him down like a dog. It has come to that, and, by Heaven! we shall protect ourselves."

He rode on. David sat down on a fallen tree for a moment, and leaned his head upon his hand. Dark days were coming, as the planter had said; nay, were already there. Was he in any way responsible for them? He tried to think. "I know not," he said at last; "but I must still go on and do the best I can. I must carry out my plan." He rose and went forward to the Corners.

A number of Jubilee men were lounging near the new store, and one of them was reading aloud from a newspaper which the Captain had given him. He had been David's brightest scholar, and he could read readily; but what he read was inflammable matter of the worst kind, a speech which had been written for just such purposes, and which was now being circulated through the district. Mephistopheles in the form of Harnett Ammerton seemed to whisper in the schoolmaster's ears, "Do you take pride to yourself that you taught that man to read?"

The reader stopped; he had discovered the new auditor. The men stared; they had never seen the master at the Corners before. They drew together and waited. He approached them, and paused a moment; then he began to speak.

"I have come, friends," he said, "to make a proposition to you. You, on your side, have nothing laid up for the winter, and I, on my side, am anxious to have your work. I have a field, you know, a cotton-field; what do you say to going to work there, all of you, for a month? I will agree to pay you more than any man about here pays, and you shall have the cash every Monday morning regularly. We will hold a meeting over at Jubilee, and you shall choose your own overseer; for I am very ignorant about cotton-fields; I must trust to you. What do you say?"

The men looked at each other, but no one spoke.

"Think of your little children without clothes."

Still silence.

"I have not succeeded among you," continued the teacher, "as well as I hoped to succeed. You do not come to school any more, and I suppose it is because you do not like me."

Something like a murmur of dissent came from the group. The voice went on:

"I have thought of something I can do, however. I can write to the North for another teacher to take my place, and he shall be a man of your own race; one who is educated, and, if possible, also a clergyman of your own faith. You can have a little church then, and Sabbath services. As soon as he comes, I will yield my place to him; but, in the mean time, will you not cultivate that field for me? I ask it as a favor. It will be but for a little while, for, when the new teacher comes, I shall go—unless, indeed," he added, looking around with a smile that was almost pathetic in its appeal, "you should wish me to stay."

There was no answer. He had thrown out this last little test question suddenly. It had failed.

"I am sorry I have not succeeded better at Jubilee," he said after a short pause—and his voice had altered in spite of his self-control—"but at least you will believe, I hope, that I have tried."

"Dat's so"; "Dat's de trouf," said one or two; the rest

stood irresolute. But at this moment a new speaker came forward; it was the Captain, who had been listening in ambush.

"All gammon, boys, all gammon," he began, seating himself familiarly among them on the fence-rail. "The season for planting's over, and your work would be thrown away in that field of his. He knows it, too; he only wants to see you marching around to his whistling. And he pays you double wages, does he? Double wages for perfectly useless work! Doesn't that show, clear as daylight, what he's up to? If he hankers so after your future—your next winter, and all that— why don't he give yer the money right out, if he's so flush? But no; he wants to put you to work, and that's all there is of it. He can't deny a word I've said, either."

"I do not deny that I wish you to work, friends," began David—

"There! he tells yer so himself," said the Captain; "he wants yer back in yer old places again. *I* seen him talking to old Ammerton the other day. Give 'em a chance, them two classes, and they'll have you slaves a second time before you know it."

"Never!" cried David. "Friends, it is not possible that you can believe this man! We have given our lives to make you free," he added passionately; "we came down among you, bearing your freedom in our hands—"

"Come, now—I'm a Northerner too, ain't I?" interrupted the Captain. "There's two kinds of Northerners, boys. *I* was in the army, and that's more than he can say. Much freedom *he* brought down in *his* hands, safe at home in his narrer-minded, penny-scraping village! He wasn't in the army at all, boys, and he can't tell you he was."

This was true; the schoolmaster could not. Neither could he tell them what was also true, namely, that the Captain had been an *attaché* of a sutler's tent, and nothing more. But the sharp-witted Captain had the whole history of his opponent at his fingers' ends.

"Come along, boys," said this jovial leader; "we'll have suthin' to drink the health of this tremenjous soldier in—this fellow as fought so hard for you and for your freedom. I always thought he looked like a fighting man, with them fine broad shoulders of his!" He laughed loudly, and the men trooped into the store after him. The schoolmaster, alone outside, knew that his chance was gone. He turned away and took the homeward road. One of his plans had failed; there remained now nothing save to carry out the other.

Prompt as usual, he wrote his letter as soon as he reached his cabin, asking that another teacher, a colored man if possible, should be sent down to take his place.

"I fear I am not fitted for the work," he wrote. "I take shame to myself that this is so; yet, being so, I must not hinder by any disappointed strivings the progress of the great mission. I will go back among my own kind; it may be that some whom I shall teach may yet succeed where I have failed." The letter could not go until the next morning. He went out and walked up and down in the forest. A sudden impulse came to him; he crossed over to the schoolhouse and rang the little tinkling belfry-bell. His evening class had disbanded some time before; the poor old aunties and uncles crept off to bed very early now, in order to be safely out of the way when their disorderly sons and grandsons came home. But something moved the master to see them all together once more. They came across the green, wondering, and entered the schoolroom; some of the younger wives came too, and the children. The master waited, letter in hand. When they were all seated—

"Friends," he said, "I have called you together to speak to you of a matter which lies very near my own heart. Things are not going on well at Jubilee. The men drink; the children go in rags. Is this true?"

Groans and slow assenting nods answered him. One old woman shrieked out shrilly, "It is de Lord's will," and rocked her body to and fro.

" No, it is not the Lord's will," answered the schoolmaster gently; "you must not think so. You must strive to reclaim those who have gone astray; you must endeavor to inspire them with renewed aspirations toward a higher plane of life; you must—I mean," he said, correcting himself, "you must try to keep the men from going over to the Corners and getting drunk."

" But dey will do it, sah ; what can we do ? " said Uncle Scipio, who sat leaning his chin upon his crutch and peering at the teacher with sharp intelligence in his old eyes. " If dey won't stay fo' you, sah, will dey stay fo' us ? "

" That is what I was coming to," said the master. (They had opened the subject even before he could get to it ! They saw it too, then—his utter lack of influence.) " I have not succeeded here as I hoped to succeed, friends ; I have not the influence I ought to have." Then he paused. " Perhaps the best thing I can do will be to go away," he added, looking quickly from face to face to catch the expression. But there was nothing visible. The children stared stolidly back, and the old people sat unmoved ; he even fancied that he could detect relief in the eyes of one or two, quickly suppressed, however, by the innate politeness of the race. A sudden mist came over his eyes; he had thought that perhaps some of them would care a little. He hurried on : " I have written to the North for a new teacher for you, a man of your own people, who will not only teach you, but also, as a minister, hold services on the Sabbath; you can have a little church of your own then. Such a man will do better for you than I have done, and I hope you will like him "—he was going to say, "better than you have liked me," but putting down all thought of self, he added, "and that his work among you will be abundantly blessed."

" Glory ! glory ! " cried an old aunty. " A color'd preacher ob our own ! Glory ! glory ! "

Then Uncle Scipio rose slowly, with the aid of his crutches, and, as orator of the occasion, addressed the master.

"You see, sah, how it is; you see, Mars King David," he said, waving his hand apologetically, "a color'd man will unnerstan us, 'specially ef he hab lib'd at de Souf; we don't want no Nordern free niggahs hyar. But a 'spectable color'd preacher, now, would be de makin' ob Jubilee, fo' dis worl' an' de nex'."

"Fo' dis worl' and de nex'," echoed the old woman.

"Our service to you, sah, all de same," continued Scipio, with a grand bow of ceremony; "but you hab nebber *quite* unnerstan us, sah, nebber quite; an' you can nebber do much fo' us, sah, on 'count ob dat fack—ef you'll scuse my saying so. But it is de trouf. We give you our t'anks and our congratturrurlations, an' we hopes you'll go j'yful back to your own people, an' be a shining light to 'em for ebbermore."

"A shinin' light for ebbermore," echoed the rest. One old woman, inspired apparently by the similarity of words, began a hymn about "the shining shore," and the whole assembly, thinking no doubt that it was an appropriate and complimentary termination to the proceedings, joined in with all their might, and sang the whole six verses through with fervor.

"I should like to shake hands with you all as you go out," said the master, when at last the song was ended, "and—and I wish, my friends, that you would all remember me in your prayers to-night before you sleep."

What a sight was that when the pale Caucasian, with the intelligence of generations on his brow, asked for the prayers of these sons of Africa, and gently, nay, almost humbly, received the pressure of their black, toil-hardened hands as they passed out! They had taught him a great lesson, the lesson of a failure.

The schoolmaster went home, and sat far into the night, with his head bowed upon his hands. "Poor worm!" he thought—"poor worm! who even went so far as to dream of saying, 'Here am I, Lord, and these brethren whom thou hast given me!'"

The day came for him to go; he shouldered his bag and started away. At a turn in the road, some one was waiting for him; it was dull-faced Esther with a bunch of flowers, the common flowers of her small garden-bed. "Good-by, Esther," said the master, touched almost to tears by the sight of the solitary little offering.

"Good-by, mars," said Esther. But she was not moved; she had come out into the woods from a sort of instinct, as a dog follows a little way down the road to look after a departing carriage.

"David King has come back home again, and taken the district school," said one village gossip to another.

"Has he, now? Didn't find the blacks what he expected, I guess."

UP IN THE BLUE RIDGE.

" Every rose, you sang, has its thorn ;
But this has none, I know."
She clasped my rival's rose
Over her breast of snow.

I bowed to hide my pain,
With a man's unskillful art ;
I moved my lips, and could not say
The thorn was in my heart.

WILLIAM DEAN HOWELLS.

I.

"INSTEAD of going through the whole book, you can read this abstract, Miss Honor."

The speaker drew forth five or six sheets of paper, closely covered with fine, small handwriting. The letters were not in the least beautiful, or even straight, if you examined them closely, for they carried themselves crookedly, and never twice alike ; but, owing to their extreme smallness, and the careful way in which they stood on the line, rigidly particular as to their feet, although their spines were misshapen, they looked not unlike a regiment of little humpbacked men, marching with extreme precision, and daring you to say that they were crooked. Stephen Wainwright had partly taught himself this hand, and partly it was due to temperament. He despised a clerkly script ; yet he could not wander down a page, or blur his words, any more than he could wander down a street, or blur his chance remarks ; in spite of himself, he always knew exactly where he was going, and what he intended to say. He was not a man who attracted attention in any way. He was small, yet not so small as to be noticed for smallness; he was what is called plain-looking, yet without that marked ugliness which, in a man, sometimes amounts to distinction. As to his dress, he was too exact for carelessness; you felt that the smallest spot on his loose flannel coat would trouble him; and yet he was entirely without that trim, fresh, spring-morning appearance which sometimes gives a small man an advantage over his larger brethren, as the great coach-dogs seem suddenly coarse and dirty when the shining little black-and-tan terrier bounds into the yard beside them. Stephen was a man born into the world with an over-weight of caution and doubt. They made the top of his head so broad and square that Reverence, who likes a rounded curve, found herself displaced; she clung on desperately through his schoolboy days, but was obliged at last to let go as the youth began to try his muscles, shake off extraneous substances, and find out what he really was himself, after the long succession of tutors and masters had done with him.

The conceit of small men is proverbial, and Stephen was considered a living etching of the proverb, without color, but sharply outlined. He had a large fortune; he had a good intellect; he had no vices—sufficient reasons, the world said, why he had become, at forty, unendurably conceited. His life, the world considered, was but a succession of conquests: and the quiet manner with which he entered a drawing-room crowded with people, or stood apart and looked on, was but another indication of that vanity of his which never faltered, even in the presence of the most beautiful women or the most brilliant men. The world had no patience with him. If he had not gone out in society at all, if he had belonged to that large class of men who persistently refuse to attire themselves in dress-coats and struggle through the dance, the world would have understood it; but, on the contrary, Stephen went everywhere, looking smaller and plainer than usual in his evening-dress, asked everybody to dance, and fulfilled every social obligation with painstaking exactitude. The world had no patience with him;

he was like a golden apple hanging low; but nobody could pull him off the branch.

Stephen's conversation - friend (every unmarried man, though an octogenarian, has his conversation-friend) was Adelaide Kellinger, the widow of his cousin and favorite boyhood-companion, Ralph Kellinger. Adelaide was now thirty-five years of age, an agreeable woman, tall, slender, and exquisitely dressed—a woman who made people forget that an arm should be round, or a cheek red, when her slim, amber-colored gracefulness was present with them. Adelaide's house was Stephen's one lounging-place. Here he came to hear her talk over last evening's party, and here he delivered fewer of those concise apropos remarks for which he was celebrated, and which had been the despair of a long series of young ladies in turn; for what can you do with a man who, on every occasion, even the most unexpected, has calmly ready for you a neat sentence, politely delivered, like the charmingly folded small parcels which the suave dry-goods clerk hands to you across the counter? Stephen was never in a hurry to bring out these remarks of his; on the contrary, he always left every pause unbroken for a perceptible half moment or two, as if waiting for some one else to speak. The unwary, therefore, were often entrapped into the idea that he was slow or unprepared; and the unwary made a mistake, as the more observing among them soon discovered.

Adelaide Kellinger had studied her cousin for years. The result of her studies was as follows: She paid, outwardly, no especial attention to him, and she remained perfectly natural herself. This last was a difficult task. If he asked a question, she answered with the plainest truth she could imagine; if he asked an opinion, she gave the one she would have given to her most intimate woman-friend (if she had had one); if she was tired, she did not conceal it; if she was out of temper, she said disagreeable, sharp-edged things. She was, therefore, perfectly natural? On the contrary, she was extremely unnatural. A charming woman does not go around at the present day in a state of nature mentally any more than physically; politeness has become a necessary clothing to her. Adelaide Kellinger never spoke to her cousin without a little preceding pause, during which she thought over what she was going to say; and, as Stephen was slow to speak also, their conversations were ineffective, judged from a dramatic point of view. But Adelaide judged by certain broad facts, and left drama to others. Stephen liked to be with her; and he was a creature of habit. She intended that he should continue to like to be with her; and she relied upon that habit.

.   .   .   .

Afar off, counting by civilization, not by parallels of latitude, there are mountains in this country of ours, east of the Mississippi, as purple-black, wild, and pathless, some of them, as the peaks of the Western sierras. These mountains are in the middle South. A few roads climb from the plain below into their presence, and cautiously follow the small rivers that act as guides—a few roads, no more. Here and there are villages, or rather farm-centers, for the soil is fertile wherever it is cleared; but the farms are old and stationary: they do not grow, stretch out a fence here, or a new field there; they remain as they were when the farmers' sons were armed and sent to swell George Washington's little army. To this day the farmers' wives spin and weave, and dye and fashion, with their own hands, each in her own house, the garments worn by all the family; to this day they have seen nothing move by steam. The locomotive waits beyond the peaks; the water-mill is the highest idea of force. Half a mile from the village of Ellerby stands one of these water-mills; to it come farmers and farmers' boys on horseback, from miles around, with grist to be ground. And sometimes the women come too, riding slowly on old, pacing cart-horses, their faces hidden in the tubes of deep, long sun-bonnets, their arms moving up and down, up and down, as the old horse stretches his head to his fore-feet and back with every step. When two

farm-women meet at the mill-block there is much talking in
the chipped-off mountain dialect; but they sit on their horses
without dismounting, strong, erect, and not uncomely, with
eyes like eagles', yet often toothless in their prime, in the
strange rural-American way, which makes one wonder what
it was in the life of the negro slaves which gives their grand-
children now such an advantage in this over the descendants
alike of the whites of Massachusetts Bay and the plantations
of the Carolinas.   When the farmers meet at the mill-block,
they dismount and sit down in a row, not exactly on their
heels, but nearly so: in reality, they sit, or squat, on their
feet, nothing of them touching the ground save the soles of
their heavy shoes, the two tails of their blue homespun coats
being brought round and held in front.   In this position they
whittle and play with their whips, or eat the giant apples of
the mountains.   Large, iron-framed men, they talk but slowly; they are content apparently to go without those finer
comprehensions and appreciations which other men covet;
they are content to be almost as inarticulate as their horses—
honest beasts, with few differences save temper and color of
hide.   Across the road from the mill, but within sound and
sight of its wheel, is Ellerby Library.   It is a small wooden
building, elevated about five feet above the ground, on four
corner supports, like a table standing on four legs.   Daylight
shines underneath; and Northern boys, accustomed to close
foundations, would be seized with temptations to run under
and knock on the floor: the mountain boys who come to the
mill, however, are too well acquainted with the peculiarities
of the library to find amusement in them; and, besides, this
barefooted cavalry cherishes, under its homespun jacket, an
awkward respect for the librarian.

   This librarian is Honor Dooris, and it is to her Stephen
Wainwright now presents his sheets of manuscript.

   "You think I have an odd handwriting?" he said.

   "Yes," answered the librarian; "I should not think you
would be proud of it."

" I am not."

" Then why not try to change it ? I might lend you my old copies—those I used myself and still use. Here they are." And she took from her desk a number of small slips of paper, on which were written, in a round hand with many flourishes and deeply-shaded lines, moral sentences, such as " He that would thrive must rise at five " ; " Never put off till to-morrow what you can do to-day " ; and others of like hilarious nature.

" Thanks," said Stephen ; " I will take the copies, and try —to improve."

The librarian then began to look through the abstract, and Stephen did not break the silence.

" Would it not be a good idea for me to read it aloud ? " she said, after a while. " I can always remember what I have read aloud."

" As you please," replied Stephen.

So the librarian began, in a sweet voice, with a strong Southern accent, and read aloud, with frowning forehead and evidently but half - comprehension, the chemical abstract which Stephen had prepared.

" It is very hard," she said, looking up at him, with a deep furrow between her eyebrows.

" But not too hard for a person of determined mind."

The person of determined mind answered to the spur immediately, bent forward over the desk again, and went on reading. Stephen, motionless, sat with his eyes fixed on a spider's web high up in the window. When, too deeply puzzled to go on, the girl stopped and asked a question, he answered it generally without removing his eyes from the web. When once or twice she pushed the manuscript away and leaned back in her chair, impotent and irritated, he took the sheets from her hand, explained the hard parts with clear precision, gave them back, and motioned to her to continue. She read on for half an hour. When she finished, there was a flush on her cheeks, the flush of annoyance and fatigue.

"I must go now," she said, placing the manuscript in her desk, and taking down her broad-brimmed Leghorn hat, yellow as old corn, adorned with a plain band of white ribbon.

"You are not, of course, foiled by a little chemistry," said Wainwright, rising also, and looking at her without change of expression.

"Oh, no," she answered; but still she crossed the room and opened the door, as if rather glad to escape, and, with a parting salutation, left him.

Wainwright sat down again. He did not watch her through the window; he took up a late volume of Herbert Spencer, opened it at the mark, and began reading with that careful dwelling upon each word which is, singularly enough, common alike to the scientific and the illiterate. The mass of middle-class readers do not notice words at all, but take only the general sense.

Honor went down the road toward Ellerby village, which was within sight around the corner, walking at first rapidly, but soon falling into the unhurrying gait of the Southern woman, so full of natural, swaying grace. At the edge of the village she turned and took a path which led into a ravine. The path followed a brook, and began to go up hill gradually; the ravine grew narrow and the sides high. Where the flanks met and formed the main hillside, there was, down in the hollow, a house with a basement above ground, with neither paint without nor within. No fences were required for Colonel Eliot's domain — the three near hillsides were his natural walls, a ditch and plank at the entrance of the ravine his moat and drawbridge. The hillsides had been cleared, and the high corn waved steeply all around and above him as he stood in front of his house. It went up to meet the sky, and was very good corn indeed—what he could save of it. A large portion, however, was regularly stolen by his own farm-hands—according to the pleasant methods of Southern agriculture after the war. The Colonel was glad when he could safely house one half of it. He was a cripple, having lost a leg at Antietam. He had married a second wife, and had a house overflowing with children. He was poor as a squirrel, having a nest in these woods and the corn for nuts, and little else besides. He was as brave as a lion, courteous as an old cavalier, hot-headed when aroused, but generally easy-tempered and cheery. He went to church every Sunday, got down on his one knee and confessed his sins honestly; then he came home in the old red wagon, sat on the piazza, and watched the corn grow. Honor was his niece; she shared in his love and his poverty like his own children. Mrs. Eliot, a dimpled, soft-cheeked, faded woman, did not quite like Honor's office of librarian, even if it did add two hundred dollars to their slender income: none of Honor's family, none of her family, had ever been librarians.

"But we are so poor now," said Honor.

"None the less ladies, I hope, my dear," said the elder woman, tapping her niece's shoulder with her pink-tipped, taper fingers.

Honor's hands, however, showed traces of work. She had hated to see them grow coarse, and had cried over them; and then she had gone to church, flung herself down upon her knees, offered up her vanity and her roughened palms as a sacrifice, and, coming home, had insisted upon washing out all the iron pots and saucepans, although old Chloe stood ready to do that work with tears in her eyes over her young mistress's obstinacy. It was when this zeal of Honor's was burning brightest, and her self-mortifications were at their height—which means that she was eighteen, imaginative, and shut up in a box—that an outlet was suddenly presented to her. The old library at Ellerby Mill was resuscitated, reopened, endowed with new life, new books, and a new floor, and the position of librarian offered to her.

In former days the South had a literary taste of its own unlike anything at the North. It was a careful and correct taste, founded principally upon old English authors; and it would have delighted the soul of Charles Lamb, who, being

constantly told that he should be more modern, should write
for posterity, gathered his unappreciated manuscripts to his
breast, and declared that henceforth he would write only for
antiquity. Nothing more unmodern than the old-time literary
culture of the South could well be imagined; it delighted in
old editions of old authors; it fondly turned their pages, and
quoted their choice passages; it built little libraries here and
there, like the one at Ellerby Mill, and loaded their shelves
with fine old works. In the cities it expanded into associations, and large, lofty chambers were filled to the ceiling with
costly tomes, which now look so dark, and rich, and ancient
to Northern visitors, accustomed to the lightly bound, cheap
new books constantly succeeding each other on the shelves of
Northern libraries. These Southern collections were not for
the multitude; there was no multitude. Where plantations
met, where there was a neighborhood, there grew up the little
country library. No one was in a hurry; the rules were leni-
ent; the library was but a part of the easy, luxurious way of
living which belonged to the planters. The books were generally imported, an English rather than a New York imprint
being preferred; and, without doubt, they selected the classics
of the world. But they stopped, generally, at the end of the
last century, often at a date still earlier; they forgot that there
may be new classics.

The library at Ellerby Mill was built by low-country
planters who came up to the mountains during the warm
months, having rambling old country-houses there. They
had their little summer church, St. Mark's in the Wilderness,
and they looked down upon the mountain-people, who, plain
folk themselves, revered the old names borne by their summer
visitors, names known in their State annals since the earliest
times. The mountain-people had been so long accustomed
to see their judges, governors, representatives, and senators
chosen from certain families, that these offices seemed to
them to belong by inheritance to those families; certainly the
farmers never disputed the right. For the mountain-people

were farmers, not planters; their slaves were few. They were a class by themselves, a connecting link between the North and the South. The old names, then, placed Ellerby Library where it stood full thirty years before Honor was born. They did not care for the village, but erected the small building at a point about equidistant from their country-houses, and near the mill for safety, that boys or idle slaves, drawn by the charm which any building, even an empty shed, possesses in a thinly settled country, might not congregate there on Sundays and holidays, or camp there at night. But the library had been closed now for thirteen years; the trustees were all dead, the books moldy, the very door-key was lost. The low-country planters no longer came up to the mountains; there were new names in the State annals, and the mountain-farmers, poorer than before, and much bewildered as to the state of the world, but unchanged in their lack of the questioning capacity, rode by to and from the mill, and gave no thought to the little building with its barred shutters standing in the grove. What was there inside? Nothing save books, things of no practical value, and worthless. So the library stood desolate, like an unused lighthouse on the shore; and the books turned blue-green and damp at their leisure.

II.

STEPHEN WAINWRIGHT traveled, on principle. He had been, on principle, through Europe more than once, and through portions of Asia and Africa; in the intervals he made pilgrimages through his own country. He was not a languid traveler; he had no affectations; but his own marked impersonality traveled with him, and he was always the most indistinct, unremembered person on every railroad-car or steamboat. He was the man without a shadow. Of course, this was only when he chose to step out of the lime-light which his wealth threw around his every gesture. But he chose to step out of it very often, and always suffered when he did.

He was for ever adding up different opinions to find the same
constantly recurring sum total of "no consequence." After
each experience of the kind he went back into lime-light, and
played at kingship for a while. He had been doing this for
twenty years.

One day he came to Ellerby on the top of the stage.
Nine Methodist ministers in the inside, returning from a missionary meeting, had made the lonely road over the mountains echo with their hearty hymns. One small brother
climbed out at the half-way station on the summit, and, after
drinking copiously from the spring, clasped his hands behind
him and admired the prospect. Wainwright looked at him,
not cynically, but with his usual expressionless gaze. The
little minister drank again, and walked up and down. After
a few moments he drank a third time, and continued to admire the prospect. Wainwright recalled vaguely the Biblical
injunction, "Take a little wine for thy stomach's sake," when,
behold! the small minister drank a fourth time hastily, and
then, as the driver gathered up the reins, a last and hearty
fifth time, before climbing up to the top, where Wainwright
sat alone.

"I am somewhat subject to vertigo," he explained, as he
took his seat; "I will ride the rest of the way in the open air,
with your permission, sir."

Wainwright looked at him. "Perhaps he was weighting
himself down with water," he thought.

The brother had, indeed, very little else to make weight
with: his small body was enveloped in a long linen duster,
his head was crowned with a tall hat; he might have weighed
one hundred pounds. He could not brace himself when they
came to rough places, because his feet did not reach the floor;
but he held on manfully with both hands, and begged his
companion's pardon for sliding against him so often.

"I am not greatly accustomed to the stage," he said; "I
generally travel on horseback."

"Is there much zeal in your district?" said Wainwright.

It was the question he always asked when he was placed next to a clergyman, varying it only by "parish," "diocese," or "circuit," according to appearances.

"Zeal," said his companion—"zeal, sir? Why, there isn't anything else!"

"I am glad to hear it," replied Wainwright.

The little minister took the remark in good faith.

"A believer?" he asked.

"Certainly," replied Stephen.

"Let me shake you by the hand, brother. This is a noble country in which to believe. Among these great and solemn peaks, who can disbelieve or who go contrary to the will of the Lord?"

Stephen made no answer, and the brother, lifting up his voice after a silence, cried again, "Who?" And, after a moment's pause, and more fervently, a second "Who?" Then a third, in a high, chanting key. It seemed as if he would go on for ever.

"Well," said Stephen, "if you will have answer, I suppose I might say the moonlight whisky-makers."

The little brother came down from the heights immediately, and glanced at his companion. "Acquainted with the country, sir?" he asked in a business-like tone.

"Not at all," said Stephen.

"Going to stay at Ellerby awhile, perhaps?"

"Perhaps."

"Reckon you will like to ride about; you will need horses. They will cheat you in the village; better apply to me. Head is my name—Bethuel Head; everybody knows me." Then he shut his eyes and began to sing a hymn of eight or ten verses, the brethren below, hearing him chanting alone on the top, joining in the refrain with hearty good will. As soon as he had finished, he said again, in a whisper, "Better apply to me," at the same time giving his companion a touch with the elbow. Then he leaned over and began a slanting conversation with the brother who occupied the window-seat on his side; but, whenever he righted himself for a moment, he either poked Wainwright or winked at him, not lightly or jocularly, but with a certain anxious, concealed earnestness which was evidently real. "Head is my name," he whispered again; "better write it down—Bethuel Head." And when Wainwright, who generally did imperturbably whatever other people asked him to do, finding it in the end the least trouble, finally did write it down, the little man seemed relieved. "Their blood has dyed the pure mountain-streams," he whispered solemnly, as the coach crept down a dark gorge with the tree-branches sweeping its sides; "but I shall go out, yea, I shall go out as did David against Goliath, and save one man—one!"

"Do," said Stephen. What the little brother meant he neither knew nor cared to know; going through life without questions he had found to be the easiest way. Besides, he was very tired. He had never "rejoiced in his strength," even when he was young; he had always had just enough to carry him through, with nothing over. The seven hours on the mountain-road, which climbed straight up on one side of the Blue Ridge, and straight down on the other, now over solid rock, now deep in red clay, now plunging through a break-neck gorge, now crossing a rushing stream so often that the route seemed to be principally by water, had driven him into the dull lethargy which was the worst ailment he knew; for even his illnesses were moderate. He fell asleep mentally, and only woke at the sound of a girl's voice.

It was twilight, and the stage had stopped at Ellerby Mill. Two of the ministers alighted there, to take horse and go over solitary roads homeward to small mountain-villages, one ten, one fifteen miles away. Brother Bethuel was leaning over the side, holding on to his tall hat, and talking down to a young girl who stood at the edge of the roadway on a bank of ferns.

"Masters is better, Miss Honor," he said, "or was the last time I saw him; I do not think there is any present danger."

"I am very glad," answered the girl with earnestness; her eyes did not swerve from the little minister's face, although Wainwright was now looking down too. "If we could only have him entirely well again!"

"He will be!—he will be!" answered Brother Bethuel. "Pray for him, my sister."

"I do pray," said the girl—"daily, almost hourly." Into her dark eyes, uplifted and close to him, Wainwright could look directly, himself unnoticed as usual; and he read there that she did pray. "She believes it," he thought. He looked at her generally; she did not appear to be either extremely young, or ignorant, or commonplace, exactly. "About eighteen," he thought.

"He has asked if his father has been told," continued the minister.

"No, no; it is better he should know nothing," said the girl. "Can you take a package, Mr. Head?"

"Yes, to-morrow. I abide to-night with Brother Beetle."

"I will have it ready, then," said the girl.

The stage moved on, she waved her hand, and the minister nodded energetically in return until the road curved and he could see her no longer. His tall hat was tightly on his head all this time; politeness in the mountains is not a matter of hat. They were but half a mile from Ellerby now, and the horses began to trot for the first time in eight hours. Brother Bethuel turned himself, and met Wainwright's eyes. Now those eyes of Wainwright were of a pale color, like the eyes of a fish; but they had at times a certain inflexibility which harassed the beholder, as, sometimes, one fish in an aquarium will drive a person into nervousness by simply remaining immovable behind his glass wall, and staring out at him stonily. Brother Bethuel, meeting Wainwright's eyes, immediately began to talk:

"A fine young lady that: Miss Honor Dooris, niece of Colonel Eliot—the low-country Eliots, you know, one of our most distinguished families. I venture to say, sir, that strike

13

at an Eliot, yes, strike at an Eliot, and a thousand will rise to beat back the blow. It would be dangerous, sir, most dangerous, to strike at that family."

" Are they troubled by—by strikers ? " asked Stephen.

" Nobody ever harms anybody in this blessedly peaceful country of ours," said the little minister in a loud, chanting voice. Then he dropped to a conversational tone again. " Miss Honor has been to the library ; she is writing some ' Reflections on the Book of Job,' and is obliged of course to consult the authorities. You noticed the old library, did you not ?—that small building in the grove, opposite the mill; her father was one of the trustees. The front steps are down, and she is obliged to climb in by a back window—allowable, of course, to a trustee's daughter—in order to consult the authorities."

" And on Job they are such as— ? "

" Well, the dictionaries, I reckon," said Brother Bethuel, after considering a moment. " She is not of my flock ; the Eliots are, of course, Episcopalians," he continued, with an odd sort of pride in the fact. " But I have aided her—I have aided her."

" In the matter of Masters, perhaps ? "

Brother Bethuel glanced at his companion quickly in the darkening twilight. He caught him indulging in a long, tired yawn.

" I was about to say, general charity ; but the matter of Masters will do," he said carelessly. " The man is a poor fellow up in the mountains, in whom Miss Dooris is interested. He is often ill and miserable, and always very poor. She sends him aid when she can. I am to take a bundle to-morrow."

" And she prays for him," said Wainwright, beginning to descend as the stage stopped at the door of the village inn.

" She prays for all," replied Brother Bethuel, leaning over, and following him down with the words, delivered in a full undertone. Brother Bethuel had a good voice ; he had preached

under the open sky among the great peaks too long to have
any feeble tones left.

"I do not believe anybody ever prays for me," was Wainwright's last thought before he came sharply into personal
contact with the discomforts of the inn.   And, as his mother
died when he was born, perhaps he was right.

The next morning he wandered about and gazed at the
superb sweep of the mountains.   Close behind him rose the
near wall of the Blue Ridge ; before him stretched the line of
the Alleghanies going down toward Georgia, the Iron Mountains, the Bald Mountains, and the peaks of the Great Smoky,
purple and soft in the distance.   A chain of giant sentinels
stretched across the valley from one range to the other, and
on these he could plainly see the dark color given by the
heavy, unmixed growth of balsam-firs around and around up
to the very top, a hue which gives the name Black Mountain
to so many of these peaks.

It was Sunday, and when the three little church-bells rang,
making a tinkling sound in the great valley, he walked over to
the Episcopal church.   He had a curiosity to see that girl's
eyes again by daylight.   Even there, in that small house of
God where so few strangers ever came, he was hardly noticed.   He took his seat on one of the benches, and looked
around.   Colonel Eliot was there, in a black broadcloth coat
seventeen years old, but well brushed, and worn with an air
of unshaken dignity.   The whole congregation heard him acknowledge every Sunday that he was a miserable sinner ; but
they were as proud of him on his one leg with his crutch
under his arm as if he had been a perfected saint, and they
would have knocked down any man who had dared to take
him at his Sunday word.   The Colonel's placid, dimpled wife
was there, fanning herself with the slowly serene manner of
her youth ; and two benches were full of children.   On the
second bench was Honor, and the man of the world watched
her closely in his quiet, unobserved way.   This was nothing
new : Wainwright spent his life in watching people.   He had

studied hundreds of women in the same way, and he formed
his conclusions with minutest care. He judged no one by
impulse or intuition, or even by liking or disliking. What
persons *said* was not of the slightest importance to him in
any way : he noted what they *did*. The service was in progress, and Honor was down upon her knees. He saw her confess her sins ; he saw her bow her head to receive the absolu-
tion ; he saw her repeat the psalms ; he watched her through
every word of the Litany; he heard her sing; and he noted
her clasped hands and strong effort of recollection throughout
the recital of the Commandments. Then he settled himself
anew, and began to watch her through the sermon. He had
seen women attentive through the service before now : they
generally became neutral during the sermon. But this girl
never swerved. She sat with folded arms looking at the
preacher fixedly, a slight compression about the mouth showing that the attention was that of determination. The preacher was uninteresting, he was tautological ; still the girl followed him. " What a narrow little round of words and
phrases it is ! " thought the other, listening too, but weary.
" How can she keep up with him ? " And then, still watching her, he fell to noticing her dress and attitude. Poor Honor
wore a gown of limp black alpaca, faithful, long-enduring
servant of small-pursed respectability; on her head was a
small black bonnet which she had fashioned herself, and not
very successfully. A little linen collar, a pair of old gloves.
and her prayer-book completed the appointments of her costume. Other young girls in the congregation were as poorly
dressed as she, but they had a ribbon, a fan, an edge of lace
here and there, or at least a rose from the garden to brighten
themselves withal ; this girl alone had nothing. She was tall
and well rounded, almost majestic, but childishly young in
face. Her dark hair, which grew very thickly—Wainwright
could see it on the temples—seemed to have been until recently kept short, since the heavy braid behind made only one
awkward turn at the back of the head. She had a boldly cut

profile, too marked for regular beauty, yet pleasant to the eye
owing to the delicate finish of the finer curves and the distinct arch of the lips. Her cheeks were rather thin. She had
no grace; she sat stiffly on the bench, and resolutely listened
to the dull discourse. "A good forehead," thought Wainwright, "and, thank Fortune! not disfigured by straggling
ends of hair. 'Reflections on the Book of Job,' did he say?
Poor little soul!"

At last the service was ended, the sermon of dull para-
phrases over; but Wainwright did not get his look. Honor
sat still in her place without turning. He lingered awhile;
but, as he never did anything, on principle, that attracted attention, he went out with the last stray members of the congregation, and walked down the green lane toward the inn.
He did not look back: certain rules of his he would not have
altered for the Queen of Sheba' (whoever she was). But
Brother Bethuel, coming from the Methodist meeting-house,
bore down upon him, and effected what the Queen of Sheba
could not have done: himself openly watching the church-
door, he took Wainwright by the arm, turned him around,
and, holding him by a buttonhole, stood talking to him. The
red wagon of the Eliots was standing at the gate; Mrs. Eliot
was on the front seat, and all the space behind was filled in
with children. Black Pompey was assisting his master into
the driver's place, while Honor held the crutch. A moment
afterward the wagon passed them, Pompey sitting at the end
with his feet hanging down behind. Brother Bethuel received a nod from the Colonel, but Madame Eliot serenely
failed to see him. The low-country lady had been brought
up to return the bows and salutations of all the blacks in the
neighborhood, but whites below a certain line she did not see.

Evidently Honor was going to walk home. In another
moment she was close to them, and Stephen was having his
look. The same slight flush rose in her face when she saw
Brother Bethuel which had risen there the day before; the
same earnestness came into her eyes, and Stephen became

haunted by the desire to have them turned upon himself. But he was not likely to have this good fortune; all her attention was concentrated upon the little minister. She said she had the package ready; it would be at the usual place. He would take it up, he replied, at sunset. She hoped the moon would not be hidden by clouds. He hoped so too; but old Marcher knew the way. She had heard that the East Branch was up. He had heard so also; but old Marcher could swim very well. All this was commonplace, yet it seemed to Wainwright that the girl appeared to derive a certain comfort from it, and to linger. There was a pause.

"This is my friend," said Brother Bethuel at last, indicating Stephen with a backward turn of his thumb; "Mr.— Mr.—"

"Wainwright," said Stephen, uncovering; then, with his straw hat in his hand, he made her a low bow, as deliberate as the salutations in a minuet, coming up slowly and looking with gravity full in her face. He had what he wanted then— a look; she had never seen such a bow before. To tell the truth, neither had Stephen; he invented it for the occasion.

"Met him on the stage," said Brother Bethuel, "and, as he is a stranger, I thought, perhaps, Miss Honor, the Colonel would let him call round this afternoon; he'd take it as a favor, I know." There was a concealed determination in his voice. The girl immediately gave Stephen another look. "My uncle will be happy to see you," she said quickly. Then they all walked on together, and Stephen noted, under his eyelashes, the mended gloves, the coarse shoe, and the rusty color of the black gown; he noted also the absolute purity of the skin over the side of the face which was next to him, over the thin cheek, the rather prominent nose, the little shell-like ear, and the rim of throat above the linen collar. This clear white went down to the edge of the arched lips, and met the red there sharply and decidedly; the two colors were not mingled at all. What was there about her that interested him? It was the strong reality of her religious belief. In the character-studies with which he amused his life he recognized any real feeling, no matter what, as a rarity, a treasure-trove. Once he had spent six weeks in studying a woman who slowly and carefully planned and executed a revenge. He had studied what is called religion enormously, considering it one of the great spiritual influences of the world: he had found it, in his individual cases so far, mixed. Should he study this new specimen? He had not decided when they came to the porch of the inn. There was no hurry about deciding, and this was his place to stop; he never went out of his way. But Honor paused too, and, looking at him, said, with a mixture of earnestness and timidity: "You will come and see uncle, I hope, Mr. Wainwright. Come this afternoon." She even offered her hand, and offered it awkwardly. As Wainwright's well-fitting, well-buttoned glove touched for an instant the poor, cheap imitation, wrinkled and flabby, which covered her hand, he devoutly hoped she would not see the contrast as he saw it. She did not: a Dooris was a Dooris, and the varieties of kid-skin and rat-skin could not alter that.

Brother Bethuel went on with Honor, but in the afternoon he came back to the inn to pilot Stephen to the Eliot ravine. Stephen was reading a letter from Adelaide Kellinger—a charming letter, full of society events and amusing little comments, which were not rendered unintelligible either by the lack of commas, semicolons, and quotation-marks, and the substitution of the never-failing dash, dear to the feminine pen. The sheets, exhaling the faintest reminiscence of sandal-wood, were covered with clear handwriting, which went straight from page to page in the natural way, without crossing or doubling or turning back. There was a date at the top; the weather was mentioned; the exact time of arrival of Stephen's last letter told. It can be seen from this that Adelaide was no ordinary correspondent.

Stephen, amused and back in New York, did not care

much about the Eliot visit; but Brother Bethuel cared, and so, with his usual philosophy, Stephen went. They talked of the mountains, of the mountain-people, of the villagers; then Brother Bethuel took up the subject of the Eliot family, and declaimed their praises all the rest of the way. They were extremely influential, they were excessively hot-tempered; the State was in a peculiar condition at present, but the Eliots held still the old wires, and it would be extremely dangerous to attack the family in any way. Stephen walked along, and let the little man chant on. He had heard, in this same manner, pages and volumes of talk from the persons who insist upon telling you all about people in whom you have not the remotest interest, even reading you their letters and branching off farther and farther, until you come to regard those first mentioned as quite near friends when the talker comes back to them (if he ever does), being so much nearer than the outside circles into which he has tried to convey you. Stephen never interrupted these talkers; so he was a favorite prey of theirs. Only gradually did it dawn upon them that his stillness was not exactly that of attention. The only interest he showed now was when the minister got down to what he called the present circumstances of the family. It seemed that they were very poor; Brother Bethuel appeared determined that the stranger should know precisely how poor. He brought forward the pathetic view.

"They have nothing to eat sometimes but corn-meal and potatoes," he said. This made no impression.

"The brook rises now and then, and they live in a roaring flood; all the small articles have more than once been washed away."

"Any of the children?" inquired Wainwright.

"Once, when the horses were lame, I saw Honor go to the mill herself with the meal-sack."

"Indeed!"

"Yes, and carry it home again. And I have seen her scrubbing out the kettles."

Wainwright gave an inward shudder. "Has she any education at all?" he asked, with a feeling like giving her money, and getting away as fast as possible: money, because he had for twenty-four hours made her in a certain way a subject of study, and felt as if he owed her something, especially if he went disappointed.

"Sir, she has a finished education," responded the little minister with dignity; "she can play delightfully upon David's instrument, the harp."

At this moment they came to the plank and the ditch.

"I will go no farther," said Brother Bethuel, "and—and you need not mention to the Colonel, if you please, that I accompanied you hither." Then he stood on tiptoe, and whispered mysteriously into Stephen's ear: "As to horses, remember to apply to me—Brother Head, Bethuel Head. A note dropped into the post-office will reach me, a man on horseback bringing the mail up our way twice each week. Bethuel Head—do not forget." He struck himself on the breast once or twice as if to emphasize the name, gave Stephen a wink, which masqueraded as knowing but was more like entreaty, and, turning away, walked back toward the village.

"An extraordinary little man," thought the other, crossing the plank, and following the path up the ravine by the side of the brook.

The Colonel sat on his high, unrailed piazza, with the red wagon and a dilapidated buggy drawn up comfortably underneath; Honor was with him. He rose to greet his visitor, and almost immediately asked if he was related to Bishop Wainwright. When Stephen replied that he was not, the old gentleman sat down, and leaned his crutch against the wall, with a good deal of disappointment: being a devoted churchman, he had hoped for a long ecclesiastical chat. But, after a moment, he took up with good grace the secondary subject of the mountains, and talked very well about them. With the exception of the relationship to the Bishop, he, with the courtesy of the South, did not ask his guest a single question : Stephen could have been a peddler, a tenor-singer, a carpet-bag politician, or a fugitive from justice, with perfect safety, as far as questions were concerned.

Honor said nothing. It was refreshing to be with a girl who did not want to go anywhere or do anything. She had really asked him to come, then, merely to please the old Colonel. A girl of gold. But, alas! the girl of gold proved herself to be of the usual metal, after all; for, when half an hour had passed, she deliberately proposed to her uncle that she should take their visitor up the hill to see the view. Now, Stephen had been taken numerous times in his life to see views; the trouble was that he always looked directly at the real landscape, whatever it was, and found a great deal to say about it, to the neglect of the view nearer his side. He did not think it necessary now to play his usual part of responsive politeness to this little country-girl's open manœuvre ; he could go if she insisted upon it, he supposed. So he sat looking down at the brim of his hat; but noted, also, that even the Colonel seemed surprised. Honor, however, had risen, and was putting on her ugly little bonnet ; she looked quietly determined. Stephen rose also, and took leave formally ; he would go homeward from the hill. They started, he by this time weary of the whole State, and fast inclining toward departure early the next morning.

He did not say much to her, or look at her; but, in truth, the path through the corn was too steep and narrow for conversation : they were obliged to walk in single file. When they had reached the summit, and Stephen was gathering together his adjectives for his usual view-remarks, he turned toward his companion, and was surprised to see how embarrassed she appeared; he began to feel interested in her again—interested in her timid, dark eyes, and the possibilities in their depths. She was evidently frightened.

"If," she commenced once, twice—then faltered and stopped.

"Well?" said Stephen encouragingly: after all, she was very young.

"If you intend to stay in Ellerby any length of time—do you?"

"I really have not decided," said Stephen, relapsing into coolness.

"I was only going to say that if you *do* stay, we, that is, I—we, I mean—shall be happy to see you here often."

"Thanks."

"The view is considered fine," faltered the girl, pulling off her gloves in desperate embarrassment, and putting them deep down in her pocket.

Stephen began his view-remarks.

"But what I was going to say," she continued, breaking in at the first pause, "was, that if you should stay, and need —need *horses*, or a—guide, I wish you would apply to Mr. Head."

"They are in a conspiracy against me with their horses," thought Stephen. Then he threw a hot shot: "Yes; Mr. Head asked me the same thing. He also asked me not to mention that he brought me here."

"No; pray do not," said Honor quickly.

He turned and looked at her: she began to blush—pink, crimson, pink; then white, and a very dead white too.

"You think it strange?" she faltered.

"Not at all. Do not be disturbed, Miss Dooris; I never think anything."

"Mr. Head is poor, and—and tries to make a little money now and then with his horses," she stammered.

"So I—judged."

"And I—try to help him."

"Very natural, I am sure."

He was beginning to feel sorry for the child, and her poor little efforts to gain a few shillings: he had decided that the Colonel's old horses were the wagon-team of this partnership, and "Marcher" the saddle-horse.

" I shall certainly need horses," he said aloud.

" And you will apply to Mr. Head?"

She was so eager that he forgot himself, and smiled.

"Miss Dooris," he said, bowing, "I will apply to Mr. Head, and only to him; I give you my word."

She brightened at once.

The golden shafts of the setting sun shone full in her face: her dark eyes did not mind them; she did not put up her hand to shield herself, but stood and looked directly into the glittering, brilliant western sky. He put his quizzical expression back out of sight, and began to talk to her. She answered him frankly. He tested her a little; he was an old hand at it. Of coquetry she gave back not a sign. Gradually the conviction came to him that she had not asked him up there for personal reasons at all. It was, then, the horses.

When he had decided this, he sat down on a stump, and went on talking to her with renewed interest. After a while she laughed, and there came into her face that peculiar brilliancy which the conjunction of dark eyes and the gleam of white, even teeth can give to a thin-cheeked brunette. Then he remembered to look at her hands, and was relieved to find them, although a little roughened by toil, charmingly shaped and finely aristocratic—fit portion of the tall, well-rounded figure, which only needed self-consciousness to be that of a young Diana. The girl seemed so happy and radiant, so impersonal in the marked attention she gave to him, which was not unlike the attention she might have given to her grandfather, that Wainwright recognized it at last as only another case of his being of no consequence, and smiled to himself over it. Evidently, if he wanted notice, he must, as it were, mount the horses. He had had no especial intention of making excursions among the mountains; but that was, apparently, the fixed idea of these horse-owners. They were, for some reason, pleased to be mysterious; he would be mysterious also.

"I hope Mr. Head's horses are good ones?" he said confidentially; "I shall need *very* good horses."

All her color gone instantly, and the old cloud of anxiety on her face again.

"Yes, they are good horses," she answered; and then her eyes rested upon him, and he read trouble, fear, and dislike, succeeding each other openly in their dark depths.

"Is it because I am a Northerner, Miss Dooris?" he said quietly. He had made up his mind, rather unfairly, to break down the fence between them by a close question, which so young a girl would not know how to parry.

She started, and the color rushed up all over her face again.

"Of course, it is all right," she answered hurriedly, in a low voice. "I know that the laws must be maintained, and that some persons must do the work that you do. People can not always choose their occupations, I suppose, and no doubt they—no doubt you—I mean, that it can not be helped."

"May I ask what you take me for?" said Wainwright, watching her.

"We saw it at once; Mr. Head saw it, and afterward I did also. But we are experienced; others may not discover you so soon. Mr. Head is anxious to pilot you through the mountains to save you from danger."

"He is very kind; disinterested, too."

"No," said Honor, flushing again; "I assure you he makes money by it also."

"But you have not told me what it is you take me for, Miss Dooris?"

"It is not necessary, is it?" replied Honor in a whisper. "You are one of the new revenue detectives, sent up here to search out the stills."

"An informer—after the moonlight whisky-makers, you mean?"

"Yes."

Wainwright threw back his head and laughed out loud, as he had not laughed for years.

" I am not sure but that it is a compliment," he said at last ; "no one has ever taken me for anything particular before in all my life." Then, when he was sober, "Miss Dooris," he said, " I am a man of leisure, residing in New York ; and I am sorry to say that I am an idle vagabond, with no occupation even so useful as that of a revenue detective."

In spite of himself, however, a touch of contempt filtered into his voice. Then it came to him how the club-men would enjoy the story, and again he laughed uproariously. When he came to himself, Honor was crying.

III.

YES, Honor was crying. The dire mistake, the contempt, and, worse than all, the laughter, had struck the proud little Southern girl to the heart.

" My dear child," said Wainwright, all the gentleman in him aroused at once, "why should you care for so small and natural a mistake? It is all clear to me now. I gave no account of myself coming over on the stage ; I remember, too, that I spoke of the moonlight whisky-makers myself, and that I made no effort to find out what Mr. Head was alluding to when he talked on in his mysterious way. It is my usual unpardonable laziness which has brought you to this error. Pray forgive it."

Honor cried on, unable to stop, but his voice and words had soothed her ; he stood beside her, hat in hand, and after a few moments she summoned self-control enough to dry her eyes and put down her handkerchief. But her eyelashes were still wet, her breath came tremulously, and there was a crimson spot on each cheek. She looked, at that moment, not more than fifteen years old, and Wainwright sat down, this time nearer to her, determined to make her feel easier. He banished the subject of her mistake at once, and began talking to her about herself. He asked many questions, and she

answered them humbly, as a Lenten penitent might answer a
father confessor. She seemed to feel as though she owed
him everything he chose to take. She let him enter and walk
through her life and mind, through all her hopes and plans;
one or two closed doors he noted, but did not try to open,
neither did he let her see that he had discovered them. He
learned how poor they were; he learned her love for her uncle, her Switzer's attachment to the mountain-peaks about
her; he learned what her daily life was; and he came near
enough to her religious faith, that faith which had first attracted him, to see how clear and deep it was, like a still pool
in a shaded glen. It was years since Stephen Wainwright
had been so close to a young girl's soul, and, to do him justice, he felt that he was on holy ground.

When at last he left her, he had made up his mind that he
would try an experiment. He would help this child out of
the quagmire of poverty, and give her, in a small way, a
chance. The question was, how to do it. He remained at
Ellerby, made acquaintances, and asked questions. He pretended this, and pretended that. Finally, after some consideration, he woke up the old library association, reopened the
building, and put in Honor as librarian, at a salary of two
hundred dollars a year. To account for this, he was obliged,
of course, to be much interested in Ellerby; his talk was that
the place must eventually become a summer resort, and that
money could be very well invested there. He therefore invested it. Discovering, among other things, pink marble on
wild land belonging to the Colonel, he bought a whole hillside, and promptly paid for it. To balance this, he also
bought half a mile of sulphur springs on the other side of the
valley (the land comically cheap), and spoke of erecting a
hotel there. The whole of Ellerby awoke, talked, and rejoiced; no one dreamed that the dark eyes of one young girl
had effected it all.

Honor herself remained entirely unconscious. She was
so openly happy over the library that Wainwright felt him-

self already repaid. " It might stand against some of my omissions," he said to himself.

One thing detained him where he was; then another. He could not buy property without paying some attention to it, and he did not choose to send for his man of business. He staid on, therefore, all summer. And he sent books to the library now and then during the winter that followed— packages which the librarian, of course, was obliged to acknowledge, answering at the same time the questions of the letters which accompanied them. Stephen's letters were always formal; they might have been nailed up on the walls of the library for all comers to read. He amused himself, however, not a little over the carefully written, painstaking answers, in which the librarian remained " with great respect " his " obliged servant, Honor Dooris."

The second summer began, and he was again among the mountains; but he should leave at the end of the month, he said. In the mean time it had come about that he was teaching the librarian. She needed instruction, certainly; and the steps that led up to it had been so gradual that it seemed natural enough now. But no one knew the hundred little things which had been done to make it seem so.

What was he trying to do?

His cousin, Adelaide Kellinger, determined to find out that point, was already domiciled with her maid at the inn. There had been no concealment about Honor; Wainwright had told Adelaide the whole story. He also showed to her the librarian's little letters whenever they came, and she commented upon them naturally, and asked many questions. " Do you know, I feel really interested in the child myself? " she said to him one day; and it was entirely true.

When he told her that he was going to the mountains again, she asked if he would not take her with him. " It will be a change from the usual summer places; and, besides, I find I am lonely if long away from you," she said frankly. She always put it upon that ground. She had learned that nothing makes a man purr more satisfactorily than the hearing that the woman in whose society he finds himself particularly comfortable has an especial liking for and dependence upon himself; immediately he makes it all a favor and kindness to *her*, and is happy. So Adelaide came with Stephen, and did make him more comfortable. His barren room bloomed with fifty things which came out of her trunks and her ingenuity; she coaxed and bribed the cook; she won the landlady to a later breakfast. She arranged a little parlor, and was always there when he came home, ready to talk to him a little, but not too much; ready to divine his mood and make the whole atmosphere accord with it at once. They had been there three weeks, and of course Adelaide had met the librarian.

For those three weeks she remained neutral, and studied the ground; then she began to act. She sent for John Royce. And she threw continuous rose-light around Honor.

After the final tableau of a spectacle-play, a second view is sometimes given with the nymphs and fairies all made doubly beautiful by rose-light. Mrs. Kellinger now gave this glow. She praised Honor's beauty.

Stephen had not observed it. How could he be so blind? Why, the girl had fathomless eyes, exquisite coloring, the form of a Greek statue, and the loveliest mouth! Then she branched off.

"What a beautiful thing it would be to see such a girl as that fall in love!—a girl so impulsive, so ignorant of the world. That is exactly the kind of girl that really could die of a broken heart."

"Could she?" said Stephen.

"Now, Stephen, you know as well as I do what Honor Dooris is," said Adelaide warmly. "She is not awakened yet, her prince has not made himself known to her; but, when he does awaken her, she will take him up to the seventh heaven."

"That is—if she loves him."

"She has seen so few persons; it would not be a difficult matter," said Adelaide.

A few days later, when she told him that she was thinking of sending for John Royce, he made no comment, although she looked at him with undisguised wistfulness, a lingering gaze that seemed to entreat his questions. But he would not question, and, obedient as always to his will, she remained silent.

John Royce came. He was another cousin, but a young one, twenty-five years old, blue-eyed and yellow-haired. He kept his yellow hair ruthlessly short, however, and he frowned more or less over his blue eyes, owing to much yachting and squinting ahead across the glaring water to gain an inch's length on the next boat. He was brown and big, with a rolling gait; the edge of a boat tilted at one hair's-breadth from going over entirely, was his idea of a charming seat; under a tree before a camp-fire, with something more than a suspicion of savage animals near, his notion of a delightful bed. He did not have much money of his own; he was going to do something for himself by and by; but Cousin Adelaide had always petted him, and he had no objection to a hunt among those Southern mountains. So he came.

He had met Honor almost immediately. Mrs. Kellinger was a welcome visitor at the Eliot home; she seemed to make the whole ravine more graceful. The Colonel's wife and all the children clustered around her with delight every time she came, and the old Colonel himself renewed his youth in her presence. She brought John to call upon them at once, and she took him to the library also; she made Honor come and dine with them at the inn. She arranged a series of excursions in a great mountain-wagon shaped like a boat, and tilted high up behind, with a canvas cover over a framework, like a Shaker bonnet, and drawn by six slow-walking horses. The wagoner being a postilion, they had the wagon to themselves; they filled the interstices with Eliot children and baskets, and explored the wilder roads, going on foot up the

steep banks above, drinking from the ice-cold spring, looking
out for rattlesnakes, plucking the superb rhododendrons and
the flowers of the calico-bush, and every now and then catching a new glimpse of the unparalleled crowd of peaks over toward the Tennessee line. Stephen went everywhere patiently;
Honor went delightedly; John Royce went carelessly; Mrs.
Kellinger went as the velvet string which held them all together; she was so smooth that they slid easily.

But, in the intervals, Wainwright still taught his librarian.

Mrs. Eliot had become Adelaide's warm friend. The
sweet-voiced Southern wife, with her brood of children, and
her calm, contented pride, confided to the Northern stranger
the one grief of her life, namely, that she was the Colonel's
second wife, and that he had dearly loved the first; anxiety
as to the uncertain future of her children weighed far less
upon her mind than this. The old-time South preserved the
romance of conjugal love even to silver hairs; there may have
been no more real love than at the North, but there was more
of the manner of it. The second month came to its end; it
was now August. Mrs. Kellinger had sent many persons to
the library; she had roused up a general interest in it; villagers now went there regularly for books, paying a small
subscription-fee, which was added to Honor's salary. Honor
thanked her for this in a rather awkward way. Mrs. Eliot,
who was present, did not consider the matter of consequence
enough for thanks. She had never even spoken to Wainwright of Honor's office of librarian, or the salary which came
out of his pocket. Money-matters were nothing; between
friends they were less than nothing. Stephen had two hours
alone with his librarian every morning, when there was no
excursion; Mrs. Kellinger had arranged that, by inventing a
rule and telling it to everybody in a decided tone: no one was
expected at the library before eleven o'clock.

"Did you do this?" said Stephen, when he discovered it.

"I did."

"Why?"

"Because I thought you would like it," replied Adelaide. He looked at her questioningly; she answered immediately to the look. "You are interested in a new study of character, Stephen; you are really doing the child a world of good too; although, as usual, I confess that my interest in the matter is confined principally to your own entertainment." She spoke good-humoredly, and almost immediately afterward left him to himself.

His mind ran back over a long series of little arrangements made for his pleasure on all sorts of occasions. "She is the best-hearted woman in the world," he thought. And then he took his note-book and went over to the library.

Their lessons would have amused a looker-on; but there was no looker-on. Honor was interested or absent-minded, irritable or deeply respectful, humble or proud, by turns; she regarded him as her benefactor, and she really wished to learn; but she was young, and impulsive, and—a girl. There was little conversation save upon the lessons, with the exception of one subject. The man of the world had begun his study of this girl's deep religious faith. "If you can give it to me also, or a portion of it," he had said, "you will be conferring a priceless gift upon me, Miss Honor."

Then Honor would throw down her books, clasp her hands, and, with glowing cheeks, talk to him on sacred subjects. Many a time the tears would spring to her eyes with her own earnestness; many a time she lost herself entirely while pleading with her whole soul. He listened to her, thanked her, and went away. Only once did he show any emotion: it was when she told him that she prayed for him.

"Do you really pray for me?" he said in a low tone; then he put his hand over his eyes, and sat silent.

Honor, a little frightened, drew back. It seemed to her a very simple act, praying for any one: she had prayed for people all her life.

One Sunday afternoon Mrs. Eliot and Honor were sitting in Adelaide's parlor at the inn, whither she had brought them on their way home from service. Royce and Stephen had been discovered, upon their entrance, in two chairs at the windows; the former surrounded by a waste of newspapers, magazines, and novels, thrown down on the floor, a general expression of heat and weariness on his face. His companion was reading a small, compact volume in his usual neat way. Big Royce was sprawled over three chairs; Stephen did not fill one. Big Royce was drumming on the window-sill; Stephen was motionless. Yet Royce, springing up and smiling, his blue eyes gleaming, and frank gladness on his face, was a picture that women remember; while Stephen, rising without change of expression, was a silent contradiction to their small power, which is never agreeable. They all sat talking for an hour, Mrs. Eliot and Mrs. Kellinger contributing most of the sentences. Royce was in gay spirits; Honor rather silent. Suddenly there came a sharp, cracking sound; they all ran to the window. Through the main street of the village a man was running, followed by another, who, three times in their sight and hearing, fired at the one in advance. One, two, three times they saw and heard him fire, and the sickening feeling of seeing a man murdered in plain sight came over them. Royce rushed down to the street. The victim had fallen; the other man was himself staggering, and in the hands of a crowd which had gathered in an instant. After a short delay the two men were borne away, one to his home, one to the jail. Royce returned hot and breathless.

"Oh, how is the poor man who was shot?" exclaimed Mrs. Eliot.

"Poor man, indeed! The other one is the man to be pitied," said Royce angrily. "He is a revenue detective, and was knocked down from behind with a club by this fellow, who is a liquor-seller here in the village. The blow was on the skull, and a murderous one. Half blinded and maddened, he staggered to his feet, drew his revolver, and fired for his life."

Honor had grown white as ivory. She shook in every limb, her lips trembled, and her chin had dropped a little. Wainwright watched her.

"But what does it all mean?" asked Adelaide.

"Moonlight whisky, of course. The detective has been hunting for the stills, and these outlaws will kill the man as they have killed half a dozen before him."

"What an outrage! Are there no laws?"

"Dead letters."

"Or officers to execute them?"

"Dead men."

Royce was excited and aroused. He was young, and had convictions. The laws should not be over-ridden and men murdered in broad daylight by these scoundrels while he was on the scene. He took charge of the detective, who, with his bruised head, was put in jail, while the liquor-seller was allowed to have his illness out in his own house, one of the balls only having taken effect, and that in a safe place in the shoulder. Royce, all on fire for the side of justice, wrote and telegraphed for troops, using the detective's signature; he went himself fifteen miles on horseback to send the dispatch. There were troops at the State capital; they had been up to the mountains before on the same business; they were, indeed, quite accustomed to going up; but they accomplished nothing. The outlaws kept themselves carefully hidden in their wild retreats, and the village looked on as innocently as a Quaker settlement. A detective was fair game: two of them had been shot in the neighborhood within the previous year, and left bleeding in the road. Would they never learn, then, to keep out of the mountains?

"But is it not an extraordinary state of things that a village so large as Ellerby should be so apathetic?" asked Adelaide.

"The villagers can do little: once off the road, and you are in a trackless wilderness," said Stephen. "Custom makes law in these regions: moonlight whisky has always been made, and the mountaineers think they have a right to make it. They look upon the revenue-men as spies."

"Yes; and they are government officials and Northerners too," added Royce hotly—"mind that!"

He had taken the matter in hand vigorously. He wrote and sent off a dozen letters per day. The Department at Washington had its attention decisively called to this district and the outlawry rampant there. It was used to it.

In a week the troops came—part of a company of infantry and a young lieutenant, a tall stripling fresh from West Point. His name was Allison; he lisped and wore kid-gloves; he was as dainty as a girl, and almost as slender. To see the short, red-faced, burly detective, with his bandaged head and stubbed fingers; Royce, with his eagle eyes and impatient glance; and this delicate-handed, pink-cheeked boy, conferring together, was like a scene from a play. The detective, slow and cautious, studied the maps; Royce, in a hot hurry about everything, paced up and down; Allison examined his almond-shaped nails and hummed a tune. The detective had his suspicions concerning Eagle Knob; the troops could take the river-road, turn off at Butter Glen, and climb the mountain at that point. In the mean while all was kept quiet; it was given out that the men were to search South Gap, on the other side of the valley.

On the very night appointed for the start, an old lady, who had three granddaughters from the low country spending the summer with her, opened her house, lit up her candles, and gave a ball, with the village fiddlers for musicians and her old black cook's plum-cake for refreshments. Royce was to accompany the troops; Adelaide had not been able to prevent it. She went to Stephen in distress, and then Stephen proposed to Royce to send half a dozen stout villagers in his place—he, Stephen, paying all expenses.

"There are some things, Wainwright, that even your money can not do," replied Royce.

"Very well," said Stephen.

Royce now announced that they must all go to the ball to divert suspicion; Allison too. But Allison had no invitation. Royce went to Mrs. Eliot, and begged her influence; Mrs. Eliot sent Honor to the old lady, and the invitation came.

"If he could avoid wearing his uniform—" suggested Mrs. Eliot to Adelaide, a little nervously.

"But he has nothing else with him, I fear," answered. Adelaide.

It turned out, however, that the lieutenant had a full evening-suit in his valise, with white tie and white gloves also. Royce surveyed these habiliments and their owner with wonder. He himself, coming from New York, with all the baggage he wanted, had only a black coat. His costume must be necessarily of the composite order; but the composite order was well known at Ellerby.

Allison was the belle of the ball. He danced charmingly, and murmured the most delightful things to all his partners in rapid succession. He was the only man in full evening-dress present, and the pink flush on his cheeks, and his tall, slender figure swaying around in the waltz, were long remembered in Ellerby. Honor was there in a white muslin which had been several times washed and repaired; there was no flow to her drapery, and she looked awkward. She was pale and silent. Mrs. Kellinger, clothed to the chin and wrists, with no pronounced color about her, was the one noticeable woman present. Royce did not dance. He found the rooms hot and the people tiresome; he was in a fever to be off. Stephen sat on the piazza, and looked in through the window. At one o'clock it was over. Allison had danced every dance. He went back to the inn with his pockets stuffed with gloves, withered rose-buds, knots of ribbon, and even, it was whispered, a lock of golden hair. The next hour, in the deep darkness, the troops started.

At five minutes before eleven the next morning, Stephen was bringing his algebra-lesson to a close, when a distant clatter in the gorge was heard, a tramping sound; men were running out of the mill opposite and gazing curiously up the road. Honor was at the window in a flash, Stephen beside her. The troops were returning. They had laid hands upon a mountain-wagon and marched upon each side of it like a guard of honor. Royce sat in the wagon, his face hidden in his hands.

"Where is Mr. Allison?" said Honor, and her voice was but a whisper. She stood back of the curtain, trembling violently.

Royce did not look up as the procession passed the library; without a word Wainwright and Honor went out, locked the door behind them, and followed the wagon toward the village. Everybody did the same; the houses were emptied of their dwellers. The whole village came together to see the body of the boy-officer lifted out and carried into the inn. Allison was dead.

The buttons on his uniform gleamed as they bore him in, and his white hands hung lifelessly down. He had fought like a tiger, they said, and had led his men on with the most intrepid, daring courage to the very last. It seemed that they had fallen into an ambuscade, and had accomplished nothing. Singularly enough, the young lieutenant was the only one killed; Royce was sure that he had seen one of the outlaws deliberately single him out and fire—a dark, haggard-looking fellow.

Stephen took Honor up to Adelaide's parlor. Adelaide was there wringing her hands. She had fastened the boy's collar for him at two o'clock the night before, when he had rather absurdly pretended that he could not make it stay buttoned; and she had tapped him on the cheek reprovingly for his sentimental looks. "This ball has spoiled you, foolish boy," she had said; "march off into the mountains and get rid of this nonsense." Ah, well, he was well rid of it now!

Honor stood as if transfixed, listening. Presently the door opened, and Royce came in. "Let me get somewhere where I am not ashamed to cry," he said; and, sinking down, he

14

laid his head upon his arms on the table and cried like a child. Honor went out of the room hastily ; she hardly noticed that Stephen was with her. When she reached the ravine, she, too, sank down on the grass, out of sight of the house, and sobbed as though her heart would break. Stephen looked at her irresolutely, then moved away some paces, and, sitting down on a stump, waited. Honor had danced with Allison : could it be—but no ; it was only the sudden horror of the thing.

Allison was buried in the little village churchyard ; the whole country-side came to the funeral. The old Episcopal rector read the burial-service, and his voice shook a little as the young head was laid low in the deep grave. Brother Bethuel had come down from the mountains on Marcher, and had asked permission to lead the singing ; he stood by the grave, and, with uncovered head and uplifted eyes, sang with marvelous sweetness and power an old Methodist hymn, in which all the throng soon joined. The young girls who had danced at the ball sobbed aloud. Honor alone stood tearless ; but she had brought her choicest roses to lay over the dead boy's feet, where no one could see them, and she had stooped and kissed his icy forehead in the darkened room before he was carried out : Stephen saw her do it. After the funeral, Brother Bethuel and Honor went away together ; Stephen returned to the inn. Adelaide had taken upon herself the task of answering the letters. Allison had no father or mother, but his other relatives and friends were writing. Royce, his one young burst of grief over, went about sternly, his whole soul set on revenge. Now troops came : an officer of the United States army had been killed, and the Department was aroused at last. There were several officers at Ellerby now, older men than Allison and more experienced ; a new expedition was to be sent into the mountains to route these banditti and make an end of them. Royce was going as guide ; he knew where the former attack had been made, and he knew, also, the detective's reasons for suspecting Eagle Knob, the detective himself being now out of the field, owing to brain-fever: the United States authorities had ordered him out of jail, and he was at the inn, having his fever comfortably on the ground-floor. Honor was with Adelaide almost constantly now. The elder woman, who always received her caressingly, seemed puzzled by the girl's peculiar manner. She said little, but sat and listened to every word, turning her dark eyes slowly from one speaker to the next. Royce came and went, brought in his maps, talked, and every now and then made the vases on the table ring as he brought down his strong hand with an emphasis of defiance.

"I can not study," Honor had said to Stephen when he made some allusion to their morning hours. She said it simply, without excuse or disguise; he did not ask her again.

The expedition was to start on Monday night. The whole village, in the mean time, had been carefully intrusted with the secret that it was to go on Tuesday. But on Sunday evening Honor discovered that before midnight the hounds were to be let slip. The very soldiers themselves did not know it. How did the girl learn it, then? She divined it from some indefinable signs in Royce. Even Adelaide did not suspect it; and Stephen saw only the girl's own restlessness. She slipped away like a ghost—so like one that Stephen himself did not see her go. He followed her, however, almost immediately; it was too late for her to go through the village alone. He was some distance behind her. To his surprise, she did not go homeward, but walked rapidly down toward the river-road. There was fickle moonlight now and then; he dropped still farther behind, and followed her, full of conjecture, which was not so much curiosity as pain. It was still early in the evening, yet too late for her to be out there on the river-road alone. This innocent young girl—this child —where, where was she going? He let her walk on for a mile, and then he made up his mind that he must stop her. They were far beyond the houses now, and the road was lonely and wild; the roar of the river over its broad, rock-

dotted, uneven bed, hid the sound of his footsteps as he
climbed up the steep bank, ran forward, and came down into
the road in advance of her.

"Where are you going, Miss Honor?" he said, showing
himself, and speaking quietly.

She started back, and gasped out his name.

"Yes, it is I," he answered, "Stephen Wainwright. I am
alone; you need not be frightened."

She came close up to him and took his hand.

"Do not stop me," she said entreatingly. "I am on an
errand of life and death!"

"I will go in your place, Honor."

"You can not."

"Yes, I can. But *you* shall not."

"Will you betray me, then?" she said, in an agonized
tone.

"No; but you will tell me what it is, and I will go for
you."

"I tell you, you can not go."

"Why?"

"You do not know; and, besides—you would not."

"I will do anything you ask me to do," said Stephen.

"Anything?"

"Anything."

She hesitated, looking at him.

"Do you give me your word?"

"I do."

"But—but it is an enormous thing you are doing for me."

"I know it is."

"Oh, let me go—let me go myself!" she cried suddenly,
with a half sob; "it is so much better."

"I will never let you go," said Stephen. His voice was inflexible. She surveyed him tremulously, hopelessly; then sank
down upon her knees, praying, but not to him. Stephen took
off his hat, and waited, bareheaded. It was but a moment;
then she rose. "My cousin, Richard Eliot, my uncle's eldest

son, has been with these men, at one of their hiding-places, for some months. My uncle knows nothing of it ; but Brother Bethuel is in the secret, and keeps watch of him."

"Your cousin is Masters, then ? "

"He is. Ask no more questions, but hasten on ; take the first broad trail which leaves the road on the right, follow it until you come to Brother Bethuel's house ; you can not miss it ; it is the only one. He will guide you to the place where Richard is, and you must warn him that the troops are coming."

"Only one question, Honor. Come out into the moonlight ; give me both your hands. Do you love this man ? "

He looked at her fixedly. She gave a quick, strong start, as though she must break away from him at all hazards, and turned darkly red, the deep, almost painful, blush of the brunette. Her hands shook in his grasp, tears of shame rose in her eyes ; it was as though some one had struck her in the face.

"Do you love this Eliot ? " repeated Stephen, compelling her still to meet his eyes.

She drew in her breath suddenly, and answered, with a rush of quick words : "No, no, no ! Not in the way you mean. But he is my cousin. Go ! "

He went. Nearly two miles farther down the road the trail turned off ; it climbed directly up a glen by the side of a brook which ran downward to the river in a series of little waterfalls. It was wide enough for a horse, and showed the track of Marcher's hoofs. It came out on a flank of the mountain and turned westward, then northward, then straight up again through the thick woods to a house whose light shone down like a beacon, and guided him.

Wainwright knocked ; Brother Bethuel opened, started slightly, then recovered himself, and welcomed his guest effusively.

"Is there any one in the house besides ourselves ? " said Stephen, ignorant as to whether there was or was not a Mrs.

Head. There was; but she had gone, with her five offspring, to visit her mother in Tennessee.

"Then," said Stephen, "take me immediately to Richard Eliot."

The little minister stared innocently at his guest.

"Take you where?" he repeated, with surprised face.

"Come," said Stephen, "you need not conceal. Miss Dooris herself sent me. I am to warn this Eliot that the troops are on the way—have probably already left Ellerby."

The little man, convinced, sprang for his lantern, lighted it, and hurried out, followed by Wainwright. He ran more than he walked; he climbed over the rocks; he galloped down the gullies and up the other side; he said not a word, but hurried, closely followed by Stephen, who was beginning to feel spent, until he reached the foot of a wall of rock, the highest ledge of Eagle Knob. Here he stood still and whistled. Stephen sat down, and tried to recover his breath. After a moment or two a whistle answered from above, and the missionary imitated the cry of a night-bird, one, two, three times. He then sat down beside Wainwright, and wiped his forehead. "He will be here in a moment," he said. In a short time, coming up as if from the bowels of the mountain, a figure stood beside them. Brother Bethuel had closed the slide of his lantern, and Wainwright could not see the face. "Miss Dooris sent me," he began. "I am to warn you that the troops are on their way hither to-night, and that they have a clew to your hiding-place."

"Who are you?" said the man.

"I am Miss Dooris's messenger; that is enough."

The man muttered an oath.

Brother Bethuel lifted up his hands with a deprecating gesture.

"You do not mean it, Richard; you know you do not.—Lord, forgive him!" he murmured.

"Well, what am I to do?" said the man. "Did she send any word?"

" Only that you must escape."

" Escape ! Easy enough to say. But where am I to go? Did she send any money ? "

" She will," said Stephen, improvising.

" When ? "

" To-morrow."

" How much ? "

" Quite a sum ; as much as you need."

" Is she so flush, then ? "

" She is, as you say—flush," replied Stephen.

Brother Bethuel had listened breathlessly to this conversation ; and when Eliot said, fretfully, " But where am I to go now—to-night ? " he answered : " Home with me, Dick. I can conceal you for one night ; nobody suspects me. The Lord will forgive ; it is an Eliot."

" Wait until I warn the fellows, then," said the man, disappearing suddenly in the same way he had appeared. Then Stephen, who had not risen from his seat, felt a pair of arms thrown around his neck ; the little brother was embracing him fervently.

" God bless you! God bless you !" he whispered. " We will get him safely out of the country this time, with your aid, Mr. Wainwright. An Eliot, mind you ; a real Eliot, poor fellow !"

But the real Eliot had returned, and Brother Bethuel led the way down the mountain. They walked in single file, and Stephen saw that the man in front of him was tall and powerful. They reached the house, and the minister took the fugitive down into his cellar, supplying him with food, but no light.

" Make no sound," he said. " Even if the house is full of soldiers, you are safe ; no one suspects me." He closed the horizontal door, and then turned to Wainwright. " What are you going to do ? " he asked, his small face wrinkled with anxiety.

" I am going back to Ellerby."

"And when will you return with the money?"

"Some time to-morrow."

"I will go with you as far as the road," said Brother Bethuel; "I want to see if the troops are near."

"Who is this Eliot?" asked Stephen, as they went down the glen.

"The Colonel's eldest son, the only child by the first wife. His father has heard nothing of him for several years; it is the grief of the old man's life."

"What is he doing here?"

"Well, he is a wild boy—always was," said Brother Bethuel reluctantly. "Lately he has been living with a gang of these whisky-men."

"And Miss Dooris knows it?"

"Yes. He was always fond of Honor when she was a child, and latterly he has—has fallen into a way of depending upon her."

"Why does he not come out of the woods, go to work, and behave like a civilized man?" said Wainwright, in a tone of disgust. "I have no patience with such fellows."

"Oh, yes, you have," said Brother Bethuel earnestly. "You are going to help him, you know."

"Well, we will send him far enough away this time—to Australia, if he will go," said Stephen. "The country will be well rid of him."

"You do not, perhaps, understand exactly," said Brother Bethuel timidly, after a moment's silence. "Eliot fought all through the war—fought bravely, nobly. But, when peace came, there seemed to be no place for him. He was not adapted to—to commerce; he felt it a degradation. Hence his present position. But he did not choose it voluntarily; he—he drifted into it."

"Yes, as you say, drifted," said Stephen dryly. "Will the other men get away in time?"

"Oh, yes; they are already gone. There is a cave, and a passage upward through clefts in the rocks to the glen where their still is; it is a natural hiding-place. But they will not even stay there; they will go to another of their haunts."

" Where ? "

" Thank the Lord, I do not know! really and truly, I do not know," ejaculated the little minister fervently. " My only interest in them, the only charge upon my conscience, has been Eliot himself. You do not understand, and I may not be able to explain it to you, Mr. Wainwright, but—I love the Eliots! I have loved them all my life. I was born upon their land, I revered them in childhood, I honored them in youth, I love them in age. They bear one of our great State names; they have been our rulers and our leaders for generations. I love them, every one." Wainwright made no answer; the little man went on : " This son has been a sad, wild boy always—has nearly broken his father's heart. But he is an Eliot still; the little I can do for him I will do gladly until I die."

" Or until he does," suggested Stephen. " One of this gang shot Allison; was this Eliot of yours the marksman ? "

Brother Bethuel was silent. Stephen turned and saw by the lantern's gleam the trouble and agitation on his face.

" He did it, I see," said Stephen, " and you know he did it. It was murder."

" No, no—war," said the missionary, with dry lips. They had reached the road and looked down it; the moonlight was unclouded now. They could see nothing, but they thought they heard sounds. Brother Bethuel went back up the glen, and Wainwright, turning into the woods, made his way along in the deep shadows above the road. He met the soldiers after a while, marching sturdily, and remained motionless behind a tree-trunk until they had passed; then, descending into the track, he walked rapidly back to the village. But, with all his haste and all his skill, he did not reach his room unobserved; Adelaide saw him enter, and noted the hour.

The troops came back at noon the next day, not having discovered the foe. Honor was with Adelaide, pretending to

sew, but her mind was astray; Adelaide watched her closely.
Stephen was present, quiet and taciturn as usual. He had
succeeded in conveying to the girl, unobserved, a slip of paper,
on which was written : " Eliot is hidden in the cellar of Head's
house. I am going out there this afternoon, and you may
feel assured that, in a day or two more, he will be out of the
mountains, and in permanent safety." But he had not been
able to exchange any worde with her.

Royce came in, foiled, tired, and out of temper.

" If it had not been for the little minister, we should have
had nothing at all for our pains," he said, when, the first annoyed heat over, he, having been left in the mean while un-
vexed by questions owing to Adelaide's tact, began to feel
himself like telling the story. " He heard us down in the road,
came to meet us, and advised us what to do. It seems that
he too has had his suspicions about Eagle Knob, and he took
his lantern and guided us up there. We hunted about and
found one of their hiding-places, showing traces, too, of recent occupation; but we could not find the men or the still.
The troops will take rations, however, next time, and make a
regular campaign of it : we shall unearth the scoundrels yet."

" But *you* will not think it necessary to go again, John ? "
said Adelaide.

" Not necessary, but agreeable, Cousin Adelaide. I will
not leave these mountains until the murderer of Allison is
caught—I was going to say shot, but hanging is better," said
Royce.

Honor gazed at him with helpless, fascinated eyes. Mrs.
Kellinger noted the expression. There was evidently another
secret : she had already divined one.

Soon afterward Honor went home, and Stephen did not
accompany her. Adelaide noted that. She noted also that
he sat longer than usual in her parlor after the early dinner,
smoking cigarettes and becoming gradually more and more
drowsy, until at last, newspaper in hand, he sauntered off to
his own room, as if for a *siesta*. It was too well acted. She

said to herself, with conviction, " He is going out ! " A woman can deceive admirably in little things; a man can not.
He can keep the secret of an assassination, but not of a clam
supper. The very cat discovers it. Adelaide went to her
room, put on her trim little walking-boots and English round
hat, and, slipping quietly out of the house, walked down the
road to a wooded knoll she remembered, a little elevation that
commanded the valley and the village; here, under a tree, she
sat waiting. She had a volume of Landor : it was one of
Wainwright's ways to like Landor. After half an hour had
passed, she heard, as she had expected to hear, footsteps; she
looked up. Wainwright was passing. " Why—is it you ? "
she called out. " I thought you would sleep for two hours at
least. Sit down here awhile and breathe this delicious air
with me."

Wainwright, outwardly undisturbed, left the road, came
up the knoll, and sat down by her side. Being in the shade,
he took off his hat and threw himself back on the grass. But
that did not make him look any larger. Only a broad-
shouldered, big fellow can amount to anything when lying
down in the open air : he must crush with his careless length
a good wide space of grass and daisies, or he will inevitably
be overcome by the preponderant weight of Nature — the
fathomless sky above, the stretch of earth on each side.
Wainwright took up the volume, which Adelaide did not conceal; that he had found her reading his favorite author secretly was another of the little facts with which she gemmed
his life. " What do you discover to like ? " he asked.

" ' His bugles on the Pyrenees dissolved the trance of Europe'; and, 'When the war is over, let us sail among the islands of the Ægean and be as young as ever'; and, 'We are
poor indeed when we have no half-wishes left us,'" said Adelaide, musically quoting. " Then there is the ' Artemidora.' "

" You noticed that ? "

" Yes."

Meanwhile, the man was thinking, " How can I get away

unsuspected?" and the woman, "How can I make him tell
me?"

They talked some time longer; then Adelaide made up
her mind to go into action.

Adelaide (quietly). "There is a change in you, Stephen.
I want you to tell me the cause."

Stephen. "We all change as time moves on."

Adelaide. "But this is something different. I have noticed—"

Stephen. "What?"

Adelaide. "No one observes you so closely as I do,
Stephen: my life is bound up in yours; your interests are
mine. Anything that is for your happiness engrosses me;
anything that threatens it disturbs me. Let us speak plainly,
then: you are interested in Honor Dooris."

Stephen. "I am."

Adelaide. "More than that—you love her."

Stephen. "What is love, Adelaide?"

Adelaide (with emotion). "It was Ralph's feeling for me,
Stephen. He is gone, but I have the warm memory in my
heart. Somebody loved me once, and with all his soul."
(Leaning forward with tears in her eyes:) "Take this young
girl, Stephen; yes, take her. She will give you what you have
never had in your life, poor fellow!—real happiness."

Wainwright was silent.

Adelaide. "Ah! I have known it a long time. You spent
the whole of last summer here; what did that mean? You
wrote to her at intervals all through the winter. You are
here again. You love to study her girlish heart, to open the
doors of her mind." (Rapidly:) "And have I not helped
you? I have, I have. Was I not the quiet listener to all
those first guarded descriptions of yours? Did I not comment upon each and every word of those careful little letters
of hers, and follow every possibility of their meaning out to its
fullest extent? All this to please *you*. But, when I came
here and saw the child with my own eyes, did I not at once

range myself really upon your side? Have I not had her
here? Did I not form a close acquaintance with her family?
Did I not give you those morning hours with her at the
library? And am I not here also to answer for her, to de-
scribe her to your friends, to uphold your choice, to bring out
and develop her striking beauty?"

Stephen. "But she is not beautiful."

Adelaide. "She is. Let me dress her once or twice, and
New York shall rave over her. I have had your interests all
the time at heart, Stephen. Was it not I who sent for John
Royce? And did you not see why I sent for him? It was
to try her. I have given her every chance to see him, to be
with him, to admire him. He is near her own age, and he is
a handsome fellow, full of life and spirit. But you see as well
as I do that she has come out unscathed. Take her, then,
Stephen; you can do it safely, young as she is, for the man
she first loves she will love always."

As she spoke, an almost imperceptible tremor showed itself around the mouth of the small, plain, young-old man who
was lying on the grass beside her; he seemed to be conscious
of it himself, and covered his mouth with his hand.

Adelaide. "But there is something which you must tell
me now, Stephen. *You* can not be in league with these outlaws; is it Honor, then? You had better tell. Her uncle
and aunt evidently know nothing of it, and the child should
have a woman-friend by her side. You know I would cut
myself up into small pieces for you, Stephen; let me be your
ally in this, too. Is it not best for Honor that I should know
everything? Shall I not be her true friend when she is your
wife—your sweet young wife, Stephen, in that old house of
yours which we will fit up for her together, and where you will
let me come and see you, will you not, your faithful, loving
cousin?" Her voice broke; she turned her head away. Her
emotion was real. The man by her side, urged at last out of
his gray reticence by his own deep longing, which welled up
irresistibly to meet her sympathy, turned over on his arm and

told her all—in a few words as regarded himself, with careful explanation as regarded Honor.

"I have the money with me now," he said, "and Head, who was so anxious to guide me, the supposed detective, *away* from Eliot, now guides me to him, relies upon me to save him."

"And Honor knows—knows, too, that he shot Allison," said Adelaide musingly. "That was the reason why she was so pale, and why she brought all her roses, and kissed the poor boy's forehead."

"She does not *know*, but fears."

"Ah! we must help the child, Stephen; the burden of this is too heavy for such young shoulders. Go; I will not keep you a moment longer; I will go back to Honor. But, first—God bless you! Do not put yourself into any danger, for *my* sake. I have loved you long, and years hence, when we are old, I shall love you just the same."

They were both standing now; she came close to him, and laid her head upon his shoulder for an instant, tears shining on her cheeks. He put one arm around her, touched by her affection; she raised her eyes, and let him look deep into them for one short moment. "He shall see the truth this once," she thought; "though nothing to him now, it will come back to him."

Adelaide Kellinger did that time a bold thing; she let Wainwright see that she loved him, relying upon the certainty that he would not think she knew he saw it, much less that she intended him to see it. She had the balance of reality on her side, too, because she really did love him—in her way.

In another moment he had left her, and was walking rapidly down the river-road. Adelaide went back to the village.

Her first step was to find out whether Honor was at home; she was not. At the library, then? Not there. "Already gone to Brother Bethuel's," she thought. She next woke up Royce, laughed at his ill nature, flattered him a little, coaxed him into good temper, and finally told him plainly that she would not stand his bearishness any longer; that he must go and dress himself anew, brush his hair, and come back and be agreeable.

"You will turn into a mountain outlaw yourself, if I do not see to you," she said.

"Oh, let me off for to-day," said Royce lazily.

"This moment!"

She had her way: Royce took himself off, followed by the injunction to come back looking like an Apollo. Now, to make one's self look like an Apollo is an occupation which no young man is in his heart above; and, when incited thereto by an expressed belief from feminine lips that he has only to try, he generally—tries. Not long afterward Royce returned to the parlor looking his best, threw himself into a chair, and took up a book carelessly. He knew Adelaide would comment. She did. She called him "a good boy," touched the crisp, curling ends of his yellow hair, and asked why he kept them so short; stroked his forehead, and said that, on the whole, he looked quite well. Her heart was beating rapidly as she chatted with him; she listened intently; everything depended upon a chance. Ten minutes before, she had executed a daringly bold action—one of those things which a woman can do once in her life with perfect impunity, because no one suspects that she can. If she will do it alone, and only once, there is scarcely any deed she may not accomplish safely. A few more moments passed, Adelaide still listening; then came a shuffling step through the passage, a knock at the door, and, without waiting for reply, the burly figure of the revenue detective appeared, wrapped in a dressing-gown, with head still bandaged, and eyes half closed, but mind sufficiently clear to state his errand.

"Beg pardon," he said; "is Royce here? I can't see very well.—Is that you, Royce? Look at this."

He held out a crumpled piece of paper.

"Seems to be something, but I can't quite make it out," he said.

Royce took it, glanced over it, cried, "By Jove!" and was out of the room in a second. The detective went stumbling along after him; he had to feel his way, being half blinded by his swollen eyelids.

"Take your pistols!" he called out, keeping his hand on the wall all the way down the passage.

Royce had dropped the paper; Adelaide had instantly destroyed it, and then she followed the detective.

"What was it?" she asked anxiously.

"Only a line or two, ma'am—from somebody in the town here, I suppose—saying that one of them distillers, the one, too, that shot Allison, was hidden in the house of that rascally, deceiving little minister, up toward Eagle Knob. They're all in league with each other, ministers or no ministers."

"Who wrote it? How do you know it is true?"

"I dun know who wrote it, and I dun know as it's true. The paper was throwed into my room, through the winder, when there didn't happen to be anybody around. It was somebody as had a grudge against this man in particular, I suppose. 'Twas scrawly writing, and no spelling to speak of. I brought it to Royce myself, because I wouldn't trust any one to carry it to him, black or white, confound 'em all!"

The detective had now reached the end of the passage and his endurance; his hand was covered with whitewash where he had drawn it along the wall, his head was aching furiously, and his slippers were coming off. "You had just better go back," he said, not menacingly, but with a dull desperation, as he sat down on the first step of the stairway which led down to his room, and held his forehead and the base of his brain together: they seemed to him two lobes as large as bushel-baskets, and just ready to split apart.

"I will send some one to you," said Adelaide, departing. She went to her room, darkened it, and took a long, quiet *siesta*.

.   .   .   .

Royce dropped his information, *en route*, at the little

camp in the grove, where the trim companies of United States infantry led their regular orderly life, to the slow wonder of the passing mountaineers. Who would not be a soldier and have such mathematically square pieces of bread, such well-boiled meat on a tin plate, such an exactly measured mug of clear coffee? Who would not wear the light-blue trousers with their sharp fold of newness making a straight line to the very boot? Who would not have such well-parted, shining hair? So thought the mountain-boys, and rode homeward pondering.

The officers in command, on principle disgusted for several seasons with still-hunting, which they deemed police-duty, were now ready to catch at any straw to avenge the death of Allison. The mountaineers and the detectives might fire at each other as long as they enjoyed the pastime; but let them not dare to aim at an army-officer—let them not dare! They were astir at once, and called to Royce to wait for them; but he was already gone.

Stephen had a start of not quite forty minutes; but, unconscious of pursuit, he walked slowly, not caring to return before nightfall. His natural gait was slow; his narrow chest did not take in breath widely, as some chests do, and, slight as his figure was, he labored if hurried. His step was short and rather careful, his ankles and feet being delicate and small. There was no produced development of muscle on him anywhere; he had always known that he could not afford anything of that kind, and had let himself alone. As he now walked on, he dreamed. Adelaide's words rang in his ear; he could not forget them. "A woman reads a woman," he said to himself. "Adelaide thinks that I can win her." Then he let his thoughts go: "At last my life will have an object; this sweet young girl will love me, and love me for myself alone; she is incapable of any other feeling." He was very human, after all; he longed so to be loved! His wealth and his insignificance had been two millstones around his neck all his life; he had believed nobody. Under every feeling that had ever come to him lurked always, deepest of all, suspicion. Now, late in life, in this far-off wilderness, he had found some one in whom he believed.

He pleased himself with the thought of the jewels he would give her; he journeyed with her in fancy through the whole of the Old World. The moisture came to his eyes as he imagined how she would pray morning and night just the same, and that he would be there to see her; he said to himself that he would never laugh at her, but would bring his unbelieving heart and lay it in her hand: if she could mold it, well and good, she might; he would be glad. So he walked on, down the river-road, his long-repressed, stifled hope and love out of bonds at last.

A sound fell on his dulled ear, and brought him back to reality; it was a footstep. "I had better not be seen," he thought, and, climbing up the bank, he kept on through the thick hillside-forest. After a moment or two, around the curve came John Royce, walking as if for a wager; two pistols gleamed in the belt he had hastily buckled around his waist, and the wrinkle between his eyes had deepened into a frown.

"It can not be possible!" thought Wainwright. But rapid reflection convinced him that, impossible as it seemed, it might be true, and that, in any case, he had not a moment to lose. He was above Royce, he was nearer the trail to Brother Bethuel's, and, what was more, he was familiar with all its turnings. "Not to be able to save Eliot!" he thought, as he hurried forward over the slippery, brown pine-needles. And then it came to him how much he had relied upon that to hold Honor, and he was ashamed. But almost immediately after rose to the surface, for the first time in his life, too, the blunt, give-and-take feeling of the man as a man, the thought —"You are doing all this for her; she *ought* to repay you." He hardly knew himself; he was like Bothwell then, and other burly fellows in history; and he was rather pleased to find himself so. He hastened across a plateau where the footing was better; he had turned farther up the mountain-side, so that Royce could not by any possibility hear him as he brushed hastily through the undergrowth, or stepped on crackling twigs or a rolling stone. The plateau soon ended, and the slanting hillside slanted still more steeply. He pushed on, keeping his breath as well as he was able, running wherever he could, climbing over rocks and fallen trees. He was so far above the road now that he could not see Royce at all, but he kept his efforts up to the task by imagining that the young man was abreast of him below—which was true. He began to pant a little. The sleeve of his flannel coat had been held and torn by a branch; he had tripped on a round stone, and grazed his knee. He was very tired; he began to lope as the Indians do, making the swing of the joints tell; but he was not long enough to gain any advantage from that gait. At last he met the trail, and turned up the mountain; the ascent seemed steeper now that he was out of breath. His throat was dry; surely, he had time to drink from the brook. He knelt down, but before he could get a drop he heard a sound below, and hurried on. Alarmed, he sprang forward like a hare; he climbed like a cat, he drew himself up by his hands; he had but one thought—to reach the house in time. His coat was torn now in more places than one; a sharp edge of rock had cut his ankle so that his stocking was spotted with red above the low walking-shoe. The determination to save Eliot drove him on like a whip of flame: he did not know how much Royce knew, but feared everything. His face had a singular appearance: it was deeply flushed, the teeth were set, the wrinkles more visible than ever, and yet there was a look of the boy in the eyes which had not been there for years. He was in a burning heat, and breathed with a regular, panting sound; he could hear the circulation of his own blood, and began to see everything crimson. The trail now turned straight up the mountain, and he went at it fiercely; he was conscious of his condition, and knew that he might fall in a fit at the house-door : never mind, if he could only get there! His eyes were glassy now, his lips dry. He reached the house, opened the door, and fell into a chair. Brother Bethuel, in alarm, sprang up and brought him a dipper full of water as quickly as hand could fill the tin. Brother Bethuel believed in water, and this time Wainwright agreed with him; he swallowed every drop.

"Where is he?" he said then, already on his feet again, though staggering a little. Brother Bethuel pointed downward, and Wainwright, with a signal toward the glen, as if of near danger, disappeared. The cellar was dimly lighted by two little windows a foot square, and the man who entered made out two figures: one was Eliot, the other Honor.

"You!" said Wainwright.

"Did you not know that I would come?" said the girl.

He had not known it, or thought of it. He turned his eyes toward the other figure; everything still looked red. He held out a pocket-book.

"Go!" he said; "Royce is on your track!"

He spoke in a whisper; his voice had left him as he gained breath. Eliot, a dark-skinned, handsome, but cutthroat-looking fellow, seized the money and sprang toward the door. But Honor sprang too, and held him back; she had heard something. The next moment they all heard something— Royce coming in above.

When the youth entered, Brother Bethuel was quietly reading his Bible; the table on which it lay was across the cellar-door.

"Welcome," said the little missionary, rising. "I am happy to see you, Mr. Royce."

The place looked so peaceful, with the Bible, the ticking clock, and the cat, that Royce began to think it must be all a mistake. He sat down for a moment to rest, irresolute, and not quite knowing what to say next. The three, close under the thin flooring down below, did not stir, hardly breathed. Stephen was thinking that, if Royce could know the truth, he too would let Eliot go. But there was not much time for thought.

Brother Bethuel brought out some apples, and began to converse easily with his visitor. After a while he said, deprecatingly:

"Will you not remove your pistols to the window-seat behind you, Mr. Royce? From my youth, I could never abide the proximity of fire-arms of any kind. They distress me."

Royce good-naturedly took them out of his belt, and placed them behind him, but within easy reach. The missionary was on the opposite side of the room.

Not a sound below. Wainwright was breathing with his mouth wide open, so as not to pant. He was still much spent.

But it could not last long; Royce felt that he must search the house, even at the risk of offending the little missionary.

"Mr. Head," he said, awkwardly enough, "I am very sorry, but—but a communication has been received stating that one of the outlaws, and the one, too, who shot poor Allison, is concealed here, in this house. I am very sorry, but—but I must search every part of it immediately."

Brother Bethuel had risen; his countenance expressed sorrow and surprise.

"Young man," he said, "search where and as you please; but spare me your suspicions."

There was a dignity in his bearing which Royce had not seen before; he felt hot and ashamed.

"Indeed, Mr. Head, I regret all this," he said; "and, of course, it is but a matter of form. Still, for my own satisfaction, and yours, too, now I must go through the house."

He rose and moved a step forward. Quick as lightning the little missionary had sprung behind him, and pushed the pistols over the sill, through the open window, down forty feet on the rocks below.

"Traitor!" cried Royce, grappling him.

But it was too late; the pistols were gone. Brother Bethuel glowed openly with triumph; he made no more resistance in Royce's strong arms than a rag. The young man soon dropped him, and, hearing a sound below, ran to the cellar-door.

"He has no pistols!" screamed Bethuel down the stair after him: "you can manage him; he is alone."

Then, setting all the doors wide open, so that escape would be easy, he ran out to saddle Marcher.

Down below, in the cellar, Stephen had caught hold of Royce's arm. Royce, full in the narrow entranceway, stood glaring at Eliot, and minding Stephen's hold no more than the foot of a fly. The light from the horizontal door above streamed in and showed Eliot's dark face and Honor's dilated eyes. The girl stood near her cousin, but slightly behind him as though she feared his gaze.

"You are the man I want," said Royce; "I recognize you!" His strong voice came in among their previous whispers and bated breath, as his face came in among their three faces—Honor's ivory-pallid cheeks, the outlaw's strained attention, and Stephen's gray fatigue, more and more visible now as he gained breath and sight. "Yield yourself up. We are two to your one."

"We are two to *your* one," answered Eliot: "that man beside you is for me."

Royce looked down with surprise upon his cousin, who still held his arm.

"No mistaken lenity now, Stephen," he said curtly, shaking his arm free. "I must have this man; he shot Allison."

"How are you going to do it?" said Eliot jeeringly, putting his hands deep down in his pockets and squaring his shoulders. "Even Honor here is a match for two Yankees."

"Miss Dooris, I will let *you* pass," said Royce impatiently. "Go up stairs. This is no place for a girl like you."

"Say lady!" cried Eliot. "She is a Southern lady, sir!"
"Bah!" said Royce; "you are a fine person to talk of ladies.—*Are* you going, Miss Dooris?"

Great tears stood in Honor's eyes; she did not stir.

"She will not go, John," said Wainwright, "because that man is her cousin—he is an Eliot."

"He is a murderer!" said Royce, filling up the doorway again, and measuring with his eye the breadth of his opponent's shoulders and muscle. "Now, then, are you with me or against me, Stephen? If against me, by Heaven! I will fight you both."

"You do not understand, John. It is Honor's cousin: that is why *I* am anxious to save him."

"And what is her cousin or anybody's cousin to me?" cried Royce angrily. "I tell you that man shot Allison, and he shall swing for it."

He sprang forward as if to close with Eliot, then sprang back again. He remembered that it was more important that he should guard the door: there was no other way of escape. If Stephen, pursuing the extraordinary course he had taken in this matter, should side with Eliot, Brother Bethuel being a traitor too up stairs, he might not be able to overcome the outlaw in an attack. He set his teeth, therefore, and stood still. His hat was off; the sunset light touched his forehead and yellow hair; the image of strength and young manhood, he confronted them in his elegant attire—confronted the outlaw in his rough, unclean garments; Honor in her old, black gown; and Stephen in his torn clothes, his tired face looking yellow and withered as the face of an old baboon. He considered whether he could keep the door until the troops came: they would not be long behind him. But, if he only had his pistols!

His eye glanced toward Stephen; but Stephen never carried arms. Eliot, probably, had only a knife; if he had had a pistol, he would have shown it before now. All this in the flash of a second.

Brother Bethuel could be heard bringing Marcher around the house. Stephen made one more effort, In a few, concise words he explained who Eliot was, and his own great wish to aid him in escaping. With his hand on Royce's arm, he called his attention, by a gesture, to Honor.

"Let the man go for my sake and—hers," he said, in a low voice, looking up at his young cousin with his small, pale-colored eyes.

Honor clasped her hands and made a step forward; she did not speak, but implored with an entreating gaze. Royce threw his head back impatiently. All this was nothing to him. He would have his man, or die for it; they all saw that.

Then Eliot, who had watched to see the result of this pleading, made up his mind.

"Stand back from the door, or I fire!" he cried, drawing out his hand, and taking aim at Royce.

He had a pistol, then!

"I give you thirty seconds!"

But Honor, with a wild scream, ran forward, and threw herself against Royce's breast, covering it with her shoulders and head, and raising her arms and hands to shield his face. He did not hold her or put his arm around her; but she clung to him with her whole length, as a wet ribbon clings to a stone.

"Leave him, Honor!" cried Eliot, in a fury—"leave him, or I'll shoot you both!"

"Shoot, then!" said Honor, looking up into Royce's face, and frantically trying to cover every inch of it with her shielding hands.

Stephen ran and caught Eliot's arm; Royce, half blinded, tried to push the girl away; then the sound of the pistol filled the room. Royce swayed and fell over heavily, carrying Honor with him as he went down; a ball had entered his lung under the girl's arm, in the little space left open by the inward curve of her waist. Eliot ran by the two, up the stair, and out of the house; but, as he passed Honor, he took the time to strike her across the cheek, and curse her. At the door he found Marcher, sprang into the saddle, and rode away.

Brother Bethuel, with white face, hurried down and stanched the blood; he had no small knowledge of surgery and the healing craft, and he commanded Royce not to utter a syllable. Honor held the young man's head in her lap, and every now and then softly took up his fallen hand. Wainwright drew away, and watched her with the deepest pain of his life gnawing at his heart. He saw her stroke Royce's hair fondly, as if she could not help it, and saw her begin to sob over his closing eyes and the deepening violet shadows under them, and then stop herself lest she should disturb him. Brother Bethuel was listening to the breathing with bent head, to find out if there was any chance for life. The house was as still as a tomb; a bee came in, and hummed above their heads.

"He *has* a chance," said the missionary at last, fervently, raising his head. "Do not let him stir." He ran up stairs for restoratives, and Wainwright sat down on a stool which had been Eliot's seat during his imprisonment, and covered his eyes with his hand. It seemed to him that he had sat there a long time, and that Honor must be noticing him now. He glanced up; she was gazing down at the still face on her lap. He stirred; she motioned impatiently for silence with her hand, but did not raise her eyes. He sat looking at her miserably, and growing old, older with every moment. His lips quivered once as he silently gave up for ever his dream of hope and love. He passed his hand over his dry eyes, and sat still. By the time he was needed he was able to help Brother Bethuel in making Royce as comfortable as possible on the cellar-floor: they dared not move him.

The troops arrived in time to hear all about it—they then went back again.

15

Wainwright returned to Ellerby that evening. The army-surgeon and a nurse had been sent out immediately to the mountain cottage, and Colonel Eliot, distressed and agitated, had accompanied them. Wainwright went to his room, attired himself anew, and sought Adelaide's parlor. Adelaide received him quietly; she said nothing, but came around behind him and kissed his forehead. He looked up at her dumbly. Her eyes filled with tears. In her strange, double, woman's way she felt sorry for his sorrow. She was conscious of no guilt; she had only precipitated matters. Honor would never have loved him, and it was better he should know it. In truth, she had saved him.

And Honor? Oh, she had the usual torments of young love! She was no goddess to Royce, only a girl like any other. He was touched by her impulsive act, and during his long illness he began to think more and more about her. It all ended well; that is, he married her after a while, took her away to the North, and was, on the whole, a good husband. But, from first to last, he ruled her, and she never became quite the beauty that Mrs. Kellinger intended her to be, because she was too devoted to him, too absorbed in him, too dependent upon his fancies, to collect that repose and security of heart which are necessary to complete the beauty of even the most beautiful woman.

Ellerby village sank back into quietude. Still the moon-light whisky is made up in the mountains, and still the revenue detectives are shot. The United States troops go up every summer, and—come back again! The wild, beautiful region is not yet conquered.

Wainwright reëntered society; society received him with gladness. A fresh supply of mothers smiled upon him, a fresh supply of daughters filed past him. He made his little compact remarks as before, and appeared unaltered; but he let the lime-light play about him rather more continuously now, and took fewer journeys. He will never swerve from Adelaide again. As they grow older, the chances are that some day he will say to her, "Why should we not be married, Adelaide?"

And she will answer, "Why not, indeed?"

This woman loved him; the other would never have given him more than gratitude. What would you have?

THE END.

CPSIA information can be obtained at www.ICGtesting.com
Printed in the USA
LVOW08s0955110913

351846LV00001B/6/P